KEEPING SECRETS

A Legal Thriller

Deborah Hawkins

Published by Deborah Hawkins
978-0-9992180-1-3 (print)
978-0-9992180-2-0 (ebook)

Contents

PART I

THE EXECUTION ORDER

"I am dying in my own death and in the
deaths of those after me"

T.S. Eliot

CHAPTER ONE

Tuesday, January 3, 2017, I-95 South from Richmond to Death Row at Sussex State Prison, Sussex, Virginia

Brendan Murphy drove south on the I-95 toward Sussex that morning with his heart aching. He glanced over at his briefcase on the passenger seat next to him, wishing he could toss it out the window. He imagined it coming to rest in a half-frozen puddle of dirty snow along the shoulder of the freeway, languishing there with Edward Wynne Carter III's execution warrant unread and unnoticed.

If only saving Ed's life could be that direct and simple. Brendan had been trying for thirty-one years to make the Commonwealth of Virginia admit that Ed had not killed his barely pregnant wife, Anne Fairfax Carter, on a cold November night in 1983, while their four-year-old son, Wynne, slept in his crib behind the locked door of his nursery. But to no avail. The Commonwealth's Attorney, Gordon Martin Fairfax and Anne's first cousin, was so hell bent on vengeance that he had thrice convicted the wrong man.

"Why did you take this case?" his wife, Emma, had asked

him last night as they sat in front of the fire in the spacious great room of their six-thousand-square-foot, three-story, brick colonial in Richmond's exclusive Windsor Farms.

They were slowing down at sixty-six. The thought made him smile as he drove. Now they liked to sit in front of the fire at night, talking and sipping good scotch, instead of going to concerts, dinner parties, and charity events. Well, he didn't mind. He'd spent his career in the Richmond office of Craig, Lewis, and Weller. He'd officially retired last October. He was still a partner, but now his name appeared in the "Of Counsel" column on the firm's letterhead. He went to his office only three days a week, and he had handed off most of his cases to other attorneys. But not Ed's. He hadn't wanted to give up his hard-charging career this early, but Emma, an accomplished pediatric cardiologist, had insisted. Stress had taken its toll, and he'd had a serious heart attack last spring.

To encourage him to back down from long hours at the firm, she had reduced her own hours at the Medical College of Virginia. She taught only one class and saw patients in her office only two days a week. Now they had time to spend with their grandchildren, five-year-old Jamie, Timothy's son, and four-year-old Gwen, Ellen's daughter. They spent days at Kings Dominion in Williamsburg and went to visit the animals at Maymont Farm. And at Christmas, Brendan had overseen Jamie and Gwen's delighted squeals as they had sledded on the softly sloping hill in the backyard that Ellen and Timothy had loved so well.

But now the magical Christmas snow was nothing but gray slush, and Brendan was on the saddest journey of his life. He glanced down and saw that the Range Rover was picking up speed too easily. He wanted the fifty-minute commute to last as long as possible to delay the minute when he'd have to look into Ed's kind, brown eyes and tell him that he would draw his last breath on Friday, March 3 at 9 p.m. in the execution chamber at Greensville Correctional Center in Jarrat, Virginia.

"Ed's mother asked me to take his case." Brendan drew Emma closer as they cuddled on the sofa under an afghan she had knitted.

"Caroline Randolph Carter?"

He nodded. "She knew me from church."

"I'm surprised the firm let you accept it."

"I wasn't. Although my section of litigation accepted only white-collar crime for our corporate clients, Craig, Lewis wasn't about to turn down the matriarch of the Carter and Wynne families of Carter's Grove Plantation."

"Why didn't you represent Ed in his first trial?"

"Caroline wouldn't help him the first time around. She thought it was beneath a Carter to get himself arrested for murder. He was represented by Brad O'Connor over at the Public Defender's Office. But when the Virginia Supreme Court threw out his first conviction, she decided she'd better spend some money to get the truth in front of a jury. But damn it, Emma, no jury has ever understood that Ed was in Charlottesville presenting a paper at a legal conference the night Anne was murdered."

Emma rubbed his cheek softly. "I know how hard this is for you. Promise you won't let the stress get to you."

He kissed her softly on the cheek. "I wish I could make you

that promise. But I only have sixty days left to save Ed's life."

"So you're going to try for a stay?"

"A stay, a commutation, a pardon. Whatever the hell I can get. He's innocent, Emma, you know that. I'm not going to let the Commonwealth murder an innocent man who's become my friend."

She laid her head on his shoulder and stroked his cheek. "I have some happier news."

He looked down at her. She was still beautiful. She cut her hair short now to accent her wide, dark eyes, always full of compassion and love. The extra pounds of middle age still sat well on her five-seven frame. She had beautiful hands with long graceful fingers that stitched together tiny hearts in the OR. She'd chosen the right profession, he thought. She was a consummate healer.

"I'd love to hear something cheerful."

"Claire is finally getting married."

"Claire? Our Claire? Tyndall's daughter? Ellen's best friend from St. Catherine's?"

"Yes! Isn't it great news?"

"Not if it's to that jerk who led her on for years and then broke her heart last summer with some woman he'd just met."

"No, it's not him. He lives in San Diego or Los Angeles. I'm not sure which. Ellen said Claire's fiancé lives in New York. She met him after she went back last spring. He's a couple of years older than Claire. Ellen said he's done very well in venture capital."

"Then he isn't marrying Claire for her money." As he spoke, he wiggled out of her grasp and started to get up, but she put out her hand.

"Why do I think you are going to the liquor cabinet for a refill?"

"Because I am."

"No, you're not. It's nearly midnight, and you said you'll be leaving for Sussex at eight in the morning. Your heart needs sleep, not more scotch."

"I don't think I can sleep."

"Try. But no more scotch. Come on, let's go to bed."

How lucky am I, he thought, as they climbed the stairs together. *I have her and Tim and Ellen and Gwen and Jamie and more money than I'll ever spend. Ed was supposed to have those things, too. I can't let him die. I can't let him die.*

CHAPTER TWO

Tuesday, January 3, 2017, Sussex State Prison, Sussex, Virginia

Tom Brower's office was too warm, but Brendan didn't care. The walk from his car to the prison entrance had been excruciating in the cold. Every breath had felt as if he were sucking needles into his lungs.

"Coffee?" Tom filled a Styrofoam cup from the Mr. Coffee on the table by the door in his gray, government-issue office and handed it to him without waiting for an answer. He was the third warden Brendan had dealt with since taking over Ed's case in 1986. He'd held the job for going on ten years.

Tom filled his own cup and sat down behind his big, steel desk, littered with stacks of folders. "This is not the way I wanted to start the new year," he said. "But that's not news to you. I've never had to execute someone whom I'm certain is innocent. Can't you get a stay?"

"I've got associates working around the clock. I called in the team yesterday morning as soon as I got the warrant. We've got sixty days. We'll spend every minute trying to stop it. But you know that."

Tom sipped his coffee, made a face, and put the cup down on his desk. "Don't drink it. My secretary can't count coffee measures. Ed doesn't know yet, does he?"

Brendan shook his head. "That's why I'm here."

"Does he even suspect?"

"I don't know. We've always talked about what we're going to try next. The last time I was here, we'd lost that habeas writ before the Fourth Circuit up in Richmond."

"That was new evidence, wasn't it?"

Brendan sighed. "That's right. The two witnesses who testified that Ed was having an affair with their roommate admitted that they had lied under oath. They had no knowledge of any affair. It was an important change in their testimony, but the court of appeal didn't see it as significant."

He remembered Judge Boyce, the lead judge on the panel in the Fourth Circuit, looking down at him from the bench and shaking his head. "I understand that these women have changed their stories. But I don't see how that helps your client. The one who told the dean of the law school that your client was having an affair with her and wanted to marry her has never changed her testimony. There was ample evidence of motive, Mr. Murphy. Your client was unhappy with his wife, and he didn't want the trouble and expense of a divorce, so he killed her."

Allison Byrd. She'd testified at Ed's first trial and then disappeared. Gordon had read her very damning testimony from that first trial to the jury in Ed's third trial as Brendan had watched her claims sway all twelve jurors in the state's direction. But she had been lying. There had been no affair. There had been no promise to do away with Anne, whom Ed still loved more than life itself. The dean had reprimanded Ed based on innuendo, hearsay, and gossip. Allison Byrd's lies had put Ed on death row.

"What about a pardon from the governor or commutation of his death sentence to life without parole?" Tom asked.

"We've tried, over and over again. Anne's family keeps buying the governor's office to make sure that doesn't happen."

"Governor Reynolds might listen, though. Ed's done so much good here. He's helped the other inmates with their cases. He's even gotten a couple of death sentences changed to life without parole."

"That's the irony," Brendan agreed. "He's been able to save others but not himself."

"I don't get that." The warden frowned.

"It's the Fairfaxes again. Gordon's right at retirement age, but he won't step down because he's constantly afraid we'll get another reversal and another Commonwealth's Attorney will let Ed plead to manslaughter for time served. That would have happened after the second reversal if Gordon hadn't been the attorney on the file."

"God, how I hate Gordon Fairfax, then. He's putting me in an impossible position."

"I know. He's stepped way over the line between professional and personal. He called me yesterday to gloat. I didn't give him a polite response."

Tom looked out the window beside his desk and studied the frozen landscape for a few seconds. Then he asked, "Does Ed's son know?"

Brendan shook his head. "I'm going to tell him as soon as

I've told Ed. Father Jim is on his way down from Richmond now to be with Ed after I've told him. We agreed that I should spend some time alone with him first, and then Jim should be with him."

Tom looked relieved at the mention of Father James Lamb, the priest at St. Stephen's in Richmond, who had been coming to see Edward Carter since Brendan took over his case. "I'm relieved to hear that."

"You're thinking suicide watch," Brendan said.

"It's required. You know that."

"How long before you take him down to Greensville?"

"Not until a few days before the execution. He'll still be here for most of his remaining time."

Brendan studied the icy world that had caught Tom's attention earlier. His eyes fixed on a puddle in the parking lot that was beginning to melt in the cold winter sun. Why take lives, he wondered, when trials were such highly imperfect mechanisms to determine the truth? He thought of Emma's steady dark eyes as he summoned his courage for what he knew he had to do. Medicine more often than law saves lives. At that minute, he wished he'd never made his way from his parents' farm near Blacksburg to Virginia Tech and then to the University of Virginia Law School.

He felt Tom watching him and brought his gaze back from the melting puddle. "This isn't going to get any easier no matter how long I sit here. It's time to go see Ed."

CHAPTER THREE

He was sitting at the long, gray, metal table in the Attorney Interview Room where they had met so many times in the last thirty years. He was staring out the window at the melting ice and snow in the prison parking lot. Brendan paused to study his client through the window in the door to give himself a few more minutes to summon his courage for what he had to do.

At sixty-nine, Edward Carter was still a strikingly handsome man. He carried his five feet nine inches with the military bearing that he had learned in college at the Virginia Military Institute. He worked out every day and managed to keep himself fit and trim even on the starchy food that constituted his prison diet. He had a high forehead and deep-set, dark-brown eyes that made his face distinguished, yet kindly. He had worn rimless glasses for most of his adult life. The glasses made him look bookish and scholarly. They had kept him from flying helicopters in Vietnam, but they had not kept him from commanding an infantry platoon as a second lieutenant. He had always been proud of bringing every one of his men home.

By this time, Brendan knew every detail of Ed's life story. He had been born in Richmond in 1948, the eldest child and only son of Caroline Randolph and Edward Wynne Carter II. His sister, Margaret, had been born in 1950. They had grown up in the sprawling, six-bedroom home in Richmond's Windsor Farms that had been the Carter family home in the time of his grandfather, the first Edward Wynne Carter. Ed and his sister had been sent to private school, Ed to St. Christopher's and Margaret to St. Catherine's.

After VMI, Ed had spent two years in Vietnam. When he came home in 1972, he had followed in his father's footsteps and enrolled in law school at the University of Virginia. In his second year, he had met Anne Elizabeth Fairfax of the rich and powerful Northern Virginia Fairfaxes. She was at UVA earning her master's degree in English.

She was tall and athletic. She had been a champion field hockey player at the then-all-female Mary Baldwin College. But she also loved music and had played the violin since she was eight years old. One night when Ed was a second-year law student, his roommate had begged him to go to a recital that his then-girlfriend was playing. The girlfriend had turned out to be Anne.

After Ed graduated in 1975, he and Anne married and moved to New York where he was an associate at Sullivan and Cromwell in white-collar crime for three years. His father had wanted him to join his lucrative corporate practice at Carter, Totten, and Randolph. But Ed had found his father's work boring, and he had wanted to make his own way in the legal world. He hadn't wanted his reputation to rest on being Edward II's son.

But by 1978, he had had enough of New York and Big Firm hours. He never saw Anne. He barely saw the light of day because he arrived at work when it was still dark and went home in the wee hours of the morning. He and Anne were overjoyed when the University of Richmond hired him as an assistant professor of criminal law. The next year, 1979, Edward Wynne Carter IV, shortened to Wynne, was born.

They were happy with their life as new parents. They bought a historic Victorian townhouse at 2425 Grove Avenue, and Anne oversaw its transformation. She liked do-it-yourself projects like painting and wallpapering, although she hired subcontractors to do the more complicated jobs. And she found a part-time position teaching English at Virginia Commonwealth University.

Caroline, Ed's mother, hadn't been happy when he'd married a Fairfax. She'd been bored and bitter after her husband died and intent on promoting petty family conflicts. But Ed and Anne wisely chose to ignore her. And she softened slightly when they produced a son to carry on the family name.

Ed discovered that he had found his true calling as a law professor. He loved teaching and writing and research. Anne was happy with her job and her house. And they both loved being Wynne's parents. They had created their ideal existence until Sunday, November 20, 1983, when Ed found her lying in a pool of blood in the hall of her beloved house, his softball ball bat beside her, matted with blood and hair and brains. Wynne had been upstairs in his room, behind a locked door, frantically crying his four-year-old heart out.

* * *

Ed turned toward the door as soon as the guard popped the latch, and Brendan began to push it open. The vacant look that Ed had bestowed on the parking lot was replaced by pure joy shining in his dark eyes behind his rimless spectacles as soon as he saw Brendan. Brendan's heart skipped a beat. *He doesn't even suspect!*

"I've got some wonderful news. Wynne is engaged!" Ed stood up as he spoke and held out his hand for a handshake, still mindful of the niceties of professional greetings even after more than thirty years behind bars.

Brendan took Ed's hand but gave him a hug instead. As he let him go he said automatically, "That's wonderful news." Except, of course, it wasn't. Nothing could be wonderful now.

"It is wonderful," Ed agreed. "He told me that he took her to Paris at Christmas to propose."

"Have they set a date?" Brendan asked cautiously.

"March 4."

Suddenly Ed's eyes were wiped clean of emotion. He studied Brendan's face carefully. "You've come to tell me something, haven't you?"

Now that he had the opening, Brendan had no words. He put his briefcase on the table, opened the pouch that contained the warrant, and handed it to Ed. He took the paper and stared down at it. Brendan watched his gentle brown eyes widen in what must have been terror as he read.

No one spoke for at least a minute after Ed finished reading the execution order.

Then he said woodenly, "March 3."

"I'm afraid so," Brendan nodded.

The two men stood looking at each other across the paper that Ed still held in his hands as if it took both of them to lift something that heavy. Silence stretched between them until Brendan said, "Let's sit down and talk about what we should do next."

He held out his hand for the order, and Ed gave it to him, his eyes still fixed as if in a trance. Brendan steered Ed gently toward the chair he'd occupied earlier. He sat down and put his head in his hands. Brendan took the chair next to him and put his hand on his shoulder.

A few minutes passed. Then Ed lifted his head and looked out at the snowy world before he turned to Brendan. His eyes were full of tears, but he said bravely, "Well, we've had a good run. Most people don't last more than seven years in here. You've kept me alive for thirty-plus."

Ed squeezed his shoulder. "It's not going to happen. I'm going to find a way to stop it."

But Ed shook his head and gave him the ghost of a smile. "Look, I know the odds. I've always known them. You don't have to make promises that we both know you can't keep."

"I can keep them. I'll find a way." Brendan tried to keep his voice calm and professional. "I've got six associates working on another writ right now."

"We don't have any new evidence. And the Fourth Circuit rejected what new evidence we did have right before Christmas."

Brendan tried not to think about Judge Boyce's final words at oral argument.

"I respect all the years you've put into this case, Mr. Murphy," the gray-haired chief judge said almost kindly.

"You've been back up here for your client more times than any attorney who practices criminal law before this court. And you've won him two new trials. But those juries have convicted him. Not to mention the first time he was convicted before you took over this case. Three juries have heard this evidence and handed down a sentence of death three times. Your client is guilty, Mr. Murphy. At some point, you're going to have to accept that."

ED

"Be still and wait without hope"

T. S. Eliot

CHAPTER FOUR

Tuesday, January 3, 2017, Sussex State Prison, Sussex, Virginia

Ed had known he would not sleep that night. What was the point of sleep when his days to be awake were now numbered?

The warden had let Father Jim spend the long afternoon with him after Brendan left to rally his troops in Richmond. The priest's tall, thin presence and soft baritone had been comforting. He had listened patiently while Ed talked about his memories of Anne, her long, dark hair, her light-blue eyes, her mischievous laugh, her love of T.S. Eliot, and the way she played the hauntingly beautiful Bach's *Partita No. 2* on her violin.

"*You are the music while the music lasts.* It was her favorite quote," Ed said to Father Jim. "We always think the music will last forever."

"*I shall not want Honor in Heaven,*" Father Jim replied, quoting Eliot, too.

"I'm not sure that I believe in Heaven." Ed shook his head.

"Doesn't matter," the priest said. "It's there waiting, all the same."

And so they had gone on talking about whatever came into

Ed's head to still the terror of what he now faced. He talked about the way Wynne had inherited his mother's blue eyes and her athletic skill and the way he'd been a star goalie in field hockey when he'd been an undergraduate at the University of Pennsylvania.

"I don't want him to postpone his wedding," Ed said.

"I think you'll have to leave that up to him."

They talked about his three trials and why the jury had found him guilty every time even though he hadn't been in Richmond the night Anne had been murdered. They talked about his mother, Caroline, and how she'd spent the family fortune trying to prove Ed's innocence.

"Do you have a will?" Father Jim asked.

Ed gave him a slight smile. "I don't have anything to leave to anyone."

"Probably better to have one, though," the priest advised. "I'll mention it to Brendan."

Now as he lay on his bunk, Ed could see a few stars through his window, but not the moon. He wished he could see the moon shining in the cold, clear night. Anne had loved the moon. In the summer, she had liked to sit outside in their tiny backyard behind the Grove Avenue house, sipping white wine in the moonlight after Wynne was asleep. Sometimes Ed would sit with her, too. But sometimes, he would not.

* * *

Ed's father had been chronically unfaithful. Paralegals, secretaries, Caroline's own friends. Edward II had had no regard for his marriage vows. The affairs had made Caroline miserable, but she had looked the other way because she had no choice.

Even before he met Anne, Ed had promised himself that he'd never be unfaithful. He hadn't wanted his wife to suffer the way his mother had. But it had never occurred to him that he would be the one who would be betrayed.

When he and Anne moved to New York in 1975 as newlyweds, Ed had had no time for affairs. The hours at Sullivan and Cromwell occupied his every waking minute. He hadn't given much thought to what Anne would do without him when he'd taken the job. But she quickly found an artsy, Bohemian crowd of friends to explore the city with. And because she was a gifted violinist, she became a part of several string quartets that played gigs at Greenwich Village restaurants and at weddings and bar mitzvahs.

Near the end of their first year of marriage and of Ed's first year at Sullivan and Cromwell, he had realized that Anne was having multiple affairs. There were a lot of signs. The phone often rang, and no one was there when he answered it. When he did get a night off, she always had plans and could not spend the evening with him. When he suggested getting theater tickets or making dinner reservations, she always put him off. The one and only social duty she was willing to perform with him was attending the firm's lavish Christmas party at the Plaza Hotel.

Ed became angry. It wasn't fair. He'd sworn himself to faithfulness even before he'd met Anne, yet somehow he had managed to marry the one woman in the world who couldn't care less about his loyalty.

And he was miserably unhappy in his job. As his second year at Sullivan and Cromwell began, he admitted to himself that he had made a mistake. Even his father's stifling corporate practice was not as boring as the tedious research assignments he had to do day after day in Sullivan's cavernous, dark library. Even as a second-year associate, he had no hope of being anything other than a glorified research assistant.

Then one afternoon, his life went from black and white to color. A curly-haired brunette with wide, dark eyes and a mischievous smile who was sitting across from him in the library leaned over her stack of books and said, "How did this ever happen to us?"

Her name was Morgan Thomas. She'd come to the firm in his class of associates. Later, after they'd figured out ways to ditch the library for coffee and then later on, for sex in sleazy, hourly hotel rooms, Ed had learned that she'd gone to law school to save her marriage. Her husband hadn't been much of a provider. He'd graduated from Duke with a Ph.D. in comparative literature but couldn't find an academic job and didn't want any other kind of work. He wrote long, dry research papers that no one wanted to publish and listened to classical music on the stereo that he'd put on their credit card. After having the phone and electricity turned off in their tiny studio apartment in Durham more than once and after the bank started calling about the missed credit card payments, Morgan had enrolled in Duke's law school and graduated number one in her class. The only things she seemed to have in common with her lazy husband were they both had graduate degrees from Duke in comparative literature, and they both spoke fluent French.

Unlike Anne, she had a wild streak. One night, she burst into his office at one in the morning as he was putting the finishing touches on a memo due on the partner's desk at eight a.m.

"Come with me! Now!" She'd shed her suit jacket and unbuttoned her silk blouse so that her lace bra was slightly visible. She came around his desk and planted a long kiss on his lips.

"Can't tonight," he managed when she let him speak. "This has to be finished when His Worship arrives in the morning." That was their nickname for the partner they worked for.

"Just give me a half hour, please."

He gave her an affectionate, but exasperated smile. "Can't tonight. Really. I'll get fired if I don't finish this. I don't perform well when I'm under this much pressure."

"It's not sex. It's something else."

He could see she wasn't going to give up. "Okay. But thirty minutes. Max."

She led him to their usual haunt, the library. But it wasn't their usual haunt at all. She'd transformed it with tiny white lights strung across some of the shelves, and somehow she'd managed to push four of the massive tables together. She turned on a tape player and jumped up onto the middle of one of them. The strains of a Strauss Waltz filled the air.

"Come dance with me!"

"Morgan, you've lost your mind. What if someone comes in?"

"We'll invite them to dance, too. Come on! Ever since I first saw these tables, I knew they were made to dance on. Ginger Rogers and Fred Astaire."

She was nuts. But he was amazed at her courage. And at this point, he hated the place so much, he didn't care if they were caught. So he joined her and steered her around her improvised dance floor until they were both laughing so hard, they had to sit down.

He smiled at the memory. A great deal of her charm was her willingness to flaunt convention in a place where being conventional was the only way to survive.

"I hate law practice," she said over and over again in the trashy hotel rooms as they dressed after sex to go back to their endless research assignments.

"Then give it up."

"Don't tempt me."

"Why not? You could leave Jay and go anywhere in the world you wanted to go. And do anything you wanted to do."

"The shock of having to support himself would kill him," she said.

"But why stay with him just so that he doesn't have to work?"

"It's not about Jay anymore. I'm still at the firm to be close to you. I'll leave if you'll leave—with me."

She didn't understand that he was in love with Anne. He told her as gently and matter-of-factly as he could, over and over. Their affair ended six months later when she got tired of her husband and tired of hearing how much he loved Anne. She walked out of the library one day without even leaving a resignation letter. Ed doubted the firm knew she was gone until her husband called three months later to find out if she still worked there.

After Morgan took off, Ed realized that he couldn't let the boredom of his job pull him into another affair. She had been funny and feisty and willing to take risks that, in retrospect, he shouldn't have agreed to. He wanted a life with Anne, and he blamed himself for allowing his job to absorb him. He didn't like her affairs, but he honestly couldn't blame her for them. He would win her back. He had no desire to make the long trek to partnership because it would mean losing Anne.

Ed began to limit his hours at the firm. He did his best to make it home by eight o'clock every night. He would hurry up to their tiny apartment, hoping to have supper with her. Sometimes he'd find her waiting, but more often he'd find the apartment dark because she was already out with her friends. When she'd announced that she was pregnant with Wynne, he'd counted up the months to see if he could actually be the father. The timing was close, so he said nothing. But there was no doubt that he wasn't the only man Anne had been sleeping with.

With a child on the way and his marriage faltering, he decided that changing his career was the only way to get things back on track. And just in case one of Anne's literary or musical friends was the baby's father, he decided to make sure the child was born far enough away that it wouldn't matter. The assistant professorship in his hometown had been a godsend in every way.

* * *

But there were things Ed had not counted on. One was Anne's new group of artsy friends. She'd auditioned for the Richmond Symphony and won a place high up in the first violin section. The string players traveled in packs, Ed soon came to realize. They hung out together after rehearsals and performances and had dinners at each other's homes. And some of them were attractive single men.

At first, he tried bravely to fly the flag of their marriage. He went to some of the couples' events even though he felt like a fish out of water. And Anne's preoccupation with her musical friends had an unexpected benefit: it gave him more one-on-one time with Wynne. The symphony rehearsed on Friday mornings. So when he went to the office on Fridays, he took Wynne with him and parked him with his toys in one corner while he met with students in the other. Afterwards, they had Happy Meals at McDonald's and fell in love with the toy du jour.

The other thing that he had not foreseen was Anne's refusal to respond to his efforts to win her back. He discovered that she was sleeping with her stand partner, a married professor of music at Virginia Commonwealth University where she was a half-time English instructor. And then there were the weekends when she took off to New York—sometimes alone, but sometimes with Wynne. His suspicion that she might be taking Wynne to see his biological father grew and grew.

He could demand a paternity test, but the tests based on blood type were only about eighty percent accurate. He'd be risking his marriage if he made his doubts known. He didn't want a divorce. He was in love with Anne, and above all, he didn't want to lose his son. Ed had seen him draw his first breath. He'd persuaded Anne to continue the unbroken line of Edward Wynne Carters. He adored his precious blue-eyed, dark-haired boy with all his heart. If he didn't carry his half of the gene pool, it made no difference to Ed. He was, in every other way, his son.

The final complication that Ed had not foreseen when he'd turned his back on Sullivan and Cromwell in hopes of keeping his family together was running into an obstacle like Allison Byrd. She was a One L, a first-year law student, and she targeted him on the first day of evidence class in the fall of 1982. Day after day, she saved her questions until class was over and lingered by his podium until all the other students had left the room. But by that time, Ed had been teaching for four years, and he had had experience with student crushes. Being a handsome, mid-thirties professor from a wealthy, Old Virginia family was a formula for creating childish fantasies in immature female heads. But keeping his distance and his wedding band visible were proven ways to dry up the fairy tales. So after class, when Allison complained that she didn't understand hearsay exceptions or the rules for authenticating documents, Ed had made impatient gestures with his left hand and told her to reread her assignments to find the answers to her questions.

She didn't react well to being told to get lost. She would purse her full lips into a pout and swing her long, dark hair over her shoulders in annoyance and flash her dark eyes and whine, "But Professor Carter, I *did* read the cases, and I don't *understand.*"

"I'd suggest you join a study group, then."

She wasn't classically beautiful like Anne. She had a wide, round face and prominent cheekbones. Her nose was broad and flat as if it had been broken and badly reset at some point. She was tall, five eight or nine, heavyset, and big-boned. Her eyes and her dark hair were her best features. She favored tight jeans and tight t-shirts; and even if she wasn't a beauty, she was a practiced flirt. Ed noticed that she commanded a lot of male attention, and he devoutly hoped that by second semester she would find herself a boyfriend and take Evidence Two from someone else. But no luck. When the new semester opened in January, she was back, hanging out at his podium after every class.

He counted the days until the end of that semester. When summer came, he wrote an article on the United States Supreme Court's decision in *Enmund v. Florida,* which held that the death penalty could not be imposed on offenders who were involved in a felony in which a murder was committed by someone else but who did not actually kill, attempt to kill, or intend that a killing take place. But he wrote at home and stayed away from his office. And he rented a cottage at Sandbridge for the entire month of August, determined to have Anne and Wynne all to himself before school started. And he hoped against hope that Anne was finished with her stand partner and those trips to New York.

BRENDAN

"What we call the beginning is often the end. And to make an end is to make a beginning."

T.S. Eliot

CHAPTER FIVE

Wednesday, January 4, 2017, 28 Liberty Street, New York, New York

Brendan sat in the waiting room of Venture Capital Assets at 28 Liberty Street, formerly the Chase Manhattan Plaza. He had a knot in his stomach. Wynne was in a meeting, so Brendan had to wait to deliver his bad news.

He'd driven straight back to his office after seeing Ed yesterday. His team of associates had been hard at work writing a writ of habeas corpus and a request for a stay of the execution. The trouble was he knew he didn't have the evidence he needed to succeed.

The door opened, and Wynne came through, smiling. He was Ed's height, five nine, but he had his mother's slender build. He had her dark hair and light-blue eyes. His face was round, like hers, and it made him look boyish even at thirty-eight. He wore the same rimless glasses that his father wore. They also made him look scholarly and intelligent.

"Sorry to make you wait!" Wynne pulled him into a bear hug. "Did Dad tell you, I'm getting married? And it's someone you know!"

"I heard about the married part, not the-someone-I-know part." Anything to put off the moment when he had to tell him.

Wynne took him by the arm and led him through the door to the inner sanctum and kept his friendly grip on his elbow as he walked him down the long corridor to his corner office. It was three o'clock, and the winter light was beginning to fade.

Wynne sat down on the sofa with the breathtaking view of Manhattan and gestured for Ed to sit beside him. He poured two mugs of coffee from a black, ceramic pot and added cream to Brendan's before handing it to him. He put one spoonful of sugar in his own cup and stirred it thoughtfully.

He's known me since he was seven years old. He's as much my son as Tim is. He knows all the little things about me including how I take my coffee. How can I tell him what I have to tell him?

"It's Claire Chastain," Wynne said, beaming. But when Brendan didn't respond immediately, Wynne's smiled faded. His blue eyes became anxious. "What's wrong? I thought you'd be thrilled because she was Ellen's best friend at St. Catherine's."

Brendan made himself smile. He was happy that two people he loved like his own children had found each other. But he hated delivering a blow to both of them at what should have been the happiest of times. "I'm thrilled. Emma will be, too. Ellen just told her Claire was engaged. She didn't say it was you."

"I asked her to let me tell you," Wynne said, his smile now back in place. "March 4. We're looking for a place in Richmond to be close to Dad. I want to take Claire to see him the day after the wedding."

Brendan sipped his coffee and looked out the window as the

day faded over New York. He felt Wynne studying him.

"You've got news about Dad, and it's not good, is it? I thought the doctor gave him a clean bill of health after they did the biopsy of that lump on his thyroid last November."

"It's not that," Brendan said. He sighed, put down his cup, opened his briefcase, and handed Wynne the order.

His face went white as he read. He threw it on the coffee table as if it burned his fingers. Tears filled his eyes. He couldn't speak for some time. Then he said, "Why now after so many years? He's sixty-nine. He can't have that much time left."

Brendan put his arm around Wynne and said quietly, "He's had three trials. There have been direct appeals after all of them. The Virginia Supreme Court reversed twice. His direct appeal after the third trial has been over for a long time, and we've been going up on writs on newly discovered evidence ever since."

"And why hasn't that new evidence ever made a difference?" Wynne demanded.

Brendan sighed. "Virginia courts are some of the most skeptical in the nation when it comes to new evidence. But I thought we finally had a shot at overturning his conviction this last time when those two prosecution witnesses admitted that they had lied in his third trial when they testified that he slept with Allison Byrd. That should have cast doubt on the prosecutor's claims that your father killed your mother to replace her with Byrd. But the Fourth Circuit wouldn't budge, and the U.S. Supreme Court has refused review." Brendan wasn't about to tell Wynne what Judge Boyce had said to him.

"It's Gordon, isn't it?" Wynne wiped his eyes with a napkin from the coffee tray.

"He's behind this order."

"I would have to say yes. But we've always known that he isn't going to rest until he gets what he believes is vengeance for your mother's death."

Wynne stared out at the city in the dimming light. Finally, he looked back at Brendan and waved his hands expansively. "All of this has been for my dad. I went to Wharton and did the joint JD/MBA so I would be able to save his life. When I graduated, I realized that going to work as an attorney wouldn't be enough. I'd be one lawyer against the slew of investigators and cops that put my dad on death row. So I built Venture Capital Assets in order to have the money to hire the best lawyers and investigators to find Gordon Fairfax's liars and make them tell the truth: my father didn't kill my mother."

Brendan sat quietly, remembering the day that fifteen-year-old Wynne had called him and said, "I need your help. I can't go on living with Aunt Jessica. I know my dad is innocent." Ed's supposed accomplice in Anne's murder, William James Miller, had just told the Mid-Atlantic Innocence Project that the police had coerced him to say that Ed hired him to kill Anne. The Fairfaxes, including Wynne's Aunt Jessica, had been up in arms because Ed was going to get another trial. Brendan had arranged for Wynne to go from Anne's sister, Jessica, to Ed's sister, Margaret Carter Randolph. And he had been sure that the Commonwealth's third attempt to convict Ed would fail. But he'd been wrong.

"What are you thinking about?" Wynne's voice brought Brendan back to the moment.

"About when you decided to leave Jessica's and go to Margaret's."

"They should have let Dad go after Miller admitted that he lied when he said my father was involved in my mother's murder."

"I wish the law had that much common sense," Brendan agreed. "A prosecutor, particularly one like Gordon, will hang on to a conviction at any cost."

"Even when he knows the person he's convicted is innocent?"

"Even then," Brendan agreed.

* * *

By the time Brendan's meeting with Wynne was over, it was nearly time to catch his plane back to Richmond. And he was exhausted by the emotional effort the meeting had cost him. But he rode the elevator up to the fifty-second floor, one of the many occupied by Craig, Lewis, and Weller's New York office, to congratulate Tyndall on Claire's engagement.

"I'm so sorry, Mr. Murphy," his secretary said. "Mr. Chastain is with his daughter this afternoon. She's picking out her wedding dress."

CLAIRE

"Whatever you want, be sure that is what you want; whatever you feel, be sure that is what you feel."

T.S. Eliot

CHAPTER SIX

Wednesday, January 4, 2017, Vera Wang, Madison Avenue, New York, New York

Through the crack in the velvet drapes in the fitting room of Vera Wang's flagship store on Madison Avenue, Claire Chastain could see her father sitting on the deep- charcoal-gray couch in the waiting area. Tyndall Chastain was studying the champagne flute in his hand. Single malt scotch was more his style, but Claire had no doubt that he was drinking the champagne that the Head Bridal Consultant, whose name tag said 'Margo,' had offered in honor of her mother. Julia had loved champagne, and she'd be sipping it now if she had still been with them. He was thinking about her mother. She could tell by the pensive look on his face.

Claire studied the layers of tulle that enveloped her and decided that they were too much. Her style had always been sleek and elegant.

The Assistant Bridal Consultant, whose name was Agnes and whose accent was French, eyed her with concern. "You don't like this one?"

Claire moved left and then right, watching the movement of the skirt in the fitting room's mirror. "No. Let's try that one." She pointed to the satin slip dress hanging on a peg above Agnes' head.

Claire peered through the curtains again while Agnes extracted her from the pile of tulle. She knew this was a happy day for her father. He had known how hurt she'd been for so many years by her hopeless love for the attorney she'd worked with for her entire career at Warrick, Thompson in San Diego, but who had, in the end, married someone else. But her father understood how easy it was to fall in love with the person you saw more than anyone else in the world. It had happened to him, too, many years after her mother's death. But as she watched him sip champagne and make small talk with Margo, she read the sadness in his brown eyes. *He's thinking that my mother should have been the one here with me now.*

Claire had always wished for a love story like the one that brought her parents together. Her hard-charging, business attorney father from a Brahmin Boston family had been swept off his feet by an elegant debutante from an Old Virginia family whose passion was art and fashion. Tyndall Chastain had been twenty-eight the summer that he had met Julia Marie Turner. He had been at Craig, Lewis, and Weller for three years, having gone straight from Harvard Law to the firm's corporate department. Many of his clients were friends of his father, who was the president of First Trust Bank of Boston. The Chastain family had owned First Trust for generations. His family's ownership of one of the firm's long-time clients meant he would inevitably become a partner, and a powerful one at that.

But her mother's family also had a history. The Turners had owned a plantation on the Rappahannock River near Port Conway before and after the Civil War. By 1893, none of the remaining Turners had wanted to go on farming, so the family had sold the plantation and moved to Richmond where they became doctors and lawyers.

Julia's father had been a tax attorney at Hunton and Williams. Julia had gone to private school at St. Catherine's and then on to Wellesley where she'd majored in art history. After college, she'd made her way to New York and used her elegance and Southern charm to finagle a job as a junior editorial assistant at *Vogue*. She was five-eight, very thin, with riveting blue eyes set in a heart-shaped face. The first thing anyone noticed about her were those eyes. She wore her chin-length, blonde hair loose by day, but put it up in an elegant chignon in the evening. Her job allowed her to borrow couture from *Vogue's* closets. French designers were her favorites. She was a blonde version of Audrey Hepburn.

Tyndall saw Julia for the first time on a hot August night in 1979. She had been in charge of a dozen models, circulating through a Madison Avenue art gallery, showing the clothes of a designer whom he had never heard of. After their wedding, Tyndall would cheerfully buy any scrap of clothing that Givenchy made if Claire's mother wanted to wear it.

Unlike her father's straight-laced, unemotional family, Julia was from a warm and adventurous clan. She was an only child, but she had seven cousins who served as brothers and sisters. She was cheerful and funny, and she loved to laugh. And she was always ready to run barefoot through Central Park in the rain.

Tyndall adored everything about her from the moment he saw her herding those models through that crowd of art patrons.

Since her engagement on Christmas Eve, Claire had reassured herself that marrying Wynne in March only three months later was not rushing things. Her utterly besotted father had married her mother in a lavish wedding in St. Stephen's Church in Richmond six months after that fateful August night. They had set up housekeeping in the four-bedroom apartment on Fifth Avenue overlooking Central Park that her Grandfather Chastain had given Tyndall as a wedding present. Julia had continued her career at *Vogue* even after Claire Marie was born in 1981.

"Here is the jacket," Agnes said as she slipped the matching jacket over the simple dress.

Claire studied herself in the mirror. Finally, she shook her head again. "It says second or third wedding to me."

Agnes nodded. "I agree. Let's try the next one."

Margo was pouring more champagne for her father. Claire was surprised that he was making small talk with her instead of pulling out his cell phone to read his messages. But although Tyndall loved his work, he had always made time for Claire. She smiled as Agnes buttoned her into another gown. She had always counted herself lucky to have him firmly on her side in all things, including putting everything else aside for her at this important moment in her life.

Her parents had wanted more children, but none had come. Still, Claire reflected as she studied the off-the-shoulder silk column with a modest pearl-encrusted train, her parents had had an extraordinarily happy marriage. Julia had had a passion for the arts: fashion, ballet, the Philharmonic, the Metropolitan Opera, and repertory theater. And Tyndall had shared that passion and had loved to contribute his family's millions to the artistic causes of Julia's choice.

And her mother's job at *Vogue,* particularly after she'd risen to Assistant Editor, had also required her to attend formal parties. Claire knew how much her father had loved arriving at those parties with Julia on his arm, dripping in the diamonds that he showered on her for Christmas and birthdays. He could spare no expense to show her how much he loved her and how happy she made him.

Julia had brought the fun and laughter into Tyndall's life that he'd always craved but had never had. When she died, all the light went out of his world. For months after her mother's death, Claire heard her father pacing in his bedroom in the wee hours of the night. His grief was an ocean that engulfed both of them. Night after night, unable to sleep herself, Claire slipped out of bed to find her father standing in her mother's enormous walk-in closet, comforting himself by touching the silks and satins and cashmeres that hung there, heavy with the scent of Chanel No. 5. Claire could hear her mother's soft, southern drawl saying, "Tyn, I love you. So, so much." Julia was the only person who had ever shortened her very dignified father's given name, and she always lingered on the "n."

Claire had been ten in 1991 when her mother died. Leukemia. She'd lasted only six months after the diagnosis. After Julia deserted them both, Tyndall debated whether to keep Claire in New York or send her south to Richmond to boarding school at St. Catherine's. In the end, he'd realized how lonely she would be in their huge apartment while he worked the hours his job demanded. At St. Catherine's, she'd be constantly surrounded by the other girls and by Julia's Turner cousins.

It had been the right decision. Claire had been happy in Richmond, and there'd been the unforeseen bonus of her friendship with Ellen Murphy. Tyndall had not known Brendan before their daughters became close friends even though they were both Craig, Lewis partners. But he could not have chosen better foster parents for Claire than Brendan and Emma Murphy. On the weekends when Claire hadn't come home to him in New York, she had stayed at the Murphys'.

Agnes finished tweaking the current dress and stepped back to view her handiwork. "It's lovely on you," she said. "I brought a veil for you to try with it."

Claire stood still while Agnes attached a long piece of tulle that ended in a single row of silk flowers that overlapped the dress' modest train. When Agnes finished and stepped back, Claire studied herself in the three mirrors that surrounded her.

Her father had thought that she would grow up to be an actor. Her height and her fascinating blue eyes, which she had inherited from Julia, made her a commanding presence by the time she was fourteen. She loved the theater and was always looking for opportunities to perform. During her summers with Tyndall in New York, he had made her take bel canto singing lessons from Anna Damero, a lesser known soprano, at the Metropolitan Opera. If you want to be on stage, he had insisted, you must learn how to project your voice. She had hated those lessons, but Tyndall had been right. Bel canto singing had taught her how to deliver a closing argument that could mesmerize a jury.

In the end, Brendan's quiet influence had turned Claire away from the risks of acting. Whereas her father's corporate practice had seemed dry as toast, Brendan's work as a litigator had set her on fire. She had watched one of his trials with Ellen when the two were sixteen, and she had immediately known that litigation was going to be her life's work. Tyndall had been overjoyed.

The curtains stirred, and Margo appeared with the champagne bottle.

"I came to see if you need anything. That's a lovely gown on you."

Claire turned to observe the back. "Yes, but it's still not quite what I'm looking for."

"I think she might like the 'Cecile,' don't you, Agnes?" Margo asked.

"Yes, it's lovely with this veil. I'll go get it," Agnes agreed.

"Let me pour you some champagne," Margo said, filling a flute as she spoke.

Why not? Claire picked up the glass as Margo left the fitting room. *It might take the edge off my nerves. Should I have nerves? Isn't this exactly what I wanted last spring when I left San Diego for New York? To meet a man I could fall in love with who wasn't Paul Curtis?*

Last October, she'd walked into *The Tempest,* the bar around the corner from her apartment building in Chelsea, to unwind over a glass of wine after a long day at Warrick, Thompson's New York office. She'd happened to sit down next to a tall, thin, dark-haired man in his late thirties, who was wearing jeans, a turtleneck, and an obviously expensive leather jacket, and who said he lived in the neighborhood, too. He had a long, thin face and lovely light-blue eyes that looked at the world through rimless spectacles. And above all, he had a warm, inviting smile.

They'd started to chat, and it hadn't been long before they'd learned that they had both lost their mothers in childhood, had spent a lot of their growing up years in Richmond, and were close to the Murphys. Wynne had told her later that he had always hated that moment when new acquaintances learned his father was on death row. But the news hadn't shocked Claire because she'd been hearing about his father's case from Brendan since the sixth grade when she had become Ellen's best friend and a regular visitor at the Murphys'.

In mid-November, during dinner at Per Se, she'd told him the story of her hopeless love for Paul Curtis. She'd felt that she should be honest with him about the painful parts of her own past. He listened thoughtfully as she explained how she'd fallen into the trap of loving an unavailable man.

"I began working for Paul on my first day at Warrick, Thompson as a new associate. He was married then and the father of a daughter. He was up for partner that year, which he made easily. Paul is a very good attorney. But he worked long hours, and his wife decided she'd had enough. By that time, I was in love with him. We worked together every day. We traveled together for work. He knew everything about me, and I knew everything about him: how he took his coffee, which judges he hated to be in front of, which judges he liked, and how he liked to surf in the mornings before work. I never had time to develop a relationship with anyone else. So when his marriage was over, I hoped he'd see how much I loved him and that we were already like a married couple because of our jobs."

"So you went on working with him?" Wynne asked.

"Yes. I kept telling myself he'd eventually figure it out. But he didn't. Last spring, a woman he'd dated in law school made sure her path would cross his again. She got herself assigned to a case that Paul and I had here in New York. She was opposing counsel. She'd only been back in his life for a few weeks when Paul asked her to marry him."

"And so you left San Diego and came to New York?"

She smiled. "I realized I needed a change."

I didn't tell him all of that story, she thought as she sipped champagne and waited for Agnes to return with the new dress. *I didn't tell him about the look in Paul's eyes when his fiancée flashed her engagement ring in my face. We'd spent all those years together; and in all that time, he had never realized I was in love with him until the moment he told me he was going to marry someone else.*

I didn't tell Wynne that I got up from the table and took the next plane back to San Diego and called Jeff because I knew he was the only one who'd realize how desperately hurt I was. I didn't tell Wynne that Jeff saved my life that night because he stayed with me and put me on the plane home to New York in the morning.

Why didn't I tell Wynne the whole story about Jeff? We've never been anything but friends. We were in the same study group in law school. I told my father that he needed a job after Warrick, Thompson fired him so unfairly. But my father didn't bring him to Craig, Lewis because of me. He wanted him at the firm because he's such a good lawyer. And he's involved with Beth Rafferty, his former client, although lately he's been traveling to Houston to see her less often. I don't want her to find someone else and hurt Jeff. He used to be a jerk about women, but he's turned out to be like my father, a man who is truly capable of love.

"More champagne, Miss Chastain?" Margo was back and already pouring.

Claire sipped and studied the five-carat diamond on her left hand. Telling Wynne about Paul hadn't put him off. He'd gone straight to Tiffany's and bought a ring and arranged for the two of them to fly to Paris for Christmas. She smiled at the memory. He'd rented a boat to take them on a private cruise down the Seine and had commissioned a champagne dinner from world-renowned chef Guy Savoy. On the stroke of midnight, he had asked her to be his wife. And after they had come back to New York, he'd told her why he wanted such a short engagement.

"I'm anxious to feel settled in a home that's truly my own," he said over a romantic dinner on New Year's Eve at the River Café. He'd booked a table next to the windows that overlooked the East River and New York's breathtaking night skyline. He reached across the table and took her hands in his and explained earnestly, "I've never had a sense of belonging in any of the families that I've lived with, and I'd given up expecting ever to start my own family until I met you. Even the money I've made, and I've made a lot, hasn't persuaded the women I've dated not to flee as soon as they found out that my father is on death row and my first priority is to save his life."

Claire squeezed his hands and said softly, "A short engagement is all right with me. I can see why you felt out of place with your mother and your father's families when you were growing up."

He sighed and studied the buildings glowing in the dark across the water before he said, "I was just a prize that the Fairfaxes and Carters competed for. Each family felt that it had to have my loyalty to prove its claim about my mother's murder. After my father was arrested, I went to live with my Aunt Jessica, my mother's sister. She drilled into me my sacred duty to hate my selfish, murderous father."

Wynne let go of her hands and sipped his wine as if he needed to fortify himself to tell the rest of his story. "But my Grandmother Carter got a court order that forced my Aunt Jessica to take me to visit my father twice a year. I couldn't find anything selfish or murderous about him. He was just a kind, scholarly man who sat behind the glass window at the prison with all the love in the world for me in his eyes and voice. We couldn't touch, but I was sure that he didn't kill my mother and that he loved me."

"It must have been so hard for you," Claire said. He was too far away for her to wipe the tears that had overflowed.

He wiped them himself, sipped his wine, then took a deep breath and went on. "When I was fifteen, that horrible Miller monster confessed that the police had coerced him to say that my father was involved in my mother's death. For the first time in my life, I could say out loud what I'd always felt: my father was innocent. But I couldn't say that in Aunt Jessica's house. So I asked Brendan to transfer my guardianship to my father's sister, my Aunt Margaret. I felt less alone there because her two sons were close to my age."

He paused and took her hands again. The tears were back in his eyes. "What I've always wanted, Claire, is for Dad to come home and for us to live together as a family in a house of our own. When I was fifteen, I figured out that with enough money, I could make that dream come true. I could find the people who'd help me prove he didn't kill my mother."

Claire held his hands tightly as if he were drowning, and she was trying to pull him to safety. She couldn't speak because of the lump in her throat.

He looked down at the engagement ring he had given her and lightly kissed the hand that wore it. He said, "And now my dream has another part. More than anything in the world, I still want to bring Dad home safely, but now I want to put the wedding band that I bought for you on your finger. Having one without the other would break my heart."

"Here is the dress," Agnes said, arriving with yet another garment bag.

She helped Claire out of the one she had on and into a column of lace with long sleeves and a narrow skirt that flared just enough to produce a short, graceful train.

Agnes pinned the long veil that ended in the modest cascade of flowers into Claire's boyishly short hair.

"What do you think?" she asked.

"I think it's perfect."

No, she told herself as she surveyed the dress from all sides, I don't have any doubts about Wynne or about this dress or about marrying him on the fourth of March.

Agnes pushed the curtains back, and Claire walked through them toward her father whose face lit up at the sight of her. He stood up and came toward her to take both of her hands.

"This is it," she beamed. "This is the dress."

He nodded. "Your mother would have agreed."

ED

"Only by acceptance of the past, can you alter it."

T.S. Eliot

CHAPTER SEVEN

Monday, January 9, 2017, Sussex State Prison, Sussex, Virginia

"They are going to postpone the wedding," Ed said. He was sitting across from Brendan in the Attorney Interview Room. Father Jim had come down from Richmond, too. He was sitting next to Ed.

"I know," Brendan said. "Claire called to tell me."

"I'm glad Wynne's marrying into your family, more or less," Ed smiled.

"Me, too," Brendan smiled back.

"I told him not to postpone." Ed frowned. "He was here the day after you were." Ed's eyes filled with tears. "I told him he has to go on with his life and be happy. He said he isn't ready to give up on saving my life."

"Postponing the wedding is their decision to make," Father Jim pointed out quietly.

Ed said nothing as he swiped at his tears.

"Claire wants to work with me on getting a stay of execution," Brendan explained. "She's on her way down from New York right now. I'll start going over your case with her tomorrow morning in my office. And Wynne has ten investigators looking for new evidence."

Ed wished Brendan and Father Jim had stayed longer because as soon as they left, the old memories took over. He was back in his classroom, facing his nightmare, Allison Byrd.

* * *

September 1983, University of Richmond, School of Law, Richmond, Virginia

She was back. She was now a Two L, sitting in the front row of his Criminal Law One course. Ed was relieved to see that the young man next to her was very attentive. He hoped she'd found a love interest at last.

But she kept turning up during his Friday morning office hours without the boyfriend. The symphony had moved its rehearsals to Wednesday evening, but Anne had joined a string quartet that rehearsed on Friday mornings at the VCU music department. The ensemble had been organized by her stand partner from the symphony, Richard Neal. When Anne announced that she'd joined Neal's quartet, Ed had realized they'd restarted their affair. The purpose of the quartet was to enlarge their time together.

Once again, he thought of confronting Anne. But his marriage had seemed to be back on solid ground all summer. They'd made love, worked on the house, gone on vacation with Wynne, and talked about trying to have another child. He just couldn't bring himself to believe that their marriage was in jeopardy again. He resolutely looked the other way and focused on his Friday mornings with Wynne. And that was how Allison Byrd finally breached his defenses. She figured out that Wynne held the key to his heart.

She came every Friday to play with him while Ed conferenced with other students. He tried to discourage her, but a four-year-old is easily bribed with toys and sweets. Ed saw what she was doing. He had ignored her, so she was using his son to gain his attention. To avoid giving her that attention, he remained polite but distant on Friday mornings. When office hours were over, he scooped up Wynne and headed for McDonald's without a backward look. Until the middle of October.

It rained that Friday. Huge drops pelted the ground, and the wind whipped at the eves of McAllister Hall where Ed had his office. The weather was so bad that no students showed, and even the ones who had appointments cancelled.

Allison took Wynne into the conference room down the hall and helped him kick a soft, plastic ball around and around the big table in the center of the room. Ed could hear Wynne's delighted shrieks as he fought Allison for the ball and won. Her ingenuity in using the conference room for soccer practice reminded him of dancing with Morgan Thomas on the tables in the Sullivan and Cromwell library.

Ed decided to pack up early and head for McDonald's with Wynne. Two hours in the office were enough on a day when no one wanted to brave the weather to see him. He could leave at eleven instead of noon. As Allison followed him and Wynne out of the building, Ed realized that she had no umbrella. He offered to let her walk under his to her car.

"I don't have a car, Professor Carter. I'm catching the bus."

He signed inwardly. The only decent thing to do in that weather was to offer to drive her to the bus stop.

Less than a minute later, Ed pulled up in front of the sheltered bench. But as Allison opened the passenger door, Wynne piped up from the back, "Can Aunt Allison come to McDonald's, too?"

Ed winced at the faux-relative name Allison had assigned herself. He waited for her to say she had other plans, but she froze with her hand on the door, her dark eyes fixed hopefully on his face. A huge gust of wind suddenly bore down on the car, pushing so hard on the door that Allison had to close it again. Although he wanted to, Ed couldn't turn her out in the storm. So he said to his son, "All right."

He learned from their awkward discourse over burgers and fries that she had grown up on a farm near Roanoke. Her father still lived there, but her mother had long ago packed a bag and vanished. She'd gone to college at Radford and then decided to set her sights on law school. Her LSATs had not been stellar. She'd barely met the qualifications for the University of Richmond.

So much personal talk made Ed uncomfortable. He tried to lead the discussion to her boyfriend. By now Ed knew he was James Watkins, the young man who always sat next to her in his class.

But Allison shrugged when Ed brought up James and handed Wynne a piece of her French fry. The gesture seemed proprietary, and it irritated Ed. "I think we are going to break up soon."

Ed felt trapped and glanced out the huge glass windows as if instinctively looking for an escape route. He was relieved that the rain had let up. "Wynne and I have to go home. My wife's expecting us." He said the words "my wife" with deliberate emphasis.

Wynne didn't like being hurried through his meal, but Ed realized he had to get away from Allison. His mind raced as he tried to think of ways to get her out of his class by Monday. A few minutes later, when he finally dropped her at the bus stop, he said, "It's really not necessary for you to come in on Fridays unless you have a reason to see me about the course. Wynne has his toys, and he's good at entertaining himself." Which was true.

Her face said that she understood his message. She nodded sullenly and got out. Ed hoped that was the last hint he'd have to give her.

* * *

But the next Friday, she returned a half hour after Ed arrived with Wynne for office hours. He was in the midst of a conference with a student when she appeared. He never had the chance to tell her to leave because Wynne brightened the minute she appeared in the doorway. He ran toward her from the corner where Ed had left him with his toys. Unlike the previous Friday, the sun was shining in all its autumn glory. She took Wynne outside, and they chased the ball that they'd chased in the conference room the previous week. And she made sure she was in full view of the long windows of Ed's office that overlooked the lawn.

Ed worked to control his anger. He didn't want any of the

other students to see how infuriated he was. He got through the morning conferences without exploding even though he wanted to.

When the last student left, he quickly gathered up his books and papers and Wynne's toys and stuffed them into his backpack. Footsteps behind him alerted him to someone entering his office. He turned, expecting to find Allison and Wynne, but Jane Birks, a full professor whose specialty was constitutional law, had entered and was studying his son and his unwanted babysitter through the long windows overlooking the lawn.

"She's here every week," she observed dryly.

"I didn't invite her," Ed replied, working to control his anger.

"Really?" Jane used the skeptical tone that she used to respond to One L's comments in her Con Law class. "Looks like she's auditioning for the role of stepmother to me."

Ed grasped the backpack to avoid slapping her. She gave him one more sarcastic smirk before she strode out of his office. He wanted to put his fist between her smug eyes.

He swung the backpack across his shoulders and headed outside. He was relieved when Wynne ran straight into his arms. "Daddy, daddy!"

Ed was overcome with the smell of the baby shampoo and dinosaur bubbles that he and Anne used for his bath. He hugged his son's small, compact body gratefully.

"I'm all done with work," he told Wynne, taking him by the hand when he released him from the hug. "Let's go."

But Wynne looked back at Allison, who was holding the ball

they'd been playing with. She was watching Ed closely. "Can Aunt Allison come, too?"

"No!" The look in those four-year-old blue eyes said that Wynne didn't understand why Ed had spoken so sharply. But he had to put a stop to this here and now. "And you only have two aunts, Wynne. Aunt Jessica and Aunt Margaret."

Wynne looked confused but said no more. He understood that his father was upset and something wasn't right. Ed led him away from where Allison was standing, still holding the ball. It was the long way to the car, but Ed didn't care.

They had gone about ten steps when she called out, "Professor Carter! Wait."

Ed steeled himself and turned to face her. She looked thoroughly intimidated, and he was glad. She held out the ball tentatively, "Wynne forgot his toy."

"That's not Wynne's," Ed said severely. "You brought it."

"But I meant for him to keep it."

"He has enough toys, thank you." Ed turned again, and this time he picked up his son so that he could get away from her faster. But her footsteps behind him told him that she was following.

He controlled himself until he reached the car. He managed to keep his emotions in check while he strapped Wynne into his car seat. He closed the car door and turned to face Allison Byrd.

"I'm very happily married," he began, "and I find your attention to me and to my son inappropriate—"

"But Professor Carter," she broke in before he could finish. "I—"

He held up his hand. "I am not the least interested in

anything you have to say. Do not come back to my class on Monday. Do not come back to my office, and above all, stay away from my son."

"But—"

"And if you don't, I'll call campus security and have you removed. Is that clear?"

She glared at him for one long, unforgettable minute. And then she turned and stalked away. It didn't help that Wynne was screaming inside the car.

CHAPTER EIGHT

Monday, January 9, 2017, Sussex State Prison, Sussex, Virginia

That afternoon, Dr. Morris, the prison doctor, pulled the EKG sensors off Ed's chest and slowly wound up the wires.

"Your heart's in fine shape," he said.

"Should that be good news?" Ed asked. "Since the state of Virginia is planning to stop it on the third of March?"

The doctor winced. A physical examination of the condemned was part of the ritual to make sure no unforeseen medical condition would interfere with death on the appointed day. Dr. Morris' job was to make sure the lethal cocktail would work without outward signs of distress for the witnesses to report to the *Richmond Times Dispatch*. If the stuff actually hurt, Dr. Morris couldn't be held responsible, and he didn't actually care. Most inmates did not talk back to him during their pre-execution exams. Trust Ed Carter to be different.

"In the Middle Ages, everyone routinely prayed for an easy death," Dr. Morris said.

"And you're saying my heart will be easy to stop? Because it's so healthy."

That was exactly what the doctor was saying, but he did not want to admit it. After all, the Hippocratic Oath's principal tenent was "First do no harm."

* * *

Mid-October, 1983, University of Richmond, School of Law, Richmond, Virginia

She was back in his class on Monday, but she sat in the last row with James Watkins and exited as soon as class was over. He wished she'd done as he demanded and dropped his course, but he had no legitimate way to force her out. Besides, she could do no harm as long as she stayed away from him and Wynne.

But she didn't. On Wednesday night, Anne was late coming home from symphony rehearsal. She usually came back by eleven because she had to teach an early class on Thursday morning. But that night, she did not return until after midnight.

Ed tried not to think about where she most likely had been and with whom. Together they tiptoed into Wynne's room to make sure he was sleeping soundly and then got into their own bed in the master bedroom and turned out the light. Anne dropped off to sleep immediately, but Ed lay awake, trying not to imagine his wife making love with Richard Neal.

The thought tormented him so much that he got up and began to pace. He walked back and forth between the two floor-length windows that faced the side street. The leaves on the oaks had started to fall, and it was easy to see shadows in the bright moonlight. A tall figure dressed in dark clothes was standing on the sidewalk, staring up at his house. The height and build told him it was Allison Byrd.

His first thought was to call the police. But if he did, there'd be a write-up in the *Times Dispatch*. He could see the headline: "University of Richmond Law Professor Stalked by Female Student." The world would assume he'd come on to her, and his reputation would be in ruins. And if a reporter found Jane Birks, she'd treat him or her to the "auditioning for stepmother" remark.

Ed stood very still for a while, waiting for the figure to move on. His skin crawled as he wondered if she could see his shadow in the window.

He had no idea how much time passed, but it felt as if he'd been staring at the shadow across the street for at least an hour. Anne was still sleeping peacefully on her side of the queen bed. But what if she woke and asked why he was staring out the window at one thirty in the morning?

He went into the bathroom and pulled on the pants he'd discarded earlier and pulled a sweatshirt over his t-shirt. He thrust his sockless feet into his loafers and tiptoed downstairs.

He felt her watching him as he slipped out the back door. She didn't move as he advanced toward her. Suddenly, he wished he had a weapon. What if she was armed?

"How did you find my house?"

She shrugged. "City directory in the library."

Damn, why didn't I list our address as confidential. "You're not wanted here. Leave!"

"I'm on a public street, and I'm not trespassing. You can't make me."

He opened his mouth to say he'd call the police and then realized that hollow threats were useless. "What are you doing here in the middle of the night? Where's your boyfriend?"

"We broke up. Tonight. I'm your neighbor now. I'm renting an apartment at 2311." She pointed up Grove Avenue toward a house in the middle of the next block that Ed knew was divided into apartments. "I'm just going for a walk to get to know the neighborhood."

"Well, now you know it. Go home."

"Your wife's having an affair."

The words hit him like bullets, but he tried not to let her detect any reaction. "That's ridiculous!"

He turned away and started back to his house. He'd feel safer inside, and he didn't want to hear any more.

"I said, your wife's having an affair!" She shouted so loudly that a light went on upstairs in the house across the street. Exasperated because he was going to have to give her what she wanted, Ed turned and went back to confront her.

"Don't wake up the neighborhood! She isn't having an affair. We are very happily married."

Allison laughed, a low, scary, crazy laugh that made him wish once again for a weapon. "I saw her come home tonight. She got out of a guy's car. They kissed for a long time before she got out."

Damn, so that's why Anne had wanted a ride to rehearsal with Richard. Her car's taillight isn't really out.

Ed raised his fist to punch Allison's smirk but regained control at the last minute.

"You're not going to hit me," she taunted.

He turned and strode resolutely toward his house, feeling defeated. He'd been beaten. And now she'd be back for more.

CHAPTER NINE

Mid-October through Early November 1983, The Carter House, Grove Avenue, Richmond, Virginia

Allison continued to come to his class; but she stayed in the back row. James Watkins pointedly returned to the front to sit with a far more attractive young woman. Ed could feel Allison's eyes boring into him for the hour that he taught the class. Their dark intensity distracted him so much that he sometimes forgot what he was trying to teach. He could see the confusion in the other students' eyes when he lost his train of thought. He felt as if he were drowning, and there was no one to throw him a life preserver.

At least Allison did not appear on the last Friday in October for office hours. Afterward, he and Wynne had their usual McDonald's lunch, and Ed was relieved that Wynne never mentioned her.

But Halloween fell on the following Monday. Anne dressed Wynne as a green dinosaur, and she and Ed walked him up and down Grove Avenue, going to the houses of the neighbors they knew to allow him to fill his treat bag. Ed was painfully aware of the tall witch who followed them every step of the way and who planted herself on the sidewalk across the street to stare up at his bedroom window for hours afterward.

Somehow he got through the rest of the week. With a heroic effort, he ignored Allison in class and managed to keep his lectures on track. And he pulled the bedroom shades down at night and refused to look out even once because he knew she wanted him to see her staring up at his window. But he could tell that she was growing more and more agitated because he was ignoring her, and that meant some sort of new confrontation was brewing.

He was relieved that she stayed away from his office and Wynne on the first Friday in November. Then on Sunday, Anne suddenly suggested they drive to Charlottesville so that she could visit a bookstore that a colleague at VCU had been raving about. Ed was over the moon with joy because it was rare that the three of them did anything together anymore.

It was one of those perfect autumn days when all the leaves were vermillion and gold, and the air was crisp and cool. They packed Wynne and his toys into their white Volvo station wagon and headed up the mountain to Charlottesville. Ed had already received the invitation to speak at the Criminal Law Symposium to be held at the University of Virginia in two weeks. He hoped that Anne's sudden interest in this bookstore would help him persuade her to come to the conference with him. He knew that all the other speakers would be accompanied by their wives.

They had lunch in the village at Le Café, Anne's favorite French restaurant. Then they drove down three miles of winding country road to find Harrington's Rare Books, which turned out to be located in a barn on a farm that the Harringtons, a British couple, had purchased and restored. The Harringtons had put floor-length windows into the erstwhile barn's walls, with views that overlooked their recently harvested hayfields. The rolled bundles of hay glowed gold in the afternoon harvest sun. A fire burned steadily in the barn's gigantic fireplace, and cups of warm, cinnamon-spiced cider were lined up in rows on a table in front of the fire to welcome visitors.

Ed took Wynne to the children's section near the fire where he read to him from *Winnie The Pooh* and let him sip cider from his own cup. Since books were Anne's passion, he wanted to give her all the time she needed to browse the hundreds that lined the shelves. She smiled her thanks at Ed, picked up a cup of cider, and wandered along the rows until she was out of sight.

Ed read and shared the warm cider with Wynne and wished the day would never end. It was one of the few days of their marriage when he sensed that Anne was content and completely happy. And then it ended.

The bell on the front door jangled, but Ed didn't bother to turn and look to see who had come in. There were one or two other people in the store, and he assumed that another book lover had heard of this unusual shop in the middle of the hayfields. But suddenly Wynne jumped up and ran straight into Allison Byrd's arms.

"Aunt Allison!"

Ed stiffened as he put the book down and got up to retrieve his son. Her dark eyes met his triumphantly as she hugged Wynne.

"Wynne!" he commanded. His voice was so sharp that it startled his little boy, who immediately disentangled himself from Allison and returned to his father. Ed took him firmly by the hand, and said, "What did I tell you about aunts?"

"Aunt Jessica and Aunt Margaret, I know."

He led Wynne back to the children's corner, seated him firmly beside himself, and started to read again. But Wynne was no longer interested in the story. Allison had hidden herself behind a nearby bookshelf and was playing peekaboo to distract him.

Panic seized Ed. He didn't want to find Anne and make her leave because leaving before she was ready would spoil the afternoon. But he needed to get Wynne away from Allison as fast as possible.

While he was trying to come up with a solution, Anne appeared, carrying several books. "Look, Ed, first editions of T.S. Eliot! *The Wasteland,* and *The Four Quartets*, and *Murder in the Cathedral!*"

"Let's get them for you," he said. "Come on, Wynne. Mommy has found the books she wants."

As Ed stood up and took his son's hand, Allison came out from behind the bookshelf. Wynne's face brightened when he saw her, and Anne noticed. Her eyes went from her son's face to Allison's and back to Ed's. The ice in her cool, blue eyes when they met Ed's hurt as if she'd stuck a knife in his heart.

He wanted to scream, *No! No! No! You don't understand.* But instead he watched Allison step toward his wife and say, "I'm one of Professor Carter's students. Sometimes I watch Wynne on Fridays during office hours."

"I see," Anne said flatly. "How nice." She put the books down and picked up Wynne, gently disentangling his hand from Ed's as she held him possessively. "It's time to go."

The magic of the afternoon was gone. Ed looked down at the books, promising himself that he'd come back and buy them for her as Christmas presents when he returned for the conference. He felt Allison's dark, angry eyes boring holes in their backs as they left the store.

The car lulled Wynne to sleep shortly after Ed started the drive back to Richmond. Anne sat beside him, eyes straight ahead. He could see that she'd clenched her fists in her lap.

"I'm not sleeping with her," he said quietly into the icy silence.

"But she'd like for you to," Anne snapped back. "That's why she followed you all the way to Charlottesville."

"She told me she didn't have a car." He briefly summarized Allison's unwanted babysitting which had culminated in that awkward meal at McDonald's. But he didn't tell her that she was stalking him at night. He didn't want to frighten her.

"Well, apparently she does."

"Apparently. Or she stole one." How he wished that were true. She'd be in jail by the time Monday's class rolled around.

"You've at least encouraged her even if you haven't slept with her. And you've let her get close to Wynne." She spat out the last sentence like an indictment.

"No, I have not. I've told her to stay away from Wynne." *And us, and our house.*

The car rolled on down the mountain in the thinning afternoon light. The rich, warm glow of the morning was gone just as the cordiality between the two of them had evaporated. *It feels as if I'm sitting next to my bitterest enemy instead of my wife.*

Out of the corner of his eye, he saw Anne's fists clench and unclench in her lap. Finally, she said, "I've ended it with Richard."

Ed thought of Allison's report that she'd seen Anne and Richard in the car that night after rehearsal and wondered if she was lying. He kept his eyes straight ahead and said nothing. Maybe that kiss had been their final goodbye.

"You knew about Richard."

Still he looked at the road and was silent.

"I've left his string quartet. I've resigned from the symphony. I'm two and a half months pregnant, Ed. You know what that means. This summer. At the cottage in Sandbridge." And then she uttered the words that would forever burn a hole in his heart and soul. "This one is yours."

CHAPTER TEN

First Sunday in November 1983, The Carter House, Grove Avenue, Richmond, Virginia

That night, Ed gave Wynne his bath and put him to bed. The trip had tired him out, and he fell asleep as soon as his head hit the pillow. Ed turned out the light and sat in the warm glow of the teddy-bear night light, studying his precious boy. The fear that had gripped him all afternoon since Anne's confession squeezed his heart tighter. It had been one thing to suspect that he was not Wynne's biological father. It was another to know that his greatest fear had come true: another man could lay claim to his son.

As he sat by Wynne's bed, he willed himself to be calm. The thought that Allison was probably across the street by now, watching his house, didn't do anything to soothe his nerves.

He got up and went downstairs and poured himself a tall Jack Daniel's. Anne had gone to bed without eating supper. Ed remembered that she'd been tired in the early days of her pregnancy with Wynne.

He sat down in one of the wing chairs facing the fireplace

and felt himself begin to relax as he sipped the whisky. Only one small light burned on the table beside him. The clock on the mantel said eight forty-five. Nothing had changed as far as Wynne was concerned, he reassured himself. He had never let Anne's infidelity interfere with his love for his son. And now her decision to give up Richard and to have Ed's child meant that she, too, wanted their marriage to continue. Ed smiled at the thought of having a second child. He'd love to have a daughter this time. What would Anne think of naming her Caroline Anne for her grandmother and mother?

He was tired, and the whisky made him sleepy. He dozed off. He woke to the sound of knocking on the kitchen door in the back of the house. He glanced up at the clock and saw that it was ten past ten. The knocking paused and then resumed. His blood froze as he realized it had to be Allison out there on his back porch, trying to get into his house.

He ran through his options and decided to call the police. Going out to see what she wanted would just fuel her obsession.

"I'm Professor Edward Carter," he told the dispatcher. "I teach law at the University of Richmond. One of my students has been stalking me. She's out on my back porch right now, trying to get into my house."

"Do you think she has a weapon?"

"I don't know. I do know she's mentally unstable. Anything is possible. My wife, who is two months pregnant, and my four-year-old son are upstairs asleep. I'm worried about their safety."

"I understand. I've got someone on the way."

About five minutes after he hung up with dispatch, he heard the police car pull up in front. A few minutes later, he could hear footsteps on the wooden porch and then a man's voice asking questions and a female's voice responding. Then he heard the sound of footsteps leaving the porch. He breathed a sigh of relief and got up to pour himself one more whisky before going to bed.

He had just finished refreshing his drink when he heard insistent knocking on his front door. He prayed it wasn't Allison. And it wasn't. When he looked through the peephole, he saw a uniformed officer on the porch.

He opened the door.

"Professor Carter?" The cop was in his mid-thirties, very fit, with closely cropped brown hair.

"Yes."

"May I come in?"

"Of course." Ed led him to the living room where his half-full glass of whisky sat on the coffee table. "Drink?" he asked the officer.

"No, thanks. I'm on duty. I just wanted to let you know you have nothing to fear from that young woman. She's got a huge crush on you, but that's all."

Ed shook his head. "There's more to it than that."

But the look on the officer's face said he was not to be persuaded. "I don't think so. She said that she's in your Criminal Law class, and she babysits your son on Fridays when you have office hours. She came over tonight to let you know she can watch him next Friday for you."

Oh, God. He's never going to see the truth. "I'm afraid that's not true, Officer. She does not babysit my son, and I've told her to stay away from him. She stalked my wife, my son, and me to Charlottesville today."

"Really? She said you invited her to meet you in a book shop there."

"She was in the book shop that we visited, but neither I nor my wife invited her to be there."

"I honestly don't think she means you or your family any harm," the officer said. "I'm not going to write this up. She's young and foolish and harmless. You can go to bed and get a good night's sleep."

Ed wanted to scream, but instead he smiled and walked the young officer to the door. Then he went back to the living room. He turned off the lights, picked up his Jack Daniel's, and peered across the street through the slats in the blinds. The tall, dark female figure staring up at his bedroom window was unmistakable.

* * *

On Monday, Allison Byrd did not appear for class, and Ed was relieved. But that afternoon, as he was getting ready to close up his office and leave for the day, Hunter Marshall Dudley, the dean of the law school, suddenly appeared. Dean Dudley, who was in his mid-forties but who looked older because he was bald and wore three-piece suits, walked in and closed the door, and Ed realized that bad news was on the way.

"I need to talk to you for a few minutes."

"All right." Ed laid his briefcase on his desk and sat down. The dean took the chair across from him, adjusting his vest as he folded himself into the chair.

"You are aware, are you not, that the law school does not tolerate sexual misconduct with students?" The dean arched one eyebrow dramatically. Ed knew that Hunter Dudley had never practiced law. Like Ed, he had languished in a Big Law library for a few boring years before escaping into academia. But Dudley liked to pretend that he had been a successful litigator before becoming a professor and part of that pretense was mugging for an imaginary jury.

The anger from yesterday that had finally died down when Ed had seen Allison's empty seat in his class that morning roared back to life. But he knew he had to hide it. "You seem to be accusing me of something."

"Jane Birks says that you're very friendly with a young woman in your Criminal Law One class. You've been using her for childcare on Friday mornings. Jane has seen you leaving campus with her."

Stay calm, he reminded himself. "And that young woman would be Allison Byrd?"

"Yes." He made the word sound accusatory.

"I gave her a ride on one occasion because it was raining. She said she had no car. But I never invited her to take care of my son. To the contrary, I told her to leave us alone."

"Really?" The dean's eyebrow was up again. His skepticism was irritating.

Don't react, he reminded himself. "Really."

"I'm afraid the young woman tells a different story."

Ed felt his gut tighten. "What story would that be?"

"I called her into my office after Jane came to me with what she'd seen. Ms. Byrd said that you'd been having an affair with her since the beginning of the semester. She said you lured her into the affair by promising that you'd leave your wife for her."

"That's ridiculous!" Ed made no effort to control his anger.

"Jane Birks doesn't think it's ridiculous."

"What does that mean?"

"It means I talked to her again after I talked to Ms. Byrd, and Jane said that, based upon her observations, the two of you were engaged in an affair."

"What observations? This is crazy!" Ed felt as if he were about to explode.

"As I said, Jane has seen the two of you in your office. She's seen Ms. Byrd with your son frequently. She's also seen the two of you in your classroom after everyone else has left."

"Don't be ridiculous! She stays after my classes to bring just this kind of attention to herself. I have told her repeatedly to join a study group."

"Stay away from her."

"With pleasure, but what do I do about the fact that she's in my class?"

"She isn't anymore. I took her out."

"Thank God!" *Finally, she's gone!*

"Consider this meeting a warning. If you even so much as look sideways at another student, you'll be fired on the spot."

"I love my wife very much, and there is no affair with Allison Byrd."

"I'm afraid that's not what my investigation shows."

Ed was now too angry to hold his emotions in check. "So you're taking a student's word over mine?" he demanded curtly.

"I'm taking Professor Birks' word," Hunter Dudley said smoothly. "She's a full professor with tenure."

"That doesn't make her accusations valid!"

"Oh, I think it does. I've known Jane for fifteen years."

"But Professor Birks does not know the whole story. This student targeted me; and when I wouldn't give her the attention she wanted, she started turning up on Friday mornings to get at me through my son. Lately, she's been stalking my house, and she followed me and my family to Charlottesville on Sunday. We were having a family outing to a bookstore my wife wanted to visit. She teaches English at VCU, you know."

"I thought you said the young woman didn't have a car. How, then, did she manage to follow you all the way to Charlottesville?"

"I have no idea. I gave her a ride to the bus stop once in the rain. I assume she borrowed a car to follow us. Or stole one."

The eyebrow went up again. Obviously the dean thought he was lying.

"And you've called the police and filed a report about this so-called stalking behavior?"

Ed remembered the cheerful officer of the night before telling him that Allison was harmless. If the dean heard that, it would further cement his belief that Ed was lying. "An officer came out to our house, but he did not file a report."

"Then it doesn't look like she's 'stalking' you to me. And how can she be stalking you when she doesn't even want to be in your class anymore?"

Ed wanted to put his fist between Hunter Dudley's smug eyes. "I'm glad you have removed her," he said.

"Then stay away from her. If you don't, the next time I come to see you, I'll be asking for your resignation."

* * *

He let himself get drunk that night after Wynne and Anne were in bed. To top off a really horrible day, he'd found Richard and Anne in the living room when he came home. Richard had come to tell her that he was leaving his wife and to beg Anne to leave Ed.

"You told him about the baby, didn't you? *Our* baby."

"If I left you, it wouldn't be for Richard," she said. "I don't want to talk about this anymore. I'm going upstairs to give Wynne his bath."

Ed's blood ran cold. Richard wasn't a threat to his relationship with his son, but his son's biological father was. That's who Anne really wanted to be with.

At ten o'clock, Ed climbed the stairs, intending to go to bed. He moved carefully and silently across his bedroom in the dark so that he wouldn't wake Anne, who was sleeping soundly. He intended to undress and get into bed and drop off to sleep. He knew he shouldn't look out the window, but he wanted to reassure himself that Allison Byrd had gotten the message and wasn't coming back. He went to the window and moved the shade just enough to see across the street. To his horror, she was there.

Fueled by the rage he could no longer contain, he hurled himself down the stairs and out the back door. He strode across the street to confront her. He grabbed her by the arm and dragged her into the light from the street lamp.

"Ow! Let go, you're hurting my arm!" Allison struggled to free herself from his iron grip without success.

"I'll hurt a lot more than your arm if you don't go back to Dean Dudley and admit that you lied!" He twisted her arm for good measure, and she howled. A light went on across the street in the upstairs bedroom, and Ed realized he'd better get control of himself. He was so angry he felt like strangling her. He let go of her in case anyone called 911. He didn't want to be caught assaulting her if the cops showed up, even though she deserved it. He said in a low, angry voice, "You lied to the dean. I have never slept with you, and I certainly never promised to leave my wife, whom I love very much, for you. If you don't go back to Dean Dudley and tell him the truth, I'll—"

"You'll what? Fail me in Crim Law One? I'm not in your class anymore." Her eyes mocked him.

Shit, she's right. I've got no leverage over her now that Dudley's taken her out of my class.

"If you want me to take back what I said, it will cost you." She crossed her arms and threw her head back slightly. She knew she had the upper hand.

"Cost me?"

"Three grand."

For a moment, he stood frozen, staring into the crazy depths of her dark, arrogant eyes. *The cop was wrong. She is dangerous. But paying her is the fastest way to get her out of my life.*

"Okay. McDonald's where we had lunch. At four o'clock tomorrow afternoon."

"Cash."

"Cash," he agreed.

The next morning, he went to the bank and withdrew the money from the joint savings account. He prayed Anne was too busy with Wynne and the coming baby to notice.

* * *

Friday, November 11, 1983, Charlottesville, Virginia

Anne wouldn't come with him to the conference. She used her pregnancy as an excuse. She was tired. She needed to rest. Caroline wasn't good with Wynne, and it would be an imposition to leave him with her.

Ed was disappointed but not surprised. Still, he drove to Charlottesville that Friday with a light heart, having paid Allison off on Tuesday and secured her promise to stay away from him and his family.

He settled himself at his hotel and then drove to the Harringtons' bookstore to buy the first editions of T.S. Eliot that he hadn't been able to buy for Anne last weekend. He decided to give them to her when he got back on Sunday. Christmas was too long to wait to see her eyes light up.

He presented his paper to the conference on Saturday at eleven a.m. That night, he went to the dinner and reception for the presenters and conference attendees. Then he went back to his hotel and went to sleep. The next morning, he drove home. He parked in the garage in the back of the alley and entered through the kitchen door, carrying his overnight bag and the books he'd bought for Anne. As soon as he walked into the kitchen, he could see something was wrong. It had been ransacked. The floor was littered with broken dishes and the placemats that Anne always left out on the table were mixed in with the broken china. The cabinet doors were flung open. The food in the pantry had been thrown down, too.

His heart began to beat faster as he walked through the kitchen and into the hall. He saw Anne's body, slumped like a discarded doll, by the front door at the same moment that he saw the bloody bat lying next to her. Then he heard Wynne crying. As he raced upstairs, the horrible truth dawned on him. *Allison Byrd had killed Anne.*

But then, as he picked up Wynne, another thought hit him. *Anne could no longer say he wasn't Wynne's father.*

CLAIRE

"For you know only a heap of broken images."

T.S. Eliot

CHAPTER ELEVEN

Tuesday, January 10, 2017, Brendan Murphy's Office, Riverfront Plaza, Craig, Lewis, and Weller, Richmond, Virginia

"The trouble is," Brendan Murphy told Claire Chastain the next morning as they sat in his office overlooking the cold, gray James River, spotted with white caps, "Ed has always insisted that Allison Byrd killed Anne. And there's no evidence at all that she did. That's why Brad O'Connor was so sure that Ed was guilty."

She'd arrived late yesterday on the train, determined to help save Wynne's father. She'd held Wynne while he cried like a child after he'd told her about the execution order. It had been the same day that she'd picked out her wedding dress.

The next day she'd gone to her father's office at Craig, Lewis near Wall Street to tell him about their decision to postpone the wedding. Jeff Ryder had also been there. He was often with her father since coming to Craig, Lewis because Tyndall liked to work with him.

"We've postponed the wedding," Claire said. "Alan Warrick has agreed to give me a three-month leave of absence so that I can help Brendan."

Tyndall frowned. "Are you sure that's a good idea?"

"I'm sure."

"But you're not a criminal defense attorney, Claire. You're a civil litigator. Brendan Murphy is one of the top criminal defense attorneys in the country, and he's got plenty of associate help," Tyndall said.

"You are an exceptional lawyer, Claire," Jeff chimed in, "but this isn't civil litigation. The odds are stacked solidly against you."

"And they were stacked against you last May when you were arrested for four murders you didn't commit."

"And a miracle saved my life."

"And I'm going to help Brendan pull off a miracle for Ed and Wynne."

So now on this frozen January day, after spending the night in the room she'd come to feel was her own at the Murphys', she focused on learning the facts of the case that had consumed Brendan for thirty-plus years.

"Who is Brad O'Connor?"

"He was head of the Public Defender's Office in 1984. He represented Ed in his first trial."

"And he thought Ed was guilty?"

"I talked to him when I took over the case in 1986. Yes, he was as convinced as the prosecutor that Ed killed his wife and unborn child."

* * *

November 1983, Caroline Carter's House, Richmond, Virginia

Ed was numb. They couldn't go back home because it was a crime scene, and he couldn't stand to be in the house that Anne had loved so much, anyway. So he and Wynne went to stay at his mother's enormous house in Windsor Farms. He cursed himself for not doing that as soon as he had realized Allison was gazing up at his bedroom window night after night. Then Anne would still be alive.

He resumed teaching on Monday. He'd only missed two days because of the Thanksgiving break. He didn't feel like teaching, but he didn't feel like doing anything else either. He hoped that the comfort of the routine would help him find some way to go on functioning.

Caroline's young housekeeper, Eva, looked after Wynne when Ed was at school. Other than that, he and his son were inseparable. He knew Wynne didn't understand the "Mommy has gone to heaven" explanation. He was convinced that Anne was coming back. Time and growing up would eventually teach him that he'd been robbed of his mother at the age of four.

Christmas fell on a Sunday. Although Caroline put up her usual nine-foot tree in the front hall where the staircase wound gracefully to the second and third floors, there was no air of festivity in the house. Ed bought presents for Wynne and wrapped them, but his despair deepened as he did. His son was certain that Santa would bring his mother home for Christmas. It was the only thing he wanted.

Detective Todd Warner and his partner, Detective Brett Monroe, appeared at Caroline's door on Friday, December 23.

Later, Ed would tell Brendan that he would never forget that date.

"Professor Carter?" The detectives were standing in the front hall. Eva had let them in, and she was standing slightly beside and behind them. She was frowning. Ed was still on the last step of the spiral staircase, having been summoned from Wynne's room by the house intercom.

At the sight of the detectives, his heart leapt with dread and joy. "You've found the person who killed Anne?" The whole sorry story of Allison's attempted affair with him would now come out. But at least she'd be brought to justice. And Wynne would be safe. He had worried she'd come back and try to kidnap him. He'd thanked the Universe numerous times that she hadn't taken him with her after she'd killed Anne.

"We think so," the detective said in his slow drawl. "We'd like for you to come down to the station with us, so we can talk about it."

"But I can't leave my son," Ed said. "We can go into the living room and chat. Eva, would you mind bringing us some coffee?"

"That won't be necessary." Detective Monroe held up one hand at the same time that he displayed a pair of handcuffs with the other. "You can come voluntarily, or we can arrest you."

Ed's head began to spin. "But you don't have probable cause."

"Oh, yes, we do," Detective Warner said.

* * *

Tuesday, January 10, 2017, Brendan Murphy's Office, Riverfront Plaza, Craig, Lewis, and Weller, Richmond, Virginia

"But I don't understand," Claire said when they resumed their places around Brendan's conference table after lunch. "Ed was in Charlottesville from Friday until Sunday morning. The coroner's report placed her time of death between one and two a.m. Ed was seventy miles away when Anne was killed."

"The detectives thought it was a murder for hire."

* * *

Friday, December 23, 1983, Richmond Police Headquarters, Richmond, Virginia

The room was tiny and cold. The officers put a paper cup full of water in front of Ed and left him for what seemed an eternity. He knew he had to calm down. He tried to imagine what sort of evidence they thought they had against him. Had they found out about Wynne's biological father? But there was no way that they could have. Anne alone knew his identity, and she'd never revealed it to anyone. *As far as you know,* a voice deep inside reminded him. *What if she had told Richard?*

When the detectives came back, they had a bag with them. They sat down, one on each side of the table with Ed at the end between them. Detective Monroe proceeded to pull items out of the bag. "Do you recognize any of these? We have reason to believe they belonged to your wife."

Ed watched in horror as they placed Anne's wedding rings on the table with an evidence tag attached to them, followed by the four-piece silver tea set that had been her grandmother's, and then the silver flatware, service for eight, that had been one of Caroline's wedding gifts.

"Those are all Anne's," he said.

"They were found in a pawn shop in Radford. Do you know why they were there?" Detective Monroe asked.

Allison Byrd. She went to college in Radford. Damn her for taking Anne's wedding rings!

"No, of course not."

"Well, we do," Detective Monroe said. "When we processed the crime scene, we saw that her rings were gone, and a silver tea service seemed to be missing. The thief left behind the small pitcher, so we figured there was more. And a drawer was empty of some but not all of a flatware service. We notified the police and pawn shops throughout the state. A pawn shop owner in Radford had a hunch that this might be what we were looking for because a man came in and pawned all of them at once. Of course, we couldn't be sure until you identified them as your wife's."

A man. Did Allison have an accomplice? But who? Not James Watkins.

"The pawn shop owner identified the person who pawned these as William James Miller," Detective Warner took up the narrative. "When we put out an APB on him, his common law wife came forward to say that he'd been working in Richmond as a handyman at the time your wife was murdered."

The house. Anne was always hiring people we didn't know to work on the house. But it has to be Allison.

"When we took Miller into custody, he confessed to Anne's murder," Detective Monroe said.

So why did you threaten me with handcuffs to make me come

down here? You could have told me that at home.

"So she was killed during a robbery?" *God, I'd have given him the stuff and bought Anne new rings if that's what he wanted.* "Then Miller will get the death penalty." Ed felt some satisfaction that Miller would pay the highest price for murdering his wife and child.

"Not exactly," Detective Warner said.

"What do you mean? It's statutory. The death penalty applies when the victim is killed during a robbery."

"That's right. And when we confronted Miller with that, he rolled over on you."

"On me? I've never met the man."

"That's not what he said. He said you paid him three thousand dollars to kill your wife."

"That's crazy. Of course I didn't."

"But Miller isn't the only person we've been talking to. We talked to Dean Dudley. Your job was in jeopardy because you'd slept with your student, that Byrd girl. You promised to leave your wife for her."

"That's a complete lie."

Detective Warner waved his hands impatiently. "Save it for the jurors. Maybe some of them will believe you. We don't."

* * *

Tuesday, January 10, 2017, Brendan Murphy's Office, Riverfront Plaza, Craig, Lewis, and Weller, Richmond, Virginia

"But how did they convict him on that evidence?" Claire frowned at Brendan. "Were they able to show that he paid Miller?"

"No. The DA on Ed's case was, and is to this day, Anne's

cousin, Gordon Fairfax. He could never prove that Ed had even met Miller, but there had been a three-thousand-dollar withdrawal from Ed's account a week before Anne was murdered."

"So did Miller have that money?"

"No, not a penny. But the jury assumed he'd spent it or hidden it or given it away. The DA put on Miller and Dean Dudley, and Byrd and her roommates, who all swore that Ed was sleeping with Allison and that he'd promised to leave Anne for her."

"Did Brad O'Connor present any evidence that Allison killed Anne?"

"No, because there wasn't any."

"Did Ed testify?"

"He did. Brad said he tried to talk him out of it, but he was adamant that he had to tell his side of the story."

"And I gather it didn't go well?"

"Brad told me it didn't when I took over the case. He said that Ed's claim that Allison was stalking him sounded contrived. The DA called the bookstore owners on rebuttal, and they testified that the encounter at the bookstore had seemed cordial. And there was only Ed's word that he went back to his hotel that night after the reception. The DA played the videos from the hotel's security cameras, and Ed did not appear on any of them."

"So the jury convicted him based upon murder for hire?"

"That's right."

"Then how did Ed come to have a second trial?"

"When it went up on appeal, the court found that Miller was an accomplice, and his testimony, particularly about the three-thousand-dollar payment, was not sufficiently corroborated because there was no evidence other than his own word, that he ever received it from Ed."

"And that's when you took over this case?" Claire asked.

"Right. Caroline relented from her earlier condemnation of Ed as a disgrace to the family and hired me. She realized he was innocent, and Brad hadn't done a good job at trial because he was convinced that Ed was guilty."

CHAPTER TWELVE

Wednesday, January 11, 2017, Death Row, Sussex State Prison, Sussex, Virginia

He's innocent. As she walked into the Attorney Interview Room with Brendan and Wynne the next day, that was Claire's first thought when she saw the handsome, white-haired man with the gentle smile sitting at the table, waiting for them. Wynne hurried over to hug him, holding him close for a long time before he turned to introduce Claire.

She noticed that behind his clear spectacles, Ed's eyes were brown, not blue like Wynne's. But Wynne had his father's height and intelligent, scholarly expression. And Ed had the same warm, captivating smile that had attracted her to Wynne that night at *The Tempest.*

The four of them settled around the table. Brendan said, "I've been filling Claire in on the details of your case, Ed."

He gave her a little smile. "I'm afraid there are a lot of details."

"We're up to the end of your first trial and the reversal."

Ed nodded. He turned to Claire. "The reversal came in

January of 1986. I was thirty-eight, the same age as Wynne now. Before the ink was dry on the Virginia Supreme Court's opinion, Gordon Fairfax announced that he was going to retry me. I was optimistic because Brendan, unlike Brad O'Connor, did not think I was guilty. And because I didn't kill Anne."

"So how did they get a second conviction?" Claire asked.

"They cheated," Wynne said.

* * *

Wednesday, September 17, 1986, John Marshall Courts Building, Richmond, Virginia

They were on day eight of Ed's second trial. Brendan and his second chair, Brian Whitby, were optimistic about an acquittal. Known as "The Two B's" by their Craig, Lewis partners, thirty-five-year-old Brendan and thirty-two-year-old Brian were considered an unstoppable team. And not only did they work well together, they enjoyed each other's company outside of work. Emma was close to Brian's wife, Mckenzie Fitzgerald, who, after working at the Public Defender's Office, had become a clerk for a federal district court judge. When Brendan remembered that fateful day eight of Ed's second trial, he always thought of the grin on Brian's face that morning when he had informed the defense team that Mckenzie had given birth to their first child in the wee hours of the morning. A son named Joel Fitzgerald Whitby.

The defense was winning that morning. Allison Byrd had eluded Gordon Fairfax's attempts to serve her with a subpoena. Hence, she had not shown up to testify. By some miracle, Brian had persuaded Judge Rolfe that Allison's testimony from Ed's first trial was inadmissible because the state had not used due diligence to procure her presence at this second trial. That meant that Hunter Dudley, Jane Birks, Paige Caldwell, and Blair Wilson could not testify because Allison Byrd's statements had become inadmissible hearsay. That left the police officers who regaled Ed's jury with all the gory details of the murder scene and the nauseating details of his wife's violent death.

Brendan objected when Gordon Fairfax called William Henry Miller to the stand, citing the Virginia Supreme Court's opinion that he was an accomplice whose testimony had not been corroborated in Ed's first trial. But Judge Rolfe rejected the defense's objection, and Miller took the stand. He gave a rambling story about being hired to kill Anne, trying to avoid mentioning the $3,000. But on cross-examination, Brendan hammered and hammered at his lie. No, Miller had to admit repeatedly, there was no evidence other than his own word that he'd received $3,000 from Ed. There was no evidence other than his own word that he'd ever met Ed. When Miller got off the stand, the defense team had been virtually certain that the jurors had not believed a word he'd said, other than his admission that he'd pawned Anne's silver and jewelry. They went to lunch feeling victorious.

But after lunch, Gordon Fairfax suddenly called a witness whom no one had ever heard of, Hiram Hill. Brendan objected strenuously, citing violation of the discovery rules, violation of the federal due process clause, and failure to demonstrate that Hill had relevant evidence to offer. But anxious to give the prosecution the chance for a comeback and a conviction, Judge

Rolfe had turned a deaf ear to the defense.

So the unknown Hill took the stand and proceeded to testify that he had been Ed's cellmate just after his arrest in December 1983. Hill claimed that Ed had described how he'd recruited and paid Miller to murder Anne. He looked straight at Ed as he testified that Ed had told him he was tired of being married and didn't want the expense of a divorce.

Ed had been outraged as he sat at the defense table between Brendan and Brian. Only his training as an attorney had kept him from showing his fury to the jury. Instead, he wrote in huge letters on the legal pad in front of him, *I HAVE NEVER SEEN THAT MAN IN MY LIFE UNTIL TODAY!!!*

Brendan demanded a sidebar to object to Hill's testimony because the state had failed to put on any evidence to support Hill's claim that he had shared a cell with Ed.

But Gordon Fairfax had come prepared with records of inmate housing at the jail. Ed and his entire defense team had stared in disbelief at the entry that said Hill had been housed with Ed in December 1983.

When the defense team huddled that night to discuss whether Ed should take the stand the next day, Ed vented his outrage.

"It's a lie! An outrageous lie! For God's sake, I'm not only a lawyer, I'm a law professor. It should be obvious that I would know better than to spill my guts to some unknown jailhouse creep! I don't care what those records say, this Hill character was never in my cell. I've never spoken to him in my life!"

"Calm down," Brendan said and put his hand on Ed's shoulder. "Of course we know that. The problem is how to discredit this guy with the jury."

"Yeah, his story that he came forward purely in the interest of justice doesn't pass the smell test," Brian observed. "Clearly the guy's being compensated in some way for the lies he told today."

"But he claimed he wasn't," Brendan said.

"That's a load of shit!" Brian shot back.

"I agree with you," Brendan said. "But how do we make the jury see that this guy's lying?"

"There's only one way," Ed said quietly. "I have to testify."

* * *

Ed took a long sip from the paper cup in front of him on the table. Then he turned toward Claire, who was on his left. "And I did take the stand," he said. "And it was an unmitigated disaster."

Brendan saw the puzzled look on Claire's face and added, "It took the jury less than an hour to convict on all charges and less than one day to decide on the death penalty—again."

CHAPTER THIRTEEN

Wednesday, January 11, 2017, The Murphys', Windsor Farms, Richmond, Virginia

That night, Claire lay awake and listened to the steady rhythm of Wynne's breathing as he slept beside her. His father was innocent. She was sure of that. She didn't practice criminal law, but she'd represented people whose negligence or fraud had harmed others. She had a sixth sense that told her who was innocent and who was lying.

She got up carefully so that she would not wake Wynne. She wrapped herself in a blanket and tiptoed across the cold wooden floor to the window where she peeked through the blinds. It was spitting snow, but the flakes were melting as soon as they hit the ground. The weight of what she had promised to accomplish settled over her. What if she couldn't save Ed's life? Every career had losses. She'd been fortunate so far, but what if this was going to be one of hers?

She shivered at the thought. Jeff had warned her not to get involved. And she respected his opinion as much as she respected her father's. Besides, he'd been a prosecutor for four years before turning to civil law. Why had she been so sure she could dive into a world she didn't know and save Ed?

Wynne stirred but did not awaken. Sometimes she wondered if she'd said 'yes' to him because she'd been intoxicated with the magic of being proposed to at midnight on the Seine on Christmas Eve. The years with Paul Curtis continued to haunt her.

It was hard not to love a man who had been part of her every day, not just from eight to five, but into the evenings and the weekends as the two of them had labored for their clients. Her father had understood. It had happened to him when Mckenzie Fitzgerald had been hired by Craig, Lewis to defend his long-time client, Fidelity International Bank, against money laundering charges. For eight years, she'd been a part of Tyndall's life. And then she'd upped and offed to Hugh Mahoney's firm in San Diego to be closer to Joel. He had been heartbroken.

She tiptoed back to bed and snuggled in next to Wynne. Tomorrow she would take him to catch the train to New York, and then she'd head to Brendan's office to hear the details of Ed's third trial.

* * *

Thursday, January 12, 2017, Brendan Murphy's Office, Craig, Lewis, and Weller, Richmond, Virginia

In the morning, Emma drove Brendan to work so that Claire could use his Range Rover to drop Wynne at Main Street Station. He held her close for a long minute on the platform before boarding the train. When he let her go, he looked into her eyes and said, "Now that you've seen death row in person, do you want to change your mind about marrying me?"

She felt guilty for thinking about Paul last night. "No, of course not."

But his eyes had said that he was still uncertain. "It's a lot to ask, Claire. It would be okay if—"

But she shook her head. "Shhh. That's enough."

Wynne pulled her close and kissed her. When he let her go, he said, "I'll miss you."

She smiled. "I'll miss you, too. But I'll be back in New York on Monday." *And I'm not going to think about the past anymore.*

She waited until the train pulled out before heading back. Then she got into the Range Rover and hurried through the morning traffic to Brendan's office to hear about Ed's third and final trial.

* * *

"So in October 1994, Miller was diagnosed with terminal throat cancer," Brendan began as they sat at the table in the corner of his office. "They told him he had three months at most. He contacted the Innocence Project at the University of Virginia, but they wouldn't listen because it involved helping Ed. The powers that be at the law school didn't want to get involved with someone they regarded as a law-professor-gone-wrong.

"Miller then wrote to me to say that he had information that would exonerate Ed. I told him to contact the Mid-Atlantic Innocence Project in Baltimore. Some of their students went to see Miller, and he gave them an affidavit that said he did not kill

Anne, and Ed did not hire him to kill Anne. Then the Project had the bat tested for DNA evidence. DNA testing was not available at the time of Ed's first and second trials."

"What did Innocence Project find?" Claire asked.

"Testing showed a DNA mixture on the bat consisting of at least four people. Ed was the major contributor but that was to be expected because he had used it to play softball with the law school's softball team. Anne was one of the minor contributors to the mixture. Miller was entirely excluded as a contributor."

"But were there others?"

"Yes, at least two more. But they could not be identified. It made sense that there would be others because even though it was Ed's bat, other people on the team had used it."

"So no DNA from Allison Byrd?"

"Well, we don't know for sure because they didn't have a reference sample for her. Ed said she didn't play softball. That meant her DNA, if it was there, would have connected her to Anne's murder. But her roommates, Blair and Paige, said she was with them all night at a party in the Fan District. Of course, they had every reason to lie for her, and they are admitted liars."

"But what if she left the party and came back without their knowledge? Ed and Anne lived in the Fan. If Allison was really at the party with Blair and Paige, she was close to the Carters," Claire said.

Brendan nodded. "It's an attractive theory, but it's just a theory. We have no DNA to connect Byrd to the bat, and we have no one who said Allison left that party. According to Paige and Blair, she was there all night.

"Anyway," he went on, "based on the DNA testing, the Mid-

Atlantic Innocence Project accepted an affidavit from Miller, denying any involvement in the murder. He said that he arrived at Ed and Anne's house that morning because Anne had hired him the week before to lay tile in the downstairs bathroom. He found her dead. The dining room and kitchen were a mess. It looked as if she'd tried to fight off her attacker. He grabbed her wedding rings and the silver because he figured the cops would think the killer had taken them. He thought if he pawned them somewhere outside of Richmond, he wouldn't be caught."

"But of course that wasn't true," Claire observed.

"Not in the least. Miller's affidavit went on to say that after the police arrested him, they pressured him to name Ed as the one responsible for Anne's death. The cops told him about a three-thousand-dollar withdrawal that Ed had made a week before the murder. They let him know that they thought Ed had hired him to kill Anne. They told him that if he'd confess to murder for hire, they'd make sure only Ed got the death penalty."

"So they essentially dictated his confession?" Claire frowned.

"That's right."

"But what about Hill's claim that Ed had confessed the murder for hire to him?"

"Completely false. After I got the report from the Mid-Atlantic Innocence Project, I went straight to the Attorney General, Robert Merriweather, demanding answers. A week later, Merriweather revealed that Hill was a paid informant who had never been in a cell with Ed."

"But what about the jail record that was used to support Hill's claim he'd been housed with Ed?"

"Merriweather would not admit outright that it was forged, but it was."

"So that's how Ed came to be tried a third time."

Brendan nodded. "Before that trial began, I moved to recuse Gordon because it was obvious that he'd suborned perjury when he put Hill on the witness stand. But I lost that motion. The Attorney General persuaded the Virginia Supreme Court to allow Gordon to prosecute Ed a third time."

"But how could they? All the murder-for-hire evidence was gone."

Brendan smiled ruefully. "And because it was, Gordon switched theories. He claimed Ed killed Anne himself."

"But he wasn't in Richmond that night. And he had no motive to kill her."

"Gordon found out that Anne had been having an affair with a music professor at VCU. He was her stand partner in the symphony. His name was Richard Neal. Neal testified that Ed had just found out about their affair and was angry because the child she was carrying might be Neal's."

"Was there any truth to Neal's claim?"

"None. Anne was barely two months pregnant which means her child was conceived in August. Neal admitted that he did not see Anne during the summer."

"So the baby was Ed's?"

"Without any doubt," Brendan said.

"Then Neal didn't help the prosecution's case very much."

"What Neal did was cast doubt on the strength of Ed and Anne's marriage. The neighbor who lived across the street was the witness who hurt the defense the most."

"How?"

"After Neal, Gordon brought the dean back. Hunter Dudley testified that he had threatened to terminate Ed if he continued his affair with Allison Byrd. I objected on the basis of hearsay, but Judge Rolfe overruled my objection. And this time, the judge let Gordon read Allison's testimony from the first trial to the jury."

"So she didn't show up to testify again?"

"No one has seen her since trial one. We've been trying to find her for years to get a DNA sample so that we can test that bat, but no luck."

"What about the roommates, Blair and Paige? Did they testify in the third trial?"

"They did. Same story: Ed was having an affair with Allison Byrd and was going to leave Anne for her."

"But you said the neighbor hurt Ed's defense the most?"

"That's right. The neighbor's name was J. Adam Winston, III. He was a Senior Vice President at Virginia Power. He and his wife were restoring their house, too; and while they didn't have much contact with Ed, they talked to Anne extensively about her work on her house."

"So he sounded sympathetic to Anne?"

"Yes, and he wasn't just some nosy neighbor. He had a lot of credibility with the jury because he was a highly placed executive in an old-line Richmond corporation who said he'd been concerned for months before Anne's death about what was going on across the street. When the windows were open, he could hear loud arguments coming from the house. I got him to admit that he couldn't hear what the voices were saying and that he was only assuming that Ed and Anne were the speakers. But I could tell that the jury had been indelibly imbued with the idea that Anne and Ed were estranged over her affair with Neal.

"But that wasn't the worst part of Adam Winston's testimony. He said that he'd seen Ed out at night on the sidewalk across from his house with what looked like a young woman, tall and slightly heavyset with long, dark hair. Sometimes it looked as if he was kissing her. Adam Winston's testimony backed up Hunter Dudley: Ed was having an affair with Allison Byrd and had promised to leave Anne for her. But then it got worse."

"What could be worse than what you've told me?"

"Adam testified that on the night Anne was murdered, he saw Ed's white Volvo station wagon parked in front of the house around one a.m. He thought it was odd because Ed had gone to Charlottesville and wasn't supposed to be back until Sunday. Winston testified that he went to bed not long after he saw the car but was awakened about thirty minutes later by tires squealing and an engine being gunned by someone leaving in a hurry. He looked out and the white Volvo was gone."

"But why would Ed leave again in the wee hours after coming back from his trip early?" Claire asked.

"Over my objection, Winston was allowed to testify that on several occasions, he'd seen Ed drive off angrily after arguments with Anne. He never stayed away very long, so Winston had assumed he'd returned within the hour. Winston went back to sleep, but when he woke up at eight the next morning, the white Volvo wasn't there. He didn't see it again until closer to noon and shortly after that, the police arrived."

Claire frowned. "So the theory of the state's case the third time around was Ed drove to Richmond on Saturday night, murdered his pregnant wife, and then went back to Charlottesville so he could return on Sunday morning and pretend to discover her body?"

"That was Gordon Fairfax's closing argument."

"But why murder the woman who was carrying his child?"

"And that was my closing argument," Brendan said. "And Ed wouldn't have driven off into the night leaving Wynne alone upstairs in a locked room with his mother dead downstairs. Ed loves Wynne beyond everything on earth."

"Did Ed testify again?"

"He did."

"How did he explain Adam Winston's testimony about his car being at the house at the time Anne was killed?"

"He denied that he was there. He denied having an affair with Allison Byrd. He testified again that Allison had been stalking him. He said those supposed trysts on the sidewalk were his demands for her to leave him and his family alone. I always thought that Allison's failure to show up to testify again after the first trial should have shown the jury that she and her roommates had colluded and lied about Ed's supposed infidelities with her."

Claire thought carefully before she asked her next question. Then she said, "Do you think that was Ed's car in front of the house?"

Brendan studied her for a moment before he answered. "The one thing you have to be prepared for in criminal law is discovering facts that you don't want to be true."

"Does that mean that you know it was his?"

"It means that we need someone who saw Ed in Charlottesville at the time of Anne's murder."

MCKENZIE

"Most of the evil in this world is done by people
with good intentions."

T.S. Eliot

CHAPTER FOURTEEN

Friday, January 13, 2017, Offices of Goldstein, Miller, Mahoney, and Fitzgerald, Emerald Shapery Center, San Diego, California

Mckenzie Fitzgerald, like most litigators, was superstitious. At five o'clock that afternoon, as she sat in her office on the twenty-sixth floor of the Emerald Shapery Center, watching the pale winter sun sinking into the Pacific Ocean, she congratulated herself on a day without a disaster. Of course, she had carefully planned it that way. She had made sure no court appearances were scheduled; no meetings with opposing counsel were on the books; and above all, she had avoided calls from her most difficult clients.

Now as she watched the sun disappear behind Point Loma, she smiled at the thought of the coming three-day weekend. The courts would be closed on Monday for Martin Luther King Day. Later tonight, she would fly to San Francisco to spend the weekend with Joel. It was hard to believe that he was thirty-one and a rising star in the litigation section of Warrick, Thompson's San Francisco office. He'd been born in the middle of Ed Carter's second murder trial in September 1986 in the wee hours of the morning on the day that Brian had said the tide had turned against them. Brian had been a senior associate on Brendan Murphy's litigation team when Caroline Carter had hired Brendan to defend her son.

The anniversary of Brian's death was only a week away. Joel had been just four months old when the airline representative had appeared at the Whitby house in Richmond's prestigious West End on January 20, 1987 to tell her that Brian wouldn't be coming home. He'd gone to Miami to check out a rumor that Allison Byrd had been sighted there. He and Brendan had been devastated by the guilty verdict in Ed's case, and they'd been working tirelessly ever since for a new trial.

She and Brian had had an agreement never to fly on small aircraft. But he'd been in a hurry to get back to her and Joel, and he'd taken a chance on a commuter airline. A chance that had left Mckenzie alone to raise their son. She was only twenty-eight.

She had finished her clerkship for the Honorable St. John Dabney and had accepted a position with Steptoe and Johnson in Washington, D.C. There had been too many ghosts in Richmond, so she fled. She had hired an excellent nanny and had thrown herself into her work. She liked civil litigation, and she was good at it. In 1994, at the age of thirty-five, she became a partner. Joel was seven

But the following year, tired of the rat race of balancing motherhood with the demands of high-powered litigation, she accepted a position at Harvard, teaching trial practice. She was thirty-six, and Joel was eight. It was the perfect time to begin spending more time with her son. Instead of weekends in hotels, skyping with him and his nanny, she drove him to soccer practice, karate classes, and scout meetings. She volunteered in his third-grade classroom once a week. When he went off to Andover for high school five years later, she gave thanks for her decision to drop out of Big Law long enough to really get to know her son.

But when Joel went to boarding school, she was lonely and suddenly tired of teaching. Five years of explaining the art of litigation was enough. She wanted to get back into the courtroom. So in 2000, when Craig, Lewis, and Weller invited her to join their New York office as a partner to defend Fidelity International Bank against charges it had laundered money from Mexican drug cartels, she jumped at the offer.

She hadn't counted on falling in love. For the first few years after Brian's death, she had been too consumed with grief to think of marrying again. She'd focused on making partner at Steptoe and on every single thing Joel did that reminded her of Brian.

When she reached Harvard, her life had been teaching and parenting. But there were several single soccer dads, and she'd dutifully gone on dates with some of them. Nothing had come of any of those evenings in cozy Italian restaurants, drinking good Chianti, and talking about their children. But the companionship had made Mckenzie wish for real love again.

When it came, it snuck up on her. Tyndall Chastain was the corporate partner at Craig, Lewis who oversaw all of Fidelity International's needs. The bank was considered "his" client. Mckenzie's role was limited to making the criminal allegations go away.

She couldn't say she felt anything the first time they met. Although he was bald, Tyndall was still a very handsome man. His best feature was his deep-set, dark eyes, which took in the world with mild kindness. He was nearly six feet tall and very fit. He adored his daughter, Claire, who was five years older than Joel; and he, too, had lost a beloved spouse and had devoted himself to work and parenting ever since.

The Fidelity litigation was being watched by all the major banks in the country. A favorable resolution could triple Craig, Lewis' white-collar crime business. For four years after she joined the firm, Tyndall's face was the first one Mckenzie saw in the morning and the last one she saw at night before going home to sleep, usually around midnight or one a.m. She and Tyndall became comrades in arms, fighting a war that was hugely important to their careers. And in 2005, the year Joel graduated from Andover and went to Yale, Mckenzie and Tyndall won an acquittal for Fidelity International on all charges. It was a stunning victory, and banks in trouble beat down Craig, Lewis' doors to get to them.

The next year, 2006, Claire graduated from law school at Stanford. Mckenzie knew that Tyndall had been devastated by her decision to go to the West Coast for law school. But he'd comforted himself with the thought that she'd come back to New York and enter the litigation department at Craig, Lewis with Mckenzie as her mentor. When she had decided to go to San Diego and join Warrick, Thompson, Tyndall had been deeply hurt. Outwardly, he'd accepted her decision with grace and enthusiasm. Inwardly, he'd felt lost and lonely, and so he'd turned to Mckenzie for friendship and comfort.

Mckenzie realized that they had become an unmarried married couple. When they weren't seeing each other at the office, they were seeing each other on dates: dinner, concerts, the theater. Tyndall had retained his wife's artistic connections through large donations to various galleries, museums, and orchestras. And Mckenzie loved the glamour of wearing evening dresses and having a witty, handsome man in a tuxedo as her escort on gala opening nights.

They did not sleep together. They never discussed it. They both knew it was too dangerous because of their professional association. If they stepped over that line, and anything went wrong, the agony of being forced together at work under the observant eye of high-end clients would be too great.

Two years after Claire broke Tyndall's heart by going west and staying, the same thing happened to Mckenzie. Joel graduated from Yale and enrolled in law school at Stanford. She followed Tyndall's example and outwardly kept a stiff upper lip. But her heart, too, was broken.

She grew even closer to Tyndall with Joel so far away. They flew to California together to visit their children. Sometimes they continued on to brief, platonic vacations in Cabo San Lucas or Cancun. She began to wonder what it would be like to marry again.

But Joel's absence hurt her more than anything had since Brian's death. When Hugh Mahoney invited her to become a name partner at his firm in 2010, defending their bank clients the way she had defended Craig, Lewis', she'd headed west to be near Joel. What she hadn't counted on was leaving so much of her heart behind in New York with Tyndall.

Now as she sat musing about her old life in New York and wondering how Claire was doing after abruptly transferring to Warrick's New York office last spring, someone knocked on her door. A moment later, Hugh Mahoney pushed it open a crack and stuck his head in.

"Got a few minutes?"

"A few. I have to go home and pack. I'm going to Joel's for the weekend."

Hugh entered and sat down in the chair across from her desk. The changes in his life since his daughter Erin's return from New York and the formation of the Andrews-Cooper Innocence Project had done him good, Mckenzie reflected. For the first time in all the years she'd known him, he was fit and trim and smiled easily. Eliminating his demanding wife and his string of mistresses had taken away his irritable edginess. He'd confided to her over dinner at his Coronado mansion that turning over the management of the firm to Mark Kelly and devoting himself to freeing the wrongfully convicted had made his life far more rewarding than being the most feared plaintiff's attorney in America.

"How is Joel?"

"Doing fine. He likes working for Alan Warrick."

"Is he working directly under Alan?"

"When Alan is in San Francisco. He spends a lot of time down here, of course, in the firm's main office; so he's given Joel a lot of responsibility on his own up there." Mckenzie smiled. "He's Brian's son. He's a born trial attorney."

Hugh's eyes lit up behind his thick glasses. "And yours, too," he reminded her. "You're no slouch in front of a jury."

"Thanks."

"Got time for a drink? We could go downstairs."

Hugh frequented the Westin hotel's bar where he loved to drink scotch. Mckenzie had spent a lot of time there, chatting with him over drinks. Sometimes their after-work meetings reminded her of the way her relationship with Tyndall had begun in New York. In the beginning, they'd formed a habit of taking a break from work around seven p.m. and having a drink at the bar around the corner from their office before going back to work until well past midnight.

"Not tonight. I haven't packed yet."

"Okay. Then I'd better get to the point. How would you feel about being nominated to fill the current vacancy on the United States Supreme Court?"

"Me?" Mckenzie's eyes widened.

"Why not you? You've got the credentials."

"But I've never been a judge."

"Neither had William Rehnquist, and he became Chief Justice," Hugh observed. "In fact, historically, serving as a judge has never been a prerequisite for elevation to the high court."

"Am I really under serious consideration?"

"You are President Mason's number one pick for the post. The White House called George and asked him to find out if you'd be interested in accepting the nomination. He called me to see if I'd talk to you about it."

Senator George Lovell was the senior senator from California, and a friend of Hugh's. Mckenzie had accompanied Hugh to several fundraisers that George had staged for himself and several other candidates. Although Hugh was less active in politics since his run-in with former President Hal Edwards, which had nearly cost him his career, Mckenzie knew Hugh liked the reigning politicians to be beholden to him. To that end, he still made large contributions to their campaigns.

"But why has David Mason focused on me? I met him once or twice when I was teaching at Harvard and he was the senator from Virginia, but they were extremely brief encounters."

"He wants to nominate someone from his home state who has a distinguished reputation as a scholar. You were born in Virginia, went to college at William and Mary, and earned your J.D. at the University of Virginia. And you've written extensively on the federal constitutional right to privacy, the First Amendment, and the permissible scope of government regulation. You're also known as an advocate for single parents of both genders in the workplace. The president's staff thinks you'll encounter little, if any, opposition in the Senate because you have a perfect professional record and because you are well known for supporting causes that are difficult to oppose."

Mckenzie looked out the window at the sky streaked with the red sunset. "I—I don't know what to say."

"'Yes' would be a good answer," Hugh smiled. "Although you'll be missed around here." There was an unmistakable personal note of affection in his voice. *How do I really feel about Hugh?*

"But Joel is in San Francisco. I left Craig, Lewis so that I could be close to him while he was still at Stanford."

"Alan would transfer him to the DC office if he asked him to."

"I don't know if he would want to go, and I don't want to go to the East Coast without him."

"Talk to Joel about it this weekend. See what he says. I'll give George your answer on Monday. And Mckenzie—"

"What?"

"Obviously this is the pinnacle of your career. I don't see how you could say no. But I don't want you to go, either."

CHAPTER FIFTEEN

Saturday, January 14, 2017, The Marina District, San Francisco, California

Mckenzie waited until Saturday night to bring up the subject with Joel. They were sitting on his gray, slipcovered sofa facing the window that overlooked the Golden Gate Bridge. The bridge's soft yellow glow stood out sharply against the night sky. Joel had cooked steaks in the newly renovated kitchen of his two-bedroom condo. Now they were sipping the last of the California merlot that he had opened for dinner. The low light in the living room and the gentle buzz of the wine made Mckenzie feel relaxed and mellow. Earlier in the day, she'd been on edge, meeting Joel's latest girlfriend, Jenny Miyamoto, for brunch at the neighborhood dim sum restaurant.

"What did you think of Jenny?" Mckenzie knew the question was important because Joel had waited all day to ask. He settled back on the sofa with his glass of wine, his eyes fixed intently on her face.

"I liked her," Mckenzie assured him. "She's very beautiful and smart."

That much had been obvious. A slender five five, with long, dark hair swept into a ponytail, Jenny had been wearing a white, open-necked shirt and skinny jeans. She'd smiled modestly as Joel had announced proudly that she had been the editor of the Law Review at Berkeley. They were very obviously in love. So much so that Mckenzie had the uneasy feeling that she had already been replaced as Number One in her son's affections. She had always known that day would come; but now that it had arrived, it was harder to accept than she'd anticipated.

Mckenzie looked out at the bridge shining in the darkness and at the thin crescent moon poised high overhead. Finally, she asked, "How did you meet? I assume Jenny works for Warrick, Thompson?"

"Nope." Joel shook his head. The gesture was pure Brian. Mckenzie felt that familiar stab of grief whenever her son did anything that reminded her of his father. "She works for Legal Aid. One of my clients bought a building and was trying to evict all of the tenants. Jenny was opposing counsel."

"You fell in love with opposing counsel?"

"Yep." Joel gave her a big grin.

He's just like his father. He's never lacked confidence.

"So what happened?"

"I'll tell if you promise never to let the state bar know. Pinky swear." Joel held out his little finger with a grin, and she accepted his challenge.

"Pinky swear."

"I persuaded my client that he should let them all stay. He didn't actually have a buyer for the building, and the monthly income from the rental covered his mortgage."

"Why is she working for Legal Aid with credentials like that?"

"Because it's what she believes in." Her son's dark eyes were bright with admiration and love. "She went to law school to help the underdog. Her grandparents, who were U.S. citizens, were in the Internment Camps in World War II."

Mckenzie winced at the mention of the camps. She'd written several law review articles on the subject, denouncing the civil rights violations that the United States had committed against its Japanese-American citizens. "I see."

"Didn't you start your career by working for Legal Aid in Richmond?"

Mckenzie winced again. "No, not Legal Aid. The Public Defender."

"Is that where you met Dad?"

"Not exactly. We met at a party for UVA and William and Mary alumni. I was about to leave the Public Defender's Office to clerk for Judge Dabney who was a District Court Judge for the Eastern District of Virginia."

"Clerking for a federal judge was a big step up," Joel observed. "But didn't you like working as a PD?"

"No." Mckenzie shook her head emphatically. "Worse job I ever had. I hated being on the losing end of guilty people's cases."

"But surely they weren't all guilty?" Joel frowned.

"And you're thinking all of Jenny's clients aren't deadbeats?" Mckenzie couldn't help casting aspersions on her rival for her son's affection.

He looked slightly sheepish. "Maybe."

"I'd be careful then," Mckenzie warned. "Don't let yourself be blinded by personal feelings when you are representing a client."

He sighed. "I know, I know. Anyway, my client didn't hang on to that property for long, and the next buyer didn't try to evict the tenants, so they didn't need Jenny."

Mckenzie sipped her wine and studied the lights of the bridge for a few minutes. Then she said, "I've got something to tell you."

"Okay, I'm listening."

"Hugh came to see me on Friday. The president wants to nominate me to fill the vacancy on the Supreme Court."

Joel put down his glass and jumped up and hugged her. "That's wonderful, Mom! Wow! Dad would be so proud!"

"Well, hold on. It's not a done deal. The Senate would have to confirm me and—"

"Oh, come on, Mom. You've never put a foot wrong in your entire professional life. There's no reason why you won't be confirmed. I'm so proud of you!" He hugged her again, and she basked in the glow of his admiration.

When he let her go, she picked up her glass and sat down again. "There's something else, Joel."

"What?" He picked up his own glass and resumed his seat on the other end of the sofa.

"Well, obviously, I'd have to move back east. We'd be separated again. Unless, that is, you'd be willing to ask Alan Warrick for a transfer to the D.C. office."

But he shook his head emphatically. "No way, Mom. I wouldn't get to work with Alan there. And Jenny would be out here."

"But with credentials like hers, she could work for Warrick, Thompson, too."

He began to look angry, and she immediately regretted pushing the wrong button. "Don't you understand? She hates Big Law! She hates the establishment! The establishment put her grandparents in the camps."

"You're making a leap that isn't supported by the facts." *Oh, God, I'm talking to him the way I used to talk to my law students. But I can't stop myself.* "Alan Warrick wasn't even alive when her grandparents were interned. And the major law firms had nothing to do with the internment. That was the government."

"But it was the government's lawyers and their outside attorneys who said it was okay to turn people out of their homes and lock them up even though they had never committed any crimes in *Koretmatsu v. United States.*"

"I know. I know. And if another case like that comes before the Supreme Court, I'll be sure to vote against the Solicitor General. But seriously, Joel, I want to accept the nomination. But I want to be sure you'll come east with me."

He shook his head. "I won't."

"But Joel—"

"Don't waste your breath. I've found the woman I want to marry. I don't want you to mess that up, Mom."

"Then the answer is simple, and it's just what I said. Everyone can come to D.C. with me."

"No, Mother."

His phone rang, and he went to his room to take the call. She guessed it was Jenny and wished he'd tell her he had to call her back. But of course, they had quarreled, and he had nothing else to say to her just then. Telling Jenny what a horrible, controlling witch his mother was would be a relief, she told herself bitterly.

She stared out at the glowing lights of the Golden Gate and thought back to the days when she'd been in Jenny's shoes. When she'd thought serving the poor would make her life meaningful. When she'd discovered that serving the poor hadn't been redemption at all. When she'd found herself in a world of liars and scam artists, bent on evading landlords and the electric company on the low end and getting away with murder on the high end.

"They're all lying, and they're all guilty," her boss, Brad O'Connor, had told her when she'd been a deputy public defender for two whole days. It was August 1983 and the ink had barely been dry on her J.D. from William and Mary. The director of the placement office had tried her best to talk her into accepting the offer from Hunton and Williams to enter the firm with their elite class of associates.

"You're at the top of your class, Mckenzie. You're wasting your talent, and you'll be making a fraction of what you'd be making at Hunton. You'll be forever sorry you made this decision. Don't do it."

But she'd pushed stubbornly on, determined to find a place where she could feel as if she was using her legal skills to help people. The trouble was, being at the top of her class and knowing how to practice law were two different things. For the first few months, while she was waiting for the results of the bar exam, she'd been a glorified clerk, unable to sign pleadings or represent clients in court. But in October, after she'd been notified that she'd passed the exam and had been sworn in as a member of the Virginia Bar, she'd been handed a docket of ten felonies and sent to court to deal with the far more experienced

Commonwealth's Attorneys. For the first time in her life, she no longer appeared to be intelligent. She stumbled over the simplest legal concepts. She begged clients to plead to avoid having to be embarrassed by her complete lack of trial skills. She woke up in a cold sweat night after night, wondering what had ever made her go to law school. Sitting in class for three years and sitting for exams twice a year on complex legal concepts had given her no training at all in how to represent clients in court. She didn't appear to be No. 2 in her class when she sat at the defense table. She looked like an idiot who didn't know what she was doing. And she didn't.

Now, as she sat listening to the steady rhythm of Joel's voice interspersed with laughter, she shivered at the memory of the day she'd realized she had to get out of the Public Defender's Office before the incompetent label was attached to her name forever.

In January 1984, the Ed Carter case had been the talk of the office. Initially, Mckenzie had been relieved when Brad O'Connor had pulled her off her misdemeanor docket to do research for Ed's defense. She wrote the kind of long, scholarly memoranda for Brad that law school had so expertly trained her to do. Day after day, she researched and wrote, and her nightmare of being and feeling incompetent disbursed. She applied for a clerkship with St. John Dabney and prayed that salvation would come quickly.

But it didn't come quickly enough. On the last day of January, on a cold, sunny morning, Brad came to Mckenzie's office holding a tape recorder.

She looked up at his lanky frame apprehensively. Brad was

in his early forties, with a pleasant round face, bald head, and a gentle drawl that juries liked. He was a good trial lawyer, and looking back, Mckenzie realized that she'd managed to learn from him even though she'd been terrified during the entire time she'd been in the Public Defender's Office.

"I've got a different kind of assignment for you today."

"But I haven't finished the memo on voluntary manslaughter that you wanted." She was doing an analysis of every published case, looking for facts similar to the Carter case.

"That's okay. This is more important. We've managed to overlook a witness who should have been interviewed. Quinn Fairchild was one of Allison Byrd's roommates. We know what Blair Keaton and Paige Caldwell have to say. They claim Ed was going to leave his wife for Allison. They're going to be prosecution witnesses. I don't know why we didn't think to track down the other one, but she's in Petersburg. I want you to go down there today and get a statement."

Mckenzie shivered at the thought of having to conduct a witness interview when she'd already learned that research and writing were the limits of her expertise. "But I'm at the very end of the memo," she protested weakly.

"It can wait. This can't." He put the tape recorder on her desk. "I'm sorry that I don't have an investigator to send with you. This will have to do."

* * *

Joel's voice continued on, steady and relaxed. Mckenzie was hurt because he wasn't in a hurry to resume their visit. She was sorry that she'd suggested a transfer to D.C., but it had seemed so logical to her. She clung to him too hard. She knew that. It was natural, but it was also wrong. She took a deep breath and promised herself she wouldn't bring up the subject of leaving San Francisco again.

* * *

She'd gotten lost three times before she'd found the ramshackle house where Quinn Fairchild lived. The wooden porch was sagging, the paint had long ago peeled off. From the looks of it, it was barely six hundred square feet.

A tall, disheveled young woman in jeans and a red sweater answered the door. Her hair was falling out of her ponytail. She wore no makeup, and her dark eyes looked sad and angry.

"I don't want to talk to you," Quinn Fairchild said after Mckenzie identified herself and then stood shivering on the shaky porch.

"Just a few minutes," Mckenzie begged, hoping she'd say no again, so she could head straight back to Richmond to her research and writing.

But no luck. "Okay. Come in."

The front door opened straight into the living room. Mckenzie sat down on a threadbare sofa and put the tape recorder on the orange crate that served as a coffee table. Quinn took the straight chair opposite.

"I don't want to talk about the Ed Carter case," she said bitterly. "It's ruined my chances of ever getting out of here." She waved her hands to display her shabby surroundings.

Mckenzie frowned. "How come?"

"Because the law school put all four of us on suspension,

claiming we'd violated the student code of conduct by cozying up to Professor Carter."

"Why don't you tell me about that?"

Mckenzie was afraid she'd show her the door, but she pulled a package of cigarettes out of her shirt pocket and lit up as if preparing herself for an ordeal. Mckenzie tried not to gag at the smell.

Quinn said, "Allison had the hots for Ed Carter. Granted he's rich and good-looking. But he wasn't interested in Allison. She tried and tried to get his attention, and nothing worked. She became obsessed with him. Finally, she started going to his office every Friday to watch his kid because she figured out that he loved his son more than anything else in the world. The kid was the way to his heart."

"Did babysitting his son ingratiate her to Ed Carter?"

"No, of course not. He hated the sight of her. You could tell whenever she'd trap him after class. But the thing was, she wouldn't give up. The more he told her to leave him alone, the more she pursued him. She moved out of our house and found an apartment on Grove Avenue just up the street from him."

"Did you stop seeing her after that?"

"No. We all had the same classes, and Allison liked to come over to our place to hang out and talk about her obsession with Ed. Paige, Blair, and I mostly ignored her."

"Well, thanks for your time." Mckenzie desperately wanted to get out in the fresh air, away from the smoke. Quinn liked to stick the cigarette in the side of her mouth, inhale deeply, and blow the smoke out through her nose. It made her seem tough. Mckenzie started to get up.

"Is that all? Don't you want to hear the rest?"

"There's more?"

"Sure. Allison is the one who killed Ed's wife."

"*What*?" Mckenzie cautioned herself to sound professional and not hysterical. "How do you know?" She reverted to her calm, measured slightly skeptical tone because she thought that's how lawyers questioned witnesses.

"Because it had to be Allison. The night his wife was killed, I was with Professor Carter. All night."

"You slept with him?"

"That's right." Quinn blew some more smoke out of her nose.

"He was in Charlottesville for some sort of law professor conference. My boyfriend at the time was a UVA law student. I went up there to see him, but we had a fight and broke up. I walked to the Unicorn's Horn, the closest pub, to find a lay. I was upset and angry, and I just wanted sex."

"Did you find anyone?"

"I hit the jackpot. I found Professor Carter. He was holding court at a table in the eating area. He'd been to some sort of reception, and when it was over, he'd come into the pub for a beer. There were five or six law students sitting there talking to him. I went over and sat down, thinking I'd try to pick up one of the single guys. But the group dwindled, and before long, it was just the two of us. Professor Carter asked me back to his hotel room, and I said yes. The truth is, I had nowhere to sleep that night. I'd come up to stay with my boyfriend. But I was also kind of curious about what it would be like to sleep with Professor Carter. And I could dangle that under Allison's nose and make her wild with jealousy."

"There were security cameras at the hotel," Mckenzie said. "We've reviewed the film, and we didn't see any evidence of anyone coming or going from Ed Carter's room that night."

"He did something to them," Quinn said. "Turned them in another direction, I think. But he made sure that they wouldn't see us going into his room."

"Did you stay all night?"

"Of course I did. Like I said, I had nowhere else to go. We had sex. It was just okay sex. But we talked a lot. I liked talking to him."

"What did you talk about?"

"He was upset because his wife had refused to come to the conference with him, and I was upset over losing my boyfriend. Ed kept saying how much he loved his wife and how he wished she'd stop having affairs. And I kept talking about all the times my boyfriend had cheated on me. He said that I was better off without him. So I asked him if he wouldn't be better off without his wife since she kept cheating on him."

"And what did he say?"

"He said that he didn't want a divorce because he still loved her. And he said he'd lose his son if there were a divorce, and he couldn't bear the thought of being separated from him."

"What happened after that?"

"I passed out because I'd had a lot to drink. The next morning, he offered to drive me back to my car. It was still parked at my boyfriend's place."

"And did he drive you to your car?"

"He did. He was a sweet man. I felt sorry for him."

"Why?"

"Because he loved his wife and his little boy so much, and it seemed like his wife didn't love him. And then, too, I knew Allison was making his life miserable."

"Did he talk to you about that?"

"No, he didn't even know that I knew her. But she was always bragging about watching his house and seeing his wife kissing another man. And she'd gone to the dean and lied about having an affair with him to get him fired."

"He slept with you. How do you know that he didn't sleep with Allison?"

"Because she never stopped complaining about being rejected. She lied to the dean to get revenge. I felt sorry for him because being in Allison's crosshairs was miserable."

"So you think Allison Byrd killed Anne?"

"Of course she did. The dean didn't fire Professor Carter, so she had to get her revenge another way: she killed his wife."

"But do you have any evidence that she was the killer?"

She blew smoke through her nostrils again. "She came to Paige and Blair after Anne Carter's body was found and begged them to say they were with her all night that night."

"Were they with her all night?"

"God, no!" She stubbed out her cigarette and immediately lit another. Mckenzie winced as a fresh cloud of acrid smoke wafted through the little room.

"Did she ask you for an alibi?"

"No, she knew I'd been in Charlottesville all weekend."

"Did you tell her you'd slept with Ed?"

"No. I had planned to before I found out she'd killed his wife. But after I realized she'd murdered Anne Carter, I was afraid that if she knew I'd slept with Ed, she'd kill me, too. She was that obsessed with him."

"When I take your statement back to my boss, he's going to want you to testify at Ed's trial."

"No way."

"But why? You can be subpoenaed and forced to testify if you refuse."

"I told you before. Allison would kill me before she'd let me alibi Ed Carter."

"But—"

"Listen!" Quinn stood up with the cigarette hanging from the side of her mouth. "I don't want to talk about this anymore. I shouldn't have told you what really happened that night. Allison is overjoyed that the cops have framed Ed Carter. She hopes he'll get the death penalty. It's time for you to go." With the cigarette still dangling, Quinn took the three steps required to reach the front door. She opened it and snapped, "Get out!"

The tone of her voice said there would be no negotiation. Mckenzie, who was still sitting on the couch, scrambled to pick up the tape recorder, her briefcase, and her coat. Without putting it on, she hurried past Quinn and out into the cold air that mercifully was free of smoke. Quinn slammed the door behind her.

She ran to her car and threw everything on the passenger seat and got in. Her hands were trembling as she started the engine and backed out of the driveway. She was halfway to Richmond before her heart stopped racing. She was hungry, but she was too upset to stop and eat. She didn't begin to feel calm until she had reached the sanctity of her office. But the moment she put the tape recorder on her desk, she realized the awful truth. She had forgotten to turn it on.

Brad appeared at that moment in her doorway.

"What did Quinn Fairchild have to say?"

Her panicked brain said she couldn't admit to a mistake as big as this one. "Nothing. She wasn't there."

And indeed, when Mckenzie drove back in a panic the next day, the saggy house was now deserted. Had Quinn been that afraid that Allison would find out that she'd talked to one of Ed Carter's lawyers?

She told herself that Quinn's statement didn't matter because the evidence showed that Ed had hired Miller to kill Anne. Two months later, before Ed Carter went to trial, Judge Dabney hired her for a two-year clerkship. Her nightmare in the Public Defender's Office was over. Unless she opened her mouth about Quinn Fairchild. But she wasn't going to do that. Brad was convinced that Ed was guilty. And Mckenzie was sure that he was right.

* * *

No, she told herself, as she watched the lights of the bridge and waited for Joel, the Quinn Fairchild statement had had no value for the defense.

At least until the day Miller had recanted his murder-for-hire claim, a voice in her head reminded her. *But I don't want to think about that. Besides, the answer was simple. Quinn had disappeared because she'd lied. She hadn't spent the night with Ed Carter because his neighbor had seen his car outside his house around the time of the murder.*

She focused on the bridge lights as they cast their steady warmth into the night and reminded herself that Quinn Fairchild had been a liar just like all the witnesses and clients she'd encountered as a deputy public defender. She'd shaken the dust of that hellish place off her feet the day she'd entered the chambers of Judge Dabney. She wasn't the person who'd forgotten to turn the tape recorder on anymore. She'd spent two years in Judge Dabney's courtroom learning how to be a litigator. And what she hadn't learned there, she'd learned from her husband, who had been widely acknowledged as one of the best trial attorneys in the country. Her heart had skipped a beat when Brendan Murphy had taken over Ed's case in 1986, and Brian had told her that he'd seen her name in Brad O'Connor's file. But when he had asked her about interviewing Quinn Fairchild, she'd repeated the lie. "There was no interview. When I got to Petersburg, Quinn wasn't there."

CHAPTER SIXTEEN

Monday, January 16, 2017, Lindbergh Field, San Diego, California

To her surprise, Hugh was waiting with his driver when she got off the plane at five o'clock.

"Hope you don't mind," he said as he opened the door of his Mercedes for her while Jose, his driver, stored her bag in the trunk. "George is anxious to hear your answer about the nomination."

She frowned as she got into back seat and put on her seatbelt. Hugh got in beside her. As they pulled away from the curb, he said, "I was hoping you'd have time for an early supper at the Hotel Del, so we could talk about your decision. From the look on your face, I'm afraid President Mason is going to be disappointed."

In truth, she wanted to go home to her cottage on First Street on the other end of Coronado Island, pour herself a big glass of wine, and stare out at the lights of the city across San Diego Bay, without thinking or feeling anything. The rest of her weekend with Joel had been tense, and he'd refused all her overtures to make things better, including nixing her suggestion to invite Jenny to brunch that morning.

"She's working today."

"But the courts are closed."

"She has files to catch up on. She doesn't have the kind of support staff that we have, Mother."

The edge in his voice said she was on dangerous ground. He was still angry with her for suggesting a move to D.C. *How do I make him understand that I'm not trying to end his relationship? Yes, I'm sad that he's transferred his loyalty to another woman, but I knew it would happen one day. I'm doing my best to accept it. Or am I?*

"Dinner sounds fine, but I'd like to drop my bag at my house first."

"Of course."

She parked Hugh in her living room with a scotch while she changed out of her rumpled flying clothes. She put on a simple, long-sleeved dress, added black pumps, and the diamond heart necklace that Joel had given her for Mother's Day last year. She needed to tell herself that he still loved her. She studied her face in the mirror as she touched up her makeup.

Most people didn't guess that she was fifty-eight. Her oval face was still smooth and unlined. She had large, dark, penetrating eyes that studied the world around her carefully and thoughtfully. Her hairdresser did an expert job of keeping her chin-length hair honey blonde. Joel, she reflected, as she refreshed her lipstick, was a dark-haired, blue-eyed copy of his father. And she was grateful for that.

* * *

It was dark, of course, when they settled at their table at 1500 Ocean, the premier restaurant at the Hotel Del. Its breathtaking view of the Pacific was submerged in the darkness, but Mckenzie could see the rush of white foam as the little waves rolled onto the wide, dark sand.

Hugh settled in with his scotch and a plate of oysters. Mckenzie chose white wine and a salad. They ate in silence for a few minutes before Hugh asked, "So what was Joel's reaction to your news?"

Mckenzie put down her fork and sighed. "He was happy about the nomination, but he wouldn't consider a move to D.C."

Hugh frowned. "But Alan would gladly—"

"I know, I know. He's got a girlfriend who works for Legal Aid. Her grandparents were interned during World War II. She apparently would never consider working for Big Law or leaving San Francisco for D.C."

Hugh raised his eyebrows. "Are they going to get married?"

"It's all very new, but at this moment, Joel is thinking about it seriously."

"And that doesn't make you happy." Hugh was also a practiced observer of faces.

"Honestly, no. Her view of the world is far too narrow. She thinks all the clients who pass through Legal Aid and the PD's office are unequivocally innocent. But she's wrong. I met more liars and cheats during the two years that I was in the Public Defender's office in Richmond than I have met since. Even my money-laundering bank clients don't lie that much."

Hugh smiled. "Erin and I see it at the Innocence Project, too, of course. But not everyone is lying, Mckenzie."

"The ones I met were." Her tone of voice said she refused to see the facts any other way, and therefore the discussion was ended.

Hugh held up his glass for another scotch, and the waiter nodded.

"I thought you'd decided to cut back," Mckenzie observed.

"This is number two. I'm cutting back," he grinned. "So give me the news, good or bad. What am I going to tell Dave Mason?"

She sighed and stared at the water for a long moment. Then her dark eyes came back to Hugh's, anxious behind his thick glasses. "Tell him yes."

Hugh smiled but still looked a little concerned. "Are you sure? You and Joel will be on opposite coasts again."

"I'll agree to speak at all the California law schools every six months," she smiled. "There are a lot of them. That should keep us in touch."

"You don't look convinced that this is the right decision."

"It's not this decision. It's knowing I have to let go of Joel." Suddenly there were tears in her eyes, and Hugh reached out and took her hand.

"I know it's hard."

She swiped at her tears and smiled. "I'm sorry. I wasn't expecting that. You're lucky you have Erin here working with you."

"I am. I take it you wanted Joel at Goldstein, Miller? We'd have been more than happy to have him."

"I mentioned it once and only once when he graduated from Stanford. He took it the way he took my suggestion about moving to D.C., only there was no girlfriend involved back then. I've clung to him too hard sometimes, I admit. This appointment, if I get it, will be a challenge, and it will force me to let Joel have the space he needs. I won't like that, but I know I have to do it."

"You might meet someone on the other side of the world and get married again."

She took back the hand that Hugh had held comfortingly and smiled. "I doubt that. I like my life as it is. And no one can be Brian." *Not even you or Tyndall Chastain?*

"Well, George and Dave are going to be very happy with your decision. George's office has already sent over the papers for you to fill out. The FBI will have an easy time with this investigation," Hugh smiled and waved at the waiter for another scotch. "You're one of the best lawyers and best legal scholars in the country. There are no skeletons in your closet."

* * *

It was only nine o'clock when she got home. She put on her pajamas, made herself a cup of tea, and called Joel.

"Hi, Mom. I don't have a lot of time. Jenny's here."

"I just wanted to say how much I enjoyed the weekend."

"Me, too," his tone softened. "I'll be down there for work in a couple of weeks. We'll see each other then."

"I called for another reason. I've decided to accept the nomination."

"Mom! That's great news!" She heard joy and relief in his voice. *I've done the right thing for both of us. He knows I'm not going to try to hang on to him.* "You'll be approved without any opposition. I'm sure of that! Wow! My mother is going to be on the Supreme Court."

"Not so fast, Joel," but she was laughing, "one step at a time."

She heard a brief whisper in the background and then Joel said, "Jenny says she's proud, too."

* * *

Her world seemed right-side up after the call. She sat on her sofa, watching the lights of the city shimmer in the water, and imagined her future. She'd have the privilege of shaping the law and the future of the country in a way that few individuals ever had. It was a big responsibility, but one she knew she was eminently qualified for.

She wanted to tell Tyndall herself. She didn't want him to read it in the papers or be surprised when the FBI agents showed up at his door, asking questions about their association. Granted it was past midnight, but he often stayed up late.

"Hello?" Her heart still fluttered a little when she heard his distinctive Boston accent.

"Tyndall, it's Mckenzie."

The pause made her heart flutter harder. Maybe he didn't want to talk to her.

But finally, he said warmly, "I'm just so surprised to hear from you. But very glad. Are you in New York?"

"No, San Diego. I've got news to share."

"And I do, too! You first."

"I'm being nominated for the vacancy on the Supreme Court."

"I can't think of a more qualified person! Congratulations! I guess that means you'll be coming east?"

"It does, of course."

"Well, the train runs every day from New York to D.C. And I'm down there often on business."

Do I want to see him again? It could complicate things. But I've missed him since the day I left Craig, Lewis. "Seeing you will be one of the job perks. What's your news?"

"Claire's engaged."

"To that friend of hers from law school? Jeff? The one you like so much?"

"No, it's Wynne Carter."

"Wynne Carter?"

"I don't know how much Brian told you about the Ed Carter case."

Oh, God, not that again tonight. "He and Brendan were upset about losing that trial."

"Wynne is Ed's son." *The little boy that Quinn said he loved so much.*

"Do you like him?"

"I do. He's achieved a lot against some substantial odds. But that's just it, Mckenzie. They've finally set a date for his father's execution. March 3. He and Claire were planning the wedding for March 4."

She was panicked at the thought but willed herself to sound calm. "Execution?"

"Ed's been on death row since 1984. But you knew that."

"I—I haven't kept up with his case. It brings back the memories of losing Brian. He went down in the plane that night because of Ed Carter." *Who Brad said is guilty as hell.*

"Well, he's exhausted his appeals, and the date has been set.

Brendan is trying frantically to stop it. And now Claire's involved."

"Claire? But she's a civil lawyer."

"I reminded her of that. And so did Jeff."

"So Jeff's still in the picture?"

"He works with me. He and Claire have been friends since they were One L's. But that's all. I like Wynne. But I don't like the idea of Claire being mixed up in all the baggage that comes with him. Honestly, I wish it was Jeff. Please don't tell anyone."

"I won't. Are they going through with the wedding?"

"For now, it's postponed."

"I see."

"I keep hoping something will save Ed. That's the only thing that will make Claire and Wynne happy. Otherwise, they'll be starting their lives together under the cloud of his death."

"Not a good omen." *She could see the cigarette smoke coming out of Quinn Fairchild's flared nostrils: Professor Carter asked me back to his hotel room, and I said yes.*

"Brendan's a good lawyer," Mckenzie said. "He'll find something to stop the execution. He's kept Ed Carter alive all these years."

"Not this time," Tyndall said. "He's run out of new claims to raise, and he's rehashing the old ones. At this point, I think Brendan's in denial. Ed Carter is guilty. But I can't tell Claire that."

Just like I can't tell Joel that Jenny's got a chip on her shoulder that skews her vision of the world. It's not as simple as rich people are bad, poor people are good.

"But that's enough about the Carter problem," Tyndall said.

"You've given me something to look forward to. When are you coming east for the hearings? I'll come down to Washington and take you to dinner."

"That sounds wonderful. I'll let you know when I'll be there."

She hung up and stared at the city lights. Her world was upside down again. Could the FBI find out that she'd committed malpractice that day in Petersburg when she'd forgotten to turn the tape on? Could they prove she'd lied when she reported back to Brad O'Connor? Surely not. Brad was dead. No one had ever questioned her story that Quinn Fairchild was not in Petersburg that day. *Unless someone found Quinn Fairchild.*

PART II

CLAIRE

"Humankind cannot bear very much reality."

T.S. Eliot

CHAPTER SEVENTEEN

*Thursday afternoon, January 19, 2017, Offices of Warrick, Thompson,
and Hayes, 200 Park Avenue, Midtown Manhattan*

"I've got an appointment with Governor Reynolds in half an
hour."

Claire breathed a sigh of relief. Wynne had headed back to
Richmond on Tuesday because the governor's chief-of-staff had
suddenly announced that his boss was willing to meet with him.
Up until that point, all of Wynne's petitions for an appointment
had fallen on deaf ears. But the governor had refused to set an
exact time because he didn't want it leaked to the press. So
Wynne had to go to Richmond and wait to be summoned.

"I'm so glad."

"He's got to listen," Wynne said. "I can promise him more
than enough money for his next campaign for whatever office
he sets his heart on. I've heard he wants to run for the Senate."

"I thought he was always in the Fairfaxes' pocket."

"He always has been. But I can offer him more. He'll listen,
Claire. I know he will. He'll stop the execution. I've got to go. I
love you."

"I love you, too." As she hung up, she glanced at the clock on her desk, four o'clock. She hoped Wynne would have time to make the last train for New York after meeting with the governor. She'd gotten home on Monday, and he'd headed out for Richmond the next morning. They hadn't had much time together lately.

As she sat at her desk thinking about Wynne and hoping the governor of Virginia would end the long Carter family nightmare that afternoon with a few strokes of his pen, she realized that footsteps were coming down the hall toward her office. She wasn't expecting anyone that afternoon.

But the footsteps continued to approach, accompanied by her secretary's voice, apparently questioning the person she was bringing to Claire's door. Claire heard what sounded like a question from Blanche, followed by a male voice apparently answering. The voice was so familiar that it seemed to penetrate every fiber of her being. Paul Curtis. Her heart skipped a beat. She didn't want to see him, but it was too late to close her door. Surely he wasn't headed her way to talk to her. But he was.

He stood in her doorway and knocked on the partially opened door. Even in a heavy, black overcoat and navy cashmere scarf in the middle of a New York winter, he looked like the blonde, blue-eyed, California surfer that he had always been. He was the only one left of the famous Pacific Beach triumvirate of teenage surfers consisting of himself, Tom Andrews, and Steve Cooper. The three of them had once traveled the world together, collecting trophies. Claire noticed at once that his handsome, square-jawed face looked drawn and tired. It was something only someone who knew him well would see. She wished she wasn't that person, but she was.

"Have you got a few minutes? I'm in town to take depositions. Thought I'd see if you had time for a drink."

Claire looked at the clock on her desk and then back into those warm, blue eyes that were making her heart race. "Not at four in the afternoon."

"Oh, sorry. I thought it was later. If I come back in say, an hour?"

His persistence disturbed her as much as his presence. "Sorry, no."

His tall figure seemed to slump a little with the blow of her refusal. Her eyes fell on his left hand. No wedding band. But he had gone through with the wedding last June. He'd sent invitations to everyone on his litigation team. She had fed hers to the shredder.

She sat silently with a look on her face that said she was waiting for him to leave.

He shifted uncomfortably from one foot to the other. "Look, I came to tell you something."

"I don't want to hear it. I don't work for you anymore. If you have any questions about a case we worked on, there's email."

"Okay, Claire. I more than deserved that. You know I'm not here about work."

"There's nothing personal between us anymore, Paul. I shouldn't have to tell you that."

"I know, I know. But—"

He won't go away until I hear him out. And I want him to go away. "Come in and sit down. I'll give you five minutes. But

I'm waiting to hear from my fiancé. If Wynne calls, you'll have to leave. And please leave my door open."

He nodded as he crossed the room and sat down. "Congratulations on your engagement."

"Thank you." She used her voice for cross-examining hostile witnesses.

He took a deep breath and said, "I lied."

"Fine. You lied. I have no idea what you lied about, and I don't care."

"Oh, God. I didn't say that right. I don't honestly know where to begin."

"You didn't have any trouble knowing where to begin when you invited me to dinner to announce your engagement last May." She knew she sounded bitter, and she didn't care.

"I know, and I'm sorry. And I realized that night what a fool I had been. Look, I lied about why I came to New York. I'm not here to take depos. I came to tell you it didn't work out with Michelle because I miss you so much. That night in the restaurant when she showed you the ring and I saw your face, I suddenly realized what I'd lost. And I didn't want the woman I was engaged to, I wanted you. And I knew I'd screwed everything up."

"So what are you asking me to do?"

"I'm asking you not to make the same mistake. Don't marry Wynne."

Claire stood up, her blue eyes flashing. "You have no right to say that to me! I've given you five minutes, now get out of my office!"

He stood up but lingered by the chair. "Claire, please listen."

"I've listened. You shouldn't have come here."

"Maybe I shouldn't have. But I had to try."

"You still don't get it, Paul. It's always been about you. For years, all I heard from you was how much you loved Kathryn Andrews and how your heart would always be broken because she'd married Tom. Then Tom died, and all I heard was how much you wanted to marry Kathryn. And all that time, you were the first face I saw in the morning, and the last one I saw at night before I went home to bed. And God help me for being stupid, not only did I listen to you, I traveled with you, and sometimes I slept with you. We were as 'married' as any couple on earth, and we spent more time together than most married couples.

"And after Kathryn married Mark Kelly, I thought you'd realize that, and I thought you'd wake up and see who really loved you. But no, you chased that ridiculous paralegal, Brandi, and you spent hours in my office talking about her. And then you ran off with a woman who hunted you down like some sort of trophy. I'm happy now, Paul, with a man who values me in a way you never did. If you're not happy, don't come and tell me about it. I'm not here for you anymore."

Her phone began to ring, and she picked it up immediately. "Claire Chastain."

"Claire, it's Wynne."

"Wait just a minute. I've got someone in my office who is on his way out." She pointed to her door and breathed a sigh of relief as Paul turned away. Then she asked, "What did Governor Reynolds say?"

"No." She could hear the tears in Wynne's voice. "He said no."

* * *

159

It was five o'clock and dark outside when her call with Wynne ended. He wasn't coming back tonight. He was heading down to Sussex to see Ed in the morning. She told herself not to be disappointed. His hours with his father could very well be numbered. Still, they'd been apart more than they'd been together since the news of Ed's impending execution had put their wedding plans on hold.

She turned away from her desk and studied the glowing cavern of midtown punctuated by the lighted spires of the Chrysler Building and the Empire State Building. The fifty-third floor afforded a breathtaking view. She had the most powerful and sophisticated city in the world at her feet and no one to share it with. What if she called Paul and suggested dinner? He would certainly accept her invitation. But to what end?

She heard footsteps advancing toward her office for the second time that day. This time it was Jeff Ryder in the black, power overcoat with a burgundy cashmere scarf who knocked on her open door. And this time her heart lurched with joy at the sight of him.

"Jeff! What are you doing here?" The tone of her voice added, *I'm so glad to see you!*

He grinned. "You won't believe this, but I was summoned by Alan Warrick and Howard to a meeting this afternoon."

"Howard? As in Morgan?"

"Yep. They've been bending my ear about what they'll give me if I come back to work for them."

Claire caught her breath. "I hope you said no! After the way they treated you last year."

Jeff grinned as he stood in the doorway. "I left them twisting slowly in the wind. I said I'd think about it."

"Did you mean that? My father would be devastated."

"No, I didn't mean it. I just wanted to get their hopes up and pull the rug out from under them because they deserve it. I don't want to leave Craig, Lewis. I like working with your father too much."

"I'm relieved to hear that."

"Why don't you come and join us? You know what it would mean to your father to have you at his firm. And it would keep Paul Curtis from lurking around your office."

"So you know he was here today?"

"Yes. I came by before my meeting with Alan and Howard to see if you wanted dinner afterward, and he was firmly planted in that chair." Jeff nodded toward the client chair in front of her desk.

"Listen, I need to get out of here and go for a walk. Wynne's down in Richmond and not coming back tonight."

"Well, it's freezing out, but we'll walk if that's what you want."

"Let's go to Bryant Park and watch the skaters."

"Okay, and then when we're good and frozen, I know a great pizza place with a big open-hearth fire where we can drink Chianti and catch up."

* * *

But when they reached the skating rink at Bryant Park, Jeff insisted on renting skates for both of them.

"I didn't know people who grew up in Southern California

knew how to ice skate," Claire said as they were lacing up their skates.

Jeff grinned. "Well, now you do. I skate, but I do not surf."

"Thank God." She took his hand, and they headed onto the ice together.

For more than an hour, they wove in and out of the sparse group of Thursday night skaters until they were tired, cold, and hungry. Claire insisted she was up for the ten-block walk to Nicolosi's, but she was thoroughly frozen by the time they were seated at a table covered with a red-checked cloth, near the warmth of the oven.

"Should I order coffee instead of Chianti?" Jeff asked.

"No! I'll leave my gloves on," she laughed. *I don't remember the last time I laughed.*

"So are you still a pepperoni, sausage, and mushroom girl?"

"Absolutely. God, Jeff. It's been so long since study group in law school. How do you remember things like that?"

He grinned and shrugged. "I don't know. Just brilliant, I guess."

After the waiter had taken their pizza order and poured the wine, Claire sat back in her chair and studied him. "How are you doing?"

He toyed with his glass and gave her a rueful smile. "I think that means 'how are you doing without Beth?'"

"Have you heard from her?"

"Not much since I was in Houston for Christmas. She's busy setting up the Christopher Rafferty Foundation to help quadriplegics and their families. She's decided to go to law school at the University of Houston because a law degree will help her run the foundation. And she's hired a young doctor to head up the medical side of things."

"And he's your rival?" Claire studied his face as she asked.

"I wouldn't put it that way. Beth and I were thrown together by some pretty extreme circumstances last year. We realized after Chris died that we needed some time to sort out where our lives were going and to figure out if they were going in the same direction. I don't see myself in Houston long term, and Beth doesn't see herself anywhere else. She feels close to Chris there, and that's where she wants Abby to grow up. We'll never say goodbye, but we have grown apart."

"So you'll be able to go to her wedding with a happy heart?"

"Well, she and Dr. Daggett haven't gotten that far yet. But yes, definitely. She deserves to be happy, especially after she devoted herself to keeping Chris alive for so many years."

Claire took a long drink of her wine. Then she said, without any attempt to keep the bitterness out of her voice, "I wish I could say the same about Paul."

"I heard that his wife has filed for divorce and headed back to New York. Did he tell you that today?"

"More or less. He wasn't wearing his wedding ring, and he was telling me not to marry Wynne."

"As if he had anything to say about it."

But Claire said nothing and stared into the depths of the fire.

"Do I take it by your silence that Paul does have something to say about you and Wynne?"

"No," Claire shook her head impatiently and gave him a little smile. "It's not Paul turning up that's bothering me."

The pizza appeared at that moment, hot and crisp from the

oven. Jeff ordered another bottle of Chianti. "You look like you need more," he said. "I'll pay for your cab home."

Claire munched pizza and drank wine and watched the orange flames in the enormous oven.

"If you want to talk about it," Jeff said, "I want to listen."

She sighed. "Am I terrible for enjoying skating with you tonight?"

"Why would that make you terrible?"

"Because Wynne's father's life is in danger."

"So you can't enjoy yourself anymore?"

"I guess that sounds ridiculous, but it's how I feel."

"Claire, maybe you should get out from under all of this for a while."

"You mean, maybe I should break off my engagement until I find out whether Ed's going to be executed?" She didn't try to keep the edge out of her voice.

But Jeff was neither offended nor ruffled. "You've got to admit, a wedding is supposed to be a joyful event, but you can't plan anything joyful under the circumstances."

She gave him a little smile. "Flying around on the ice tonight was a break from all the black clouds hanging over Wynne and me. But ending my engagement would make Paul think I want him back in my life. And I don't."

"I'm relieved to hear that."

She laughed. "The way that I'm relieved to hear that you aren't going to go back to work for Howard and Alan."

He smiled. "We'd be in the same firm again if I did."

"I'd rather have you where I know you're appreciated."

"Look, Claire, maybe you shouldn't get involved with

Brendan's work on Ed's case. You're too emotional to be objective."

"And didn't I say the very same thing to you last year when you were representing the Raffertys and in love with Beth?"

"Okay, I admit that you did."

"And you didn't give up the case even though you were waist-deep in feelings for your client."

"No, I did not."

"Well, I'm not going to give up Wynne or his father's case. But I will admit I feel lost when I try to figure out how to help Brendan. The state's theory of why Ed is guilty has changed over the course of his three trials."

"That's probably a good sign," Jeff said. "When I was a prosecutor, having to switch theories meant my case wasn't all that strong. Has Brendan suggested what you can do to help?"

She shook her head. "He's got all of his associates churning out writs right and left. The trouble is, all of them are based on evidence that's already been rejected by the courts, both state and federal."

"So he's spinning his wheels in the same old mud?"

"I don't know if he thinks so, but I do. Maybe that means my civil background won't let me be of much use."

"As far as being a civil lawyer goes, I think that's actually an advantage here."

She frowned. "I don't understand what you mean."

"I mean you've got a fresh set of eyes, and you won't be taking anything for granted. After you practice in an area for a long time, you start to make assumptions rather than look at the facts."

She considered what he'd said for a minute, and then said thoughtfully, "You've given me an idea of how to help."

"What are you going to do?"

"What you did last year in the Rafferty case. Look for the real killer."

"And who would that be?"

"Allison Byrd, the student who was stalking Ed at the time Anne was killed. Ed has said all along that she killed Anne."

"Then why hasn't Brendan looked into that before?"

"He has. But he says there's no evidence that she's the killer. But it has to be her. She's the only one with a motive. When you said my background makes me look at everything for the first time, I realized I need to go back over everything the way you did in the Rafferty case. I know where to start now."

"Where?"

"With those former students who admitted that they lied at Ed's trials. Blair Keaton and Paige Caldwell. I'm going down to Richmond to talk to both of them."

Jeff smiled and squeezed the hand that wore the five-carat diamond. "Wynne and Ed are lucky to have you on their side."

CHAPTER EIGHTEEN

Monday, January 23, 2017, Law Office of Blair Keaton Wilson, Richmond, Virginia

"I'm tired of talking to people about this case," Blair Wilson said at two o'clock on Monday afternoon as she studied Claire, who was sitting in the chair opposite Blair's desk. Paige Caldwell had refused to return Claire's calls, but Blair had agreed to a meeting. She and her husband, John Wilson, practiced family law from the third floor of a sleek glass low-rise office building not far from the Chesterfield County Courthouse. Blair looked unhappy and every one of her fifty-seven years. She had let her hair go gray, and her middle-age bulk seemed uncomfortable in the black suit and white blouse she had worn to court that morning.

Claire's weekend had been devoted entirely to long conference calls between Wynne and his various investigators and the DNA expert who was going over all the previous results and testing the DNA samples taken from the murder weapon again. Dr. Laurence Vom Saal, Wynne's Ph.D. biologist from New York University, had confirmed the earlier tests results which showed William James Miller's profile was not on the bat. He was now trying to identify the other, so-far-unidentified DNA profiles that had been found on the murder weapon.

"Thank you for meeting with me," Claire said.

Blair's dark eyes softened momentarily as she studied her visitor. "You said on the phone you're engaged to Wynne."

"Yes."

"That's the only reason I agreed to see you." Blair's expression hardened again. "I don't like reliving the days of the Ed Carter scandal. The law school kicked us out because they claimed we'd violated the code of student conduct with him. Paige and I had to hire attorneys to force them to reinstate us; and then when it was time to take the bar, we had to get all sorts of affidavits to prove that we hadn't been involved with him."

"I didn't know that. How unfair."

"So you can see why I'm through talking to people about Ed Carter. But Wynne was such a cute little boy, and I felt so sorry for him because he lost his mother and his father. So I said I'd talk to you. Once."

"You knew him back then?"

"Everyone in Professor Carter's classes knew Wynne. He brought him to his office hours on Fridays because his wife had some sort of rehearsal that morning. She was a musician. The one thing I can say for Professor Carter, he adored Wynne."

"Still does," Claire smiled.

But Blair refused to smile back. "Look, let's get this over quickly. I've already admitted that I lied under oath at Professor Carter's first and last trials. I'm not proud of that. He was not having an affair with Allison Byrd."

"Why did you lie about that?"

She sighed and looked out the window. "Because he's so guilty, and I was afraid he wouldn't be convicted. It was my misguided attempt to give the state a boost to make him pay for what he did."

"But why are you so convinced that he is guilty?" Claire thought of the gentle white-haired man she'd met at the prison who'd seemed incapable of any form of violence.

Blair leaned across her desk and studied Claire for a moment. Then she asked, "Do you really want to hear the truth from me? I can see how much you love Wynne, and I'm sure his father has charmed you, too. But that charm was his downfall. You may not want to hear any more."

"I came to hear the truth."

"Well, then, here it is. Ed Carter wasn't sleeping with Allison, but he was having affairs with his students. He had a motive to kill his wife because he wasn't happy with her. He was sleeping around."

This can't be true, Claire told herself. *Brendan said that Anne was the one who was having affairs, and Ed put up with them because he loved her.*

"And how do you know that he was having affairs with his students?"

"Because he came on to me and to Paige. We both said no, and he was a gentleman about it. He didn't try again. But there were others. He was very attractive, and he always gave the ones who said yes an 'A' in his class."

"How many others?"

She shrugged. "I don't know for sure. At least four because

169

they were friends of mine. Paige and I would have been numbers five and six if we'd said yes."

"Do you think there were more than that?"

"I doubt it. He was discreet. He didn't want word to get around."

I don't want this to be true. How can I tell Wynne?

"But you never told anyone about this?"

"No." Blair shook her head. "I didn't want to drag anyone else down. Everyone who actually slept with him kept quiet so they wouldn't get kicked out of school. It was easier for me to lie about Allison to help the state convict him of killing his wife than to tell the truth: he never slept with her."

"Just exactly how did Ed Carter invite you to have an affair with him?"

"Well, invite is too strong a word. It was more a process of innuendo. A smile, an invitation to coffee, a chance meeting that wasn't chance. Allison didn't get that. She came on too hard and too strong. She was obsessed with him. She lived with me and Paige in a house near the law school, and we were all in his evidence class during our first year. Ed Carter was all she talked about."

"What made her focus on Ed?"

"I think she saw him as some sort of Prince Charming. She grew up on a farm, and her family was poor. He was handsome, rich, and from an old Virginia family. He had an adorable little boy, and he obviously loved being a father. All of that fed her fantasies. She got this totally crazy idea that she could make him leave his wife for her and have babies with him. The more Ed told her to leave him alone, the more she pursued him. She stole her ex-boyfriend's car so she could follow him and his family to Charlottesville that Sunday. She was determined to show him that Wynne missed her and wanted to see her. Ed was so upset because she'd followed them, that he paid her three thousand dollars to leave them alone. She took the money, but instead of leaving town the way she'd promised, she went to the dean and tried to have him fired by claiming he'd been sleeping with her. She was mentally unstable and horribly vindictive."

Claire's heart was racing. "All of this is exculpatory evidence. If Allison was desperate enough to steal a car, she was desperate enough to kill Anne. Why didn't the prosecutor turn this evidence over to Brendan?"

"Because he never had it. Gordon Fairfax made it clear to me and to Paige that he didn't want to hear anything that wouldn't help the state's case. If a lie would help him convict Ed Carter, he wanted to hear the lie."

"But didn't Brendan and Brian Whitby try to interview you?"

"They tried. But Gordon said we didn't have to talk to the defense if we didn't want to. And we didn't want to."

"What about now? This evidence could save Ed's life."

Blair shook her head. "I'm not giving you any declarations for your habeas petitions."

"But Ed's going to die, and he didn't kill Anne."

"I want him to die. Despite what you think, he did kill his wife. Look, I know you're looking for something that will save him. But I was in court the day that neighbor testified about seeing his car at his house the night Anne was killed. I think Allison's lie made him decide to get rid of his wife. Even though

171

there was no affair with Allison, Ed's marriage was on the rocks. He and his wife were sleeping around." Blair stirred restlessly in her chair. Then she said, "I don't want to talk about this anymore. I know what I know. Ed Carter is guilty. I'll be glad when he's gone because people won't come around asking questions. I can finally put it behind me."

Claire shivered inwardly at the thought of Ed's death but managed to keep her face emotionless. She didn't want to be shown the door before she'd gotten all the information she'd come for. "I understand, but I only have two more questions."

"What are they?"

"Could you call Paige Caldwell and ask her to talk to me?"

"I will call her. I can't make any promises. She's even more bitter about Ed Carter than I am."

"Thank you. Second, do you have any idea where Allison Byrd is?"

"The last I heard, she was cleaning toilets at a bed and breakfast down in Port Conway at a plantation called Belle Grove."

* * *

That night, Claire sat in front of the fire with Brendan and Emma in the great room of their house, sipping after-dinner scotch with them and describing her interview with Blair Wilson. Brendan was deeply upset.

"All these years, he's denied being unfaithful to Anne." He stared at the fire as he spoke.

"I wouldn't put too much stock in that," Emma said. "We know that Anne was having an affair with that music professor. He was hurt. I'm sure that's why he did it."

"Probably." Brendan spat out the word, and Claire could see the anger smoldering in his eyes.

"But it still bothers you," she observed.

"Yeah." Brendan spoke sharply and got up to refill his glass.

Emma frowned. "You shouldn't have more than one."

"I'm sure you're right. But at this moment, I don't care." He jerked open the drinks cabinet and angrily poured another scotch. He came back to the sofa and resumed his seat next to Emma. He said, "I've believed every single thing Ed has ever said to me for thirty years. Now I'm wondering what else he's lied about. He never told me that three-thousand-dollar payment went to Allison Byrd. He testified under oath in all his trials that he withdrew that money to make a temporary loan to a friend."

"Well, she wasn't a friend, and it wasn't a loan, but you can't blame him for paying her off to get rid of her," Emma said.

"She was tormenting him," Claire added.

He frowned and took a long pull of his scotch. Claire could tell that he was still upset by the truth of Ed's affairs with his students.

Finally, Emma said, "But surely you don't think he killed Anne?"

"I'm not sure of anything at this moment." He tossed back more scotch. "I keep thinking about the white Volvo outside of the house that night. And not one single person has ever said that he or she saw Ed in Charlottesville during the time of the murder."

"You've never questioned him before," Emma said.

"I didn't know that he was lying to me before."

* * *

173

Wynne was quiet for a long time after Claire told him about her meeting with Blair Wilson. When he called, she was curled up on the bed in her room at the Murphys', drinking the cup of tea Emma had insisted would help her sleep.

"Brendan's very upset. He thought your father didn't have any secrets from him."

"I thought he didn't, either. I knew my mother was having an affair with that Neal character. I had no idea Dad was sleeping with his students. Nor did I know that he tried to pay off Allison Byrd. He should have told Brendan about all of this."

"He should have, but he didn't."

"I wonder why," Wynne said. "Maybe because it made him look guilty. Is that what Brendan thinks? Does he think Dad is guilty because he didn't tell him everything?"

"I don't know," Claire sighed. "Emma and I tried to talk him out of that."

"God, Claire. I'm so tired of being caught in the middle of all this. I can't bring myself to believe Dad killed my mother."

"I know."

"Listen, I want to ask you something."

"What is it?"

"Honestly, I'm also tired of feeling so alone. Neither my mother's family nor my father's seem like my real family."

"I understand. But you aren't alone. You have me."

"And that is what I wanted to ask you about. What if we don't wait to get married? What if we do it right away? Then, whatever comes, we'll be our own family."

"I—" *I should be able to say 'yes' at once. What's wrong with me?*

174

"That's okay," he said. "It's too much to ask."

"No, no. It's not." *Are you sure?* "But my father would not be happy about a justice of the peace ceremony at the courthouse. And I can't blame him. I'm all he has."

"And I don't want that for us, either," Wynne said. "But what if we find a place that feels right? You know, like 'meant to be.' We could have a small ceremony with your father, the Murphys, and our closest friends."

"Okay. If we find the right place."

"Thanks for even considering it."

"I love you."

"And I love you, too. Are you coming back to New York tomorrow? I miss you."

"Before I come back to New York, I'm going to see if Paige Caldwell will talk to me, and then I'm going down to that bed and breakfast in Port Conway to find Allison Byrd."

"Why, Claire? She's not going to confess to murdering my mother."

"I know, but if I can finagle a DNA sample from her, Dr. Vom Saal can test the murder weapon."

"Don't go alone, then. Blair Wilson said she was mentally unstable back then, and I'm sure she still is."

"I'll be fine."

CHAPTER NINETEEN

Tuesday, January 24, 2017, Law Offices of Paige Caldwell Marshall, Richmond, Virginia

Blair Wilson called Claire at nine the next morning to let her know that Paige Caldwell had agreed to see her that afternoon. She had relented for the same reason that Blair had. She had been moved by her memories of the little boy who had played with his toys in his father's office every Friday morning.

Claire arrived at a neo-Colonial office building not far from the Henrico County Courthouse at three o'clock. A bored assistant led her down a musty smelling hall to an office at the back of the building with a parking lot view. The sign on the wall next to the open door said, "Paige C. Marshall, Attorney At Law, Trusts and Estates."

A tall, thin, middle-aged woman in a navy dress that hung loosely on her slender form rose from her desk to greet her. She had deep lines on her forehead and around her mouth. Her hair was gray, and her dark eyes seemed dull and tired. She looked ten years older than Blair. "I'm Paige," she said, "and you must be Claire, Wynne's fiancée. Please sit down. I've had my assistant make coffee."

Claire took the chair opposite Paige's desk and accepted the Styrofoam cup of warm brew. She tasted it and found that it was surprisingly good. "Thank you for seeing me."

Paige shifted in her chair uncomfortably. "Look, you're wasting your time here, Ms. Chastain. I can't do anything to help Ed Carter, and even if I could, I wouldn't. I hate that man. I'm sure Blair told you the damage he did to our careers before they even got started." She waved her hands around her seedy little office and went on, "Blair landed on her feet because she married John Wilson, who had built a solid family law practice on his own before they met. But I've always had to struggle. Things didn't work out with my kids' father, and I raised the two of them on my income alone. It hasn't been easy because I'm 'that lawyer who was mixed up in the Ed Carter scandal.' I'm a pariah. No one wants to work with me or send me referrals. It's been tough to build and maintain a practice all these years."

"Why did you help convict Ed?" Claire asked.

"Because he is guilty," Paige said.

"But you lied."

"We lied about who he was having an affair with. It wasn't Allison, but I'm sure Blair told you the real story. He was guilty of having affairs."

"Didn't the two of you also lie about being with Allison on the night Anne Carter was killed?"

"Yes, we did. We said we were at a party in the Fan with her. Blair and I were at that party, but Allison wasn't. I have no idea where she was. Probably watching the Carter house the way she always did."

"Why did you agree to give her an alibi?"

"Because we knew Ed was guilty. We didn't want to let the defense complicate things by suggesting that Allison killed Anne Carter. We wanted to give Gordon Fairfax a neat, clean case against Ed. Don't you understand, he killed his wife and he ruined three innocent lives?"

"He didn't ruin Allison Byrd's life."

"I didn't mean Allison. She brought it on herself. But Blair and Quinn and I were sucked into the scandal, and our lives have never recovered."

"Who's Quinn?"

"She was our fourth roommate."

"Did she sleep with Ed?"

"God, no! She had a boyfriend."

"Then how was her life ruined by Ed Carter?"

"Because she got kicked out of school, too. Guilt by association even though she had nothing to do with any of it."

"Where is she now?"

"No idea. She didn't have the money to hire an attorney to fight for reinstatement. She went back to Petersburg, and no one ever heard from her again."

"Why wasn't she a witness?"

"Probably because she disappeared early on, and no one went looking for her because no one needed her. She couldn't give Gordon Fairfax any more information than Blair and I had given him. And she had nothing to offer the defense."

"I know this has been difficult for you," Claire said. "Thank you for seeing me."

Paige stood up and came around her desk to walk Claire back

down the musty hall to the exit. As they reached the doorway of her office, Paige paused.

"One more thing. I know you didn't come here looking for personal advice. But I can see you're a good person, trying to do what you think is fair and right. And I have no doubt that you love Wynne. I can't let you leave without saying this. The Carter scandal has never done anything but destroy the lives it has touched. Don't let it destroy yours, too."

* * *

"What did you learn from Paige Caldwell?" Brendan asked that night during their after-dinner scotch ritual.

"That she's even more bitter than Blair. She told me they had a fourth roommate named Quinn Fairchild. The law school kicked her out, too."

"Was she one of the students Ed slept with?" Emma asked.

"No. Paige said she had a boyfriend."

"Did anyone ever interview her?" Brendan asked.

"I don't think so. Blair said she didn't know anything that would help either side. She disappeared after the law school expelled her."

"Another dead end," Brendan sighed.

"Don't worry," Claire told him. "I'm going to Belle Grove tomorrow to find Allison Byrd."

CHAPTER TWENTY

Wednesday, January 25, 2017, Belle Grove Plantation Bed and Breakfast, Port Conway, Virginia

The plantation where, in Blair's less than elegant phrase, Allison Byrd had last been seen scrubbing toilets, was a little over an hour from Richmond, about twenty miles south of Fredericksburg, at the end of a lane lined with oaks. Around ten o'clock the next morning, the Range Rover emerged from the shelter of the trees into the clearing in front of the magnificent house. Claire stopped the car to stare at the graceful, yellow, two-story mansion with green shutters and white porticos that looked like frosting that had been applied along the front, upstairs and down. James Madison had been born in the original house that stood on this site. But that structure was long gone, and the present building was the house her mother's family had owned from 1839 to 1893. Julia had told her stories about the house and about the family during the Civil War. The eldest Turner daughter, Carrie, had etched her name and that of her Union soldier fiancé on one of the windows in the upstairs bedrooms.

Claire parked in the gravel lot to the left of the entrance and walked across the drive to the front door. She was arriving unannounced because she didn't want her quarry to have time to flee.

She knocked, and a few minutes later, a pleasant-faced, dark-haired, thirtyish woman, in gray slacks and a red sweater, opened the door.

"Come in," she smiled, beckoning Claire inside. The hall was warm and inviting. "I'm Sally Lane, the event coordinator. Are you here for an appointment with our wedding planner?"

She noticed the ring. "No, I'm Claire Chastain. I'm an attorney. I don't have an appointment, but I need to talk to someone who works here on behalf of a client."

Sally frowned. "Then you'll have to speak to Michelle. She owns the bed and breakfast, and she makes all the decisions about employees. She's in the kitchen going over the menus with the chef. I'll go get her."

Claire studied the vibrant turquoise walls and highly polished floors while she waited. An archway, painted white, framed the graceful staircase that led to the second floor. *I'm connected to this house. How ironic that saving Ed brought me to a place where I feel close to my mother.*

Suddenly Claire heard footsteps tapping on the wooden floors, and a moment later, Sally and another woman emerged from the dining room to Claire's left. The owner had a round, kind face and a warm smile. Her royal-blue dress accented her friendly, brown eyes. Claire felt welcome at once.

"I'm Michelle Darnell," she said, taking the hand that Claire had extended in more of a friendly clasp than an actual handshake. "Sally says you are looking for someone who works here."

"I need to talk to Allison Byrd. I was told she is employed as a housekeeper. This is a picture of her. It's very old. She'd be middle-aged by now." She held out a photo that Brendan had given her from his file.

The warmth in Michelle's eyes turned to concern. "Let's go into the parlor and talk. I'll make some tea."

"I'll make it and bring it to you," Sally said. She, too, looked wary as she turned away.

Claire followed Michelle into the parlor where the innkeeper sat down on one of the two high-backed Victorian settees and motioned for Claire to take the seat beside her. The late morning sun warmed the red walls of the parlor, accented by white woodwork, a brass chandelier, and two graceful arches on either side of a fireplace covered by a brass peacock screen. There was a pianoforte under the window that overlooked the Rappahannock River that flowed behind the plantation. The parlor had the same graceful elegance and tranquility of the front hall. *That's how I remember my mother. Elegant and tranquil. And beautiful.*

Sally appeared with a tray containing a blue-and-yellow-flowered china teapot and matching cups with gold rims. Michelle thanked her and poured two cups of tea.

"Cream, sugar, lemon, or all three?" she asked.

"Lemon, please." Claire accepted the cup from Michelle and began to sip the dark tea with a hint of orange and spice. The brew was warming and friendly like the house. She held out the picture again.

Michelle took the photo and studied it for a moment. Then she said, "I see the resemblance although this picture is very out of date. I can tell you that when Allison Byrd worked here, she called herself 'Anne Carter.'"

"What? Oh my God!" Claire set the cup down on the table in front of the sofa because she was too excited to drink more tea.

Michelle put the picture on the table next to Claire's cup and frowned. "I don't understand."

"Anne Carter is the woman I think Allison Byrd murdered in Richmond in November 1983."

"Then I'm glad I let her go."

"How long was she here?"

"I hired her in early November. The Thanksgiving and Christmas holidays are very busy at Belle Grove. We always need some extra help. But I had to tell her not to come back just before Christmas."

"What happened?"

"In a word, she was stealing. Thank heavens she didn't take anything that belonged to our guests. But she helped herself to quite a lot of our silver and some rare books from the library. At first, I thought they'd been misplaced, but then I got a call from the owner of a pawn shop in Fredericksburg who told me that he had some items that looked like they belonged to Belle Grove. He had brought his wife here to celebrate their twenty-fifth wedding anniversary, and he recognized the silver. Wanted to know if I'd sold anything to this Anne Carter who had brought them in to pawn."

"Did you notify the police?"

"Not at first. I just told her that we didn't need her anymore. I didn't want any bad publicity for Belle Grove. But she wouldn't go away. She kept coming back and sitting out front in her car, just watching the house. So finally, I had to call the sheriff and have her arrested. When he ran her ID, he came up with her real name, Allison Byrd."

"Did she get any jail time?" Claire asked, hoping she'd still be in custody.

"No. She had a public defender who struck a deal for her. She pled to some sort of lesser charge and promised to leave us alone."

"And she hasn't come back?"

"No. Thank heavens. Who told you she was here?"

Claire explained her conversation with Blair Wilson and Ed and Anne's story.

"So your fiancé's father is going to be executed on March 3 if you can't prove that Allison is the one who killed his wife?"

"That's right. I'm looking for evidence to prove Allison killed Anne Carter. I was hoping for a DNA sample from Allison."

"Sorry, I can't help you there. I can tell you that I questioned my decision to hire her from day one. There was something not quite right about her."

"Someone who knew her years ago said she was mentally unstable."

"I'd agree with that. Menacing is the word I would use. She'd appear out of the shadows and just stare at me with a blank look on her face. It was creepy. I'd say 'go back to work' and she would. But everything about her just seemed off. I should have told her to leave long before I did."

"Thank you," Claire smiled. "I've taken up enough of your time."

"Before you go, would you like a tour of the house?"

"Yes. My mother told me about an etching on one of the windows upstairs. Is it still there?"

"Of course. It's the bedroom that we've named 'The Turner Suite.' When was your mother at Belle Grove?"

"I'm not sure. She died when I was only ten years old. Her family once owned the house. They were here during the Civil War. She told me a lot of stories that had been handed down about what happened when Belle Grove was the headquarters for the Union Army. Apparently, that's when the oldest daughter met the man whose name she engraved on the window with an engagement ring. My mother said girls used to do that back then to prove the diamond was real."

"What was your mother's name?" Michelle asked.

"Julia Marie Turner."

"Oh my!" Michelle got up and came over to Claire and gave her a big hug. "Sally!" she called out. "We've got one of the Turners at Belle Grove! Come help me give her a tour!"

BRENDAN

"Birth, copulation and death. That's all the facts when you come to brass tacks."

T.S. Eliot

CHAPTER TWENTY-ONE

Thursday, January 26, 2017, Sussex State Prison, Sussex, Virginia

Brendan watched Ed sign the will that he had prepared for him. He didn't want to think about how and when this document would be needed. When Ed finished, Father Jim signed as a witness and Ed's senior associate, Robert Weaver, signed as the second witness. Then Ed, Father Jim, and Robert signed the self-proving affidavit, and Tom Brower's secretary notarized it. Brendan carefully folded the completed document, put it in a protective sleeve, and handed it to Robert Weaver, who was headed back to the firm.

As he handed it to Robert, Brendan broke the solemn silence that had surrounded the execution of the will. "See that this gets into Ed's file," he said.

"Of course." Robert put the will into his briefcase, said his goodbyes, and left with Tom's secretary, who was his guide to the Warden's Office and ultimately to the prison's exit.

After the door closed behind them, Brendan resumed his seat at the table opposite Ed. He wished Father Jim had departed with the others instead of sitting down next to Ed again.

Brendan had been seething ever since Monday when Claire had come back from her interview with Blair Wilson with the information about Ed's affairs, and he was determined to confront him. But he'd pictured venting his righteous indignation without an audience.

"You lied to me," Brendan began a low, accusatory tone.

Ed's dark eyes peered at him quizzically through his professorial spectacles. "About what?"

"About being faithful to Anne. And about who you gave the three thousand dollars to."

Ed shifted uncomfortably in his chair and looked over at Father Jim, whose long, narrow face remained calm and compassionate. "I—"

"Don't lie anymore," Brendan cut him off angrily. "You paid Allison Byrd three thousand dollars, and you never told me that. And you weren't faithful to Anne, and you never told me that, either. I've been defending you for thirty years. You aren't supposed to keep secrets from me."

"How did you find out?"

"Blair Wilson and Paige Caldwell. They told Claire about your payment to Allison Byrd and about the way you propositioned your students, including them. They opened up to Claire because they felt sorry for Wynne."

Brendan saw Ed flinch when he mentioned his son's name. But he said nothing and kept his face impassive except for the guilty look in his eyes. Ed's silence fed Brendan's anger the way air feeds a fire. He leaned across the table and said in a low, furious voice, "I've believed in you for thirty years. And now it turns out you've lied to me. So what else have you lied about?"

"I didn't kill Anne, if that's what you mean," Ed said slowly. As he spoke, he looked at Father Jim again.

"I didn't say that you did," Brendan shot back. He could hear Emma's voice whispering in his ear, *"Don't raise your blood pressure any higher than it already is."*

"Not in so many words," Ed said slowly. "But every jury is admonished that a witness who has been shown to be a liar about some things can be deemed to be a liar about everything. You're saying that since I didn't tell you about the affairs and about paying off Allison Byrd, I also didn't tell you that I murdered my wife."

"Did you murder Anne?" Brendan demanded, still too angry to end the interrogation.

Suddenly Ed took off his glasses, put them on the table, leaned back, and covered his hands with his face. His dignity seemed to crumple like paper under Brendan's steely gaze. Brendan saw tears slipping through his fingers.

The priest spoke for the first time. "I think you're being too harsh, Brendan," he said in his even, quiet baritone. "Ed talked to me about all of this in recent days because it was on his conscience, and we agreed that he should set the record straight with you. But I remain completely convinced that Ed did not kill Anne."

Ed uncovered his face and swiped at his tears. His pain was obvious and raw, and suddenly Brendan was struck with remorse for his anger. But Ed did not give him the chance to speak. Instead, he resumed his customary military bearing and said quietly, "I didn't talk about the affairs with my students because they are irrelevant. And I never slept with Blair Keaton or Paige Caldwell. It's true that they flirted with me, and I thought they were interested. But they said 'no' and I realized I'd been mistaken, and that was the end of it."

"But why were you unfaithful?" Brendan asked.

"I was hurt because Anne was having affairs. They started in New York when I was working at Sullivan and Cromwell. I couldn't blame her too much because I was always at work and we were never together. So I decided to take the teaching job because I could spend more time with her. The trouble was, she didn't want to spend more time with me."

"Did you have affairs in New York, too?"

Ed gave him a rueful smile. "Just one. I've never told anyone about it other than Father Jim. She was a fellow associate who was as bored as I was. It went on until she pressured me to leave Anne. I refused, and she just walked out of the firm library one day and never came back. I have no idea what happened to her. It doesn't matter. We were bored and unhappy, and I never loved anyone except Anne. And Wynne."

"Why did you lie to me about where the three thousand dollars went?"

"Because I was ashamed of giving in to blackmail, and because paying Allison off made me look guilty. Brad O'Connor was so sure that I was guilty. I was afraid you'd think that I was having an affair with her if I told you the truth about the money. But there was no affair with Allison, and I didn't kill Anne. Although, at this point, I'm not sure if it matters anymore whether I did or I didn't. Either way, the State of Virginia is going to kill me on the third of March."

"No, Ed! I'm going to—"

"Don't say 'save your life' to me one more time!" Ed's voice rose. Now he was the angry one. "You're not going to. Just last week, the Fourth Circuit rejected our latest habeas petition explaining how these off-market drugs that they use in executions torture people to death. The governor has told Wynne that not even his millions will buy me a pardon. Or even a commutation to a life sentence. Face it, Brendan, I'm a dead man."

The room was silent as if a bomb had gone off. Brendan sat very still, wishing he had held his temper in the first place. He could hear Emma saying, *Why bring all this old stuff up now? None of it matters.*

He wished he'd listened to her. There was only one thing he could do. "Ed, I'm sorry for what I said. You're right. The affairs are irrelevant. I know you didn't kill Anne."

"And our baby," he added softly.

The room went silent again. Brendan looked at Father Jim, whose eyes were fixed on Ed. Brendan wondered if the priest could absolve him of the sin of disloyalty. He wished he could cut out his tongue in penance. Ed had lost a much-loved wife and very-wanted child.

Ed was staring vacantly toward the window overlooking the parking lot. Brendan realized that he was thinking about something. Finally, Ed said slowly, "I intended to tell you about the affairs today. Father Jim and I had agreed that I needed to get the lie off my conscience. You've stuck by me all these years, Brendan. No one could ask for a better lawyer. Or friend."

Brendan felt his own eyes tear up because Ed had forgiven him. In response, he wanted to speak some words of comfort and hope, but what could he say? Ed was right. They were out of options.

Claire, bless her heart, didn't realize that even finding Allison Byrd wouldn't help them so late in the proceedings.

But Ed wasn't finished. He studied Brendan's face for a moment before he said, "Father Jim and I think there's something else you need to know."

"What is it?" Brendan braced himself for a confession to Anne's murder after all.

"It's Wynne," Ed said, his eyes still fixed vacantly on the world outside the glass. "He's not my son. And he doesn't know."

* * *

Thursday, January 26, 2017, The Murphys', Windsor Farms, Richmond Virginia

"If I say no more scotch, will you listen to me?" Emma asked that night as Brendan got up from the sofa to refill his glass for the second time. He was relieved that dinner had been just the two of them. Claire had gone back to New York. He needed to talk about Ed's bombshell without her presence.

"No, I won't."

She sighed. "I figured. You're upset."

"Of course I'm upset," he agreed as he sat down beside her again. "I lost my temper with Ed today, and I'm ashamed of that."

She stroked his arm gently. "I don't see how anyone could blame you, sweetheart. You've put your heart and soul into this case. He kept things from you. Important things."

He sipped his scotch. "I've wanted to win it for Ed all these years. But I've wanted to win it for Brian, too. He believed in Ed so much that he wouldn't have done the stupid thing I did today."

"You're going to need grief counseling when this is all over."

Brendan's eyes teared at the thought. "Maybe. I don't know. I don't want to think that far ahead. I wish I could hold out hope the way Claire is doing. She's deluding herself, but she feels better than I do."

"And you're saying there isn't any hope?"

Brendan shook his head. "Not at this point."

They sat in silence watching the fire. Finally, Brendan said, "He wants me to tell Wynne."

"That he's not his father?"

"Yes."

"I don't think he should put that on you."

"Neither do I."

"What did you tell him?"

"That I'd think about it."

"What if Ed's wrong?" Emma asked.

"You mean, what if Wynne really is his son?"

"It's cruel to bring this into question so late in their relationship."

Brendan sighed. "I think Father Jim has some crazy idea that Wynne might find his birth father after—" He couldn't bring himself to say "the execution." "He's counseled Ed that this is necessary for him to pass in peace."

"Humph! I'm not so sure about that," Emma shook her head. "It's going to break Wynne's heart more this way. He'll be losing Ed twice."

"That's what I think, too."

"Can't you talk him out of it?"

"I tried. But Jim got to him first and convinced him that he owes it to Wynne."

"You know," Emma said, "I'd tell Ed that Wynne's DNA expert should do a test to determine the truth before anyone talks to Wynne. Claire could get a sample without telling him."

"But I'd have to tell her."

"She's going to find out that there's a question about Wynne's father one way or the other. I'm sure she'd rather make sure Wynne isn't hurt if he doesn't have to be."

"You're right. I'm going to tell Ed that's what we have to do."

"Now put the scotch down and come to bed."

I'd be so lost without her, Brendan thought as he followed her upstairs.

MCKENZIE

"There will be time, there will be time
To prepare a face to meet the faces that you meet"

T.S. Eliot

CHAPTER TWENTY-TWO

Monday, January 30, 2017, Ristorante I Ricchi, Dupont Circle, Washington, D.C.

At seven p.m., Mckenzie and Tyndall decided to walk to the Metro from the Willard Hotel where she was staying and take the Red Line to Dupont Circle. From there it was only a few blocks to their favorite restaurant, I Ricchi, on Nineteenth Street. They'd decided to take the Metro instead of hailing a cab because it felt like old times when they'd been on the road together, defending Fidelity International.

"Soon you'll be too famous to do this," Tyndall joked as they found a seat on the subway car.

"I doubt it." Mckenzie smiled. But she had used the service exit from the hotel in case any reporters were lurking out front.

It feels as if we haven't been apart for seven years, she thought as they followed the maitre d' to their table in a quiet corner of the restaurant. The warm-beige walls, white-linen topped tables with yellow roses in white vases, and the dark-wood accents made I Ricchi feel like a cozy, family dining room in Tuscany.

They consulted over which bottle of Italian red wine to

order, settling on one they both liked. After they ordered Caprese salad with heirloom tomatoes, lobster risotto for Tyndall and pasta Florentine for Mckenzie and after the wine had been poured, Tyndall raised his glass.

"To your success tomorrow."

"Thanks. But I'm not going to be asked any questions until Wednesday," she smiled. "The members of the committee are going to spend tomorrow making speeches about how much they love me or hate me."

"And I know you'll be ready for them."

"I am. It's been quite an experience to go back and read every article that I've written since the beginning of my career." She gave him an ironic smile. "Some of them could have been authored by Joel's new girlfriend."

"The one who works for Legal Aid and who thinks poor people never lie?"

"That very one. I was quite a firebrand in the early days of my career, arguing that litigation, whether civil or criminal, favors the rich."

"That's not news," Tyndall observed mildly. "We all know that it does."

"But we aren't supposed to say so in print," Mckenzie smiled. "Only young lawyers who think the unwritten rules of the profession are nonsense are frank about the inequities in access to the courts."

"That's true," he agreed.

I used to say we were one brain in two bodies. He always understood. Why did I leave him and Craig, Lewis? For Joel. For my career. For the chance to be a name partner with Hugh Mahoney.

"So the senators will grill you on your early indiscretions starting on Wednesday?"

"That's right. But I'm ready for them. I'll say, 'Perspective changes with experience. Now I see that justice truly is available without regard to wealth.'"

"Which is not true," his warm-brown eyes teased her.

This is the way it used to be. Sparring back and forth about the ironies of the legal business. I don't talk to anyone else the way I talk to him. Not even Hugh.

The salad arrived, and they were lost for a few minutes in the glory of aged olive oil, tangy tomatoes, and creamy cheese. As the plates vanished and the waiter added more wine to their glasses, Tyndall observed, "I'm guessing your writing on the death penalty is going to be the most difficult subject for you to defend."

We used to prepare for oral argument this way. He had a razor-sharp instinct for the jugular. Yes, my opposition to the death penalty will outrage some of the senators on the committee. Can't be helped. I am entitled to think civilized people don't take lives in the name of vengeance. After all, trials are not an exact science: it's too easy to execute the innocent.

"They'll definitely go after me. I've written in opposition to the death penalty many times, as you know."

"And they aren't going to confirm a death penalty opponent."

"True, but the current court is questioning its continued viability under the Eighth Amendment. After all, no one has yet figured out a humane way to kill someone in the name of the state."

"But you're not going to say that to the committee," Tyndall observed as the waiter appeared with their entrees.

"Of course not. I want to be confirmed." She smiled as she savored the pasta.

"I'll give them the correct answer. My private views must give way in the face of precedent which has affirmed the constitutionality of the death penalty many times. As a justice, I must be bound by existing law."

Tyndall took another bite of his risotto before giving her a mischievous grin. "It is the correct answer, but it sounds like double talk. Our profession is so good at that, isn't it?"

"Now you sound like Jenny Miyamoto."

"The girlfriend?"

"Yes. She'd just love to clear all the double speak out of the law single-handedly in one clean sweep."

"She's headed for a rude awakening."

"I know. I had mine working for Brad O'Connor. Poor people do not always tell the truth, and they are not always innocent."

"Does Brad know you've been nominated?"

"He passed away five years ago. But Judge Dabney called to give me his support. He's retired, of course."

"Any chance Joel will come east with you?"

"None."

"Because of the girlfriend?"

Mckenzie put her fork down for a moment and considered his question thoughtfully. "That, and I've hung on to him too hard. He's rebelling now. I didn't mean to hold him too close. But I did. I think the girlfriend is one way of telling me to keep my distance."

Tyndall's face softened. "I admire you for being honest."

She picked up her fork and smiled again. "At least I'm allowed to be honest in my private life."

"You can't blame yourself, though, for holding on to Joel."

"Because I lost Brian?"

"I still hang on to Claire because I lost Julia. I'm lucky that she hasn't pushed me away as hard as Joel has pushed you. But that's not to say she won't eventually."

She smiled. "More honesty."

"You don't like Joel's new girlfriend?"

"I'm not sure. She's a brilliant, beautiful girl, and I can see that Joel is infatuated. Maybe it will last, maybe it won't. But what I can say for sure is that she makes me feel competitive."

"For Joel?"

"For Joel. Even though I know that I have to let go of him, it's hard. A new job, a new place will help me do the right thing and let him live his own life and let them figure out what their relationship is going to be."

The waiter came for their empty plates, and Tyndall suggested coffee.

"Yes, please." *I'm not ready for this to end. I like confiding in you. I feel so alone most of the time.*

"I'm going through the same thing with Claire," Tyndall said as the waiter poured the dark, rich brew for them. "I don't like what Wynne's putting her through. I wish she'd just end it with him."

Oh, God, that case. Stay calm. Don't show any emotion. "Surely Brendan's been able to get a stay by now? I thought the courts had decided those black-market drugs they use in executions violate the Eighth Amendment's ban on cruel and unusual punishment."

But Tyndall shook his head. "No, Claire said Brendan's writ on those grounds has been denied."

God, I didn't expect that. Brendan has kept him alive for thirty years. Surely that isn't going to change. "Is Claire still working with Brendan?"

Tyndall nodded. "She's got her hopes up because some woman who was a prosecution witness opened up to her about things she's never told anyone. Based on that, Claire went down to a plantation near Port Conway where the woman who she thinks actually killed Anne Carter was supposedly working. She wasn't there anymore, but Claire found out that she has been using 'Anne Carter' as an alias."

I'm afraid to ask her name, but I have to. "What's her real name?"

"Allison Byrd."

Thank God no one's found Quinn Fairchild. Yet.

"Didn't you work on that case when Brad O'Connor had it?"

"I just did research for him." *And that's my story if anyone brings it up during the hearings.*

Tyndall sighed. "Claire is convinced this Allison Byrd is the killer."

"Then she's been listening to Ed Carter. Brad told me that was Ed's story, but he said there was no evidence to back it up. He was sure that Ed was guilty, and the jury's verdict did not surprise him. You're in the same position with Claire that I am with Joel. I know that Jenny Miyamoto has a chip on her shoulder the size of a redwood, and Joel can't possibly be happy with someone who's so bitter. But he won't listen if I try to tell him. And you know that Claire can't possibly save Ed Carter's life because he's guilty. But you can't tell her that."

"That's right." Tyndall looked sad. "For so many years, I wanted her to get over Paul Curtis and marry someone else. And now I'd be glad if Paul could talk her out of marrying Wynne. He came to New York and tried, but she wouldn't listen."

"What about the one you like so much? The one who used to be with Alan Warrick and who got arrested for four murders last year only to be found innocent at his preliminary hearing?"

"Jeff Ryder. I'd be thrilled if he and Claire got together. They've been friends for a long time, and I think she'd be happy with him. He sees her the way I see her and the way I saw Julia. Unique. Beautiful. Compassionate and loving. But I don't think there's any chance of that now."

"Why?" Mckenzie frowned. "Surely this is the worst possible time for a wedding."

"It is. But that plantation where she went looking for the Byrd woman is the one that Julia's family owned during the Civil War. Wynne had asked her to go ahead with the wedding if they found a place that felt right."

"Oh, God," Mckenzie put her coffee cup down. "Are they going to get married in a hurry?"

"You mean before Ed's execution?"

"It sounds so horrible when you say that." *Why in the world hasn't Brendan found a way to stop it by now?*

"It is horrible. It's the last thing I want for Claire. I told her she shouldn't even think of getting married under a cloud like this."

"What did she say?"

"She said Wynne wanted to go see the plantation, and then the two of them would make up their minds. All I can do is hope that they realize it's not a good time."

He signaled for the check, and they put on their coats and went outside. It was too cold to walk back to the Metro, so they hailed a cab to take them to the Willard.

When they reached the hotel, Tyndall accompanied her to the elevator and punched the button for her floor. When the doors opened, he smiled and hugged her. "It'll be good to have you on this side of the world again, Mac."

She leaned over and gave him a swift kiss on the cheek. He was the only one who had ever given her a nickname. And she liked it.

* * *

She put on her pajamas and brewed a cup of tea. She settled herself on the sofa in her suite and tried to concentrate on her notes. But she kept thinking about that day in that cold shack in Petersburg and about the smoke flaring out of Quinn Fairchild's nostrils when she'd said that Ed Carter had been with her on the night of Anne's death. She'd told herself when Ed was tried the first and second times that Quinn's information, even if true, hadn't been important. The state had claimed that Ed had hired Miller to kill Anne, so of course he hadn't been there when it happened.

But by trial three, when the story had become that Ed traveled to Richmond on Saturday night and killed his wife, Quinn's statement could have made all the difference in the jury's verdict. But Quinn had been lying, she told herself. Ed had driven to Richmond and killed Anne when everyone thought he was in Charlottesville. The neighbor had seen his white Volvo. Mckenzie didn't know why Quinn Fairchild had made up her crazy story about sleeping with Ed. *Probably because I looked so naive and inexperienced that day. And probably because she noticed that I forgot to turn on the tape recorder. She realized that she could lie her head off and no one would know.*

No, I did the right thing to stay quiet, Mckenzie reassured herself as she got into bed. Lawyers made mistakes. Some were important, but this one wasn't. Brad had been right. Ed Carter was guilty. If only Tyndall could talk Claire out of marrying Wynne.

But as she set her alarm for six a.m., a thought nagged her. What if Quinn had been telling the truth? What if she picked up the phone right this minute and woke Brendan and offered her sworn statement?

You know that's Ed Carter's only hope of staying alive. But she'd lose everything if she did. And she'd worked too hard to let that happen. She was on her way to a lifetime appointment as a United States Supreme Court Justice. Brian would have been so proud. And no woman vying for Joel's attention could top that achievement. She wasn't going to sacrifice her career for a man who'd murdered his wife.

* * *

Friday, February 3, 2017, Room SH-216 of the Hart Senate Office Building, Washington, D.C.

It was four thirty, and the hearings were nearing an end. Mckenzie was tired but happy. Hugh, who had been watching from the public seats all three days, had told her she'd given excellent answers even to the toughest questions. Senator Mary Sue Austin, the senior senator from Virginia, was the last to question her. She was forty-six and a University of Virginia law grad who had left a partnership at Hunton and Williams to run for the Senate. She had expressed her respect for Mckenzie's academic career in her opening statement but was opposed to her nomination because of her writings on the death penalty. They had been round and round all afternoon about whether Mckenzie would vote to uphold death convictions that came before the Court. Mckenzie had resolutely refused to state how she would vote on any individual case, the answer every nominee gave when questioned about how he or she would rule in the future.

Mckenzie kept her eyes focused on Senator Austin's thin, narrow face as she waited for her next question the way a tennis player focuses on his opponent who is about to serve. The senator's brown eyes had drilled holes in Mckenzie all afternoon as if daring her to tell the Committee that she was lying about her willingness to be bound by existing law.

"I appreciate your appearing here today," Senator Austin's soft accent, the opposite of her sharp face, intoned.

Good, we're near the end.

"I have one last question for you, and it is an important

question for the people of Virginia, who have so much invested in the justice system of our state."

Oh, God, no more Eighth Amendment questions, please. She knows the Fourteenth Amendment binds the states to observe the rulings of the Supreme Court on death appeals. I've told her I can't say how I'd rule on a future case. Can't she move on to something else?

Senator Austin looked down at her notes and then her dark eyes met Mckenzie's and held them for what felt like a long time before she asked, "I think you are familiar with the murder trial of Edward Wynne Carter, III?"

Why did she have to bring that up? Stay calm. Don't show any emotion. Could she know about Quinn Fairchild? Please God, no. This is national television.

"I am."

"Your late husband, Brian Whitby, was one of Mr. Carter's defense attorneys, was he not?"

"He was."

"And are you aware that Mr. Carter is going to be executed by the State of Virginia for the murder of Anne Fairfax Carter on March 3?"

I am aware that the Fairfaxes contributed millions to your campaign.

"Yes."

"So it is possible, even likely, that you will be on the Court at the time that Mr. Carter's last appeals are presented for review. That is, *if* you are confirmed."

"If that is a question, the answer is yes. I could be a sitting justice at that time."

"And how would you handle that matter, Professor Fitzgerald, since you have a personal connection to that case?"

"I—" It was the first time she'd stumbled in three days of hearings. The thought had never occurred to her. If she could issue a stay of execution, even a temporary stay, maybe Brendan could find a way to save Ed. For Wynne. And for Claire.

Senator Austin's dark eyes bored into her like lasers. *She hates me, and she thinks she's trapped me. But she hasn't.*

"I'm sorry, Senator. I hadn't considered the matter previously. But of course, I'd have to recuse myself."

"Thank you, Professor Fitzgerald. I have no further questions."

I'm powerless to save him. Unless I confess. But remember what Brad said. You'd be giving up everything for nothing.

She was suddenly awash in a sea of flash. The photographers had taken over. She smiled graciously until all of them had the shots they wanted. Then she turned toward the public seats and saw Joel sitting next to Hugh. Both of them were smiling proudly.

CLAIRE

"What we know of other people is only our memory of the moments during which we knew them. And they have changed since then."

T.S. Eliot

CHAPTER TWENTY-THREE

Friday, February 3, 2017, U.S. Route 301 North to Belle Grove Plantation Bed and Breakfast, Port Conway, Virginia

Claire swung the Range Rover off of I-95 North and picked up U.S. Route 301 North at ten thirty that morning. She was on her way to meet Wynne at Belle Grove. He was driving up from Sussex where he'd been with Ed. When Claire had thought about planning her wedding, she hadn't expected to be driving alone to inspect a potential venue. This hurry-up and just-get-it-done approach wasn't what she'd imagined as she'd drifted down the Seine on Christmas Eve.

Her father had called from D.C. this morning, and their conversation had poured gasoline on the fire of her nagging doubts about marrying Wynne in a hurry. And it had opened a new avenue of worry about Tyndall.

"I had dinner with Mckenzie on Monday night at I Ricchi."

"Was that a good idea?" Claire asked.

"Yes, a very good idea. We are still friends."

"But she broke your heart when she went west," she reminded him.

"And you did the same thing when you went to Stanford and accepted that job at Warrick, Thompson. And I still take you to dinner at our favorite restaurants."

"You're making fun of me." But she was relieved to hear the laughter in his voice as he teased her. *He is really over her. I don't have to worry,* she told herself.

"I've got meetings here today, and then I'm headed back to New York. We can have dinner at La Grenouille if you'll be back tonight."

"I'd love to." *And I would. God, wouldn't it be wonderful to be with someone who cares about me who's not involved in Ed Carter's case.* "But I'm headed down to Belle Grove to meet Wynne today and then back to Richmond tonight." The pause on the other end of the line told her that her father was about to say something she didn't want to hear.

"Claire, I know you don't like advice from me unless you ask for it. But I want you to be happy more than anything else in the world. Don't give in to pressure from Wynne to get married this quickly."

* * *

A truck ahead of her was loaded with bags of fertilizer and not in any hurry to make its way down Route 301. Claire wanted the trip to take as long as possible, so she decided not to pass it.

As March 3 loomed closer without any evidence to stop the execution, she felt as if she were on the bow of a ship sinking faster and faster. Then Brendan had asked her to get that surreptitious DNA sample from Wynne. A thought had nagged her as she had pulled several hairs out of Wynne's brush for

Brendan to send to Dr. Vom Saal. Ed and Anne's marriage had been in trouble, and Ed couldn't have divorced Anne without losing Wynne if he wasn't his son. And Ed clearly didn't want to lose Wynne because he loved him with all his heart. At that point, he loved him more than the unborn, unknown child Anne had only begun to carry. Blair's firm conviction that Ed was guilty weighed on Claire. And then, there was the matter of the white Volvo.

It was clear that Wynne was everything to Ed and that he had everything to lose if he divorced Anne, and everything to keep if he killed her. These were the doubts that had begun to torment Claire. And they tormented her even more because they were doubts that she could not share with Wynne.

* * *

Following the truck had made her late. Wynne was standing by his rental car, waiting for her as she parked in the gravel lot across from the house.

Her heart turned over at the sight of him, tall and slender, yet powerful in his black cashmere overcoat. He was wearing the red wool scarf that she'd given him for Christmas. Although the snow had finally melted, the temperature was hovering just above freezing, and his cheeks were flushed from the cold. The light, but chilly wind blew his dark hair across his forehead, and he swiped at it with his black-leather-gloved hand. His blue eyes behind his round, clear spectacles lit up when she got out of the car. He hurried across the gravel to take her in his arms. For a moment he said nothing, but Claire could feel all the emotion that came with that hug.

He stepped back, still holding her, and studied her face. "I was afraid for a minute that you'd changed your mind and weren't coming."

"I was behind some slow traffic. How's your father?"

The light in Wynne's eyes went out. "He's not sleeping or eating much. He seems tired and old and confused. I've never seen him like this. But he's never been this close to dying before."

The joy that Claire had felt at meeting Wynne trailed off into sadness, but she didn't let it show. Instead, she smiled and took his hand as they crossed the gravel drive to the house. They went up the front steps and rang the bell. As they stood waiting for someone to answer the door, Claire had the odd feeling that they were being watched. She turned and looked toward the Summer Kitchen and the outbuildings to their right.

Wynne followed her gaze. "What's wrong?"

"Oh, nothing." She turned back toward the front door just as Michelle, the innkeeper, opened it. "Come in, come in," she said, stepping aside to let them enter the front hall. "I'm so happy to have you back at Belle Grove, Claire. And this must be Wynne. Tea is waiting in the parlor. Come in and warm up, and we'll talk about what sort of wedding you two would like to have."

Michelle led the way into the elegant red parlor where a pink-and-green-flowered teapot and cups were waiting on the mahogany table between the two gold velvet settees. Michelle sat down on one of the settees and began to pour tea for everyone. Claire found a seat opposite Michelle, but Wynne didn't take the seat next to her. Instead, he walked over to the box piano under the window and began to play a rambling, haunting melody.

Claire listened in amazement as the notes tumbled out, each one sadder than the one before. *It's like listening to his heart breaking.*

Suddenly he stopped and turned to Claire and Michelle. "I hope you don't mind."

"No, of course not," Michelle said as he crossed the room to take the seat beside Claire. She handed him a cup of tea. "What were you playing?"

"The beginning of Bach's *Partita No. 2*. It was my mother's favorite piece to play on her violin. She'd play at night after she'd put me to bed, and I'd fall asleep to it."

"I didn't know you played the piano," Claire said.

Wynne smiled as he sipped his tea. "I inherited my mother's looks and her musical talent. But I don't play the piano very often anymore because it makes me sad. And we aren't here to be sad. We're here to plan our wedding. What are our options?"

"We do everything from elopements to large weddings at Belle Grove," Michelle explained. "Claire said you were thinking of under twenty guests."

"That's right. Just close family and friends."

"Then let me show you the library. It would be an ideal place for a cozy, family ceremony."

She led them out of the parlor and into a warm, book-lined room with a magnificent view of the Rappahannock through the winter-bare trees. The sunlight cast soft shadows on the Persian rug and the polished wooden floor.

"I love it," Wynne said. "What do you think, Claire?"

"Beautiful," she agreed.

They followed her back down the corridor and across the front hall to the spacious red dining room, whose windows also overlooked the rear lawn that sloped down to the river behind the house.

"And if the guest list is small enough, we could seat everyone in here for lunch or for an early evening meal, depending on the time of the wedding," Michelle said. "If you choose early evening, we could set up the parlor for dancing afterward." She smiled at Claire. "I hope I'm not overwhelming you with ideas."

"They are all very good ones," she smiled back. "Could Wynne and I walk through the house on our own and talk it over?"

"Take your time, and go outside and walk the grounds, too. The back lawn is a lovely place for a wedding, but I think it will be too cold this time of year. When you are finished, I've arranged for the three of us to have lunch in the dining room to talk over your plans. I'm going to the kitchen now to make sure everything is ready when you are finished touring the house."

Hand in hand, they wandered through the first floor again, looking at the parlor and the library, and the two-bedroom suites on that floor. Then they took the graceful staircase to the second floor and wandered through the Madison and Turner Suites. When they reached the Turner Suite, Claire showed Wynne the etching on the glass.

"Your ancestor?" he smiled.

"Carrie Turner, yes."

Wynne bent down to read the inscription: "Carrie Turner, M Van Der Burgh, May 18, 1869."

"A Union soldier. The house was a Union headquarters."

"So she met him during the war, and then he came back for her in 1869?"

"That's the story that has been handed down in the family," Claire said. "My mother told me when I was little. Back then, I thought it was like a fairytale. After the war, the handsome soldier came back for the girl he fell in love with."

Wynne studied the writing on the glass for another moment, and then said, "You can't tell if Van Der Burgh's first name starts with a 'W' or an 'M.'"

"It doesn't matter, anyway," Claire said. "She wound up marrying someone else."

Wynne took her hand and smiled. "Sounds sad, but I don't feel sad here. Let's go outside and look at the grounds."

The pale winter sun was doing its best to bring some semblance of warmth to the early afternoon. Claire let Wynne draw his arm through hers as they walked across the lawn that ended in the steep bank that led down to the river.

Wynne paused and looked at the lawn with its magnificent view of the Rappahannock. "This would be the perfect place to have a big reception in the summer for all our friends, since our actual wedding is going to be so small."

"Yes." *It feels as if someone is watching us. No, that's ridiculous. Michelle is probably looking out to see if we're headed back for lunch.*

He continued to study the lawn and then he turned to gaze at the back of the house. "It's so tranquil." His eyes smiled down at her as he spoke. All the tumult of the last few weeks had been erased from his boyish face.

He's found peace here, Claire thought. *Then it's meant to be. We'll get married at Belle Grove.*

Wynne put his arm around her shoulders and smiled at her. "Let's go back inside and have lunch and make our plans."

As they turned away from the river back toward the house, Claire thought she saw a shadow in the grove of trees to their left. *But that's ridiculous. No one is standing outside on a cold day like this, watching two people walk by a river.*

* * *

The dining room was warm and inviting after being outside. Michelle had set one end of the long mahogany table for the three of them.

"Isn't the lawn beautiful?" she asked as she put three plates on the table. "This is one of our breakfast dishes, but I thought you'd enjoy it for lunch. Potato and rosemary hash with onions and shaved brussel sprouts, topped with a crab cake, poached egg and hollandaise sauce. And I have tea or coffee to warm you up."

Claire accepted a cup of coffee and began on her lunch. "This is delicious," she said to Michelle after a few bites.

"Wonderful," Wynne echoed.

"So now that you've had a chance to talk it over, what are your plans?" Michelle asked.

"I think it should be a mid-morning ceremony in the library with lunch afterward in here," Wynne said. "What do you think, Claire?"

"That would be lovely." *And it would. He always has exquisite taste.*

"For twenty people?" Michelle asked.

"Tops twenty," Wynne agreed. "And then, in the summer, we'll come back and have a huge blowout on the lawn."

"Do you need someone to conduct the ceremony?" Michelle asked.

"No." Claire smiled at Wynne. "I'm sure Father Jim will be willing. I used to go to church with the Murphys when I was at St. Catherine's. He knows me. And of course, he knows your father."

Wynne nodded. "I'm sure he'll be happy to do it."

"So, then, we need to set a date," Michelle said.

"How about a week from today?" Wynne asked. "It will be Valentine's Day."

Michelle smiled indulgently. "While we can put together a very bare bones wedding that fast, I think the two of you are wanting a bit more than we can come up with in a week."

"How long do you need then?" Wynne asked.

"I would say three weeks, minimum."

"So that would be February 24," Wynne observed.

"Yes."

"Then February 24 it is!"

MCKENZIE

"Liberty is a different kind of pain from prison."

T.S. Eliot

CHAPTER TWENTY-FOUR

Tuesday, February 7, 2017, Offices of Goldstein, Miller, Mahoney, and Fitzgerald, Emerald Shapery Center, San Diego, California

It was good to be back in San Diego, away from D.C.'s winter chill. Mckenzie studied the cobalt water of San Diego Bay, shining in the warm winter sun as she sat at her desk and reflected on her triumphs before the Senate Judiciary Committee.

"Best job I've ever seen," Senator Lovell had enthused when he'd taken her, Joel, and Hugh to dinner Friday night after the hearings had ended. "You'll be confirmed immediately."

And as soon as I am on the Court," Mckenzie reflected that morning, *I'm going to find a way to stop Ed Carter's execution. Brian would want me to.*

Her phone rang, and her secretary told her that Tyndall was calling. She smiled as she picked up the phone.

"Are you in San Diego, I hope?" she asked.

"No, I wish I were. It's freezing in New York. I called to congratulate you on your success before the Committee and to tell you that Claire's getting married on February 24. She and I want you to come."

Mckenzie glanced at her calendar. That was exactly a week before the execution. "Does that mean there's good news about Wynne's father?"

"I'm afraid not."

"Then why are they going ahead with it?"

"Wynne has put pressure on her. And she feels as if he'll be alone when Ed dies if she doesn't agree."

"Where is the wedding?"

"At Julia's ancestral home, Belle Grove, down at Port Conway. The wedding is going to be very small, only about twenty guests."

"I'm flattered to be asked, and I'll be there."

"You'll be Justice Fitzgerald by then, I bet."

"I'm planning on it. And soon as I've got the robes on, I'm going to find a way to stop that execution."

* * *

She had just put down the phone when there was a knock on her door, and Hugh Mahoney opened it slightly to say, "Do you have a few minutes?"

"Of course."

"Senator Lovell called this morning. The vote on your confirmation is going to be delayed."

"Delayed? But after the hearings, he said he thought they'd vote this week."

"That was before Mary Sue Austin started calling in favors."

"Ah, yes, Senator Austin. She doesn't like me."

"It's more about not trusting you. She thinks you'll do something to keep Ed alive. She claims her constituents have an interest in his death."

Mckenzie shivered. "How barbaric. It's not her constituents. Its Anne Fairfax's family. So is she going to block my confirmation?"

"She doesn't have the votes to do that. And a majority of the committee are for you according to George Lovell. So it will just be a delay."

"How long?"

"It's set to come up on March 6."

"That's the Monday after—" She couldn't bring herself to say the words.

"Exactly," Hugh nodded.

* * *

The minute Hugh left her office, her personal cell phone rang. It was Joel.

"Hey, Justice Mom."

"Thanks, but I've just been told that Senator Austin is conspiring against me."

"Because of Dad's client who's on death row in Virginia?"

"That's right."

"So is the move to D.C. off?"

"No, just postponed. Until Senator Austin makes sure the Fairfaxes get what they want."

"So Senator Austin was afraid you'd find a way to stop it as soon as you were on the Court? She didn't believe you'd recuse yourself?"

"Truth to tell, I lied about that. I was going to find a way to issue a stay." *Because I feel guilty about botching that recording.*

"Is there anything we could do to stop it?"

"You and me?"

"Yeah, Dad would want us to try."

"I can't think of anything the two of us can do. But if I do, I'll let you know."

"Okay. Jenny belongs to an anti-death penalty group here in San Fran. They are going to hold a series of candlelight vigils for Ed Carter every Friday night from now until March 3. I'll be there, too, of course. Maybe you should come?"

"I wish I could. But as long as I'm still a nominee, I can't do anything that would express my personal view about an issue that could come before the Court."

"Of course."

After she hung up, she realized that it would also be better if her son didn't express any personal views on the death penalty in public while her nomination was pending. But since Jenny was involved, he wouldn't listen if she suggested not attending one of her rallies. Besides, she was happy that people were speaking out against something so cruel and irrevocable.

She watched an aircraft carrier pull away from the dock and head toward the open sea with its helicopter escort. She willed herself to slow her racing thoughts and do what she was best at doing: analyzing the problem.

She thought back to first-year ethics class. An attorney could not disclose the contents of a client's communications except when the client had made a credible threat to someone's life.

"But even then," bluff, gruff Professor Phillips had cautioned them, "the preferred method of disclosure is an anonymous tip."

So what if she could send Brendan Murphy an anonymous tip that he should talk to Quinn Fairchild? Granted Quinn would probably reveal Mckenzie's awkward incompetence that had failed to net the defense team a recorded statement. But Brendan wouldn't tell the rest of the world. Her nomination to the Court would be safe, and Quinn's information would stop Ed Carter's execution. And even better, Senator Austin would be none the wiser.

Mckenzie's heart stopped racing. She knew she'd come to the correct conclusion. But there was one problem with her anonymous tip solution. She had no idea if Quinn Fairchild was still alive.

She picked up her phone and called Hugh.

"I need a favor."

"Anything. How about dinner tonight?"

"Dinner would be wonderful. I need a few hours of Joe Sanders' time. It's for a client who needs to find an important witness."

"He's busy, but I'll tell him to give your request priority."

"Thanks."

"Pick you up at seven at your place?"

"See you then."

CLAIRE

"I will show you fear in a handful of dust."

T.S. Eliot

CHAPTER TWENTY-FIVE

Friday, February 10, 2017, Vera Wang, Madison Avenue, New York, New York

"But your dress is not finished, Ms. Chastain," Margo, the Head Bridal Consultant, wailed, "and we cannot have it by February 24. I am so sorry, but it takes six months to create one of our gowns."

Claire stared out at the cold, dark street jammed with five p.m. traffic and remembered Father Jim Lamb's words over the telephone on Monday. "I'm sorry, Claire. I know these are difficult circumstances. But the Episcopal Church has its rules about marriage, and one of them is not to rush into it. We don't have enough time to do the counseling the Church requires. I can't perform the ceremony if you insist on February 24."

Was the Universe telling her this wasn't the right time to marry Wynne? Michelle had told them she had someone who regularly performed weddings at Belle Grove. That would have to be the answer.

Claire turned back to the troubled Margo. "What if I wear the sample dress?"

Margo looked blank. "The sample dress?"

"Yes, the one you use for try-ons. It was a perfect fit."

"I—I suppose you could. No one has ever suggested that. I think you'd have to give it back, though. It would only be on loan."

"Of course. We're having a larger party in the summer. I can wear my own gown then."

"I'll check to be sure if we can lend the sample, and I'll call you tomorrow."

"Thank you." Claire gave her the warmest smile she could muster, hoping that would encourage her to grant her request.

She wrapped herself in the black cashmere Dior overcoat that had once been her mother's and headed out onto Madison Avenue, awash in rush hour traffic. The taxis that whizzed by were all full. She would have to take the subway home to Chelsea.

The platform was teeming with impatient people just off from work and intent on catching the train as quickly as possible. Claire was tired and discouraged, and she hated being jostled by the crowd. She peered down the dark subway tunnel, hoping the train would come quickly. Suddenly she felt a swift, hard shove from behind and a sharp pain in her left shoulder. She struggled to keep her footing but to no avail. The dark hole of the subway tracks was rising up to meet her. She heard the sound of the approaching train and blacked out.

* * *

New York-Presbyterian Hospital, Weill Cornell Medical Center, New York, New York

When she opened her eyes, she saw Jeff Ryder surrounded by a white halo. She blinked, and the halo seemed to grow smaller. She blinked again and saw her father standing beside Jeff.

Her head ached, and there was a searing pain in her left shoulder than ran all the way down to her left wrist. She looked down and saw the cast around her left forearm.

"What happened?"

"Someone snatched your purse and pushed you onto the tracks," Jeff said. "Luckily, there were a couple of quick-thinking guys who pulled you out in the nick of time. The police found the Vera Wang receipt in your coat pocket and figured out who you were and who to call."

Tyndall leaned over and kissed her cheek. "How do you feel?"

"Like I'm floating outside my body. But I can still feel my head hurting, and my shoulder and wrist are on fire."

"The floating feeling is from the pain meds," her father said. "You've got a mild concussion, and you broke your left wrist when you fell. Your left shoulder is deeply bruised from your purse strap breaking, and you hit on that side when you went down."

"Did you see anyone near you just before it happened?" Jeff asked.

"Not really. It all seemed to come from behind. The platform was very crowded."

"It looked like a heavyset male in a beanie on the surveillance tape," Jeff said. "As soon as he uses one of your credit cards, the cops will have him."

"Spoken like an ex-prosecutor," she gave him a little smile.

"Thank God, he didn't make off with your sense of humor," he grinned back.

Claire felt herself drifting toward sleep again, although she wanted to stay awake. Her eyes were heavy, and she was fighting to keep them open.

"We'd better let you rest," her father said and gave her another kiss on the cheek. "I'll be back in the morning. The doctor said you could probably go home. You should stay with me for a few days until you feel better."

"Maybe. I'm tired. I don't know. Wynne—"

"I called him," Jeff said. "He's on his way back from Sussex. He'll be here in the morning, too."

Her lids were too heavy. She couldn't stay awake. She closed her eyes and was gone.

* * *

When she opened them again, it was dark. The clock above the door said three a.m. She looked around the tiny room and realized Jeff was sitting on a chair by the end of her bed, dozing.

"Jeff?"

He opened his eyes. "What?"

"Why are you still here?"

"Your father was going to stay. I told him to go home and rest."

"I'm fine. Go get a good night's sleep and come back in the morning."

"Can't do that. I promised your father I'd stay."

"But you don't have to."

"Yes, I do. I've read enough med malpractice cases to know you shouldn't leave anyone alone in the hospital overnight who's been hit on the head. Do you need more pain medication?"

"Not right now. This reminds me of that night."

"What night?"

"The night you stayed with me. After Paul announced his engagement."

"You weren't safe that night, either."

"I'm safe."

"No, you're not. Now go to sleep."

CHAPTER TWENTY-SIX

Saturday, February 11, 2017, Claire's Apartment, 100 11th Avenue, Chelsea,New York

By eleven the next morning, Claire was at home, settled with Wynne on the sofa in her living room. They cuddled together as they looked out at Claire's magnificent, thirtieth-floor view of the Hudson River and the city. Her father had begged her to come home to his Fifth Avenue apartment where she'd grown up, but her building was secure, and she wanted to be at home and alone with Wynne. He'd arrived at the hospital at seven that morning along with Tyndall, who had thanked Jeff profusely for staying all night.

"How's your head?" Wynne asked.

"Better. The docs said the headache would go away pretty quickly, and it has."

"Don't get any ideas," he cautioned. "You need to rest for a few days."

"How's Ed?"

Wynne sighed. "Bearing up. I don't see how he manages to stay so calm. We need a break in his case, Claire."

"I know. I keep hoping the Fourth Circuit will finally grant one of Brendan's writs."

"Me, too. They're a tough bunch up there."

Claire's cell phone rang, and she looked down at the caller ID. "It's Brendan," she said. "Could you make me a cup of tea while I talk to him?"

"Of course." Wynne disentangled himself and headed for the kitchen.

"Thank God, you're okay," Brendan said. "Emma and I didn't sleep all night because we were so worried."

"Mild concussion. Broken left wrist. I was lucky. Who told you about it?"

"Wynne. I was with him at Sussex when Jeff Ryder called to say you'd been in an accident."

"I hope you didn't tell Ed. He has enough to worry about, and I'm fine."

"We haven't told him yet."

"Well, don't then."

"I wanted to be sure you were okay, but that's not the only reason I called."

"Please give me some good news."

"I wish I could, but not this time. Dr. Vom Saal has the test results. Ed was right. Wynne isn't his son."

"Oh, God!"

"I know."

"That means he hasn't any relatives except the Fairfaxes, and he's cut all of his ties to them."

"And there's something else, Claire. It means that Ed had a motive to kill Anne."

"To keep from losing Wynne."

"Right."

"I don't want to believe that."

"I told you in the beginning, when you practice criminal law, you have to be prepared to find out things are true that you don't want to be true."

At that moment, Wynne came back with her mug of tea. He smiled as he put it on the coffee table and rearranged her pillows.

"Tell Brendan 'hi,'" he said.

Claire studied Wynne's kind, blue eyes. He loves me. That's the one thing I can be sure of in a world that seems to be coming apart at the seams.

"Brendan says 'hi' back. And he wants to talk to you."

Claire sipped her tea and watched Wynne's face change as Brendan told him that he was needed urgently at the prison.

"Brendan says I have to go back to Sussex tomorrow."

"I know," Claire said. "He told me."

"I don't want you to be alone."

"I won't be. I can call my father or Jeff. I'll be fine. And Wynne, please don't tell Ed about this. He doesn't need any more bad news."

CHAPTER TWENTY-SEVEN

Sunday, February 12, 2017, Claire's Apartment, 100 11ᵗʰ Avenue, Chelsea, New York

"Pepperoni, sausage, and mushroom from Nicolosi's," Jeff said when he set the pizza box on the coffee table in Claire's living room at seven p.m. "And I've brought a bottle of Bordeaux."

She laughed. "Only you would bring French wine to go with pizza."

He grinned. "There was a time last year when I thought I was out of the French wine business for good. How are you feeling?"

"Better. No more headache. The cast is annoying, and my wrist hurts."

"Where's the rock?"

"The rock?"

"Your engagement ring?"

"In my jewelry box. My finger is still too swollen to put it on."

"Have you considered whether that might be a sign?"

"Oh, no. Don't you start, too. My father has been a veritable

Greek chorus of 'Postpone, postpone.' By the way, I was disappointed that we weren't going out for dinner."

"Well, you did get thrown off a subway platform forty-eight hours ago. I thought a restful night at home might be more the thing. Since I've disappointed you, let me get some plates for us. You go back to being cozy on the couch."

Claire laughed and stretched out on the sofa again. She pulled the white cashmere throw over her feet while he went to the kitchen. *I haven't laughed like this since the night we went skating.*

He was back in less than five minutes with plates and glasses. He opened the bottle of wine and poured it for them. Then he handed her a plate with three big slices of pizza.

"Here, you look hungry."

"Well, maybe not this hungry."

"I'm betting you eat all of that and more."

"What do you win if you're right?"

His steady, blue eyes met hers, and they were serious instead of teasing. "The right to talk sense into you."

"Don't, Jeff. I know what everyone thinks, but everyone doesn't know the truth."

She bit into a slice of pizza and stared pensively at the lights over the Hudson.

"Are you willing to let me in on the truth?" He had taken the chair opposite the sofa and was attacking his own slice of pizza.

"Of course." Her eyes came back to his. "Wynne is on his way to Sussex because Brendan told him it was urgent."

"I wondered why he left you at a time like this."

"He didn't have a choice, although he won't know that until tomorrow."

"What's going to happen tomorrow?"

"Ed is going to tell Wynne that he isn't his biological father."

"What? That's crazy."

"I wish it were." Claire explained Father Jim's insistence that Ed tell Wynne the truth as well as her role in the DNA testing.

"Well, it was smart to be sure before springing something like that on him," Jeff said.

"I was so hoping Anne Carter was wrong when she said Wynne wasn't Ed's son."

Jeff shook his head. "You always know who your mother is. Your father—that's more of a crapshoot."

"For Wynne it is."

"It was a lousy idea to dump this on him now."

"Brendan and I thought so."

"What was that priest thinking?"

"We're not sure. Brendan said Father Jim thought Wynne could connect with his biological father after—I can't say it."

"No, I know. What a blow for Wynne, though."

"Unnecessary in my opinion. No one could love Wynne more than Ed does. You can just feel it when you're in the room with them. Wynne isn't going to be able to reconstruct that with some stranger."

"Father Jim doesn't sound very compassionate."

"Oh, he is in some ways. Just not when it comes to all the problems that Ed's situation is creating."

"You mean he's done more than convince Ed to hurt Wynne with the so-called 'truth' at a time like this?"

"Yes. Father Jim has been Ed's spiritual counselor since Brendan took over his case in 1986. He's very close to Ed. And Wynne. And he won't agree to perform our wedding."

Jeff frowned. "He knows you, too, doesn't he?"

"Right. He's as close to a parish priest as any of us have. And he won't do this for us."

"Why?"

"Says the church requires more time for counseling."

"Well, I can't disagree with that," Jeff said.

Claire finished the second slice of pizza and started on the third. She felt Jeff watching her. "Don't say anything."

"Looks like I'm winning this bet."

"Okay. Talk sense into me."

"Same thing the priest was saying. You and Wynne are rushing into this."

Claire sighed and picked up a fourth slice of pizza from the open box. "Would it make you feel better if I told you that I know?"

"Yes."

"Well, then, I know we're taking this too fast."

"So stop it."

"How?" Her eyes met and held Jeff's for what felt like a long time. Then she went on. "How do I stop it? Tomorrow he finds out that he's a Fairfax, but not a Carter. He hates the Fairfaxes, and they hate him for supporting Ed. When he gets back to New York late tomorrow night, do I say, 'I've changed my mind? We're taking this too fast? I'm deserting you when you need me the most?' Even if I didn't love Wynne, and I do, how could I do that to him?"

Jeff sighed and refilled their glasses. Then he said, "You can't. You're right."

Claire took a long sip of her wine. "Thanks for understanding."

"It's a dilemma, though, because I see the part of you that isn't sure about marrying Wynne."

"Well, then, I hope no one else does because I don't have a way out."

"Why do you have doubts?" Jeff asked. "Paul?"

"In the beginning, yes," Claire admitted. "But I've come to realize what a selfish narcissist Paul is. Maybe I do know more about him than anyone else does, but one day I'll know more about Wynne than any human being on earth."

"Then where are the doubts coming from?"

"I'm not sure. Wynne is very sweet, and he loves me. But he comes with some very heavy baggage that I wasn't counting on. He's never going to love anyone the way he loves Ed. And now he's about to find out Ed hasn't told him the truth all these years. And I'm wondering what else Ed has lied to Wynne about."

"I'm not so sure I'd accuse Ed of lying to Wynne about the identity of his father. For all intents and purposes, Ed Carter is Wynne's father," Jeff said definitively. "DNA isn't going to change that."

"Which is exactly why I thought they should have left well enough alone. Because it also raises the question of did Ed kill Anne so he wouldn't lose Wynne? He couldn't divorce her without losing him."

They were quiet for a few minutes as they studied the glorious view of the river at night as they ate. Finally, Claire put her plate on the coffee table and leaned back against the cushions.

"You didn't finish the crusts," Jeff observed. She was glad he was trying to lighten the mood.

"I never do."

"But they're the best part."

"Then they're all yours."

He picked up her discarded plate and began on the crusts. Claire studied him as he munched.

"What's wrong?" he asked. "Why are you looking at me like that?"

"Because I'm wondering what you're going to say when I ask you something."

"Will I be your maid of honor? Of course."

She laughed. "Actually, that's not a bad idea. You're my closest friend."

"You could ask Paul and torture him."

"No, thanks."

"I think you should ask your friend Ellen. She's the nearest thing you've got to a sister."

"Good point."

"Okay, now that we've settled that, what were you actually going to ask me?"

"Will you help me save Ed's life? It's the only thing that's going to fix this whole mess and keep Wynne from being miserable for years to come."

Jeff stopped finishing the crusts and put the plate on the coffee table again. He studied her face.

"Why are you staring at me?"

"To see if your pupils are the same size. Your head hit those tracks pretty hard."

"My pupils are fine. I told you, my head doesn't even hurt anymore. Will you help me?"

"I thought that's what you said," Jeff agreed. "But I was afraid it might be the concussed part of you talking."

"Will you stop it? I need your help."

"Of course I'm willing to help you, Claire. By now you know I'd do almost anything for you, short of putting a bullet in Paul Curtis. But how much time have we got left to save Ed Carter? Less than two weeks?"

"Nineteen days."

"Well, then plenty of time."

"Be quiet and listen. It might be."

"I'll listen, but I want you to listen to me first."

"I started this conversation. I get to go first."

"If you want my help, you'll listen to what I have to say."

"Okay." She gave him a pretend pout and sipped her wine.

"I stayed with you at the hospital because of all those malpractice cases we had to read in law school, but there's another reason I stayed."

"And that would be?"

"I think the person who pushed you in the subway was Allison Byrd. I think she'll be back to try again."

"That's preposterous."

"No, it isn't. I asked the cops to let me see that surveillance tape again."

"And?"

"And I was wrong when I thought the figure was a male. I saw a person in a long coat—the kind a woman would wear in the winter—enter the subway a few minutes after you. She followed you to the platform, and she got close enough to push you over. It all looked very deliberate on the tape."

"But you couldn't see her face."

"Yes, I could. There's a brief close up from camera three that I found when I replayed the video for the fourth time."

"But you don't know what Allison Byrd looks like."

"Yes, I do. I found her mugshot on a law enforcement database that I still have access to. She was arrested last year at your family's former plantation and allowed to plead to misdemeanor stalking."

"I know. Michelle told me."

"Michelle?"

"Michelle Darnell, the innkeeper."

"Okay, so I stayed with you in the hospital, and I intend to stay here tonight, because I think Allison Byrd tried to kill you on Friday afternoon."

Claire stared out at the river and the lights and said nothing for a few moments. Her gut told her Jeff was right. "But Allison Byrd doesn't know me."

"I think she does. I think she saw you and Wynne visiting Belle Grove to plan your wedding."

Claire's eyes came back from the night skyline and held Jeff's concerned blue gaze. "You could be right. The day we were there, it felt as if we were being watched. Wynne and I walked outside on the lawn by the Rappahannock after we toured the house. I thought it might be Michelle watching us from the dining room because she was waiting for us to come in for lunch. But it felt sinister. I thought of Allison Byrd at the time but discounted it. She signed a stay-away order, so she shouldn't be at Belle Grove. But she's always been a stalker. Port Conway is a small community. She could have found out that Wynne and I were coming back to book the house for our wedding."

"Then it's highly likely she was there. And she's dangerous. She became obsessed with Ed and thought she could replace his wife. Which would explain why she murdered Anne. And since you are now going to marry Wynne, she's fixated on you."

"So in her crazy brain, he's now Ed, and I'm now Anne."

"Right."

Claire studied Jeff's earnest face. "I wish I could say you don't have a point, but you do."

"So I'm sleeping in your guest room tonight, and I'm keeping you in sight until Wynne comes back."

"Okay. But you're going to help me, aren't you?"

"Of course. What exactly am I going to help you do?"

"Get a sample of Allison Byrd's DNA. Because I'm sure it's on that bat. If you're right and she's coming after me again, it will give us a chance to prove she killed Anne."

"Well, if you get close enough to get a sample, you'll be dead. So that's not an option. We don't know where she's staying in New York or even where she lives, so we can't break in and steal her toothbrush."

"Please be serious."

"I am serious. I'm trying to work out a way to get you what you want. She was wearing a scarf in the surveillance video. It was draped loosely around her neck. In a place as crowded as the subway, it might be possible to cut a piece off or even grab it and run. But to do that, you'd have to hire an investigator to find and follow her, looking for the right opportunity. And I'd have to agree to let you go back down in the subway. Which I might not do."

"You can't stop me, so don't even think about it. Wynne's got a whole stable of investigators working for him on Ed's case. Marvin Silverman's good, and I've worked with him before. He can help us. But I don't want you to worry Wynne with your suspicions about Allison Byrd."

"I think you should tell him," Jeff said.

"Not now. After tomorrow, he's going to have a lot of heavy duty emotions to process. We might be wrong. That surveillance footage is not very clear. I don't want him to worry needlessly. Or to get his hopes up if it isn't Allison, and we can't get a sample. I don't think we should say anything to him until we've gotten her DNA, and Dr. Vom Saal has connected her to the murder weapon."

"But won't Wynne know if we use one of his people?"

"No. Marvin will understand the importance of keeping quiet until we have something."

"Okay. I disagree with you. If I were Wynne, I'd want to know that you're in danger. But you're calling the shots, so I'll keep quiet."

"And don't say anything to my father, either. I don't want him to worry."

"Well, he's already worried."

"Then we don't have to tell him."

Jeff smiled. "You've always been able to beat me in oral argument. Now let's get some sleep. You look tired. I'll wrap up the rest of the pizza and put it away. I'm surprised there's any left."

BRENDAN

"There will be time to murder and create."

T.S. Eliot

CHAPTER TWENTY-EIGHT

Monday, February 13, 2017, Sussex State Prison, Sussex, Virginia

Brendan sat with Wynne in the Attorney Interview Room, waiting for the guards to bring Ed in at eleven a.m. Wynne had arrived at the Murphys' late last night, and Brendan had driven the two of them down from Richmond that morning.

The door opened, but instead of Ed, it was Father Jim Lamb. Brendan felt a moment of extreme irritation. Wynne's world was about to shatter because of him. Brendan wished the priest had stayed in Richmond.

After brief greetings, Father Jim sat down next to Brendan. Wynne was opposite them. Brendan studied Wynne's thin, tired face and saw in it the anxious, skinny fifteen-year-old who had asked to live with the Carters because he believed in the innocence of the man whom he thought was his father.

This isn't the right time to do this, Brendan thought. *When it's over and Ed's gone, we could have given him the news.* He looked over at Father Jim who was checking messages on his cell phone. *I'd like to strangle him. Wynne is as much my son as Tim. I don't want him to be hurt like this.*

The door stirred again, and this time it was Ed shuffling in between two guards who placed him in the chair next to Wynne and locked his chains to the nearest table leg.

"Please take the cuffs off," Brendan ordered. The guards gave him a sullen look but complied. It was a breach of regulations, but they knew Brendan was friendly with the warden. If they refused, Tom Brower would give Ed's attorney what he wanted.

They lingered by the door as if to show Brendan that they were in charge. But he dealt them a second blow. "This is a confidential interview covered by attorney-client privilege."

The two gray shadows withdrew sullenly. Ed's now-freed hands took Wynne's.

"I've got something to tell you, son. Something that is going to be hard for you to hear."

"I'm listening."

He looks so vulnerable, Brendan thought.

"Father Jim and I have talked a lot about what I'll leave behind. It won't be money, as you know. The Carter money went to pay my legal fees."

"That doesn't matter, Dad," Wynne said. "I've made more than I'll ever spend."

"I know," Ed smiled, "and I'm proud of you. But there's something that I've never told you that Father Jim and I think you should hear from me. And not from someone else."

"What?"

"Your mother's affair with Richard Neal was not the only affair she had during our marriage. When we lived in New York, she had several lovers. You were conceived during that time. When I found out that she was pregnant, I made myself believe that I was your father. But I'm not, Wynne."

"That's ridiculous! Of course you are!"

Ed shook his head slowly. "No, I'm not."

"But how do you know?" Wynne demanded.

"Because Dr. Vom Saal did a DNA test."

"When? How? I didn't know anything about it."

"I asked him to," Brendan interrupted, keeping his voice steady and calm in the face of Wynne's anger. "Ed had told Jim that he had always had doubts that he was your father, and Jim thought you should be told. I didn't want to tell you unless we were sure. I asked Claire to send Dr. Vom Saal some hairs from your brush. She and I didn't want you to be hurt unless it was absolutely necessary."

"Well, it wasn't necessary!" Wynne shot back. He held on tightly to Ed's hands.

"I refuse to believe this. Dr. Vom Saal is wrong. And even if he isn't, it doesn't matter. You're my father, and you always will be." Wynne paused and gave Father Jim a look of pure hatred before he went on. "And I will always hate you, you useless priest, for stirring this up. You refused to officiate at my wedding, but you had no scruples about hurting me and my father at a time like this."

"Wynne, I—" Father Jim started to say.

"I don't want to hear from you!" Wynne snapped. "I want you to get up and leave this room and stay out of my sight forever."

Ed disentangled his hands from Wynne's grasp and put one of them on his shoulder. "Calm down," he said. "Father Jim and I both thought you should know. If you are going to blame him, you have to blame me, too."

"I refuse to do that!" Brendan watched Wynne's jaw work in angry, little circles.

"There's one more thing I think you should know," Ed said.

"I don't want to hear it."

"We couldn't find out who you father is. Dr. Vom Saal ran the DNA databases and didn't find a match. But I do know one thing: he was the love of your mother's life."

Wynne frowned. "How do you know that?"

"Because Richard Neal begged her to leave me for him, and she told me about it. She said that if she left our marriage, it wouldn't be for Neal. She used to take off to New York on weekends after we moved to Richmond. Sometimes she went by herself, but sometimes she took you. I guessed she was taking you to see your father. So I think what she was telling me that night when she told me that she had turned down Neal was that if your father had asked her to live with him, she would have."

"So you think he didn't want her or me?" Wynne spoke slowly.

"Yes," Ed said. "And I was so glad because I wanted both of you."

"But the baby she was carrying when she was killed, you were the father?" Wynne asked.

"Yes. Her exact words were, 'This one is yours.'"

* * *

The trip back to Richmond seemed endless to Brendan as he drove. For a long time, Wynne said nothing as he stared out the window.

"Just for the record," Brendan finally broke the silence, "I was opposed to this. Jim was the instigator."

"I know." Wynne looked over at him and smiled.

"Everyone in both families has always said you looked like Anne, not Ed. Did that ever make you wonder?"

"About who my father was? No. I didn't know she was having affairs in New York, and obviously Neal couldn't have been my father."

"I'm sorry that Jim talked Ed into telling you."

Wynne shrugged. "At this point, it doesn't matter. In fact, nothing matters right now. The State of Virginia is going to kill my father. It's too bad that one of his affairs didn't produce a half-brother or sister for me."

Brendan gave him an ironic smile. "I never thought of that."

They drove in silence until Wynne suddenly said, "What do you know about Claire and Jeff Ryder?"

Brendan was startled. "Claire and Jeff? They met in law school. They've always been friends, but nothing else."

"Are you sure? He stayed all night with her in the hospital. That seems like more than friendship."

"I don't think so. He stayed with her the night after she found out about Paul Curtis' engagement because she was so upset that he didn't think she should be alone. That news hit her very hard. He talked her into coming back to New York the next day and then transferring to Warrick, Thompson's New York office. She's told you about how much Paul hurt her, hasn't she?"

"She has. But she didn't mention that she turned to Jeff."

"Why are you asking now?"

"I think because everything that I thought was true has turned out to be a lie. My mother didn't love the man I thought

257

was my father. But he loved her. I love Claire. But what if she is in love with Jeff Ryder and not me?"

"I think you're reading way too much into all this," Brendan said.

"But you'd tell me, wouldn't you? If you knew there was something between Jeff and Claire?"

Would I? I don't know. That would be for Claire to tell him. But I don't know of anything.

"I have no reason to think there is. But Claire doesn't confide in me. I do know Tyndall is very partial to Jeff."

"As in he wishes she'd picked him instead of me?"

"You'd have to ask Tyndall."

* * *

"How did Wynne take the news?" Emma asked that night as they sat in front of the fire with their after-dinner drinks.

"About as well as can be expected. Nothing will shake his loyalty to Ed."

"I'm glad," Emma said. "I've never known Father Jim to put a foot wrong, but now he has."

"Agreed," Brendan nodded. "The news didn't damage his relationship with Ed, but it's caused him to doubt Claire."

"Claire?"

"He asked me on the way back about her relationship with Jeff. He stayed the night at the hospital with her the other night."

"Well, that was just good judgment," Emma said. "She was hurt, and she shouldn't have been alone. Hospitals make mistakes at night."

"I know. But he said, 'What if she's in love with him and not me?' And I made the mistake of telling him that Tyndall is partial to Jeff."

Emma shrugged. "I'm not sure you were telling him anything he didn't already know or couldn't have seen for himself. Tyndall brought Jeff to New York, and they work together."

"True, but Claire instigated that."

"It was only to help a friend," Emma said. "I'd do the same for any of my friends from med school if they were out of work and being treated unfairly."

Brendan put his empty glass on the coffee table, and said, "Only one tonight. I'm tired."

"Good." Emma kissed his cheek. "Let's go to bed."

PART III

CLAIRE

"Time for you and time for me, and time yet
for a hundred indecisions"

T.S. Eliot

CHAPTER TWENTY-NINE

Tuesday, February 14, 2017, Claire's Apartment, 100 11ᵗʰ Avenue, Chelsea, New York

"Why didn't you tell me?" Wynne demanded over dinner at Claire's apartment. He had arrived on the last train from Richmond, and Claire could see at once that he was too exhausted and depressed to go out for dinner. She hated to cook, but she'd hailed a taxi and taken him straight home where she'd made a couple of wobbly omeletes and opened a good bottle of California cabernet to make up for the so-so food.

"Because we all thought the news should come from Ed—he was right. We wanted him to be wrong."

"But he wasn't!" Wynne tossed back a half a glass of wine, and Claire reflected that at this rate of alcohol consumption, he'd be asleep before long. And she'd be glad of that. He was edgy, and she was in no mood for a fight.

"Does it matter?"

"Does what matter?"

"That you do not share Ed's DNA."

"No, of course not. But I'm glad that ridiculous priest said he wouldn't marry us. I never want to see him again." Wynne polished off his wine and poured more.

Claire studied him as he chugged it down. As a rule, he wasn't a big drinker. And he hadn't even asked her how she was feeling since he'd gotten off the train. Normally, he was always concerned about her and very attentive. She took a deep breath and asked, "What else is wrong?"

His eyes met hers sharply. "Tell me about you and Jeff Ryder."

"Jeff? There's nothing to tell, other than what I've told you already. We were classmates in law school. We both went to work in San Diego. Alan Warrick treated him very unfairly last year, and my father hired him at Craig, Lewis because he's a good lawyer, and he deserved much better."

"What about the night you found out about Paul Curtis' engagement?"

"I flew back to San Diego and called Jeff. He is and was my best friend. That's all."

"Are you sure?"

"Why are you suddenly cross-examining me about my friendship with Jeff?"

Wynne was wearing his dark suit pants and a white shirt. He'd taken off his suit jacket and hung it over one of the empty chairs when they'd sat down in Claire's dining room. He leaned over and took his cell phone out of the inner pocket of his jacket. He unlocked the screen, scrolled to his text messages, and when he found the one he was looking for, he handed the phone to Claire.

"Take a look at this. I received it while I was on the train coming back from Richmond."

Claire looked down at the screen and read:

Your mother was a whore. And so is she. I watched them both with their lovers. She was sleeping with someone while you were gone. Don't make the mistake your father did. Don't marry a whore and spend your life in prison. Love, Aunt Allison

She laid the phone on the table and said calmly, "Jeff was here on Sunday night. And he stayed over. In the guest room. It's not the first time. He slept on the couch in my condo in San Diego last year when he realized that I was in shock over Paul's news. He didn't think I should be alone that night, and he didn't think I should be alone on Sunday night, either."

"Why did he think you shouldn't be alone? Do you share secrets with him that you don't share with me?

Claire sipped her wine thoughtfully for a second or two, trying to decide why he was so suddenly and unexpectedly jealous. Her wrist was throbbing in the cast, and she wished she could just go to bed, go to sleep, and avoid being cross-examined about Jeff. Finally, she said, "Jeff was here on Sunday to warn me that he'd gone back over the surveillance video from the subway, and he thinks Allison Byrd was the one who pushed me off the platform."

"But he doesn't know what she looks like."

"Yes, he does. He found her mugshot when she was arrested for stalking down at the plantation. And he saw a close-up of the person who pushed me on camera three, and he said that person looked like the mugshot."

Wynne looked down at his phone again and then back at Claire. She could see that his attitude toward Jeff was softening. "He could be right. And this message means she's watching your apartment. I remember she wanted me to call her 'Aunt Allison' when I was little, and that upset my father."

"I didn't think she could get into this building," Claire said.

"Well, it looks like you're wrong. She not only got in, she saw Jeff coming and going last weekend."

Claire shivered at the thought of Allison watching her front door.

Wynne got up and draped his coat around her shoulders. "Here, you're cold."

"No, I'm not. But the idea of Allison Byrd in that hallway out there makes my skin crawl."

"Mine, too. It's not a good idea for you to stay here."

Claire looked out at her spectacular view of the river and the city and sighed. "I guess you're right."

He reached out and took her hand. "You should go to your father's until we're sure you're safe. I would rather have the two of us stay at my place, but I've got to go back to Richmond tomorrow."

"Tomorrow? But you just got back."

"I came to see you," he smiled, "because it's Valentine's Day. But I haven't had time to buy you a present."

"Doesn't matter." She smiled and squeezed his hand. "Why are you going back?

"I've upped my offer of campaign contributions to Governor Reynolds so that he'll commute Dad's sentence to life. That would give me more time to finally prove he's innocent. The governor has realized that he's facing challenges in the primaries for that Senate seat from some strong candidates. Suddenly, he's willing to talk."

"Does that mean I'll be going to Belle Grove by myself on Friday to make the final arrangements with Michelle for the wedding?"

"It might." He let go of her hand and poured the last of the wine into their glasses. "Ask your father to go with you if I can't make it."

She sipped her wine but said nothing.

"What's wrong?"

"I feel as if you should be with me on Friday."

"I should," he agreed, "but I also should be negotiating with Reynolds to save Dad."

Claire looked out at the lights shining on the river. She said, "We're apart now more than we're together."

"I know." His tone was matter of fact.

"And we never laugh anymore."

"I know."

They sat in silence, studying the view. Finally, Wynne's blue eyes came back to hers. He said, "Please don't call off the wedding. Please."

"I just keep wondering if we'll ever get back to the way things were when we were in Paris. We could smile then. And laugh."

"Is that what you and Jeff were doing on Sunday night?"

"I told him I felt guilty."

"I didn't mean to do this to you," Wynne said.

"I know. Listen, there is something else I talked to Jeff about."

"What?"

"The only way this will get better is to prove Allison killed your mother. Since she's in New York, we have a shot at getting a DNA sample."

"True, but how?"

"Jeff and I talked to Marvin Silverman."

"Jeff talked to Marvin, too?"

"I've asked Jeff to help me prove that your father is innocent. He's a former prosecutor, Wynne, and a really good criminal lawyer. We need his help."

"So what did Marvin say?"

"He said he would see if he could find where Allison is staying in New York and try to finagle a DNA sample. I was thinking that we should show Marvin this text message. It might help him figure out her location."

"You'd need cell tower information for that," Wynne said.

"Right," Claire agreed, "and Marvin could get it for us."

They cleared away the few dishes together and got into bed. Wynne put his arms around her and said, "I'm sorry jealousy got the better of me."

Claire smiled at him in the dark. "I know what a hard time this is for you right now."

"Brendan has managed to keep Dad alive all these years. I thought that would never change."

"I know."

"I can't imagine life without him. I can't imagine waking up on March 4 and knowing he's gone."

"I know." Claire hugged him.

"I wish that priest hadn't put all that confession stuff into Dad's head."

"I wish he hadn't, either."

"Do you see the irony in all this? Edward Wynne Carter IV is a Fairfax and not a Carter, and he's moving heaven and earth to save a Carter?"

"I think you are a Carter," Claire said. "You are whoever you think you are. And nothing can change the bond between you and Ed."

Claire lay still, listening to Wynne's breathing become regular. Wine, travel, and emotion had taken their toll. He was asleep. But Claire lay awake in the dark, wondering if Allison Byrd was, at that moment, outside in the hall. And remembering what Paige Caldwell Marshall had said. *"The Carter scandal has never done anything but destroy the lives it has touched. Don't let it destroy yours, too."*

CHAPTER THIRTY

Wednesday, February 15, 2017, Claire's Apartment, 100 11ᵗʰ Avenue, Chelsea, New York

The alarm woke Claire at six. She rolled over and used her cast to hit the off button and realized that Wynne was already in the shower. It was still dark outside and would be for another hour. She was tempted to go back to sleep.

But at that moment, he emerged from the bathroom, wrapped in a towel. He leaned over and kissed her. "I didn't mean to wake you up."

"You didn't. The alarm did."

"Go back to sleep. You don't have to be at the office this morning."

He's right. I don't have to be there. But I miss being there. I miss knowing my clients need my help. I don't like this leave of absence. I miss my life before I got involved in all of this. "Are you on the early train?"

"Yes. I was tempted to take the company jet this time. I'm tired of that long train ride."

"Why didn't you?"

"Couldn't get a flight time out of La Guardia where the plane is. Would have had to have it flown to Teterboro. Just too complicated all around."

"Do you see Reynolds today?"

"No, at eight a.m. tomorrow."

"Are you staying with Brendan and Emma?"

"Yes. Brendan is going with me to talk to the governor."

"That's good."

"You know, Claire, I'm worried neither he nor Dad are going to survive this."

"I am, too."

She watched him dress and put his belongings in his small travel bag. He was thin to begin with, but he'd grown thinner in the last month.

He felt her watching him and looked over and smiled. "What are you thinking?"

"That you're too skinny."

"I've been skinny all my life. That's why I couldn't get any girls."

She smiled back. "Well, you have one now."

He leaned over and kissed her. "I do. And I'm glad. Tell you what. We'll go to Paris in April for the whole month. French food will fatten me up."

He means well. But I want to go back to work. I can't leave my clients forever, or I won't have any to go back to. But this wasn't the time to tell him. She yawned and stretched as she put her feet on the floor and pulled on her robe. "I'll go get the paper."

She padded down the hall in her bare feet and crossed her living room to the front door. She opened it. But instead of *The*

New York Times, a bloody softball bat was sitting in front of her door.

Terror seized her. She looked up and down the hall but saw no one. She slammed the door and called, "Wynne!"

"What's wrong?"

"You need to see this."

He was already in his suit pants and shirt, but his tie was missing, and he was in his sock feet. "What is it?"

"Look." Claire opened the door again.

"Oh, my God!" Wynne hurried over and looked down at the bat. "Close the door! Allison is probably still out there."

Claire shut the door and leaned against the wall. She closed her eyes for a moment.

Wynne put his arms around her. "Are you okay?"

She nodded. "I'm fine."

"Listen, I'm not leaving until you're safe at Tyndall's. I'll take the later train. Go pack your things while I call the police."

"No," Claire shook her head. "I'll go pack. But don't call the police."

"Why not?"

"Because they'll take that bat, and we won't get to swab it for Allison's DNA. Don't you see? She's been stupid enough to give us exactly what we need: a reference sample. There are some gloves in the bathroom that my cleaning lady uses. While I pack, put them on, and put that bat in a clean, plastic bag. I'll take it to Dr. Vom Saal myself."

"I don't think you should go alone."

"You're probably right. I'll ask Jeff to go with me."

* * *

Wednesday, February 15, 2017, New York University Biology Department, Washington Square, New York, New York

Claire found Dr. Vom Saal's office on the second floor without difficulty at eleven a.m. She had called ahead to let him know she and Jeff were coming.

"I see why you didn't call the police," Jeff said when he met her at her father's apartment. "But you're taking a risk."

"All of this is a risk," she said as she handed him the plastic bag. "So much so, that I've stopped thinking about risk at this point. Let's go find a cab."

Dr. Vom Saal welcomed them into his office, strewn with papers and scientific journals. He was a short, slight man in his early fifties, with kind, brown eyes and gray hair that he allowed to grow slightly below his ears. He was wearing a plaid shirt and blue jeans. *He looks like a scientist,* Claire thought.

He called in one of his research assistants to take the bat before they sat down. The assistant was in his mid-twenties, also in jeans and a plaid shirt. Dr. Vom Saal sent him off with instructions to test the bat for DNA.

Dr. Vom Saal sat down at his desk and motioned for Claire and Jeff to take the chairs in front. She had already explained how they had made their grisly discovery that morning when she telephoned to say they were bringing it to his office.

"I'm thinking that's animal blood," he said, "but if it's human, we'll have to notify the police. And you haven't put yourself in the best position if that turns out to be the case."

"I realize that," Claire said. "But it would take the police a long time to process it. And we don't have time to wait."

"You're expecting us to find a single female profile?"

"Yes."

"But how can we connect it to this woman whom you suspect killed Wynne's mother?"

"Her profile should be in the FBI's CODIS database," Claire said. "She was arrested for stalking in Virginia last year. Virginia takes DNA samples even from misdemeanor stalkers."

Dr. Vom Saal nodded. "That's good to know. I hope we find what you're looking for."

"When will you have an answer?" Jeff asked.

"We're giving it priority, of course. I'm hoping by this time tomorrow. Should I call you or Wynne with the results?" Dr. Vom Saal asked Claire.

"Call me," Claire said. "Wynne's in negotiations with the Governor of Virginia tomorrow, trying to get Ed's sentence commuted to life. His phone will be off while he's in those meetings." She handed him her business card with her telephone number.

"All right," Dr. Vom Saal agreed as he stood up, indicating the meeting was over. "I'll call you the minute I know anything."

* * *

Wednesday, February 15, 2017, Café Espresso, Greenwich Village, New York, New York

"You look like you need to go skating in Bryant Park," Jeff said as they left the Biology Building. The cold, crisp winter air made Claire think about what it would be like to glide around the ice in the bright midday sun.

"I do," she smiled. "But I can't right now. I need to get in touch with the private investigator."

"Marvin?"

"Yes."

"Something else has happened? Besides the bat?"

"Yes."

"Feel like telling me?"

"I would love to tell you."

"Let's go for coffee, then. Café Espresso is two blocks away."

Claire chose a table by the window while Jeff fetched lattes for them. She watched the people go by on the sidewalk until he returned with their coffee.

"Here."

"Thanks." She smiled at him as he took the seat opposite.

He put a paper sleeve that contained a gigantic chocolate chip cookie on the table between them. "Lunch. To share." He took a sip of his coffee and went on, "So what's going on besides some lunatic leaving a replica of a murder weapon at your door?"

"The lunatic has sent a text to Wynne. Read this." She handed him her phone with the message that Wynne had forwarded to her.

Jeff's eyes darkened as he read. When he finished, he handed the phone back to Claire. "So this Allison character was in your building last weekend, too?"

"Your hunch that she took my purse was accurate. That told her where I lived, and she's been spying on me ever since."

"The way she spied on the Carter house before Ed's wife was killed."

"Exactly."

Jeff sipped his coffee and broke off a piece of cookie and munched it thoughtfully. "Well, I'm glad you're at your father's place for now. The security is better in that building."

"True."

"I'm going to show the people at the security desk that mugshot so they'll know what that Byrd character looks like."

"Thanks, that's a good idea."

"So what do you need Marvin for now that you've got the bat and Dr. Vom Saal is testing it?"

"I wanted to see if he could give us some idea of where Allison Byrd was when she sent this text to Wynne."

"You don't need Marvin for that. It's obvious she's been hiding out somewhere in your building."

Claire broke off a piece of cookie. "Nice lunch, by the way. Reminds me of those meals we shared last year in San Diego."

"You mean when I was starving, and you footed the bill for those amazing dinners?"

"Well, now you're returning the favor."

"One cookie is not the equivalent of dinner at the Italian Kitchen in La Jolla."

She smiled. "I see your point. About the cookie and about Marvin. All he could do would be to confirm what we already know."

"Was Wynne upset by the message?"

"Of course. He started asking me questions about you."

"And you told him what?"

"The truth. That you're my closest friend."

"And he said?"

"Eventually he apologized for being jealous."

"He's going through a difficult time."

"He is. But you don't have to worry about the maid of honor thing anymore. Ellen has let you off the hook."

Jeff smiled. "Good news." But he immediately became serious again. "You have to tell your father now about what's going on. And about who tried to push you off the subway platform."

She sighed. "I know. I thought of that this morning when I was taking my suitcase up to his apartment. And he'll have to go to Belle Grove with me on Friday to make the final wedding arrangements."

"Because Wynne will still be talking to the governor?"

"He thought it might take that long to get an agreement. And then he'll go straight down to Sussex to see Ed."

"How are you getting to Belle Grove?"

"We'll fly to D.C. on Friday morning and rent a car and drive down."

"But Tyndall, at this moment, does not know he's going with you?"

"No. He doesn't know I've moved back home, either."

"I've got a meeting with him in half an hour. Come with me, so you can tell him everything. Oh, and the last bite of cookie is yours."

She smiled and took the last piece. "Thanks. It will actually be easier to tell him what's been going on with you there."

"Why?"

"He gets so emotional about me because I'm all he has. You're good at getting him to be logical."

"I'm glad he listens to me. But there's one more thing I think I should do."

"What's that?"

"Go with you and Tyndall on Friday."

"Why?"

"Because the two of you will be focused on making the final wedding plans. I can devote my undivided attention to watching out for Byrd or anyone else who seems to be suspicious."

"My father will be thrilled to have you." *And so will I.*

CHAPTER THIRTY-ONE

Thursday, February 16, 2017, Tyndall Chastain's Apartment, Fifth Avenue, New York, New York

"I'm sorry," Dr. Vom Saal said when he phoned Claire at noon the next day, "we didn't find a profile on the bat. And the blood is chicken blood."

"Are you sure?" Claire stared out at Central Park from her bedroom window.

"Very sure."

"But how can that be true?"

"Probably wearing gloves," Dr. Vom Saal said.

"I see."

"We'll run it through one more layer of analysis, but we're not optimistic."

Since Wynne, at that moment, was tied up in negotiations with the governor of Virginia, she phoned Jeff at his office.

"Dr. Vom Saal couldn't find a profile," she told him.

"How disappointing."

"I was already drafting a habeas writ in my head."

"I know. Listen, maybe connecting Allison Byrd to the

murder weapon isn't the way to go."

"What do you mean?"

"You're running out of time, and getting a sample from her seems less and less likely."

"So?"

"You need to find someone who can say Ed wasn't there when his wife was killed."

"True. But I have no idea how to find someone who could say that wasn't Ed's Volvo parked at the Carter house that night."

"I'd walk the block if I were you the next time you're in Richmond. Talk to the neighbors. See if any of them remember anything."

"Maybe you'd go with me tomorrow after we come back from Belle Grove?"

"Of course, I will."

* * *

Friday, February 17, 2017, Bell Grove Plantation, Port Conway, Virginia

"It makes me think of Julia," Tyndall said as they turned into the circle in front of the plantation at one o'clock the next day. "Elegant and beautiful."

Jeff parked the rental car, and the three of them crossed the gravel lot to the front door. Michelle welcomed them into the front hall.

"I bet you haven't had lunch," she said. "There's tea and coffee and sandwiches in the parlor."

Claire sat next to her father on one of the gold velvet settees, and Michelle and Jeff occupied the other. Michelle poured tea or coffee for everyone and passed the plate of sandwiches. Claire wasn't hungry, but she took two to be polite. She noticed that Jeff piled his plate high. She was glad someone was there to show appreciation for Michelle's hospitality.

"So everything is arranged for you next Friday," Michelle smiled at Tyndall and Claire. "Tamara will be here to conduct the ceremony at eleven, and then we'll have lunch in the dining room for twenty guests. Do you know if all twenty are coming?"

Claire's mind went blank. "Honestly, I've been so busy with other things, I haven't checked the RSVPs."

"That's okay," Michelle was unperturbed. "If you find you have fewer, just give me a call. Here's the proposed menu." She handed all three of them a printed card.

Claire looked down at the card, but the letters swam before her eyes. She felt Jeff watching her. *He knows I'm not focusing on this.*

Tyndall nodded and handed the card back to Michelle. "Looks fine to me. Claire?"

"Delicious." She handed hers back, too.

"I should take you through the upstairs rooms," she said, "so you can decide who will be where to dress for the ceremony."

Jeff set his cup on the sofa table and said, "While you do that, I would like to take a walk around the grounds."

"Of course," Michelle said. "I'll show you the way outside."

"No need. The back door is opposite the front door. I saw that when I came in."

* * *

It took Claire and her father about thirty minutes to wander through all the suites, upstairs and down. The Turner Suite was the last on their tour, and Tyndall lingered, studying Carrie Turner's etching on the glass. Claire watched him touch the writing with one finger as if to make sure it was real.

"So she's one of Julia's ancestors?"

"Yes," Claire said. "I haven't had time to work out the exact connection."

"And this was to commemorate her engagement?"

"Yes, but she didn't marry him."

Tyndall turned from the window and studied her closely for a moment. She knew what he was about to say and didn't want to hear it. Fortunately, Michelle appeared in the doorway.

"Do you have any questions or need any help?"

"No," Claire smiled, "we've figured out where everyone will dress. Since it's informal, no one needs much space." She'd decided to forgo the formal Vera Wang gown in favor of one of her mother's vintage Givenchy suits. The white suit seemed more appropriate for a small wedding in the library, and the suit jacket would do a better job of hiding her cast.

She glanced through the windows and saw Jeff standing on the lawn, studying the river. Suddenly she wanted to escape her father's doubts about her future with Wynne. She said, "I'm going to go outside for a few minutes while you and Michelle settle the last details."

She hurried downstairs and grabbed her mother's black Dior overcoat that she'd left in the parlor. She slipped it on and walked back into the hall. She opened the back door, crossed the porch, and hurried down the steps to the lawn.

"Jeff!"

He turned and smiled as she crossed the grass to reach him. "What are you doing out here?" he asked. "It's cold."

"You looked lonely standing here staring at the river," she said.

"Well, I'm not lonely now."

"What do you think of Belle Grove?"

"It's a beautiful place for a wedding. Now I'm sorry that Ellen has replaced me as maid of honor."

She laughed.

"I'm glad I can still make you do that."

"Me, too."

He had the same expression in his eyes that her father had; but she knew he wouldn't ask her again about her doubts. *Everyone has doubts before a wedding. It's normal.*

"I'm glad I came out for a look around," he said, "because I've found something we're going to want to take back to Dr. Vom Saal. Maybe we still have a shot at a DNA profile."

Claire felt a sudden rush of joy. "Really? Are you sure?"

"Come and see."

He took her hand and led her across the lawn toward the dilapidated outbuildings across from the side of the main house. He stopped in front of a rectangular building that had two doors, one in each half of the building.

"This is the old Summer Kitchen," Claire said. "Michelle is trying to raise money to restore it."

"Well, it looks as if someone's been staying in part of it."

"Are you sure?"

"Yes, although I don't know when."

Jeff led her through one of doors into the bare interior. When Claire's eyes adjusted to the lower light, she saw discarded cans of soup and chili in one corner and some dirty bedding.

"Anything that identifies who's been here?"

"No, but there's always the possibility that it was Allison Byrd. I thought you'd want to take some of this back to New York for Dr. Vom Saal to test."

Claire nodded. "It fits her profile of being a stalker. She was told to stay away from the plantation."

"And she's doing her best to watch the places where you and Wynne are going to be. Vera Wang, your apartment, and the place you're going to be married."

"Well, we know she's in New York now," Claire said. "Because she's been in my apartment building."

"Agreed. This stuff doesn't look recent."

"We should go inside and tell Michelle and get a clean bag to put it in. And we're still going to see if we can find any neighbors on Grove Avenue who remember anything about that night before we go back to New York."

"This looks like a promising find," Jeff said. "I think our luck is changing. We're going to find a neighbor with a memory, too."

"I hope so for Wynne's sake."

"And for yours," Jeff said and squeezed her hand gently.

* * *

It was close to five o'clock when they returned to the Murphys'. Tyndall had decided to fly back to New York that night, so Claire had given him the additional items for Dr. Vom Saal. She snuggled into her bed at eleven o'clock, hoping that she and Jeff would find someone in the Carters' old neighborhood whose memory extended back to the night of Anne's death.

CHAPTER THIRTY-TWO

Saturday, February 18, 2017, corner of Grove and North Davis Avenue, The Fan District, Richmond, Virginia

Jeff parked the Murphys' Range Rover on North Davis Avenue at the corner where it intersected with Grove at ten o'clock the next morning. Claire slipped out of the passenger's door and hurried to the corner to gaze up at 2425 Grove Avenue. She wrapped her coat around her tightly. The sun was out, but it was cold. She could hear Jeff's footsteps behind her.

"Is this it?" he asked when he reached the spot where she was standing.

"Yes. This is the house Anne was restoring when she died."

Claire gazed up at the two-story brick house with the wide, white porch gleaming in the mid-morning winter sun. There were two white wicker armchairs on either side of the front door. To the left were bay windows upstairs and down.

Claire pointed at the upper window. "That was Ed and Anne's bedroom."

"So Allison Byrd stood where we're standing to watch the house?"

"No," Claire shook her head. "Over there on Davis. There's a window on the side that was in their bedroom, too."

"Oh, I see," Jeff agreed. "She stood across the street on Davis and looked up at that window on the side up there."

He pointed, and Claire nodded. "She stood under that street light, right there on the corner."

Jeff looked back at the house again. "Do you know who lives here now?"

"A family purchased it a couple of years ago. Hastings, I think is their name. It was a rental for a long time after the murder. Someone bought it for a song and divided it into apartments."

"Wish we could go inside and take a look," Jeff said.

Claire shrugged. "It wouldn't hurt to ask. Come on."

A woman with a pleasant face, dark hair, and striking blue eyes, answered the door. She was wearing a simple black dress with a blue scarf around her neck. Her eyes and hair made Claire think of Anne. "I'm Claire Chastain, and this is Jeff Ryder," Claire told her. "We are attorneys looking for information about the Carters who used to live here back in 1983."

"I'm Frances Hastings," she said. "I'm afraid I don't know anything about the Carters. My husband and I bought the house from Tom and Louise Finch."

"Would you mind if we just walked through the house?" Claire asked. "We might see something that would help us."

Frances sized them up carefully before she said, "Well, I suppose it would be all right for the two of you to come in for a few minutes. My husband has taken the children to the park, so I can show you the upstairs, too."

They followed Frances through the parlor to their right, into the dining room behind it, and into the modern, gleaming kitchen. The house was furnished in a mixture of Victorian and eighteenth century antiques. Claire imagined that Anne would have approved.

From the kitchen, they headed up the backstairs to the second floor.

"This isn't the original master suite," Frances said as she opened a door that led toward the back of the house. "My husband and I had the area that was once the rear apartment redesigned for us."

"Where is the original master suite?" Jeff asked.

"This way."

They followed her to the front of the house where she opened a door on the left. "In here."

They entered an enormous children's playroom full of miniature furniture and lined with bookshelves full of toys. The bay window that overlooked Grove Avenue had a specially built window seat littered with books and stuffed animals.

Frances smiled. "I'm afraid this room is never neat. But my little boys have fun here."

"How many do you have?" Claire asked, thinking of Wynne.

"Three. Two, four, and six. They're a handful."

Jeff had wandered over to the window that overlooked Davis Avenue. Claire watched Frances' eyes follow him as he looked out.

"You know," she said softly after a minute or two of watching Jeff, "there is something that happened when we first moved in that you might be interested in."

Jeff turned from the window. "What?"

"A woman used to stand out there under the streetlight at night and stare up at that window. It was creepy."

Claire tried to keep her voice calm although she was excited by the news. "Do you know what she looked like?"

"Yes, as a matter of fact, I have a picture in a file downstairs. We kept it in case she came back. I'll give you a copy."

"Thanks," Claire smiled. "Did you get a name, too?"

"Byrd," Frances said. "I'm not sure of the first name. It started with 'A.'"

"Allison?" Claire asked.

"That sounds right. I wrote it down on the pictures of her that my husband took."

"Does she still come around?" Jeff asked.

"No. My husband went down there one night after we'd been here two months, and we'd seen her staring at our window most nights. He told her to leave and not come back. She told him a crazy story. She said that his wife, Anne, was having an affair. She called him 'Ed' and said she knew that he was really in love with her. She begged him to get rid of Anne and marry her."

"What did you do?" she asked.

"My husband called the police. We stood up here and saw them talking to her. I don't know what they said, but she never came back. It was unnerving while it lasted. We hadn't converted this room for the boys yet, and we were sleeping in here. It felt like an invasion of our privacy to have someone watching our bedroom window all night."

"Thank you," Claire said. "You've been a great help."

"You're thinking this Allison woman had something to do with that old murder, aren't you?"

"We are," Jeff told her.

"Well, I wouldn't be surprised. The police who came out that night told us to increase our security because she seemed mentally unstable. Let me get that picture for you. And if you need any more help from me or my husband, we'd be glad to give it to you. I don't doubt that she could have killed Anne Carter."

* * *

The eleven o'clock sun was slightly warmer as they resumed their walk down Grove Avenue, but the air was still crisp and cold. Claire linked her arm through Jeff's, and he smiled at her. "Don't worry."

"Does it show?"

"It shows." He took her hand for a moment and gave it a little squeeze. "You said you were going to get Ed and Wynne a miracle. You're getting closer."

They went house to house, knocking, explaining, and thanking everyone who answered the door. But no one knew anything about the Carter murder. At the very end of the street, an elderly lady said she remembered the police cars and the ambulance that had come that morning to take away the body. But 2425 was at the far end of the street, and she had not known Ed or Anne.

So they worked their way down the other side until they came to the house directly opposite 2425 where J. Adam Winston, III had lived. They knocked, and a pleasant-faced man who appeared to be in his early thirties answered the door and said his name was John Winston.

Claire introduced herself and Jeff, and explained their mission.

John frowned slightly. "My father is eighty-one. His arthritis has him in a wheelchair. I'll ask him if he's willing to talk to you."

As they waited, Claire studied the view of 2425 across the street. Jeff watched her focus on the Grove and Davis intersection.

"The Winstons had a good view of the front of the Carter house and of Allison watching the bedroom window from Davis," he observed.

Claire nodded. "I was wishing we'd find something to undermine Adam Winston's claim about the Volvo, but he could see it."

"If it was there." Jeff smiled.

John Winston appeared at that moment and opened the door for them to come in. "My father said he would talk to you."

He led them down a long, narrow hall, identical to the hall at 2425. The floor plan was the same, staircase to the left, dining room, kitchen, and parlor to the right. But this house had a master bedroom with a sitting room downstairs at the very end of the hall.

"Since Dad can't go upstairs anymore, I had the back of the house remodeled for him a few years ago," John said.

Adam Winston was sitting in his wheelchair by the fire. The mahogany side table next to him held a coffee cup and the *New York Times*, *Washington Post*, and *Wall Street Journal*. He reminded Claire of Ed because he had a full head of white hair and wore the same rimless spectacles. He looked very distinguished in a small, gray, checked shirt, dark slacks, and black cardigan sweater.

He motioned for Claire and Jeff to take seats on the sofa opposite his chair. Claire was on the side by the fireplace and the warmth felt good.

"My son says you're looking for information about the Carters who used to live across the street?"

"Yes, I'm engaged to Wynne," Claire said. "Ed is going to be executed in thirteen days unless we can find a way to stop it."

"I'm sorry to hear that. Wynne was such a well-behaved little boy. Both of his parents loved him, but I remember seeing him with Ed the most. There was something really special about that relationship."

"It would help if you could tell us what you saw the night that Anne was killed," Jeff spoke up.

"She was such a sweet, talented woman. I used to hear her practicing her violin. Such beautiful music. When I found out how she died, it hurt me for a long time."

"Did you know her well?"

"Me? Not really. My wife, Marion, talked to her all the time. Marion was renovating this house, and Anne was working on theirs. Sometimes we used the same people."

"Did you ever use William James Miller?" Claire asked.

"Who?" Adam frowned.

"The man who claimed he was paid to kill Anne and then recanted."

"Oh, yes. I remember all that. He laid tile, I think. It seems like he did a bathroom for us, and Marion recommended him to Anne. But I'm not sure."

"Could we ask your wife what she remembers?" Jeff asked.

"I'm afraid not," Adam shook his head. "She passed away five years ago."

"We're sorry," Claire said.

"I'm surprised I'm still here. That was the other thing about what happened across the street. Anne was only thirty-three. She had her whole life ahead of her."

"What do you remember seeing on the night she was killed?" Claire asked.

"I heard a car door close around one a.m., and I looked out and saw a man get out of a white Volvo station wagon and go into the Carters' house."

"Where were you when you saw him?" Jeff asked.

"Upstairs. Our bedroom had a sitting room on the front of the house. It had a good view of the street and the Grove and Davis intersection. That's where I used to see Ed with that tall girl under the streetlight at all hours of the night. I had trouble sleeping so I used to work late at my desk in front of the window."

"Did you see him with that girl that night?" Claire asked.

"No, I didn't."

"I think you testified that the car you saw was Ed's?"

"Yes, it was."

"Could you see a license plate? Is that how you knew?"

"No, I couldn't see the plate."

"What about the height and build of the person who got out of the car?"

"The man was Ed's height, and very fit like Ed."

"How did he get into the house? Did he use his key?"

"That, I didn't see. I assumed it was Ed."

"So you were never sure the man you saw was Ed Carter," Jeff asked.

"No, I wouldn't say that. There was never another white Volvo wagon in front of that house except his."

"What kind of car did Anne drive?" Claire asked.

"She had some sort of Volkswagen with a hatchback. A Rabbit or a Golf. Blue."

"Did you see it parked in front that night?"

"No, she always parked on Davis and not in front of the house."

"What happened after the man in the Volvo went inside?" Jeff asked.

"Nothing for a while."

"How long a while?"

"I would say twenty-minutes. Maybe a half-hour. I thought Ed had come home early from his out-of-town conference and had gone to bed."

"What did you hear after that?" Jeff asked.

"Nothing. I went to bed and went to sleep. Then about thirty minutes later, squealing car tires and the sound of an engine being gunned out front woke me up."

"Did you look out and see the car leave?"

"No, by the time I got to the window it was gone. I figured Ed and Anne had fought again, and he was going to find a bar and have a few drinks to calm himself down before he came back."

"Did you hear them arguing?"

"Not that night. It was cold so we all had our windows closed."

"And you're sure it was Ed?" Claire asked.

Adam gave her a sad smile. "I'm so sorry to tell you this; but yes, I am sure. It was Ed's Volvo, and it was Ed."

* * *

Jeff drove the Range Rover to Sugar and Twine in Careytown, twelve minutes away from Grove and Davis. Claire glanced up at the marquis of the movie theater as they walked to the coffee shop and wished life were normal enough for popcorn and a movie.

Jeff pointed to a table by the window and said, "Have a seat, and I'll bring back coffee and lunch."

Claire smiled. "Okay." She pulled out her phone as she waited for Jeff and called Wynne, who had gone to Sussex to tell Ed that Governor Reynolds had not agreed to a deal to commute his sentence to life.

But Wynne didn't answer. So she studied Jeff as he negotiated his purchase at the counter. He wasn't thin anymore. He worked out regularly at the firm's gym, and his striking blue eyes were relaxed and happy as he talked to the clerk about the menu.

Our timing was always off, Claire thought.

He returned with a tray containing two lattes, a turkey sandwich, and a pastry with what looked like raspberry jam in the center and two plates.

"Looks amazing," she said.

"The girl at the register promised me you'd be impressed. I figured we'd split everything except coffee."

"Perfect."

They settled into the food, and Claire was surprised to realize that she had actually been hungry.

"You're eating," Jeff smiled. "That's a good thing."

"I always eat."

"No, you don't. And now you're a bride-to-be. They don't eat."

"Well, I'm eating. I think Brendan should try again for a stay."

"Why?" Jeff frowned.

"Because Allison has to be Anne's killer."

"But we don't have her DNA on the murder weapon."

"But we have other evidence. Blair told us that Allison lied to the dean about having an affair with Ed. And she had a crazy idea that Ed would leave Anne and marry her. She stole her boyfriend's car to follow Ed to Charlottesville that Sunday. And after Ed paid her to leave him and his family alone, she continued to stalk them.

"Michelle said Allison stalked the plantation after she was fired. And Michelle said Allison didn't seem to be all there mentally. There was something off about her.

"And then we have the surveillance tape that proves that she followed me from Vera Wang to the subway station and pushed me off the platform. She sent Wynne that text message, claiming you and I were having an affair. And even if there was no DNA on it, we know who left the bloody bat in front of my apartment door. And now we know that Allison stalked the Hastings' bedroom after they moved in, and she made that crazy remark to Mr. Hastings about 'his wife's' affair. And Frances had no doubt that Allison could have killed Anne. I think all of this is enough to cast doubt on the jury's murder verdict in Ed's case."

With great concentration, Jeff cut the pastry in half and put a piece on her plate.

"Why aren't you saying anything?"

"Because I'm eating dessert." He picked up his half and bit into it.

"That's not the reason. You don't want to tell me you don't agree with me. Why don't we have enough evidence to try again for a stay?"

"Because of the conversation we just had with Adam Winston."

"Explain." Claire nibbled at her share of the raspberry pastry.

"Okay, but you won't like it. Obviously Ed and Anne had a fight between one and one thirty, and Ed left the house in a rush."

"And Allison saw Ed leave because she always watched the house. After he left, she went in and killed Anne."

"She had no way into the house."

"She could have knocked and persuaded Anne to let her in."

"Could have, but she didn't."

"How do you know?" Claire frowned.

"Because her DNA isn't on the bat. Ed's is."

"But she was pregnant with his child."

"But she had the power to take Wynne away from him. Even if Ed could visit his own baby, Wynne would no longer see him as his father."

"And that would have devastated Ed. Oh, God!"

"She must have said something to him that night when he came back from Charlottesville that made him think she was going to leave him."

"I can't believe that. Ed's a gentle soul. He's not capable of killing."

"Except where Wynne's concerned."

Claire stared out at the street, aghast by Jeff's suggestion.

He reached out and put his hand over hers. "Listen, Claire. I know how hard this is for you. But sometimes the truth isn't what you want to hear."

"Brendan said that. When I first started working on Ed's case."

"Those were wise words."

She leaned back in her chair and kept her eyes fixed on the street as they filled with tears that began to overflow. Jeff handed her a napkin, and she dabbed at her eyes. "Sorry."

"Don't be. Brides-to-be cry, too."

"Poor Wynne. He'll be devastated. He's not Ed's son. And Ed killed his mother."

"You don't have to tell him what Adam said," Jeff observed quietly.

Claire wiped her eyes again and gave him a teary smile. "You're right. And maybe Dr. Vom Saal will be able to get Allison's DNA off those cans and find it on the bat."

Jeff squeezed her hand again and smiled. "Maybe."

"And maybe Adam Winston is wrong about whose car was in front of the Carter house that night."

MCKENZIE

"We die to each other daily."

T.S. Eliot

CHAPTER THIRTY-THREE

Sunday, February 19, 2017, Coronado, California

Mckenzie went for a long run that morning on the beach at ten o'clock. She wanted to work out some of the anxiety she felt over Joe Sanders' silence. Ten days since Hugh had told him to give her search for Quinn Fairchild priority, yet no news. What if she was dead?

Breathless, she stopped in front of the Hotel Del Coronado and looked out at the surfers hovering in the water, waiting to catch a wave. One of those black spots was Joel. Work had brought him down for the weekend. Without Jenny. She sensed tension in that relationship. He'd turned his phone off at dinner last night, something he wouldn't have done if there hadn't been some sort of problem between them.

Oddly enough, it made her sad. She'd come to accept the idea of Joel with the talented, fiery Legal Aid lawyer. Someone was going to replace her as Number One in her son's life. It was inevitable. And Jenny, with her compassion and spirit, even if some of her views of the world were too narrow, was a good choice.

She watched the waves and wished she could guess which speck was Joel. Surfing was dangerous. She was glad he didn't do it often.

Why no word from Joe Sanders, she wondered. Nothing, not even an update. She decided to walk up to the Hotel Del and have an espresso on the patio.

She had just settled at a table where she could still see the surfers and had ordered her coffee, when her phone rang. She fished it out of her fanny pack and saw that it was Tyndall. She smiled and clicked the accept button.

"I'm calling to see when you're coming for the wedding," he said. "If you're going to be here on Thursday night, I want you to come to the rehearsal dinner."

"So there's going to be a rehearsal?"

"Not really. There's nothing much to rehearse. I will escort Claire into the library, and then take my seat next to you and Brendan and Emma. They will say their vows, and we'll have lunch in the dining room. But Brendan and Emma are having a dinner on Thursday night at their house for Claire and Wynne and his Aunt Margaret and Tim and Ellen and the grandchildren. And Jeff."

"And Jeff?"

"Claire insisted. The two of them are on their way back from Richmond today. They walked Grove Avenue together yesterday, looking for anyone who might remember the night of Anne's death. I'm glad he's with her. Wynne is preoccupied with Ed."

Mckenzie felt a burst of renewed hope. Maybe Quinn Fairchild would not matter after all. "Did they find anything?"

"Not much. Claire sounded discouraged when she called this morning to say they'd be back tonight."

"How is she after that accident in the subway?"

"I can't even begin to explain," Tyndall said. "It wasn't an accident."

"What?"

"She was pushed. By that crazy woman who killed Anne, Allison Byrd. She's been stalking Claire. She's developed a delusion that Claire has become Anne Carter because she's marrying Wynne. Claire has had to leave her apartment and come stay with me. I'd give anything if she'd call off this wedding and put the Carters behind her. I feel sorry for Wynne, but not sorry enough to risk Claire's life."

Quinn said Allison killed Anne. And Quinn said she was afraid Allison would kill her if she found out she'd slept with Ed. Dear God, Tyndall is right to be worried. Why can't Joe find Quinn?

"I'm taking the red-eye to D.C. on Tuesday night."

"Let me know your flight number, and I'll meet you. Why are you flying the night haul?"

"Because I'm meeting with Senator Lovell and Senator Austin on Wednesday morning. George is trying to persuade her to go ahead with the confirmation vote."

"God, I hate that woman," Tyndall volunteered. "Governor Reynolds was on the verge of commuting Ed's sentence to life, until the good senator stepped in and convinced him his career in politics would be over if he did."

"So no commutation?"

"No. Looks like the Fairfaxes have won the last round. They're moving Ed down to Greensville a week from tomorrow."

"Greensville?"

"The execution chamber is at the Greensville Prison at Jarrat."

"Oh." Mckenzie shivered in the bright, warm sun. "Can't Brendan do anything to stop it?"

"It doesn't look like it. He called me this morning about that little bit of evidence Claire and Jeff found on Saturday. Allison stalked the family that bought the Carter house on Grove Avenue when they first moved in. Neither he nor I think it's enough to change things, but he's going ahead with another request for a stay tomorrow. This is all so horrible, Mac. This isn't the way Julia and I pictured Claire's wedding."

"I know," she sighed.

"I'll be at Dulles on Wednesday morning," Tyndall promised. "I'm so glad you're coming. I need your help to get through this."

And what would you think if you knew the truth? I've been sitting on Ed's alibi for over thirty years.

Guilt overwhelmed her. Mackenzie dialed Joe Sanders.

"I was getting ready to call you," he said.

"I hope you've got good news."

"Mixed."

"Give me the good news first, then."

"I've found her. She's a paralegal. She worked for a couple of firms in Richmond for about ten years, and then she moved up the road to D.C. She worked for King and White's D.C. office, and then she moved to their office in San Francisco. She transferred down here to San Diego and retired from that office five years ago. She's in bad health."

Mckenzie's heart beat faster. "And she's still here?"

"Yes. She's living in an apartment in Pacific Beach."

"Well, that's not bad news. There's a lawyer back in Richmond who needs to talk to her right away to save his client's life. Brendan Murphy. I'll text you his number."

"Here's the bad news: she won't talk to Murphy or anyone else."

"What do you mean?"

"I mean she won't talk to anyone."

"Are you sure?"

"Positive. I contacted her at her apartment and told her you'd sent me to find her. And she was adamant she wouldn't talk. What is all this about anyway?"

"Brendan Murphy has a client on death row in Virginia who will be executed on March 3 if Quinn Fairchild won't verify that he was with her all night on the night his wife was murdered."

"And you know this how?"

"Never mind how. I know."

"So a man's life hangs in the balance, and Quinn won't cooperate. Does she know that the situation is life or death? I mean, I didn't tell her because I didn't know until this moment."

"Probably not."

"Do you want me to go back and tell her?"

Mckenzie thought of Tyndall and of Claire. And above all of Brian and Joel. "No, I should go. Give me her address."

* * *

"What's wrong, Mother?" Joel studied Mckenzie as they walked to her car parked on Ocean Boulevard near the Hotel Del.

"Nothing."

"Your face doesn't look like nothing." Joel stowed his surfboard in the back of her BMW SUV.

Mckenzie took her keys out of her fanny pack and considered what to tell him.

"What if I told you that I committed malpractice thirty-four years ago when I was working for the public defender in Richmond?"

"I'd say you were lying."

"And what if I told you that means I've been sitting on Ed Carter's alibi evidence for over thirty years?"

"Now I know for sure you're lying. You would have told Dad in a heartbeat if you'd had anything at all that would help Ed Carter."

"And what if you're wrong? What if I lied to save my reputation because I thought your father was such a good lawyer that he'd find a way to save Ed without me having to confess my mistake?"

Joel, who was now seated in the passenger seat, looked over at her as she sat behind the wheel. She felt his dark eyes, Brian's eyes, studying her. "I'd ask what you intended to do to make it right."

* * *

They drove back to her cottage on First Street, showered, and changed. Mckenzie was dressed first, in jeans and a gray hoodie. Joel came into the living room five minutes later in jeans and a black sweater.

"You don't look like a lawyer," he observed.

"Good. Then maybe she'll talk to me."

"I'm going with you."

"Don't you think two of us might be intimidating?"

"No. You need backup. And besides, I'm not intimidating," Joel grinned. "I'm charming."

"You've got a point," she smiled. "And I hope you can charm Quinn Fairchild into talking to us."

* * *

Mckenzie was tense as she drove across San Diego to Pacific Beach. She willed herself not to think about how much was riding on this interview. She found a place to park on Feldspar Street. She and Joel got out and walked to 8201 Ocean Terrace. Apartment No. 2 was up a flight of wooden stairs.

"She's got an ocean view if she cranes her neck around this corner of the building," Joel observed as they stood on the small balcony outside the front door, waiting for Quinn to respond to the doorbell.

"I can't believe she's been right under my nose all this time," Mckenzie said. "What's taking her so long to answer?"

"Be patient," Joel said.

After what seemed like an eternity, a heavy-set, middle-aged woman opened the rough wooden door, which was painted bright green. Mckenzie could still see in her face the tough, smart-mouthed young woman whom she had met in Petersburg in 1983. Her dark eyes still looked sad and angry. She was wearing a loose, brightly patterned red dress and an oversized beige cardigan.

"You've got the wrong apartment," she hissed. "Go away. I don't know you."

"We've met," Mckenzie said. "A long time ago in Petersburg."

Quinn's eyes studied her curiously for a few seconds. Then she shrugged, "I think you're lying. But even if you aren't, I don't remember you, and I don't want to talk to you."

She started to close the door, but Joel suddenly thrust his foot across the threshold.

"Wait!"

Quinn's eyes went from Mckenzie's face to Joel's and then to his Nike blocking her threshold. She said slowly, "Who are you?"

"I'm her son. My father was Brian Whitby. He worked on the case my mother has come to see you about. He died trying to help this client, the one we're trying to help now."

"Which client?" Her eyes narrowed suspiciously.

Joel removed his foot from the doorway and said, "Ed Carter. My father was one of his defense attorneys in his second murder trial."

"Were you the ones who sent that private investigator here last week? Saunders? Sanders? Something like that?"

"Yes," Mckenzie agreed. "I needed to find you to talk to you."

"Well, I'm not going to talk about the Ed Carter case. I gave you a statement that day you came to my place in Petersburg. Why are you bothering me now?"

"The tape was lost," Joel lied quickly. Mckenzie felt a burst of gratitude toward her son. "We need a new statement. Ed's going to be executed on March 3 if we don't find some evidence that will show he didn't kill his wife."

Quinn's mouth twitched as if she were considering whether

or not to speak. Suddenly she was lost in a fit of deep, hoarse coughing. "Oh, damn," she wheezed when she could speak. "I've been off my oxygen too long. You can come in for a minute."

Mckenzie stepped in first. The apartment was one large room with a kitchen in one corner, a small table for eating in another, and a sofa and two chairs in front of a television set in another. She could see the entrance to a small bedroom and presumably a bathroom beyond in the fourth corner. The smell of stale cooking grease was overwhelming.

Quinn sat down on the sofa and inserted her nasal cannula. As she and Joel took the chairs opposite, Mckenzie thought of the tough-girl way Quinn had smoked that cigarette in that tiny shack in Petersburg.

Quinn studied Mckenzie's face for what felt like a long time. Finally, she said, "I remember you now. You were working for the public defender. You were just out of law school, and you had no idea what you were doing."

Mckenzie flinched under her accurate appraisal. "Well, all that's changed in thirty years. Right now, I need to get that statement again from you."

"What statement?"

"The one you gave me about sleeping with Ed Carter in Charlottesville the night his wife was killed in Richmond."

"Did I say that?"

Mckenzie suppressed an urge to tell her to cut the BS. She could tell Quinn was enjoying playing cat and mouse with her. "You said that and more."

"Hmm. My memory is not what it used to be."

"But surely you remember something as important as that," Joel prompted.

Quinn shrugged. "Maybe I do, maybe I don't. But for sure I don't want to get involved in any legal stuff. I'm on disability because of my COPD. I don't feel like flying across the country and testifying in a courtroom."

"But you could save Ed's life," Joel pleaded.

"Why would I want to do that? He destroyed mine. I got kicked out of law school because of him."

"The school did that," Mckenzie said. "Ed personally had nothing to do with it."

"Look, I don't care what you say, I'm not going to get involved."

"But you know he didn't kill his wife," Mckenzie begged.

"No, I don't. They said he hired some guy to do it."

"And then that guy recanted. And his DNA wasn't on the murder weapon. So they changed the story to say Ed did it. But he couldn't have done it. He was with you."

"Maybe." Quinn shifted her gaze to the large window behind Mckenzie and Joel. Mckenzie turned to see what she was looking at and realized that this sad little apartment had a full ocean view that didn't require craning any necks to see around corners.

"Beautiful, isn't it?" Quinn's eyes met Mckenzie's again. "It calms me when I think about all the things that could have gone right in my life that went wrong. Things that weren't my fault."

"Look, if you won't help Ed, what about Wynne, his son?" Joel asked.

He's just like Brian. He knows how to read a potential witness. I'm lucky he decided to forgive me for what I did.

"Wynne? The little boy? The one he brought to the office every week?"

"He's a thirty-eight-year-old man now, on the verge of losing his father," Mckenzie said. She could see Quinn beginning to soften.

"Okay, tell you what. I won't talk to you. But I'll talk to him."

Mckenzie pulled out her phone.

"What are you doing?" Quinn demanded.

"I don't have Wynne's number, but I know who I can get it from."

But Quinn shook her head. "No phone calls. Face to face or nothing."

Mckenzie's heart sank. "I don't think he can leave Ed right now. They only have a few days left together."

"Well, then, tough luck."

"Wait," Joel said. "Would you talk to Wynne's fiancée? She's a lawyer, and she's looking for evidence to save his father."

"That little boy is getting married?"

"Yes, next Friday, as a matter of fact," Mckenzie said.

"Okay, I'll talk to the bride-to-be. But only if she comes here to me. What's her name?"

"Claire Chastain."

* * *

"You don't have to tell Brendan the whole truth," Joel said as soon as they got in the car.

"What do you mean?" Mckenzie pulled out onto Feldspar Street and headed for I-5 South. "I'm going to have to tell him

313

that I screwed up and sat on that mistake all these years. He's got to understand that it's worth sending Claire this far on the eve of her wedding."

"Of course," Joel agreed. "But you don't have to tell him about your mistake. You're a good lawyer, Mom. You've done a lot of good for a lot of people. And the Supreme Court needs you. Lawyers are human. They make mistakes."

"Maybe, but this one seems unforgivable to me at the moment, although Brad O'Connor, my boss, insisted that Ed was guilty. And I have never been sure that Quinn was telling me the whole truth about that night."

"And we don't know that now," Joel said. "Look, leave the mea culpas out of it, Mom. Tell Brendan that Dad once thought she might be an alibi witness for Ed, and you happened to remember that and decided to help out by having Joe track her down. You know that Tyndall's worried about Claire, and you wanted to help."

"I see why Alan Warwick thinks you'll make partner by age thirty. You could convince anyone of anything." She glanced over at him and smiled.

He grinned back. "I love you, Mom. You're always my hero. Nothing and no one will ever change that."

Her eyes suddenly filled with tears. *She'd been wrong to think their bond would ever be broken or that he couldn't forgive her. I'm sad for Ed and Wynne and Tyndall and Claire, and even for me because I'm not perfect. But this is still one of the happiest days of my life.*

CLAIRE

"Let us go then, you and I,
When the evening is spread out against the sky"

T.S. Eliot

CHAPTER THIRTY-FOUR

Monday, February 20, 2017, Tyndall Chastain's Apartment, Fifth Avenue, New York, New York

"I don't want you to go," Tyndall said as Claire was stuffing last minute items into her suitcase.

"I don't have a choice" she insisted. She wished she'd been able to call a cab for the airport before he found out about her trip to save herself the stress of confronting his opposition.

"Of course you do. You're getting married on Friday. You don't have time to go to San Diego and back and be at Brendan's for dinner on Thursday night."

"I'll be back by Friday for the wedding. Emma will understand if I don't make it for dinner on Thursday. Wynne will send a plane for me if I can't get a commercial flight back in time."

"Claire, this is crazy!"

"No, it isn't, Papa." She stopped packing and put her hand on his arm. He was dressed for work in his usual navy suit. Her childhood name for him brought tears to his eyes. She hugged him. "Brendan needs me to go to San Diego. There's an alibi witness for Ed who won't talk to anyone but me or Wynne."

"Then take Wynne with you."

"I can't. He's reopened negotiations with Governor Reynolds. He's intent on showing him that he can beat any campaign contribution the Fairfaxes can come up with."

"This isn't your fight, Claire."

"No, Papa. It is. I made it my fight when I agreed to marry Wynne." She saw the despair in his face and hugged him again. "I love you."

"And I love you. And Wynne and the Carters and their death row baggage are not what I want for you."

She sighed and sat down next to him on the small sofa in her bedroom. "It's not what I want either. So if this alibi pans out and we get a stay, I'll be able to tell Wynne I need more time to think about the future."

"Does that mean you'll call off this wedding if Brendan can get a stay?"

"Postpone," Claire smiled.

Tyndall looked relieved, but his dark eyes were still troubled. "Well, then, if you have to go to San Diego, promise me you'll take Jeff. I don't want you out there by yourself."

"Don't worry, Papa. He's meeting me at La Guardia. He wasn't going to let me go alone, either."

* * *

The big jet roared into the sky and turned west on its long, cross-continent voyage.

Jeff summoned a flight attendant as soon as they were moving around the cabin.

"Scotch, please. Two." He pointed to Claire who was seated next to him, midway back in first class.

"You didn't ask what I wanted," she observed.

"True. But as your maid of honor, it's my job to see that you are properly looked after until Friday morning when I turn that responsibility over to Wynne. You need scotch so you'll sleep. We have to get going first thing in the morning to find this Quinn person."

"Ellen is my maid of honor."

"I'm subbing for Ellen on this trip."

She smiled. "You're funny."

"I'm glad one of us is."

* * *

Tuesday, February 21, 2017, Lindbergh Field, San Diego, California

The scotch made Claire sleepy. When she woke, it was eight a.m. on Tuesday morning, and the plane was descending in preparation to land. She looked over at Jeff, who was already awake.

"We're nearly home," he smiled.

"Is this home?" she asked.

"It is for me. You know my family's here."

"Funny, it feels like home to me, too."

"Good."

"What's the plan?"

"We're checking into a two-bedroom suite at the U.S. Grant because your father and I don't think you should be alone, Claire. We think you're in danger. And then we're meeting

Mckenzie at her office. She's going to drive us to meet Quinn Fairchild."

* * *

Tuesday, February 21, 2017, Offices of Goldstein, Miller, Mahoney, and Fitzgerald, San Diego, California

At eleven thirty, Claire and Jeff were standing in the gray marble lobby of Goldstein, Miller, waiting for Mckenzie Fitzgerald. As soon as she emerged from the doors to the inner sanctum, she hurried over to Claire and gave her a hug.

"Thank you for coming!"

Claire stepped back and studied the face of the woman her father loved. *Why so much anxiety in her eyes?* She said, "Have you met Jeff Ryder? He works with my father."

Mckenzie smiled. "Of course. He has mentioned you many times." She shook Jeff's hand. "My car is downstairs in the garage. Quinn lives in Pacific Beach. I'll drive you there and introduce you. But after today, you'll be on your own. I'm leaving for D.C. tonight for meetings on Wednesday, and then I'll be at your wedding, Claire, on Friday with Tyndall."

The sun was out in full force as they drove to Quinn Fairchild's apartment. Claire realized how much she had missed sunshine when she was back in New York's gray winter. She noticed that Jeff, who was sitting beside her in the back seat, looked pensive. She wished she could ask why but it was neither the time nor the place.

Traffic was light, and they made it to 8201 in twenty minutes. Mckenzie parked in front of Quinn's building, and the three of them walked up a flight of wooden stairs. Mckenzie knocked on the bright- green door.

A gray-haired woman with a sallow face and an oxygen cannula in her nose opened it. Her hard, dark eyes immediately focused on Claire. "Is this the fiancée?" she demanded.

"This is Claire Chastain and a close friend, Jeff Ryder," Mckenzie said.

Claire watched the suspicious eyes shift to Jeff. "She isn't marrying him. What's he doing here?"

"Wynne is talking to Governor Reynolds of Virginia," Claire said in the soft, melodious bel canto tones that soothed and charmed jurors. "He sends his deepest thanks to you and hopes that you can help us save his father's life."

"Well, come in then." Quinn motioned for them to enter.

Claire looked around the sparse room, and her heart ached for this woman who was so obviously suffering. She sat down beside her on the shabby sofa. Jeff and Mckenzie took the opposite chairs.

"What does he look like now?" Quinn asked.

"Ed? He's an old man. White hair, but still maintains his military bearing," Claire said, surprised by her question.

"No, the little boy."

"Oh, Wynne," Claire smiled. She opened her phone and pulled up a picture of herself with Wynne in Paris. She handed it to Quinn, whose eyes misted over as she studied it.

Finally, she handed it back to Claire. "He's grown up to be so handsome."

"He's devoted his life to saving his father," Claire said. "Will you help?"

Quinn sighed deeply. "Yes, I guess. I hate Ed Carter. I suppose she told you about that." She nodded toward Mckenzie, who did not flinch at the accusation.

"Yes," Claire agreed, still softly bel canto. "And you have a right to feel that way. But so many people will be hurt by Ed's death, most of all Wynne."

Quinn softened. "Okay. Well, here's the story of that night."

"Wait," Jeff held up a small digital voice recorder. "Do you mind if we record this? We'll need to get a signed statement later, but the recording will help us make an accurate writing for you to sign."

"That's fine," Quinn said. "The story is simple, really. I was in Ed's classes in law school. I was taking criminal procedure from him that fall. It was my second year. I ran into him in a pub in Charlottesville around nine or ten o'clock the night his wife died."

"Why were you in Charlottesville?" Claire asked.

"My then-boyfriend was in law school at UVA. We broke up that night."

"What was his name?" Claire asked.

"Trevor James Trewitt, Jr. He went on to become a big-time lawyer in D.C. Anyway, I was upset, and I wanted a hook up. I ran into Ed, who was alone and unhappy because his wife had refused to come with him to the criminal law conference where he was presenting a paper."

"So you slept with him?" Claire asked. Her heart was beating very hard. She could hardly wait to call Wynne.

"Yes. All night. He drove me to my car the next morning, and that was it. I felt sorry for him because he loved his wife and little boy so much, but his wife didn't seem to love him."

"Why didn't you come forward when he was arrested?" Jeff asked.

Quinn shrugged. "Because I didn't care what happened to him after I got kicked out of school. I had to go back to Petersburg and live in a shack. I never got to be a lawyer, the way I'd planned. And besides, I knew Allison would kill me if I did anything to save Ed."

"How did you know that?" Claire asked.

"Because Allison killed Anne Carter because she was obsessed with Ed. She was jealous of anyone he slept with. So if I'd said that I slept with Ed, she'd have killed me, too."

Claire reached out and took both of Quinn's hands in hers. She knew there were tears in her eyes, but she didn't care. "Thank you for this," she said. "It's enough to save Wynne's father. I'm sure it is. Thank you."

* * *

Claire spent the afternoon turning the recording of Quinn's statement into an affidavit for her to sign. Jeff went to El Cajon to visit his father and his brother. When he came back at six o'clock, he found her in the living room of their suite.

"Did you call Wynne and tell him the news?" he asked.

"I called," Claire said, "but he's in with the governor and can't be disturbed."

"Even with the news that we've got the evidence to get a stay?" Jeff frowned.

"Never mind. I called Brendan instead. He's ecstatic. How's your family?"

"Very well. My brother and his wife are expecting again. Everyone is hoping for a girl this time. And my father has a lady friend who's moved in with him. She's very nice, and he's really happy."

"That's good. I've finished writing out an affidavit for Quinn to sign. Should we take it over there to her tonight?"

"No, I have a better idea. Let's go to *Over the Moon* and celebrate. We'll have plenty of time in the morning to go to Pacific Beach before we catch the red-eye back to Washington."

Claire smiled. "Last time I was at *Over the Moon*, I was a basket case over Paul."

"And Carrie Moon talked you into going on with your life and putting him behind you," Jeff reminded her.

"True. And I did. And I have. It was a beautiful little place. I loved the music."

"Well, then we'll go. Besides, this is the closest thing to a bachelorette party that you're going to have."

She laughed. "You take those maid of honor duties seriously, don't you?"

"I do, indeed."

"You know, I could ask Wynne to postpone the wedding, now. My father wants me to."

"I thought of that when Quinn gave us her statement. With Ed out of danger, the pressure goes away."

"Honestly, I'd like some more time."

"I know." Jeff smiled.

"How do you always have me figured out before I figure me out?"

"Well, I wouldn't go that far. But we've known each other a long time."

"We have, haven't we? Longer than I've known Wynne. We have more history, you and I."

"True."

"Jeff, why never you and me?"

He looked startled, and she was afraid she shouldn't have asked. But he smiled and said, "Timing, mostly. For a long time, I knew you were perfect wife material, but I didn't want one. By the time I got over that, Paul Curtis and Beth were in the way. By the time I got over that, Wynne was in the way."

"And Beth isn't in the way anymore?"

"No, she'll always be married to Chris. That's what the Chris Rafferty Foundation is really all about. It's wonderful and beautiful, and I love going there and seeing all the larger-than-life pictures of Chris. They're on all the walls in every room. And a lot of pictures of the family, too: Chris and Beth and Abby. But in the end, Beth will always be Chris' wife in my eyes. And when I do find a wife, I don't want to feel as if she belongs to someone else."

"Makes sense."

"Good. I'm glad. Now let's go eat Carrie Moon's amazing food and listen to Stan Benedict if he's playing. And dance. We've finally got something to celebrate!"

* * *

Tuesday, February 21, 2017, Over the Moon, A Jazz Club, Seaport Village, San Diego, California

It hadn't been a whole year, Claire realized as they wandered along the path of tiny white lights, since she'd come here with Jeff, shattered and broken-hearted over Paul's engagement.

Time did heal wounds, and quickly if you were willing to move on. Carrie Moon, ever the beautiful, red-haired hostess with the fascinating green eyes, hugged Claire and Jeff and gave them a table where they could see the stage, but still talk. She sent them a bottle of champagne and oysters on the house.

"She's seen the ring, and she's gotten the wrong idea," Claire whispered to Jeff when the champagne arrived.

He grinned. "Sorry. I guess I'm to blame. I told her we had something to celebrate. I didn't realize she would assumed it was you and me."

"Well, it doesn't matter," Claire said. "We are celebrating you and me. We've saved Ed's life."

"Be careful, though," Jeff cautioned. "The criminal law is not a logical beast."

"I don't understand. We have an alibi for Ed. Surely the State of Virginia isn't going to execute him now."

Jeff shook his head. "The prosecutor will question it."

"You mean Gordon Fairfax will say Quinn is lying?"

"Yes."

"But why?"

"To hang on to the conviction."

"But that's ridiculous."

"Is it? What if Quinn isn't telling the truth?"

Claire frowned. "Of course she's telling the truth."

"But why, then, was Ed's car in front of his house the night Anne died? And why did Ed take off in a hurry and not return until mid-morning on Sunday?"

"Because Adam Winston was wrong about what he saw."

"You're saying there was no white Volvo?"

"There couldn't have been because Ed was in Charlottesville all night. Adam and his wife were close to Anne. He believed Ed was having an affair with Allison because he saw them together. Like Blair and Paige, he wanted Ed to be convicted after the murder-for-hire theory fell through."

"Makes sense," Jeff admitted, "but you're making some big assumptions about Adam Winston's motives."

"I don't think so. Quinn is telling the truth. Come on, let's dance. Stan's playing one of my favorite songs."

"Which is?"

"Phil Collins. 'Two Hearts Until the End of Time.'"

CHAPTER THIRTY-FIVE

Wednesday, February 22, 2017, La Jolla Shores, La Jolla, California

Claire talked Jeff into a walk on the beach at La Jolla Shores before they drove to Quinn's apartment in next-door Pacific Beach. There were plenty of parking spaces to choose from in the lot at the Shores on a Wednesday morning at ten a.m. Claire took off her Manolo Blahniks and carried them across the soft sand to the water's edge. She stared out at the vast expanse of the Pacific and breathed in the cool, salty air. Overhead, the seagulls sang their throbbing, haunting tale of woe. The winter sun cast Jeff's shadow in front of Claire, although he was standing behind her.

"You can't ice skate here," he observed.

"No," she agreed without turning. "And you do not surf."

"I absolutely do not. But I like to walk through the little waves at the edge of the tide."

"Me, too." She reached out and took his hand. They walked a long way down the beach without speaking. She remembered the times in law school when she'd felt attracted to Jeff, only to be put off by his penchant for party girls. But the Rafferty case had changed him. No more up hook ups, and he had learned to control the impulsive streak that had constantly gotten him in trouble.

"It's getting close to eleven," Jeff said as they passed the last lifeguard station. We'd better get over to Quinn's and get that affidavit signed."

"Right." But she was sorry that they had to turn around. She wished they had nothing else to do except walk in the tiny waves washing up on the sand.

* * *

Wednesday, February 22, 2017, 8201 Ocean Terrace, Pacific Beach, San Diego, California

Jeff was able to park their rental car in front of Quinn's building. They hurried up the wooden stairs only to find her bright-green door ajar. There were red smears around the handle. Claire started to push it open to go inside, but Jeff grabbed her arm.

"Wait! Don't touch that. It looks like blood."

She stepped back and watched him use his elbow to widen the opening. He called out, "Quinn! Quinn!"

But there was no answer.

"Okay, you stay here," he told her.

She stood on the porch for what seemed an eternity, waiting for him to come back. When he did, his face was ashen.

"She's dead."

"No!"

"I'm afraid so."

Claire moved toward the door to go inside, but Jeff held her back.

"You don't want to see it. There's brains and blood everywhere."

"What?"

"Whoever it was used a baseball bat."

"Oh, God, Allison. But how did she know? How could she have followed us here?" Suddenly, she was in tears. Jeff put his arms around her and held her while she cried.

"It's okay, Claire. But try to get a grip. We've got to call the police."

"I know. I know." She stepped back, and he let her go. He pulled out his cell phone and called 911.

* * *

Wednesday, February 22, 2017, Office of the District Attorney, Hall of Justice, 330 West Broadway, San Diego, California

Claire felt numb as she sat next to Jeff in front of Bart Stephenson's massive desk in the District Attorney's Office. Jeff had called him after the police arrived at Quinn's apartment, and Bart had invited him downtown to talk about finding Allison Byrd before she left town.

"So she was the one witness you needed to stop this execution on the third of March?"

"Yes." Claire listened as Jeff gave Bart the rundown of Ed's case and Allison's involvement.

"So she's the real killer?" he asked when Jeff finished. Bart was tall and lean, with a military-style haircut that made him look bald, and dark eyes that seemed to bore holes in anyone he observed for more than a few seconds. But Claire could see that he liked and respected Jeff.

"Yes. And Quinn could alibi Ed," Jeff said. "Allison's been following Claire in New York, but we never expected her to follow us here."

"I don't see how she managed a cross-country flight," Claire said. "She's unemployed as far as we know and was working as a housekeeper at a bed and breakfast before that."

"Stolen credit card, probably," Bart waved his hands. "What airline did you fly?"

"American," Claire said, "Why?"

"Because I bet her name is on the passenger list of your flight from New York or on the one right after yours."

"She uses the alias 'Anne Carter,'" Jeff said. "It's her sick way of claiming Ed Carter's wife's identity."

Claire watched Bart write that down on his legal pad. Then he looked at Claire and smiled for the first time, and she realized that his stern face could be warm, too. "I'm sorry this has happened. We're going to do our best to get this Byrd woman in custody before she slips out of town. If there's anything my office can do above and beyond this investigation, just let me know."

"It might help if you gave us an affidavit," Jeff said, "reciting the details of the murder and stating that Allison is your chief suspect."

"You're thinking you might use that to try to stop the execution?"

"The similarity between Quinn's murder and Anne Carter's ought to cast doubt on Ed's conviction," Jeff said. "It's our best shot at getting a stay now that Quinn's statement has become nothing but hearsay."

"You recorded her?"

"Yes, but we can't use it because we can't produce her as a witness."

"I'll write something up for you," Bart said. "When are you headed back to New York?"

"We missed our flight this afternoon. I think we can make the red-eye tonight," Jeff told him.

"Then I'll fax it to your office, and it will be waiting when you get back."

"Even better, fax it to Brendan Murphy in Richmond. He's Ed's attorney." Claire handed Bart one of Brendan's cards as Jeff spoke.

Bart nodded as he took the card. "I'll see that he gets it. Good luck to the two of you. And there's a job here for you, Jeff, any day you want to come back."

* * *

Midnight, Wednesday, February 23, 2017, The Red-Eye to Washington, D.C.

"And do you want to go back to the District Attorney's Office?" Claire asked after the big jet had roared into the midnight sky and turned east for the long flight.

"No."

The flight attendant stopped to put two scotches on their tray tables. Jeff smiled at her, and Claire noticed she lingered for a moment longer than necessary. But he didn't react to the attention as he once would have. He just smiled and thanked her again as she left.

"Drink that."

"I know. So I'll sleep."

"And so I can sleep, too. We have a busy next two days."

Claire sipped her scotch thoughtfully. Finally, she said, "You won't tell anyone I thought about calling the wedding off? Please."

"I wasn't planning on it. But you still could."

"I don't see how."

"Honestly, I don't either. Have you talked to Wynne?"

"Yes. He's upset about Quinn but grateful you asked Bart for that declaration."

"We could try to use her hearsay statement. Claim it fits the dying declaration exception."

"That would be an act of desperation."

"It would be better than nothing."

"We'll see what Brendan thinks," Claire said. She sipped her scotch and wondered if she would be able to sleep.

"Where are the two of you going after the wedding?" Jeff asked. "Some place romantic and restful?"

"No, down to Sussex to see Ed. It could be the last time I see him. They're taking him to Greensville on Monday."

Jeff winced. "Claire, even if Wynne doesn't understand, stop this thing now. A wedding isn't supposed to turn into a funeral."

"But how do I tell him he's alone in the world when he thought he could count on me?"

"Oh, God. I wish you hadn't put it that way."

"I wish it wasn't that way."

"We're not going to sleep. We might as well have another scotch and watch the movie."

CHAPTER THIRTY-SIX

Thursday, February 23, 2017, The Murphys', Windsor Farms, Richmond, Virginia

Claire was late for the party that night. She and Jeff had arrived at Dulles at ten a.m. and then had driven through choking traffic on the I-95 south, not reaching the Murphys' until three in the afternoon. No one had been home. Brendan had been at his office, and Emma had been at the hospital seeing patients. Claire had used her key to let them in. Jeff had gone straight to his guest room to rest, and she had collapsed in her own room, grateful for a few hours' sleep before she had to face the ordeal of dinner. She woke with a start at five thirty and realized she only had a half hour to wash the travel dust off and dress for dinner. So by the time she came downstairs in a simple black Chanel sheath, everyone had already gathered in the Murphys' great room with their drinks.

Wynne was standing by his Aunt Margaret and her husband, William Randolph, talking earnestly to Brendan and his son, Tim. Her father, Mckenzie, and Jeff were deep in conversation with Emma. Ellen and Tim's wife, Liz, were overseeing five-year-old Jamie and four-year-old Gwen's efforts at new coloring books, which were supposed to distract them while the grown-ups had their dinner party.

Everyone looked up when Claire came in, but Jeff's eyes caught and held hers for a moment before Wynne hurried across the room to put his arm around her.

"You look beautiful."

"Thank you." She offered him her cheek to kiss as Emma pressed a glass of red wine into her hand, and her father kissed her other cheek.

"Here. I'm sure you need this after the last couple of days," Emma smiled. "At least you've come back with good news."

"To the bride and groom and to good news!" Brendan raised his glass of scotch, and everyone joined the toast.

Claire's eyes went to Jeff's again, and he shook his head slightly. *Oh, God. They don't know. He hasn't told them. And if Bart Stephenson sent Brendan that fax, he hasn't read it yet.*

Mckenzie, who was standing next to her father, was beaming. "Congratulations on getting that affidavit from Quinn."

"The writ's been drafted," Brendan said. "All I have to do is attach her statement after the wedding tomorrow and file it. I'm expecting the Fourth Circuit to issue a stay on Monday in time to keep them from moving Ed to Greensville."

Claire had a knot in her stomach. She took a sip of wine and then looked over at Jeff, who said, "I think we should get this over with before dinner. It's not something the little ones should hear."

Tim's wife, Liz, looked up, and Claire saw her quickly evaluate the situation. "I'll take them in the kitchen and get them started on their supper."

As soon as the door closed behind them, Jeff said, "It would be a good idea for everyone to sit down."

Brendan, Emma, and Tim sat down on one of the two enormous white linen sofas. Mckenzie, Tyndall, and Ellen sat across from them on the other one. Margaret and William took the two oversized club chairs. Wynne remained standing by Claire and Jeff, but his blue eyes were fixed on Claire.

"What's happened?" he asked.

"When we got to Quinn Fairchild's apartment about mid-day yesterday, we found her dead."

"Dead?" Brendan shook his head. "But how?"

"Someone beat her to death with a baseball bat. It was a very bloody crime scene," Jeff said.

Tyndall's eyes went straight to Claire. "Don't worry," she said. "Jeff wouldn't let me go in."

Mckenzie looked stunned. She said slowly, "So we only have her recorded statement now?"

"Right," Claire agreed.

"And I can't use it because it's hearsay," Brendan shook his head.

"It's a copycat version of my mother's murder."

"Yes," Jeff agreed.

"So it had to be Allison," Wynne said.

"Yes. Claire and I met with the District Attorney, Bart Stephenson. He guessed she used a stolen credit card to book a flight when she realized where Claire and I were headed. They are trying to arrest her before she leaves San Diego. Bart is faxing Brendan his own affidavit saying that he believes it's a copycat killing. That's not as good as Quinn's alibi evidence, but it's worth a try. It should be in your office right now."

"I'm sure it is," Brendan said. "I left a little early tonight because of the party. I'll revise the writ after the wedding. I can still have it filed before the court closes tomorrow."

Claire looked over at her father. The lines in his face were deeply etched, and his dark eyes were troubled. He looked at her and shook his head slightly. She looked away toward the kitchen where the grandchildren were eating their carefree supper.

A moment later, Wynne squeezed the hand that wore the diamond gently, and whispered in her ear, "If you want out—"

He looked so alone and vulnerable. "I don't," she lied. His face broke into a relieved smile.

She felt eyes on them and looked over to see Emma watching their exchange. She gave Claire a reassuring smile. Then she said, "Okay, that's enough. We're here to celebrate Claire and Wynne. Dinner is ready, and the champagne is waiting. Come on, let's eat!"

* * *

The first knock on Claire's door came at midnight. She had just come upstairs after the party, and she hadn't had time to undress. She hoped it was Jeff, but it was Mckenzie, also still in full evening dress.

"May I talk to you for a few minutes?"

"Of course."

She came in and took one of the two chairs that occupied the bay window. Claire took the other.

"I have to tell you about Quinn. All of this is my fault."

"No, it isn't. Don't be ridiculous."

"No, I knew that Allison Byrd would kill her if she talked. I just never dreamed that she'd be able to cross the continent to get to her if I told you and Jeff about her."

"But how did you know that? Was that in your husband's file, too?"

"I lied," Mckenzie said. "I was the one who interviewed Quinn when I was in the Public Defender's Office. I forgot to record her, and when I went back to talk to her again, she had disappeared. So I lied to cover up my mistake."

Claire listened as Mckenzie told her the story of how she had used Joe Sanders to find Quinn and then had confessed the whole story of her incompetence to Joel.

"He told me that I am a good lawyer and the Supreme Court needs me. And then he asked me what I was going to do to make it right. So the two of us went to see her."

"And that's when she said she wouldn't talk to you?"

"Right. It had to be Wynne or you."

Claire sighed. "I'm kicking myself because Jeff and I didn't go back that night after we taped her statement."

"You couldn't have known. Besides, she might have already been dead by then."

"Maybe. I don't know."

"Claire, it would be fine to call off the wedding."

"I—"

"Don't make excuses. The only person in that room who doesn't see your doubts is Wynne."

"Every bride has doubts."

"Not like the ones you're having."

"Please, I don't want to talk about it."

"Well, then, I should let you get some sleep. But remember, it's not too late to call it off in the morning."

* * *

Claire had just enough time to put on her pajamas and robe and wash her face before the next knock came. She opened the door to find her father in the hall, wearing his pajamas and bathrobe.

"I need to talk to you."

"Okay," she invited him in, and he took the chair that Mckenzie had occupied earlier.

"Claire, please. This is madness. You can't go through with this tomorrow."

His face was a portrait of worry and grief. He had looked exactly the same way when her mother had been dying and he had been wearing out his knees, begging the Universe for a miracle to save her.

"Papa, I have to. Wynne is going to lose Ed next week. He won't have any family to turn to if I walk away."

"He's got Margaret and William."

"That's not the same thing."

"I don't care. I don't want your life endangered any more than it already has been. Wynne's a very nice and remarkable young man, but the circumstances that surround him are too dangerous."

"I'll be fine, Papa."

"Not without Jeff."

"You know very well that Jeff has never wanted a wife."

"Jeff has changed, and you're the one who changed him."

"Not me. Beth Rafferty."

"But you played a part, Claire. I remember when he called me from San Diego that night when you were so upset over the other jerk's engagement."

"We've been friends for a long time."

"And he loves you, and he doesn't come with a woman in his life who wants to kill you."

"She's stranded in San Diego, right now. And the police are looking for her. She's not a threat to me, Papa."

"We don't know that for sure, Claire. Please, at least postpone it."

She got up from her chair and went over to the other one and gave him a big hug.

"I can't do that to Wynne. You can see how all this has taken its toll. He's thin and tired, and he's trying so hard to stay strong for Ed. I'd never forgive myself if I walked out on him at a time like this. He loves me, Papa. The same way you and Jeff do. Now, I need to sleep. I was on a red-eye last night. I'm exhausted."

* * *

She had just turned off the light and snuggled into bed when the third knock came. She got up and cracked the door. Jeff was standing there.

"No more tonight," she said. "I'm being bombarded with advice not to get married tomorrow."

"That's not why I came. Please let me in for a minute."

"Okay," she sighed, opening the door wide enough for him to enter. He was wearing sweatpants and a long-sleeved T-shirt that passed for pajamas. "Why, then?"

"To tell you I'm no longer maid of honor."

"I thought we'd settled that."

"Well, just in case we hadn't, I'm now the best man."

"But Brendan—"

"Has been demoted to co-father of the bride. The strain of the wedding plus trying to get a stay of execution at the same time is taking its toll on him. Emma insisted, and Wynne asked me. He thought it would make you happy."

"It does."

"Good. Now go to sleep."

"I keep trying, and people keep knocking on my door."

"As the new official best man, I'll make sure no one else does."

"Thank you."

"I'm driving you and Tyndall down to the plantation tomorrow morning. Early. Eight sharp."

"What about Mckenzie?"

"She's tagging along with Emma. Says she wants to give Tyndall his last father-daughter moments with you before the wedding. Now get some sleep."

CHAPTER THIRTY-SEVEN

Friday, February 24, 2017, Belle Grove Plantation Bed and Breakfast, Port Conway, Virginia

Jeff drove Brendan's Range Rover through the soft, persistent rain next morning with Claire in the passenger seat and Tyndall in back. The mood in the car was as somber as the weather. Claire tried to lighten the atmosphere by remarking that rain on her wedding day was good luck, but although Jeff smiled briefly and agreed, her father remained quiet, eyes fixed on the road.

They had just exited I-95 and picked up Route 301 North toward the plantation when Jeff's cell phone, which was sitting on the console, announced a text message. "Can you check that for me?" he asked Claire. "The password is my birthday."

"I know," she said as she picked up his iPhone and punched in the numbers. "It's a message from Bart Stephenson."

"Read it to me."

"He says, DNA on the Quinn Fairchild murder weapon is a one hundred percent match with Allison Byrd's profile in the CODIS database. There are no other DNA profiles. Has yet to apprehend her but thinks she's still in San Diego. The airlines have not reported an 'Anne Carter' bound for Richmond or New York. He says he will send Brendan an updated affidavit with the DNA information for the Carter writ."

"Wow," Jeff grinned, "that's fantastic news. The good luck has already begun!"

But Claire was deeply aware of her father's silence. She glanced back at him, and he nodded to acknowledge the news, but said nothing. *He thinks we shouldn't be thinking about a murder investigation on my wedding day. And he's right.*

They reached Belle Grove at nine forty-five because of the rain and the traffic. Michelle met them in the front hall, smiling and welcoming as always.

"I've put Claire and her maid of honor in the Turner Suite upstairs," she announced in her soft South Carolina accent. "Mr. Chastain, you have the Madison Suite, also upstairs. Wynne, his best man, and his aunt and uncle have the Conway Suite on the first floor because it's closer to the library. They haven't arrived yet. Why don't you all put your things in your rooms, and then we'll meet in the library to make sure everything is the way you want it."

Claire hung her mother's white Dior suit next to the full-length mirror in the Turner Suite and studied Carrie Turner's etching on the glass for a few minutes. She wished for her mother's presence, and for a marriage as happy as her parents' had been. Then she turned and headed downstairs to see if everything was ready for the wedding.

She was the first to arrive in the library where a simple podium had been set up in front of the window facing the river. There was a single row of chairs facing the podium and the window. She counted them. Ten. They hadn't even made it to twenty guests after all. It wasn't the sort of wedding that needed arches and huge vases of flowers. But there was a tasteful vase of white roses and orchids in front of the podium where she and Wynne would stand to take their vows.

She stood watching the gray mist curl over the river and felt her nerves begin to steady. Everything was going to be fine. She'd be happy with Wynne. Eventually.

Her nose picked up the smell of a five-star kitchen. Something delicious was cooking for their luncheon after the ceremony. It was probably the lobster Benedict that Michelle had suggested. There would be wedding cake, too, although she couldn't remember what she'd finally ordered. And a lot of Veuve Clicquot.

Her father appeared and then Jeff. Tyndall looked around and then said, "It's very plain."

"We'll have a much bigger, fancier party on the lawn in the summer," Claire assured him.

He studied the rain falling softly on the river and the lawn but said nothing.

The front door opened, and Claire heard the Murphys enter the hall. She heard Sally Lane say, "They're in the library, inspecting the arrangements." And a minute later, the small room was filled with Brendan and Emma, Tim and Liz, and Ellen, and her husband, Tom.

"Oh, it's beautiful," Ellen said as she looked around the library. "So cozy and intimate! Now I wish we'd brought Jamie and Gwen, don't you, Liz? They would have thought they were coming to a magical palace."

Liz smiled. "I'm sure they would have. But that wouldn't have made them sit still during the ceremony."

"You're right," Ellen agreed.

Michelle appeared in the doorway. "It's ten thirty, and the groom has just arrived. I'm keeping him outside until the bride has a chance to go back upstairs to dress for the wedding."

"Come on, Claire," Ellen said, picking up the garment bag she'd laid over a chair when she came in to admire the library. "Let's make sure Wynne doesn't see you before the ceremony."

"You'll find champagne waiting for all of you upstairs," Michelle said. "And the photographer is here to take the pre-wedding pictures."

Did I order a photographer? Claire asked herself. *I don't think so.* She looked over at her father and realized it was his doing.

When they reached the Turner Suite, Ellen poured champagne for them. It reminded her of that day at Vera Wang when she'd been choosing what she thought was going to be her wedding dress. Before the news of Ed's impending execution had changed everything.

"Mmm," Ellen sighed, "this is good. This is the most wonderful place to have a wedding, Claire. And to think your mother's family once owned it."

She nodded, smiled, and drained her glass of champagne quickly and poured another. The photographer appeared, and she and Ellen posed for pictures. Then her father entered, wearing his perfectly tailored navy suit and serious maroon silk tie, and the photographer took a father-daughter portrait.

Just as they finished, Michelle appeared at the door.

"Everyone is in place, downstairs. They're waiting for you."

"We're ready," Claire said. "Ellen, you go down first. Papa and I will follow."

Ellen nodded and hurried downstairs. Claire could hear her high heels clicking on every step as she descended to the front hall and the parlor.

"Claire, I have something to say before we go down."

"Don't, Papa. The decisions have all been made. I know how you feel about Wynne and about Jeff. This isn't the time to talk about it."

"That wasn't what I was going to say."

"I'm listening then," Claire smiled at her father.

"I've always been proud of you, but never more than today."

"Thank you, Papa." She kissed his cheek. "Let's go downstairs."

* * *

They paused for a moment in the hall to allow time for Ellen to take her place to the left the podium where Tamara, the officiant waited. Claire was amazed to hear the soft strains of a harp because she had forgotten to hire anyone to play.

Tyndall read the surprise in her face and whispered in her ear, "Michelle suggested the harpist."

"I'm glad she did," Claire smiled.

"Looks like they're ready for you," her father said. "Are you ready?"

"Yes." Claire took a deep breath and strode firmly into the library, her arm linked through her father's. As they crossed the room, she had a quick impression of eyes on her from all sides: Wynne's Aunt Margaret and her husband, William; Brendan, Emma, Tim, and Liz on the other side of the room.

Tyndall and Claire paused in front of the podium. Tamara began to chant the age-old words: "Dearly beloved, we are gathered together here today—"

Claire tried to keep her eyes on Wynne, but she couldn't help looking at Jeff, standing just behind him. Jeff's blue eyes were calm and encouraging.

Suddenly the door to the Hipkins-Bernard Suite burst open, and a tall, gray-haired woman in a dirty, blue dress, holding a 9mm semi-automatic pistol strode across the room toward Claire and Wynne. Claire's heart skipped a beat. Allison Byrd. She had snuck into the house and hidden in the only unoccupied suite, the one adjacent to the library.

Michelle, who had been standing by the entrance, pulled out her cell phone and turned toward the hall, obviously intent on calling for help. But Allison whirled on her and commanded, "Drop that phone, and come back in where I can see you and put your hands up."

Michelle let the phone slide onto the rug and obeyed.

"Who are you?" Tamara asked.

"I'm his Aunt Allison," the woman said, gesturing toward Wynne with the gun. Suddenly she grabbed Claire and twisted the arm that wore the cast behind her, making her drop her bouquet. Red, searing pain ran along her left shoulder and wrist. A second later, she felt the gun between her ribs.

"You're coming with me!"

"No, she's not!" Jeff lunged toward Allison. Claire felt the gun leave her rib cage long enough for her to fire a shot at Jeff. She saw him fall. She assumed that she was going to be next.

But Allison put the gun against the small of her back instead and hissed, "Get moving."

With the gun pressing against her spine, Claire walked out of the library and down the hall. When they came to the front door, Allison opened it and pressed the gun harder against Claire's back. She could see a dirty, white van sitting in front of the house.

"Get down those steps and get in!"

With the gun pressing hard against her back, Claire obeyed. As soon as she was inside, Allison covered her eyes with a smelly rag and ordered her to lie down on the floor of the back seat. A few minutes later, the van pulled away from the house. Claire lay still and tried to calm her racing heart. Surely it wouldn't take long for the police to find her or for her to escape from this madwoman. But how badly was Jeff wounded?

PART IV

JEFF

"If you aren't in over your head, how do you
know how tall you are?"

T.S. Eliot

CHAPTER THIRTY-EIGHT

Friday, February 24, 2017, Belle Grove Plantation Bed and Breakfast, Port Conway, Virginia

Jeff lay still and watched everyone moving around the room. Brendan had had a heart attack and wasn't breathing. Emma was doing CPR, but his face remained a horrible shade of gray.

Wynne had rushed out the front door and taken off after Allison Byrd, squealing the tires of his rental car as he accelerated. Jeff realized that was not a smart move since she had a gun and he did not, but no one had asked his advice.

Suddenly the room was full of paramedics and deputy sheriffs and the sheriff himself. One team of EMTs went to help Emma with Brendan; the other hurried over to him.

"I'm okay," he said as they cut off his coat and shirt and began looking at the wound. "Claire's father is over there. He needs you more than I do. He doesn't look good."

"We'll get to him in a minute," the EMT who was looking at him said. He narrowed his eyes and surveyed the damage to Jeff's left shoulder. "You're lucky. The bullet just grazed the skin. I'll clean it up and give you a tetanus shot. Sam," he said to his companion, "this guy's right. He's fine. But the gentleman over there seems to be having trouble breathing." He nodded toward Tyndall, who was still seated and gasping for air. Mckenzie held his hands and spoke softly, trying to calm him.

As the EMT worked on Jeff's shoulder, he could hear the EMT helping Emma say,

"Thank God, you're a doctor. You've got his heart going again."

"But he's just barely with us," Emma said. "Our only chance is to get him to Medical College in Richmond. We need Air Transport. We don't have time for an ambulance."

Jeff watched Sam put an oxygen mask on Tyndall as the EMT with Emma picked up his cell phone to summon the helicopter for Brendan. He listened intently to whatever the dispatcher was telling him. When he ended the call he said, "Air Transport will be airborne in fifteen minutes. Flight time after that is fifteen to twenty, depending on the winds. The pilot will want to land on the back lawn if there's room," he said to Michelle. "We need to keep the distance we have to move him to a minimum. We don't want his heart to stop again."

* * *

Two FBI agents from Richmond arrived at one thirty. By that time, Wynne was back, upset that he had found no trace of Allison Byrd, and Tyndall had recovered enough to take off the oxygen mask and talk calmly to the sheriff and his deputies about Allison's identity and the reasons why she would want to kidnap Claire. The remaining Murphys had headed back to Richmond where Brendan was fighting for his life in the ICU.

Wynne's aunt and uncle had stayed behind, waiting on Wynne's return.

Michelle had gathered them all in the parlor and served them coffee, tea, and sandwiches while Mike Parker and Fred Harrison, the two FBI agents in their mid-forties in gray suits, interviewed them in turn. Jeff knew the agents could only monitor the situation until there was evidence that Claire had been moved across state lines. But Allison could very well have headed north to D.C. or even south toward Jarrat near the North Carolina border.

When the agents finished interviewing Wynne, Jeff, whose interview was also over, suggested a walk on the lawn. He could see that, while everyone in the room was upset, Wynne was close to the breaking point.

Jeff retrieved their overcoats from the Conway Suite, and the two of them went down the back steps to the lawn. Jeff walked toward the river, which was still gray under the early afternoon clouds, although the rain had stopped. He remembered walking with Claire on the day they'd come to finalize the arrangements for the wedding.

"I should have had security here," Wynne said. The glasses that usually made him seem scholarly now made him seem frail and tired. He was so angry that he was trembling. "And I should have been able to chase that horrible woman down and stop her from leaving with Claire."

Jeff gave him a reassuring pat on the arm. "We all thought Allison Byrd was still in San Diego. And we had no idea that she'd sneak into the house and hide in the empty suite next to the library. But she's worked at Belle Grove. She knows the house. She figured out a way to get in without any of us seeing her. I'm sure she would have known how to get past security guards if they had been here."

"Claire didn't want to go through with the wedding, did she?" he shook his head sadly. "You knew she had doubts."

"She felt keeping her promise was more important than her doubts," Jeff said quietly. "She knew how alone you'd be otherwise."

He stared at the gray water, his face as bleak as the winter landscape. "I need to do something to help find her, but I don't know what to do."

"The sheriff has brought in the dogs. If Allison is hiding Claire close by, they'll find her. The FBI agents think we'll get a ransom demand before long."

But Wynne shook his head. "I don't think Allison Byrd is after money. She's obviously mentally ill. We've got to find Claire before she harms her. Now we know for certain that she killed my mother."

Jeff watched a lonely hawk soar over the river. He said slowly, "I wish we did know that, but we still can't place her at the scene of your mother's murder."

Wynne sighed. "I guess you're right. Dr. Vom Saal hasn't identified her DNA on the bat. But she's done so many things that say she's the killer, including killing Quinn."

"I know," Jeff agreed.

They walked toward the edge of the lawn overlooking the river. When they paused at the edge, Wynne said, "You're admitted to practice in Virginia, aren't you?"

"I am. I had a case down here for Fidelity National, and I

was admitted to the bar in Virginia based upon my D.C. bar admission. Why do you ask?"

"Because Dad's without a lawyer now."

"I'm sure one of Brendan's Richmond partners will take over for him."

But Wynne shook his head. "It won't be the same without Brendan. He's been Dad's rock all these years. You're the only person who can fill his shoes. I want you to take over."

Jeff was silent for a few moments while he thought about the responsibility he was being asked to assume. But he knew what Claire would want him to do. "Okay," he nodded. "I will."

"Brendan was working on a writ that he planned to file on Monday with motion for a stay."

"I know," Jeff nodded. "It was based on Quinn's statement, but without her signed affidavit, it's worthless."

"Maybe you can find a way to use it?" There was a glimmer of hope in Wynne's tired eyes.

"We'll see."

CHAPTER THIRTY-NINE

Saturday, February 25, 2017, Brendan Murphy's Office, Riverfront
Plaza, Craig, Lewis, and Weller, Richmond, Virginia

At eleven a.m. the next morning, after a sleepless night in his
guest room at the Murphys', Jeff sat at Brendan's desk in the
Richmond office of Craig, Lewis, reading the draft writ that
Brendan's team of associates had written based upon Quinn's
affidavit and the one that Bart had sent, outlining the
similarities between Quinn's murder and that of Anne Carter.
It was a stretch, he realized, to claim that Quinn had given her
statement believing that she was about to die. They actually had
no idea that Allison had followed them to San Diego and to
Quinn's apartment. Yet knowing that Quinn was afraid that
Allison would kill her if she told the truth to save Ed made it
possible to believe that Quinn was aware that giving her
statement might make death eminent. Besides, Jeff told himself,
arguing Quinn's statement as a dying declaration was the only
chance he had to use it to stop Ed's execution.

He had begun his day at eight that morning in the waiting
room on the cardiac floor at Medical College. Sitting with

Emma, waiting for news of how Brendan had passed the night, reminded him of sitting with Beth Rafferty last year when Chris was in the hospital in La Jolla. He felt that same desperate sense of urgency as he willed Brendan to live as he had once willed Chris to live for Beth and Abby.

Eventually the nurses allowed him a few minutes to sit by Brendan's bedside. He used every one of them to promise Brendan that he'd do everything in his power to save Ed. And Claire. God, how he wished for news of Claire.

Suddenly his cell phone began to ring, and his heart skipped a beat when he saw that Wynne was calling. "Have they found Claire?" he demanded without a greeting.

"Not yet," Wynne replied. "The FBI agents are getting worried because we're coming up on twenty-four hours gone without contact from the kidnapper."

Jeff's stomach tightened because he knew that the extended silence made it more likely that Claire had been harmed.

"How's Brendan?" Wynne asked.

"About the same. I spent some time at the hospital this morning. He's hanging on, but just barely."

"I'm calling to give you Dr. Vom Saal's number," Wynne said. "I thought you should get in touch and let him know you've taken over Dad's case."

"That's a good idea. How's Tyndall? He stayed at the Murphys' last night, but he wasn't up when I left for the hospital this morning."

"He finally agreed to take some Valium that Emma offered. He's hanging by the phone, the way we all are. Mckenzie is with him, trying to keep his spirits up, but she's afraid, too. Just like the rest of us."

"As soon as you know anything at all about Claire, call me."

"Of course," Wynne agreed.

Jeff hung up and looked around Brendan's office. It was full of family pictures. Brendan and Emma. Emma alone. Emma, Tim, and Ellen. Tim and Ellen and the grandchildren. And Claire. There were pictures of Claire and Ellen, and Claire and Tyndall, and Claire with Brendan and Emma.

His eyes suddenly filled with tears. He remembered the night Claire had come to find him in his ratty Mira Mesa apartment almost a year ago to the day, and the way she'd insisted on taking him to that amazing, expensive dinner at the Italian Kitchen in La Jolla when he'd been starving. But above all, he remembered the way she'd stood up for him and believed in him when the rest of the world had called him a liar and a cheat.

He wiped his eyes and told himself he didn't have time for feelings. He picked up the phone and called Dr. Vom Saal.

"I've been waiting to hear from someone connected to the Carter case."

Jeff gave him a brief rundown of where things stood.

"So you're in charge now?"

"I am. What can you tell me about what you've found so far?"

"Well, the items from the plantation contained DNA that was consistent with the profile of Allison Byrd that is in the FBI's CODIS database."

"So we know that at some point, she was staying in the old outbuildings at Belle Grove," Jeff said.

"That's a reasonable assumption."

"What about the DNA on the bat? Have you linked any of the profiles to her?"

"I'm afraid not yet."

"Damn!" Jeff couldn't help himself.

"I'll keep trying."

* * *

Work, Jeff had learned a year ago during the Chris Rafferty case, was the only way to stay sane in the midst of desperate times. After he hung up with Dr. Vom Saal, he went back to the writ and the motion for a stay. He explained why the court should grant an exception to the rule that only one habeas petition could be filed for a prisoner. He explained that Quinn's evidence could not have been discovered previously and that no reasonable fact finder who had had that evidence could have found Ed guilty of Anne's murder under the federal constitution's due process clause. The work absorbed and comforted him. He wrote and edited and re-wrote and edited until the sun had set, and he could barely make out the cold, choppy waves of the river below Brendan's window.

He put on his overcoat and started to turn off the brass desk lamp that sat in the middle of the desk. But he thought better of it. He wanted to leave it on as a symbol of hope. He flipped off the overhead lights and headed down to the parking garage.

He had just gotten into the Range Rover and started the engine when his phone rang.

"Where are you?" Wynne asked. "How fast can you get to the Murphys'?"

"I'm in the car, on my way out of the garage. I'll be there in ten minutes. What's happened?" *Please say they've found Claire, and she's safe.*

"We've heard from Allison Byrd. The call's been recorded. We want to know what you think since none of us are criminal lawyers."

"Just tell me if Claire's all right."

"We don't know," Wynne sighed.

Jeff was tempted to go through red lights, but he decided it wasn't worth the risk of being stopped by the police. It was seven o'clock, and there was little traffic.

Mckenzie opened the front door and hurried him into the great room where Tyndall and Wynne sat with Mike Parker who was operating the recording equipment. Emma was still at the hospital.

He sat down on the sofa without taking off his overcoat. "How long ago did Allison Byrd call?"

"About forty-five minutes," Mike said. "She used a burner phone."

"But you could still get a location, couldn't you?" Jeff tried to keep his anxiety in check.

"Not one that helps us. Byrd picked an area out toward Powhatan where there aren't as many cell towers so we couldn't get triangulation, and her phone didn't have GPS. Her location was approximate. The sheriff is out there now, but so far his deputies are just tromping through fields. They haven't seen a place where she could be hiding Claire."

Jeff's heart sank. "What did she say?"

"Listen." Mike started the recording.

"Wynne, it's Auntie Allison." Jeff shivered when he heard the flat, hard voice with the thick twang.

Wynne replied, *"Where is Claire? I won't talk to you unless you tell me where she is and promise she's safe."*

"I had to take her for your own good, son. She's a whore. She's been sleeping around. I saw that other guy come out of her place, and I saw them at that hotel in California. I couldn't let you marry her." Jeff shivered again when he thought of Allison Byrd following him and Claire around New York and San Diego.

"Tell me where she is," Wynne repeated.

"Oh, you won't listen for nothing. You're gonna wind up in prison like your daddy if you marry that girl. I can't help you!"

Mike paused the recording for a second. "At that point we were afraid she'd hang up. So Wynne changed tactics." He started the recording again.

"Why don't you tell me why you called?" he asked.

"I figured you'd want her back. You're such a romantic fool. So, here's what you have to do. Are you listening to your auntie?"

"I am," Wynne agreed.

"Ya'll got that statement from that no-good Quinn. Made me so mad that I didn't get to her and shut her up before your so-called fiancée and her boyfriend persuaded her to talk."

"Are you admitting that you killed Quinn?" Wynne asked.

"I am not admitting anything," the angry, aggressive twang shot back. *"I'm telling you, if you use that statement to stop Ed Carter's execution, you'll never see your prissy whore of a fiancée again."*

"Tell you what, then. You give me Claire, and I'll give you Quinn's statement," Wynne offered.

"Oh, it doesn't work like that, son." They were listening to pure evil, Jeff thought. *"You'll give me a copy, and then you'll go ahead and take that original one to the court. I wasn't born yesterday. I'm not falling for that. No, I'm not. You listen here, son.*

363

And you listen good 'cause I'm only gonna tell you once. If you or anybody else does anything to stop that execution on Friday, I'll execute this good-for-nothing girl. It's real simple. If your no-account daddy dies on Friday, the girl lives. If he doesn't, she dies instead. Although I'd be doing you a big favor if I just got rid of her for you now. She's never going to be the wife you deserve."

The line went dead, and Mike turned off the recording.

Mckenzie was handing Jeff a scotch. "Here, you look like you need this."

"I do." He tossed back a big gulp and set the glass on the coffee table. He unbuttoned his overcoat, slipped it off, and then picked up the glass and drank some more. He looked at Mike Parker. "So what does the FBI make of this call?" he asked.

"We're very worried. We know this Byrd woman has killed before, so there's no doubt she's prepared to carry out her threat."

Tyndall, who had been sitting next to Mckenzie on the opposite sofa, spoke for the first time. "We don't even know for sure if Claire is still alive."

The statement hung stark and bare and terrifying in the room.

Jeff said, "We have to believe that she is and make our decisions accordingly. I am almost finished with the writ and request for a stay. I was planning to file them on Monday in the Fourth Circuit."

"Monday is the day they take Dad down to the execution chamber at Greensville," Wynne said.

"Could you still file on Monday," Mckenzie asked, "but file under seal?"

"The clerk would never go along with that," Jeff said, "because the Commonwealth's Attorney has to be able to respond to whatever I file. And the newspapers would move to open a sealed filing. So Byrd would know."

Wynne looked over at Tyndall who sat ashen-faced next to Mckenzie. Wynne said, "I think I'm the one who has to make the call here. I haven't told Dad about Allison's attacks on Claire or about Quinn's death. I didn't want to put any more stress on him because facing death is stressful enough. He's holding on, but not by much. So I haven't told him anything other than we're working hard for a stay."

"But you have to tell him about Brendan," Jeff said. "So he'll understand why I'm now suddenly his lawyer."

Wynne nodded. "Yes, and I was going to go down to Sussex and explain it all tomorrow."

"I should be with you," Jeff said. "If we cease trying to stop the execution, I'll need his consent."

Wynne nodded. "That's true. Of course, he'll give it."

"What we really need," Mark Parker observed, "is for Byrd to take Claire across state lines so the FBI can get fully involved."

CHAPTER FORTY

Sunday, February 26, 2017, Sussex State Prison, Sussex, Virginia

At one in the afternoon, Jeff sat next to Wynne in the Attorney Interview Room, waiting for Ed and wondering how he was ever going to fill Brendan Murphy's shoes. The door stirred and the guard ushered in a kindly faced, brown-eyed man with a full head of white hair. Even in handcuffs and shackles, he looked like a legal scholar and a teacher, not a killer. Jeff suppressed a shiver at the memory of the real killer's voice on the recording last night, threatening to kill Claire.

Ed look startled when he saw Jeff. "Where's Brendan?" his alarmed eyes went straight to Wynne's. "And where's Claire? Wasn't she coming with you to see me after the wedding?"

"Brendan's in the hospital," Wynne said.

"What's wrong?"

"He had a heart attack," Jeff said as he motioned to the guard and said, "Please unshackle his hands. And then leave. This is a confidential interview."

The guard looked unhappy but obeyed.

"Has something happened to Claire, too?" Ed looked from

Wynne to Jeff and back to Wynne.

"Yes," Wynne said gravely.

"Is she all right?"

"We don't know," Jeff shook his head.

Ed sat back in his chair and closed his eyes for a moment. When he opened them, he said, "You all have been keeping things from me, haven't you?"

"We have," Wynne agreed. "We didn't want to worry you if we didn't have to. But now we have to. Mckenzie Fitzgerald has been sitting on Quinn Fairchild's alibi evidence all these years. She interviewed her back when she worked for Brad O'Connor when she was just out of law school. Quinn told her she was with you all night the night my mother was killed. Mckenzie forgot to tape the interview, and then Quinn disappeared. So she panicked and didn't tell anyone."

Ed shook his head slowly. "That didn't matter, though, because I was accused of hiring Miller to kill Anne. Telling the jury that I was sleeping with a student would have made me seem that much guiltier. I'm lucky she didn't tell Brad."

"But why didn't you tell Brendan and Brian about Quinn when they tried your case for the second time?" Jeff asked.

"Because I was still being accused of hiring Miller. Sleeping with Quinn still made me look guilty, and I was ashamed of my affairs with my students."

"But why didn't you tell Brendan during your third trial when they claimed you drove to Richmond and killed Anne yourself? Quinn Fairchild on the stand could have rebutted Adam Winston's testimony that the white car in front of your house was yours."

"I thought the jury would believe me when I said I was in Charlottesville on Saturday night. I was afraid if Brendan called Quinn, the prosecutor would make the jury think that she was lying because she had had a romantic involvement with me even if it lasted only one night."

"So there was no affair with Quinn?"

"That's right. Just two people who ran into each other in a bar on a lonely Saturday night. And admitting to the jury that I had slept with a student would have just enhanced Gordon Fairfax's picture of me as an unfaithful husband who wanted his wife dead."

"But Quinn's story is true, isn't it? You were with her all night the night Anne was killed?" Jeff asked.

Ed nodded. "I was. But there was nothing to back up my alibi except Quinn's statement."

"What about the security cameras at the hotel? Wouldn't those cameras have picked up you coming and going with Quinn?"

"They would have if they'd been pointed at the door to my room. But I changed their direction so that the surveillance footage would not show Quinn and me together. The prosecution played that video to impeach my testimony that I was in the hotel that night because the cameras never picked up an image of me."

"So by tampering with those cameras, you turned evidence that could have helped you into evidence that hurt you," Jeff observed.

"That's right. But how did you find Quinn?"

"Mckenzie found her and tried to get a statement," Wynne explained. "But Quinn said that she would only talk to me or to

Claire, and since I was negotiating with Governor Reynolds, Claire and Jeff went to San Diego to talk to her."

"And she gave us a statement last Tuesday that we recorded," Jeff added. "But Allison killed her before she could sign the affidavit. I was still going to try to get her evidence in front of the court by arguing it was admissible as a dying declaration."

"That's a stretch," Ed said.

"A long one, I know. But it was all I could think of."

"But now we can't even try that," Wynne broke in, "because Allison hid in one of the empty rooms at Belle Grove and abducted Claire just as the wedding ceremony began. She's threatened to kill her if we use Quinn's statement to stop the execution on Friday."

Ed's eyes teared up. "Since the first day that woman walked into my classroom, she's been a poison that has threatened me and everyone I love. And the hell of it is, I've never been able to do anything to stop her."

"We'll stop her," Jeff said. "As soon as we find Claire, I'm going to file this writ. It's ready to go."

"Do you have any idea where Allison is holding her?" Ed asked.

"All we know is that Allison called me from a burner phone that pinged off some cell towers out in rural Powhatan. No exact location. The sheriff went out there with dogs and deputies, and they scoured the location, but haven't found any trace of Allison or Claire yet."

"Tell me Brendan is going to be all right," Ed said.

But Wynne shook his head. "Right now, we just don't know."

* * *

They were within ten miles of Richmond, when Jeff's phone rang.

"It's Tyndall," Wynne reported.

"Answer it for me."

"This is Wynne," Jeff heard him say to Claire's father. "Jeff is driving and can't talk right now. Okay, okay. I see. But no sign of her? What about Brendan?"

Wynne pushed the end call button and looked over at Jeff. "The sheriff found the white van abandoned not far from where GPS says Allison made that call yesterday. They traced the plates, and it was reported stolen about a week ago. They're processing it now, but so far no sign of blood. So we can go on hoping Claire hasn't been hurt."

"That's some good news," Jeff said. "What about Brendan?"

"Emma says his heart rhythms are steadier, but he's still unconscious. Possibly there's been brain damage. They just don't know."

"What are your plans now?" Jeff asked.

"Brendan had planned to stay in Richmond to be near the court, so that he could make all the last-minute filings. I was going to go down to Jarrat to be near Dad at the prison."

"I should stay in Richmond then," Jeff said.

"Of course. I'm just having trouble deciding where I need to be. If they find Claire—"

"When they find her," Jeff corrected, "Tyndall is going to be the first one who needs time with her. I think you should be with your father. He needs you."

"You're right," Wynne agreed. "I feel as if I need to apologize to Tyndall for putting Claire in danger. I never meant to."

"He knows. She wanted to help you and Ed. This isn't a good time for blame, anyway. I keep thinking about that Volvo in front of the house. We know that Allison stole her boyfriend's car to follow Ed and Anne to Charlottesville."

"True. But she didn't need a car to get to my parents' house. She lived around the corner."

"But if she was planning a murder that night, she needed a faster getaway than being on foot."

"So you're thinking of locating the boyfriend?"

"His name must be in the file somewhere. Or Mckenzie probably knows."

CHAPTER FORTY-ONE

Monday, February 27, 2017, The Law Offices of James Watkins, Richmond, Virginia

"I wish I could help you," James Watkins said at eleven o'clock on Monday morning after Jeff sat down across from his desk in his office in a building near the Chesterfield County Courthouse. He had the same soft, southern accent that Ed had. Those r-less vowels immediately sounded friendly. He was heavyset, with a paunch that hung over his belt, suggesting beer was his drink of choice. He had just come from a court appearance and was wearing his dark suit pants and a heavily starched white shirt and navy tie. His suit coat was hanging on a hook on the back of his office door.

"Thanks for making time for me on short notice."

"Of course. I read about your fiancée's kidnapping in the *Times Dispatch* over the weekend. Allison was always crazy as a loon."

"Actually, not my fiancée. Wynne Carter's."

"Ed's son?"

"Yes."

"Wow! Now I see. That's just the kind of sicko thing that Allison would do."

"How long did you date her?"

"Not long. A few months during our second year of law school. She was obviously nuts. Has anyone told you that she stole my car?"

"Yes."

"That was after I stopped dating her."

"What kind of car did you have?"

James chuckled. "A beat up, five-year-old Ford Mustang. Bright red. It was a heap of trash. I reported it stolen, and the cops found it parked in front of Allison's apartment on Grove. She made up some story that I'd let her borrow it."

"Was she prosecuted for car theft?"

"Nah." He shook his head. "It wasn't worth it. I got the car back in one piece. It was on its last legs anyway. You look disappointed."

Jeff explained what he'd been hoping to hear.

"Sorry, no Volvo wagon. The only people who drove those were people who had kids. Like Ed Carter."

* * *

Jeff headed back to the Murphys' where Wynne was about to leave for Jarrat.

"Any luck?" he asked as Jeff entered the front hall.

"None."

Wynne handed Jeff his cell phone and a piece of paper and said, "I'm leaving this with you. This is the phone that Alison Byrd called on Saturday. If she calls again, I'll be too far away for Mike to monitor the call. And here's my alternate number so you can reach me with any news."

"Okay. I'm assuming you haven't heard anything new."

"No. I talked the sheriff in Port Conway into taking the dogs out again around Belle Grove because you uncovered evidence that Allison had been squatting in the outbuildings at the plantation. But so far, no news. It's a very long shot because I don't see how she could get Claire into those buildings undetected."

"Right," Jeff agreed. *But she could be there alone if something's happened to Claire. No, I'm not going to let myself think that.*

* * *

That afternoon, Jeff drove to Charlottesville where he had discovered Trevor James Trewitt, Jr. had retired from his Washington D.C. law practice to a farm near Keswick in horse country. Trewitt lived in a brick colonial revival mansion with a white-columned porch at the end of a long drive, lined on each side with pastureland, populated by half a dozen magnificent chestnut horses. Trevor came out on the porch when Jeff pulled up in the Range Rover.

Whereas James Watkins had been a typical beer-drinking, Southern good ol' boy, Trevor had a tall, lean aristocratic bearing. He was wearing jodhpurs, riding boots, and a University of Virginia sweatshirt. He came down the steps to greet Jeff.

"Come on in, and I'll get us something to drink." Although he didn't look at all like James Watkins, he had the same warm, friendly accent.

Jeff followed Trevor down a long, marble hall into a den at the back of the house. It was lined with dark-paneled shelves filled with books and furnished with a red leather sofa, chairs, and an antique mahogany desk. Although it was large, the room seemed cozy and inviting.

"Have a seat over there," Trevor suggested, pointing to the sofa. He walked over to the drinks tray and poured two whiskys and handed one to Jeff as he sat down next to him. "It's three o'clock. That's close enough to five for a drink."

Jeff would have preferred coffee because he had the drive back to the Murphys' ahead of him, but he didn't want to refuse Trewitt's hospitality. "Thank you."

"I'm really sorry to hear about your girlfriend," Trevor said.

"Actually, she's Wynne Carter's fiancée."

"Oh, Ed's son. That's too bad. I've just read the stories in the papers. Sounds like this Allison woman is a real nut job."

"And then some," Jeff agreed.

"Well, I'm happy to meet with you," Trevor said, "but I went to UVA for law school, so I don't know much about Ed Carter and all that stuff down in Richmond."

"I know," Jeff agreed. "Coming up here is a real long shot, but I had to try."

"And I am delighted to help you if I can," Trevor smiled, ever the Southern gentleman.

"You dated a woman named Quinn Fairchild when you were in law school."

"Ah, yes, tough little Quinn, from the wrong side of the tracks in Petersburg."

"Do you happen to remember the night you broke up with her?"

Trevor frowned. "When would that be?"

"November 19, 1983, to be precise."

"Wow, I couldn't have told you that."

"Ed's wife, Anne, died that night or in the wee hours of the morning of the twentieth."

"Oh, now I remember. Not the date, but the story. It was all over the news the next day. Yeah, Quinn came up from Richmond to see me that weekend. And I broke up with her."

"She told me and Claire Chastain that she slept with Ed that night. She picked him up in a pub called the Unicorn's Horn."

"That could very well be true. The pub was just around the corner from the apartments where I was living. I had to tell her that our relationship was over. She was in Richmond; I was up here. We didn't really have much in common except for being second-year law students. And truth to tell, I had met someone else who lived here in Charlottesville."

"So you let her drive all the way up from Richmond to tell her to get lost?"

"Well, I never thought of it in quite those terms. I cooked dinner for the two of us at my apartment and tried to tell her nicely that it wasn't going to work out. She stormed out, and that was the last I saw of her until the next morning."

Jeff suddenly was on high alert. "What did you see the next morning?"

"Well, to be honest with you, I was worried about her. I offered her a place to sleep that night because she didn't have anywhere else to go, and she'd driven up here counting on staying with me. But she left in a huff and didn't come back all night, and I was afraid something had happened to her. So you can imagine how relieved I was to look out the next morning and see her getting out of a white Volvo station wagon."

"Did you see who was driving the car?"

"It was a man. That was all I could tell."

"So he never got out of the car?"

"You know, now that you mention it, he did. He got out and opened the door for Quinn and kissed her on the cheek. Then he got back into the Volvo and drove off."

"According to Quinn, that man was Ed Carter," Jeff said.

"It could very well have been," Trevor agreed. "But I didn't see his face, and I didn't know Ed Carter at the time."

"But you've seen his picture since, haven't you?"

"In the papers, yes. But I was too far away that morning. All I know is that a man with brown hair, five nine or maybe six feet at the most, was with Quinn that morning. If you think my declaration will help you get a stay of Ed Carter's execution, I'll be more than happy to write one out before you go."

"Yes, thanks," Jeff smiled.

CHAPTER FORTY-TWO

Tuesday, February 28, 2017, The Murphys', Windsor Farms, Richmond, Virginia

"Jeff!"

He opened his eyes and saw the faintest thread of light through the blinds.

"Jeff!"

Tyndall's voice. *Oh, God! Claire. No! Please, no.*

"I'm coming." The guest room alarm clock said six a.m. He pulled a sweatshirt over the T-shirt and sweatpants that he had slept in and hurried barefoot to open the door. Tyndall was standing in the hall in his robe, looking pale and drawn.

"What is it?"

"The Richmond police are here with the sheriff from Powhatan and Mike Parker from the FBI. They're waiting for all of us downstairs."

Jeff's gut tightened. *Claire's not dead. She can't be dead.*

He followed Tyndall down to the great room where Mckenzie, also in robe and slippers, was pouring coffee for Detective Hampton, Sheriff Bass, and Mike Parker. He was surprised to find Emma there, too, although she was already dressed so Jeff guessed that she was on her way to the hospital.

"We've got news," Detective Hampton began when everyone was seated. He pulled out a manila envelope and took out some eight by ten photographs. "Do you recognize the ring in these pictures, Mr. Chastain?"

Jeff saw Tyndall flinch as he looked at the pictures. When he had finished, he laid them on the coffee table and said, "That's Claire's engagement ring."

Detective Hampton and Sheriff Bass exchanged a look. Then Sheriff Bass said, "A woman who fits the description of Allison Byrd pawned this ring at Quick Pawn in Radford yesterday. The shop's surveillance video caught her coming and going at four thirty in the afternoon."

"Radford," Jeff said. "That's where Anne Carter's wedding rings were pawned."

"Right," Detective Hampton said.

"Is this all you know?" Jeff asked. "Do you know anything about where Claire is?"

"No," Sheriff Bass shook his head.

"But you're not optimistic that she's safe, are you?" Tyndall asked.

"We've been worried, as you know, from the beginning. The more time that passes, the more worried we become," Mike Parker said in his quiet, professional baritone.

"Any chance that Allison has taken Claire to Radford?" Jeff asked.

"Of course there's a chance," Sheriff Bass said, "but you know as well as I do that moving a hostage is risky."

"So you're thinking Claire was left behind in Richmond or Powhatan?" Jeff asked.

"We're afraid to think that," Detective Hampton said, "because if that's the case, she's been harmed."

Tyndall leaned back in his chair and put his hand over his face. Mckenzie got up and knelt by him and put her arms around him.

Jeff stared out at the brown winter lawn and tried to grasp the fact that Claire could be dead. After a few seconds, he said to Detective Hampton, "Have you let Wynne Carter know about this?"

The detective shook his head. "Not yet. We thought he was going to be here with the rest of you."

"He's down at Greensville with his father," Jeff said. "I have his cell phone upstairs. I'll go get it. I think you and Sheriff Bass should tell him what you've told us."

* * *

An hour later, Mckenzie, Tyndall, and Jeff gathered around the Murphys' landline with Wynne on speakerphone. Emma had asked her housekeeper to make blueberry muffins and more coffee for everyone before she left for the hospital. Brendan's life was still hanging by a thread.

"How are things there?" Jeff asked Wynne.

"I can't even begin to explain. Dad's in this tiny little cell next to the execution chamber. The doctors have prodded and probed to be sure he'll be easy to kill on Friday. They won't let me see him except through a glass window. The only person who can be in the room with him is Father Jim. And since Dad's taking some comfort at having him near, I've decided to forgive him for the DNA fiasco."

"I've got some new evidence," Jeff said. He quickly gave Wynne a rundown of his meetings with James Watkins and Trevor Trewitt.

"It's not great, but it's something," Wynne observed.

"If we put it with Bart's copycat killing declaration, it sounds persuasive," Jeff said.

"What we really need is DNA on that bat," Wynne said.

"I've got an idea," Mckenzie spoke up.

"Let's hear it," Wynne said.

"Let's get Jeff in to see Governor Reynolds with all this new evidence. Byrd is watching the court filings. She won't know if Jeff has a private meeting with the governor."

"It's worth a try," Wynne agreed. "I'll call his chief of staff right now and beg for a time today."

After Wynne hung up, Jeff looked over at Tyndall who was still in shock. Jeff said, "I don't think Claire's been harmed, Tyndall."

"What makes you say that?"

"Because Alison Byrd needs her as a bargaining chip to tie our hands so that we can't help Ed with Quinn's statement. At least until nine on Friday night, Byrd has no motive to murder Claire."

"But after that?"

"There won't be an after that," Jeff insisted. "We're going to find her before then."

* * *

Tuesday, February 28, 2017, The Murphys', Windsor Farms, Richmond, Virginia

At eight that night, Jeff returned from his meeting with Governor Reynolds.

He was surprised to see Emma in the great room sitting in front of the fire with Tyndall and Mckenzie.

"How's Brendan?" he asked as soon as he walked in.

"He was fully conscious for a little while this afternoon. He asked about Ed, and I told him you were taking care of it," Emma said. "He seemed relieved to hear that. His heart rhythms are better. Fingers crossed."

"How did it go with the governor?" Mckenzie asked.

"So-so. He took the folder of new evidence and promised to study it. He reminded me that he wants to run for the Senate when his term expires, and I reminded him that Wynne's willing to fund his campaign."

"And that wasn't enough to persuade him to commute Ed's sentence or grant a stay?" Tyndall demanded.

"It wasn't enough for anything other than a promise to consider what we have. Any news on Claire?"

"Someone in Powhatan thought they saw Allison go through a fast food drive through out there. Detective Hampton ran the license plate that the witness called in, but couldn't trace it to her," Tyndall said. "Most likely it was her in another stolen car."

"There must be someone who knows where Allison lives," Emma said.

"Detective Hampton doesn't think she has a place to live. She seems to just squat in abandoned buildings."

"Like she did in the outbuildings at the plantation," Jeff observed.

"Right. The sheriff still has his deputies looking in the area where Byrd made the call to Wynne. But so far, no sign of her out there."

After supper, Emma went back to the hospital to be with Brendan. Mckenzie talked Tyndall into trying to get some sleep. Afterward, she and Jeff sat in front of the fire, finishing the last of the wine from dinner.

"I'm to blame for all this," she began.

"I doubt that. You have no idea whether or not the jurors would have believed Quinn if she'd testified at Ed's third trial."

"Why wouldn't they?"

"Because Adam Winston saw the white Volvo there that night."

"So you're saying Quinn could have been lying after all?"

"You thought she was lying," Jeff reminded her. "And she didn't stick around to talk to you after she realized the recording didn't happen."

"And those are all the reasons why I've told myself all these years that I didn't commit malpractice by forgetting to turn the tape on."

Suddenly Wynne's phone began to ring, and Jeff answered it. "Wynne Carter's phone, Jeff Ryder speaking."

"Mr. Ryder, Sheriff Bass. I've got some news about Miss Chastain."

"Tell me you've found her, and she's okay."

"I'm afraid I can't say that. But I can say we found an old shed behind a house out here in Powhatan where it looks like she was being held. There's a pair of white shoes that look like bridal shoes and some bedding."

"Size six and a half, white satin Manolo Blahniks covered in pearls?"

"That's right."

"Text me the exact address," Jeff said, "I'm on my way."

"What is it?" Mckenzie asked when Jeff ended the call.

"Sheriff Bass has found Claire's shoes in a shed out in Powhatan in the area where Allison called from. I'm going out there."

"I want to come, too. And Tyndall. I'll go get him."

Jeff took the keys to the Range Rover off the peg in the kitchen and walked to the front hall where he took his overcoat out of the closet and put it on. He heard the sound of footsteps and looked up to find Mckenzie coming down the stairs alone, buttoning her overcoat and wrapping a knitted scarf around her neck.

"He's asleep," she said. "It's the first time he's had any deep sleep since all this happened. I don't want to wake him."

Jeff nodded. "He's exhausted. We should let him rest."

They got into the Range Rover and headed out into the night, which seemed especially cold and dark. Although it was the first of March, the temperature was right at freezing.

There was little traffic on the roads, but it took forty minutes to travel from the Murphys' across Richmond to the Huguenot Trail exit off 288 North. Jeff turned onto the 711, a dark, twisty road that wound down an even darker hill. Then all at once, Route 607 appeared out of the darkness, lit by the only streetlight for miles. Jeff had to hit the brakes hard and swerve a little in order to make the left turn. They were immediately plunged into more darkness. Jeff navigated the big car down an unlit, unpaved, single-lane road.

"Where in the world are we?" Mckenzie whispered. "There are hardly any houses out here."

"Nearly there according to the navigation," Jeff said. "The address is 1815 Huguenot Springs Road."

Suddenly there was an open field in front of them with a large house at the end of the open space. The house was surrounded by sheriff's cars and large lights which had been brought in to illuminate the scene.

"Looks like we're here," Jeff observed.

He parked next to the line of deputy sheriffs' cars, and he and Mckenzie got out. The attention of the crowd of law enforcement officers was fixed on the garden shed behind the house. Mike Parker saw them approaching and came to meet them.

"Glad you're here," he said. "She was being held in that shed. Come have a look at the shoes we found."

They followed him over to the entrance to the shed. A pair of white satin pumps encrusted with pearls had been packaged in a clear evidence bag and placed in an open evidence storage container.

"Do you recognize those?" Mike asked.

"They're Claire's," Jeff said. "They're her wedding shoes."

"That's what we thought."

"What else have you found?"

"A sleeping bag and a pillow. Some fast food containers and empty paper bags. Have a look."

The inside of the shed had been illuminated by one of the portable lights. Jeff saw the wadded up bedding on the concrete floor and a plastic bag that held the discarded food wrappings.

"There's no evidence that she's been harmed," Mike said. "We haven't found any blood or weapons."

"Who lives in the big house?" Jeff asked. "Didn't anyone see Allison here with Claire?"

"The house isn't occupied," Mike said. "The owners use it for family gatherings and parties. We think Allison was squatting there and keeping an eye on her hostage out here in the shed."

"Unoccupied spaces. That's her typical pattern," Jeff observed.

"Any idea where she's gone?" Mckenzie asked. "And is she still holding Claire?"

"We assume she's still in the area. Someone saw a car come down here around ten o'clock last night, but didn't bother to call it in until tonight. We believe Allison must have seen the stories in the newspapers that reported we'd picked up her license number in that drive through and decided to move Claire. We don't believe she could have gotten very far."

"So you're looking for another empty house around here?" Mckenzie asked.

"Yes. We've knocked on doors asking if anyone is aware of any vacant property. No luck so far."

* * *

Tyndall was awake and worried when Jeff and Mckenzie returned to the Murphys'.

"We thought it best not to wake you," Mckenzie said. He listened closely as she explained what the sheriff had found.

When she finished, he shook his head. "I just want her home safely and miles away from everything to do with the Carters."

"It isn't Wynne's fault," Jeff reminded him gently.

"I know," Tyndall said. "But I don't care. No more Carters in our lives."

Mckenzie's eyes met Jeff's, and she shook her head slightly as if to say, *Don't argue with him. He's not rational right now.* "Let's get some sleep," she suggested. "Maybe the sheriff will have found Claire by morning."

MCKENZIE

"This is the way the world ends.
Not with a bang but a whimper."

T.S. Eliot

CHAPTER FORTY-THREE

Wednesday, March 1, 2017, The Murphys', Windsor Farms, Richmond, Virginia

Sunlight and the hum of voices woke Mckenzie at six a.m. As she opened her eyes, she realized her cell phone was ringing.

"Are you watching the news?" Hugh demanded.

"The news? No, it's six a.m. You woke me up. Why are you awake at three in the morning?"

"Because Gil Carlyle of the *L.A. Times* just called. A major story is breaking about you on the East Coast as we speak. It will be on the West Coast in the next three hours. By that time, the whole country will know that you're guilty of ineffective assistance of counsel in the Ed Carter case."

"*What?*" Mckenzie got up and walked over to the window. She moved the blinds just enough to see at least ten news vans parked on the Murphys' lawn in the early morning light. "Oh, my God! There's a huge press contingent camped on the front lawn."

"Well, it's just going to get bigger. George Lovell is planning a news conference as soon as it's light here to demand your withdrawal as a nominee for the Court."

"But—"

"Do you know someone named Jenny Miyamoto?"

"She is, or was—I'm not sure of their present status—Joel's girlfriend."

"She called the *New York Times* yesterday and gave Sol Goldmeir an earful about you. Then she called Gil at the *L.A. Times* and gave him the same earful."

"About me?"

"She claims that you were prepared to let an innocent man be executed for the sake of your career."

"God! No! Did she really say that?"

"And more. I'm emailing you the article as we speak."

Mckenzie quickly booted up her laptop and opened Hugh's email. "Oh, God." She groaned several times as she read it.

"She's even blaming you for Claire Chastain's kidnapping," Hugh observed. "She says if you'd told the truth about interviewing Quinn Fairchild in 1983, Allison Byrd would have been apprehended decades ago."

"Except her DNA is not on the murder weapon."

"Doesn't matter. DNA does not always transfer; and even when it does, it does not always survive."

"Right. I know. There's no question that Allison killed Anne Carter, DNA evidence or no DNA evidence. What should I do, Hugh?"

"Fall on your sword. Give Ed's current lawyer a declaration under penalty of perjury admitting ineffective assistance. Then issue a mea culpa press statement and resign as the nominee."

"Resign?"

"Resign. You don't have a choice."

* * *

"Mom, it's three in the morning," Joel groaned two minutes later. "Call me when the sun comes up."

"The sun is up in Virginia," Mckenzie said, "and the Murphys' lawn is full of press thanks to Jenny."

"Oh, God. No! Don't tell me. She blew the lid off the Quinn Fairchild story?"

"She certainly did. Senator Lovell is calling for my resignation as a nominee for the Court based upon ineffective assistance of counsel. How did she find out about that unrecorded interview with Quinn from 1983?"

"It's all my fault," Joel said. "I told her about it one night when I'd had too much to drink. I thought she was in love with me, and that it was safe to tell her anything. I was proud of you for admitting your mistake and helping Jeff and Claire find Quinn."

"But she betrayed your confidence."

"I didn't think she would. Maybe she felt free to snitch because we broke up."

"When did that happen?"

"A week ago. I asked her to marry me, and she said no."

"Why did she turn you down?"

"She said she could never marry anyone who worked for Big Law. I was hurt at first, but then I realized she was a hypocrite. She complained about racial and socio-economic bias, but she was judging me and you, too, based on bias. Her view of things was too narrow. You can't say that all poor people are good, and all rich people are bad."

Well, at least he's figured that out.

"Look, Joel, I don't mind losing the Court nomination. Maybe I'm not right for the job, anyway. But she's put Claire's life in danger. That crazy woman kidnapped her at the wedding, and then she called Wynne and threatened to kill her if we tried to use Quinn's alibi evidence to stop Ed's execution. We haven't been able to find out where she's holding Claire."

"Oh, God!"

"Why didn't Jenny at least tell you that she was going public with this as a courtesy?"

"Because she's a fanatic, Mom. She thinks she's right about everything. Even if she'd known that Claire was in danger, I doubt it would have stopped her."

* * *

As soon as Mckenzie hung up with Joel, Tyndall called through her closed door,

"Mac? Are you all right. What's going on outside?"

She opened the door to find him in the hall in his robe and slippers. "You'd better come in," she said.

They sat down in the chairs under the window. The shades were down, but they could hear the reporters milling around on the lawn.

"What's this all about?" Tyndall asked.

"Joel's ex-girlfriend has given the press a story about Quinn's alibi evidence and my failure to record it in 1983."

"What? But Claire—"

"Please don't say it. I know. She's in danger. Look, we've got to take this one step at a time. Hugh called and said George is planning a news conference to demand my withdrawal as a nominee to the Court."

"No! Don't do that!" Tyndall looked hurt. "You're the best possible choice for that job."

"Maybe. But not now. Jenny's made me look ruthless and ambitious."

"Not true."

"Thank you. But the only way to combat this is to issue my own press release, resigning. I'm going to get dressed and go downstairs and tell the world I'm withdrawing. Then I'm going to draft a declaration stating that I provided ineffective assistance to Ed when I was employed in the Public Defender's Office and give that to Jeff to take to the Fourth Circuit. Now that the information is public, I have no choice but to put it before the court."

Tyndall was silent for a few moments. Then he said, "You're right. I'll wake Jeff while you write your statement for the press and make the arrangements to deliver it."

"And you need to go tell Emma why her front lawn is full of reporters."

JEFF

"Where does one go from a world of insanity?
Somewhere on the other side of despair."

T.S. Eliot

CHAPTER FORTY-FOUR

Wednesday, March 1, 2017, Brendan Murphy's Office, Riverfront Plaza, Craig, Lewis, and Weller, Richmond, Virginia

Jeff hung up the phone and put his head in his hands and stared at the clock on Brendan's desk. Four thirty. Judge Boyce's clerk had just called to say that the request for a stay based upon Mckenzie's declaration had been denied. *It should have been enough,* he thought. *Ineffective assistance based on alibi evidence should have been enough. And if that wasn't enough, what was?*

He picked up the phone again and called Wynne at Jarrat. "It's a no go," he said.

Wynne was silent for a long time. Then he said, "That was our best shot. It didn't take them long to knock it out of the water."

"I know. The judges have their minds made up in favor of guilt. How's Ed?"

"Resigned. They finally let me sit with him for a few minutes. Any news on Brendan and Claire?"

"Brendan is holding his own. Sheriff Bass has his dogs out again, searching the area where they found her shoes, and the sheriff down in King George County has his K-9s out again, too."

Suddenly Jeff's cell began to ring, and he could see the call was from Tyndall. "Hang on, it's Claire's father. Maybe there's some good news."

But a few minutes later, he picked up the line again and said to Wynne, "I've got to get to the Murphys' ASAP. Claire's wedding suit has been found. And it's covered in blood."

* * *

The Murphys' drive was full of cars from the Richmond Police Department and a couple of Chesterfield County Sheriffs' cars. Some news vans had lingered after Mckenzie's dramatic statement on the steps that morning, acknowledging the mistake early in her career, and withdrawing her name as a nominee for the Court.

One of the reporters ran up to him. "I've just heard the news that your request for a stay has been denied again by the Fourth Circuit."

"We're in the process of appealing that decision to the United States Supreme Court," Jeff said. He gave thanks for Brendan's army of associates who were at work on the filing as he spoke.

Another reporter appeared. "We understand that Allison Byrd's hostage has been killed in retaliation for your attempt to save Ed Carter."

"I don't know that to be true," Jeff said, trying to mask his terror that it might be. "Now if you'll excuse me, I have to go inside."

Emma met him in the front hall. "Brendan's better. Mckenzie called me because she's worried about Tyndall."

Jeff followed her into the great room where Sheriff Bass and Detective Hampton were sitting on the sofa, talking to Claire's father, who had obviously been crying. Mckenzie was sitting beside him, holding his hand. Everyone looked up when Jeff entered.

"Tell me what's happened," Jeff said.

"We found what we think is Ms. Chastain's suit. Mr. Chastain is too upset to identify it. We were waiting for you," Detective Hampton said.

"Where did you find it?" Jeff asked.

"In the bathroom of a fast food restaurant in Powhatan. Byrd planted it there and phoned the sheriff to tell him to look for it. We have her on surveillance camera walking in with the box."

"Any information on the vehicle she was driving?" Jeff asked.

"No. She parked out of range of the cameras in the parking lot."

"I'd better take a look at it," Jeff said.

He followed Detective Hampton into the dining room where a medium-size cardboard box sat on the table. He made himself look inside. Claire's white suit was wadded up, torn in places, and covered in blood.

He looked away quickly. "It's Claire's. Byrd threatened to kill her if we used that alibi evidence."

Detective Hampton nodded. "That's what we were afraid of. I'm going to send this with the CSI people now. I'm hoping they can get a report back by this afternoon."

Jeff walked over to the sofa opposite where Tyndall and

Mckenzie were sitting with Sheriff Bass and sat down. Emma had poured a scotch and offered it to him, but he shook his head. "I've got to go back and work on the appeal to the Supreme Court. If you have coffee, that would be great."

"We don't know anything for sure until we find a body," the sheriff said. "We've still got the dogs out."

Emma handed Jeff a cup of coffee. He took a sip and said, "Call me with any news, no matter what time. I'll be up all night."

"Will do."

The room was quiet after all the law enforcement personnel had left. Tyndall accepted a cup of coffee from Emma and looked at Jeff. He said, "I'm coming back to the office to help you with Ed's appeal to the Court."

"Is that a good idea?" Emma asked.

Jeff remembered how working on his own case and Claire's support had gotten him through the Chris Rafferty nightmare. "It's a great idea."

"And I'm coming, too," Mckenzie said. "Now that I'm no longer a nominee, I can get back to work."

CHAPTER FORTY-FIVE

Thursday, March 2, 2017, The Murphys', Windsor Farms, Richmond,
Virginia

Jeff heard his cell phone ringing and struggled to open his eyes. He realized that he'd fallen asleep on the couch in Brendan's office at four a.m. after Brendan's senior associate, Robert Weaver, had left for D.C. to make the filing at the Supreme Court. He glanced at his watch as he reached for his phone. Ten after ten. The request for a stay should be filed with the Court by now.

Jeff punched the accept button on his phone and heard a familiar voice. "Mr. Ryder, this is Detective Hampton."

"Yes, Detective."

"Mr. Chastain wanted me to call you." Jeff's heart began to beat faster. He'd sent Tyndall and Mckenzie back to the Murphys' at three.

"Have you found Claire?"

"No, but the lab analyzed the blood on the suit, and it's not human blood."

Jeff took a deep breath. "Thank God! Allison did this before when she was watching Claire's apartment in New York."

"Well, it's better news than we expected. But it doesn't mean that Ms. Chastain hasn't been harmed."

"I know."

After he hung up, he realized that although Jenny Miyamoto's press release had provoked Allison to frighten them with the bloody suit, she still had a motive to keep Claire alive to hobble their efforts to get a stay. If the motion he'd sent up to the Court with Robert this morning was successful, the next message from Allison wouldn't be covered in animal blood.

A sense of futility overwhelmed him. He didn't want to admit that he was out of options to save Ed and that he was helpless to rescue Claire. He drove back to the Murphys' to find the house empty and a note that said everyone had gone to visit Brendan. Exhausted by the thought of what was coming tomorrow, he went upstairs and threw himself on the bed in his guest room and went to sleep.

* * *

His cell phone went off at exactly one o'clock. Jeff reached for it without looking at the caller ID. His eyes felt sandy, and he felt the fatigue that goes with sleeping during daylight.

"Jeff, it's Dr. Vom Saal."

"Tell me you've identified one of those DNA profile on the bat as Allison Byrd's."

"I'm afraid not."

"But you aren't giving up, are you?"

"It's very old DNA, Jeff. We've tried everything to match what's there to Byrd, but if her DNA is there or ever was there, we can't identify it."

"Please try again."

"Okay. But we don't have much cellular material left to work with."

CLAIRE

"There was a door. And I could not open it.
I could not touch the handle."

T.S. Eliot

CHAPTER FORTY-SIX

Thursday, March 2, 2017, Huguenot Springs, Powhatan, Virginia

Claire guessed that it must be close to midnight. She had counted the sunrises and sunsets carefully, and she knew that tomorrow was the day that Ed Carter would die. And she realized that this madwoman intended to kill her as soon as Ed's execution was a certainty. She had heard Allison tell Wynne what would happen if they tried to save Ed. And the talking heads on the blaring televisions that Allison loved to leave on day and night, when she was in a place that had one, repeatedly assured the world that there would be no reprieve for Ed Carter.

It was also clear that Allison was insane. She constantly referred to Claire as "Anne." And she harangued her about her supposed infidelities with Jeff and repeated the same delusional story about seeing Anne's murder over and over.

"You're a whore. You're not good enough for Auntie Allison's Wynne. Like father, like son. Wynne didn't have any judgment, just like his daddy. He picked you just like Ed picked that whore, Anne. He should have picked me. The minute I saw him and Wynne, I knew we were meant to be a family. I would have given him a houseful of babies." She patted her fat stomach for emphasis. "I knew he was in Charlottesville that night, and I went there to kill her. I thought with her gone, Ed would understand that we were meant for each other. But I didn't have to do it, because Ed came back from Charlottesville and did it himself. I was watching their house the way I always did, and I heard them shouting about how Ed wasn't Wynne's daddy. She made a fool of him. Wynne wasn't his son. And so he killed her. He deserves to die."

Claire had been sure during those first forty-eight hours that the police would find her. When that hadn't happened and she had realized just how hopelessly insane Allison was, she had concentrated on finding a way to escape. But as the days went by, Claire began to see that escape was going to be more difficult than she'd first thought. Allison did not sleep much, and when she did, she was easily awakened. And she kept moving Claire from one unoccupied house in rural Powhatan to another so that the conditions of her imprisonment kept changing.

The closest Claire had come to success had been when Allison had driven them to Radford to pawn Claire's engagement ring. Allison had rented a cheap motel suite with one of her many stolen credit cards. She had locked Claire in the bathroom while she went to pawn the ring. The window had been too tiny to squeeze through, so Claire had tried to figure out how to unlock the flimsy door. She had been close to success with a bobby pin that someone had left behind when Allison had come back with a huge bag of marijuana.

Claire had nearly choked on the smell of the smoke as Allison had gotten high that night, staring at the blaring television. But eventually her eyes had closed, and she had looked as if she'd passed out. Claire had crept out of the bedroom and across the suite's living room, praying that Allison really was out cold. But as soon as Claire's hand had closed around the handle of the front door, Allison's eyes had popped open. She had jumped up and grabbed Claire by her cast and dragged her into the bedroom where she had locked her in for the night. It had been a second floor room with no window wide enough to squeeze through.

Now on the day before Ed's execution, they had doubled back to the unoccupied house at Huguenot Springs where Allison had first held Claire. But this time, instead of leaving her alone in the shed, Allison had locked Claire in one of the upstairs bedrooms.

Claire sat by the window in the big room, staring into the night. The moon was full, so she could see the ground below quite clearly. Although it seemed trivial under the circumstances, Claire longed for a hot shower and clean clothes. She was wearing a pair of sweatpants, a sweatshirt, and ill-fitting sneakers that Allison had shoved in her face nearly a week ago.

She tried to figure out a way to get out the window and down to the ground without breaking another bone. Her cast made her left arm clumsy and interfered with grasping things like the gutter that she'd need to slide down to make her escape.

Claire knew that Ed's request for a stay had been turned down by the Supreme Court. Allison had turned the television up very loud and uttered a whoop when the news had been announced an hour ago. Since then, Claire had heard her moving around the house, gathering up her belongings for yet another move. Now that Ed was on his way to certain death in less than twenty-four hours, Claire knew that her hours were numbered, too. Unless she could find a way down from this window.

But luck was not with her. A few minutes later, Allison appeared with the ever-present gun and ordered Claire downstairs and into the back seat of the ancient white Camry that she'd stolen in Radford and had been driving without plates ever since.

"I'm taking you back to where I found you," Allison said as she turned the car to head out of the gravel drive. "You're good for nothing, and I'm sick of the sight of you."

As they drove through the moonlit night, Claire fought to hold back her rising panic. Allison was headed north on I-95, and Claire had no idea where they were going this time. But after about thirty minutes, Allison got off the interstate, and Claire realized that she had taken the exit that brought them to Route 301. She was, indeed, taking Claire back to where she'd found her. She was headed for Belle Grove.

Claire knew that Allison always kept the gun on the front passenger seat, within easy reach. She realized that her only chance was to jump out of the car when Allison slowed for the turn into Belle Grove's oak-lined drive and to run as fast as she could toward the house, using the trees as shelter. Even though the moonlight was a disadvantage, staying close to the trees would make her a more difficult target.

Allison slowed the car to five miles per hour and made the turn. Claire reached for the door handle and prepared to make her desperate bid for freedom. But suddenly, the car came to a full stop and Allison said, "This is where your free ride ends. Like I said, I'm sick and tired of you. Get out."

Claire pulled up the door handle and pushed the door open. At the same moment, she saw Allison reach for the gun in the moonlight. Claire began to run as soon as her feet hit the ground. She wove through the trees just as she'd planned. Her lungs burned, and she struggled to run harder and faster through the silver light, but her ill-fitting shoes felt like bricks attached to her feet. Bullets were whizzing past her. She saw the house ahead and realized that she was about to emerge from the shelter of the trees. As she prepared to make a last frantic dash across the gravel to the house, she went down.

JEFF

"Without some kind of God, man is not very interesting."

T.S. Eliot

CHAPTER FORTY-SEVEN

Friday, March 3, 2017, Greensville Correctional Center, Jarrat, Virginia

Jeff left the Murphys' at six a.m. in a drizzle of freezing rain. By the time he reached the prison a little over an hour later, he realized that the entire day was going to be overcast and frozen. Winter was refusing to yield to spring. He sat in Brendan's Range Rover and stared up at the bare, unforgiving cement façade with the huge blue letters that said, "Greensville Correctional Center." Barbed wire and a gigantic guard tower loomed to the left. He wondered how he would be able to get through the day.

But he had to find the strength to do the job that Brendan would have done. He owed it to Ed and to Wynne, and above all to Claire. His heart ached at the thought of her. She'd been missing a week. That wasn't a good sign.

Wynne was already in the lobby when Jeff went inside. A guard showed them to the warden's office where they waited with weak cups of coffee and mounting nerves.

Ronnie Ray Wright, the warden, strolled in ten minutes

later. He was wearing a rumpled gray suit and a navy tie, and his long, lean face was tense.

"So you're here instead of Mr. Murphy," he said to Jeff.

"Yes. He's in the intensive cardiac care unit at Medical College in Richmond."

"Sorry to hear that. But this certainly isn't the place for him today with his heart in bad shape. I've talked to Mr. Carter here about the procedure. Are you familiar with it?"

"No. I've been trying my best to keep it from happening."

"I'd better go over it with you, then. Ed's in a cell next to the execution chamber. I'll walk you over there after this so that you can be familiar with the layout of the execution room before tonight. It will take place promptly at nine. There's a phone in there with a direct line to Governor Reynolds. He can order a stay at any time. Or we can receive word from the court that a stay has been granted.

"Normally, family visits are limited to one contact visit today. But since you are an attorney, Mr. Carter, and part of your father's defense team, it seems pointless to stick to that. You and Mr. Ryder and Father Lamb can be with him pretty much up until he's taken into the execution room at eight thirty. They'll start the IV lines then, and if there are no orders from the court or the governor, the lethal injection will begin on time at nine, after the curtains are opened for the witnesses to view the execution.

"Your father has refused to order a last meal," the warden said to Wynne. "He can change his mind, but if he does decide to eat, his meal has to be completed by five. He can shower at seven if he wishes. I'll walk you over to the execution chamber now and show you the layout."

Jeff felt sick to his stomach as he followed Warden Wright down the halls and through the various secure corridors until they reached L-Building. The warden opened the door to a mostly bare room with a gurney in the center, a red telephone on the wall, medical equipment to administer IV drugs, and a heart monitor.

"I've seen enough," he said to Warden Wright. "I want to talk to my client."

"Of course."

They retraced their steps to the adjacent cell where Ed was praying with Father Jim, who had been with him since sunrise. He got up to embrace first Wynne and then Jeff.

"How's Brendan?" he asked.

"Much better," Jeff smiled. At least he could give him some good news.

"And Claire?"

"We're still waiting to hear," Wynne said.

* * *

As the day wore on, Jeff wished that he could somehow grasp all the clocks in the world and stop time. He worked on his laptop while Wynne and Ed talked quietly together about family history that Wynne had never heard. Although Jeff's requests for a stay had been rejected yesterday, he'd instructed Brendan's associates to immediately refile them in the Fourth Circuit and the U.S. Supreme Court. *Surely at least one justice will see reason,* Jeff told himself.

Ed shook his head when a lunch tray arrived. Wynne persuaded him to take a bite or two, but that was all.

Just before one o'clock, Jeff's cell rang. His heart leaped when he saw Mckenzie was calling. Her job had been contacting Governor Reynolds that morning. He made the guard let him go into the hall outside the cell so that he could answer the phone.

"Has the governor agreed to issue a stay?" Jeff asked as soon as he picked up the phone.

"No, he wouldn't budge. I'm calling about Claire."

"Tell me she's back home safely." He could barely breathe as he waited for her answer.

"I'm afraid not. Last night, after Allison heard that the Supreme Court had refused to grant a stay, she drove Claire back to Belle Grove and let her out in the lane that leads to the mansion. Then she shot at her as she tried to run to the house. Near the end of the lane, two bullets took her down. Allison assumed that she was dead and left. She wasn't found until one of the overnight guests was leaving around mid-morning."

"But why didn't anyone hear the gunshots?"

"Michelle thinks they didn't hear them because it's cold, so all the windows were closed; and only the rooms on the river side of the house were occupied."

"So how is she?"

"She hasn't regained consciousness. Air Transport took her to Medical College in Richmond. She's in surgery."

"Oh, God!" Tears burned his eyes. He fought to stay calm. He couldn't forget his responsibility to Ed. "How's Tyndall?"

"He's trying to bear up under all of this, but he's close to the breaking point."

"It's good that you're with him."

"I hope so, but I can't stop thinking about the role that I've played in all this. Brian wouldn't be proud of me right now."

"What about Brendan?"

"He figured out what day it is and started asking questions. Emma agreed with the cardio team's recommendation to keep him lightly sedated."

"I'm relieved to hear that."

"How are things there?" Mckenzie asked. "How's Ed?"

"Very calm and stoic. He's determined to live up to his military training. Robert Weaver is in charge of Brendan's team at Craig, Lewis. I'm going to text you his number. Will you call over there and see if there's been any movement with either the Fourth or the Supremes?"

"Of course. And I'll write an affidavit for him to make a supplemental filing on the ground that Byrd has demonstrated she's a killer not once but twice in the past month, and therefore it's far more likely that she killed Anne."

"Good idea. Thanks. And the minute you know anything about Claire—"

"Absolutely. That goes without saying."

"Should I tell Wynne now, do you think?"

"I'd wait until we know more about her condition."

"Makes sense. What about Allison Byrd? Have they found her?"

"It's the usual story," Mckenzie sighed, "not yet."

* * *

Jeff paced the hallway in front of Ed's cell for a few minutes, trying to regain control of his emotions. When he felt calm enough, he asked the guard to let him back in.

Wynne and Father Jim looked up hopefully when he entered. Ed's brown eyes remained calm and resigned.

"Any news?" Wynne asked.

"Nothing yet from either court. Mckenzie called to say she's going to give Brendan's team another affidavit to bolster our supplemental filings."

Wynne gave Jeff a dispirited smile. "Thanks."

* * *

The hours passed too quickly, Jeff thought. He could hear footsteps passing in the hall outside and voices shouting various bits and pieces of words and phrases. He knew that the staff was rehearsing the execution. They had already examined Ed's veins to see if they would make inserting the IV lines difficult. When they had asked permission to take him to the infirmary to insert stents to make it all go faster, Jeff had angrily ordered them out.

But now all was calm in the small cell. Ed and Father Jim were absorbed in prayer and Wynne, too, had closed his eyes and was moving his lips silently.

Any bits of hope that had remained at the beginning of the day had worn away as the remaining hours of the afternoon dissolved one by one. What remained was a death watch like the one he and Ethan and his father had made as his mother had struggled out of life.

That was the thing, Jeff thought as he scoured his memory for any lingering bits of Catholic prayer from his boyhood that he could pull into service. *The body doesn't easily let go of life. Even when death comes in the natural course of things, death is not a quick or easy process. In truth, what the law was refusing to recognize was the immutable law of survival. The state had no humane way to end Ed's life because his body was going to fight those drugs just as hard as his mother's body had fought the cancer.*

Jeff made himself stop thinking about the mechanics of death. He cobbled together what he could remember of a "Hail Mary" and an "Our Father" and hoped the Universe would not mind his silent, imperfect recitations. Over and over, he offered his bits of prayer until something else dawned on him. The atmosphere in the cell had progressed from calm to unshakably tranquil. It was the same unearthly feeling of peace that he had experienced during his mother's deathbed watch. And he remembered what his father had said that night to everyone's amazement.

Vic had opened his eyes as they all sat praying around Helen's bed and had observed matter-of-factly, "An angel has come to help her pass. I can see bright light and wings."

Jeff had assumed that grief and strain had caused his father's hallucination. Vic Ryder was a hard-headed Bronx boy and anything but a mystic. But as he sat with Ed, Father Jim, and Wynne in prayer as the last minutes of Ed's life were ticking away, he felt as if a mystic, loving presence had come into the room.

Suddenly his phone vibrated, and he asked to be let out into the hall again. It was three o'clock.

"Hi, Jeff." His heart beat faster at the sound of Robert Weaver's voice.

"What news?"

"We've got a temporary stay from the Supreme Court."

Jeff's knees were weak with relief. "Oh, God. It's a miracle!"

"Well, not quite," Robert went on. "It's only temporary. Justice Moreno is questioning the drug protocol. You better get to the warden's office fast to hear what he and the Attorney General have to say for themselves."

But Warden Wright had already sent one of his assistants to fetch Jeff to the conference room where Lucian Shelby, the Deputy Attorney General, was telling Justice Paula Moreno over the speakerphone why Virginia's choice of death-dealing drugs was humane.

"I want to hear from Mr. Carter's attorney," Justice Moreno said when Shelby paused for breath.

"Jeffery Matthew Ryder for Ed Carter," Jeff said.

"Good afternoon, Mr. Ryder. I've just heard from Deputy Attorney General Shelby that your client can be executed without violating the Eighth Amendment's ban on cruel and unusual punishment. I assume you disagree."

"Absolutely, Justice Moreno." Jeff went on to explain the scientific reasons why the drugs the state had chosen would cause Ed an agonizing death. He would be put to sleep, but only briefly, and then likely would awaken, paralyzed and unable to express the extreme pain that the procedure of stopping his heart and breathing would inflict.

"I see," she observed when Jeff concluded. "Do you have anything to add as rebuttal, Mr. Shelby?"

"Yes, Justice Moreno. The initial drug will put Mr. Carter completely to sleep, and he will not awaken during the procedure."

"Can you be sure?" the justice asked. "Haven't there been executions when the inmate has not been fully unconscious?"

"We see no possibility of that here," the deputy attorney general insisted stubbornly.

"I have one more question for Mr. Ryder. I've just received a declaration from Mckenzie Fitzgerald supporting your earlier claims that a woman named Allison Byrd is the true killer. Ms. Fitzgerald says that this Byrd woman has, in the past month, committed one murder and attempted another and that both acts of violence are related to this case."

"That's correct, Justice Moreno. Quinn Fairchild was with Ed Carter all night on the night his wife was killed. Allison Byrd killed her to try to prevent her statements from reaching the courts. And Allison kidnapped Ed's future daughter-in-law at her wedding and threatened to kill her if we brought forward Quinn's alibi evidence. When Allison felt certain that Ed's execution would go forward, she attempted to kill Claire."

"Do you have physical evidence that demonstrates Allison Byrd murdered Anne Carter? Fingerprints? DNA?"

"We know that Byrd lived near the Carters' house and stalked the Carters constantly. We also have a DNA expert working on the murder weapon."

"But he hasn't found Ms. Byrd's DNA on it, right?"

"He's still looking."

"I see."

Jeff's heart was hammering hard now.

"I'm going to take all of this under consideration," Justice Moreno said. "I'm leaving the temporary stay in place."

Jeff heaved a sigh of relief. He felt as if he'd managed to walk through a fire unscathed.

The call ended, and Warden Wright said to Jeff, "Because the stay is only temporary, we're going forward with the procedures on the assumption that it will be lifted before nine p.m."

"I see," Jeff said. *They're always so sure of themselves. But I was, too, when I was a prosecutor because I always won.*

* * *

As he followed the guards back to Ed's cell, his phone rang again. Mckenzie. He stopped in the hallway and answered it.

"We've got a temporary stay," he told her. "I just got off the phone with Justice Moreno and the AG."

"That's good news."

"Justice Moreno was focused on your supplemental declaration."

"I'm glad it helped. I've got more good news for you. Claire is out of surgery, and she's going to be okay."

"Thank God!" Jeff suddenly had tears in his eyes.

"She's been rambling about things Allison Byrd said to her."

"Such as?"

"Such as Allison told her that she was watching the Carters' house the night Anne was murdered. She said that she had planned to kill Anne because she knew Ed was away, but Ed came back and did it himself."

"Claire's under some pretty heavy sedation, isn't she?" Jeff asked.

"She is."

"And we both know that Allison is insane."

"That's true," Mckenzie agreed.

"Then we shouldn't pay any attention to the ravings of a madwoman. We know that Ed was with Quinn that night, and Quinn had to be telling the truth because Allison killed her to keep her quiet. I've got to go tell Ed and Wynne that, for now, the stay is in place. Allison killed Anne. All we need is time to prove it."

* * *

But before going back to Ed's cell, Jeff called Dr. Vom Saal.

"I was just going to call you to report the final results on the bat," he said.

"What are they?" Jeff's heart began to beat faster as he waited for the answer.

"No DNA from Allison Byrd."

"Are you sure?" Jeff's heart accelerated again.

"Positive. The only other profile I can identify is one that is consistent with Wynne's."

"But he was too little to swing a bat that size."

"Of course. But it belonged to his father. I'm sure he had contact with it."

"Never mind. That's not important. So you are one hundred percent sure Allison Byrd's DNA is not on that bat?"

"Yes."

ED

"Death has a hundred hands and walks by a thousand ways."

T.S. Eliot

CHAPTER FORTY-EIGHT

Friday, March 3, 2017. The Execution Chamber, Greensville Correctional Center, Jarrat, Virginia

At eight thirty p.m., Warden Wright opened the door to Ed's cell and allowed Ed to walk into the execution chamber on his own. No handcuffs, no ankle chains, no restraints of any kind. As he walked toward the gurney in the center of the room, he had a blurred impression of a bare, gray floor, white-washed block walls, and one wall covered by a heavy blue curtain.

He lay down on the gurney, and the guards secured his arms and legs. His arms were strapped to extensions on either side of the table the way that Jesus' arms had been nailed to the cross. The room was unbearably cold. Father Jim, who had already given him the last rites in his cell, read the Twenty-Third Psalm in a soft voice. Ed focused on the words, "*the valley of the shadow of death.*"

The guards on either side of him had placed tourniquets around his arms to make his veins easier to find. He felt a sharp sting as first one needle entered his left arm and then the other entered his right. The guards snapped the tourniquets as they were released. Ed smelled the acrid smell of the alcohol wipes they'd used before puncturing his veins. The way was open, now, for the poison to flow. He began to whisper the words of the psalm with Father Jim: *"I will fear no evil, for thou art with me."* His line of sight was limited because he was strapped down on his back. He heard shuffling and rustling in the room. Someone asked, "Should we open the curtain," and someone else said, "Not yet. It's only eight forty-five. He's got fifteen more minutes."

"Thou preparest a table before me in the presence of mine enemies." Ed closed his eyes and thought about Wynne.

* * *

When Jeff had told him at six thirty that Justice Moreno had lifted the stay and had given the green light for the execution to take place as scheduled, Ed had not been surprised. For the next half hour, he had agonized over whether he should tell Jeff exactly what had happened the night Anne died. He had told himself that, at this point, the truth made no difference. He was going to die, regardless. But finally, at seven, he had asked to be alone with Jeff.

"I don't want Wynne ever to know what I am about to tell you," he began after Father Jim and Wynne had left the cell.

"I won't tell," Jeff promised.

"I wasn't with Quinn all night."

"But she said you were."

"She'd been drinking a lot. She passed out just before midnight. I lay there in the dark, miserable and lonely, thinking about Anne and hating myself for sleeping with yet another student because my wife didn't love me. I knew that all I really wanted was to be at home with Wynne and Anne.

"I got up and put all my things in the car and left Quinn a note saying the room had been paid for, and she could just leave in the morning. I drove home and parked in my usual spot in front of the house. It was just before one o'clock."

"So the car Adam Winston saw was yours?"

Ed nodded. "I could see that the lights were on in the front living room. I wondered why she was up so late because she tired easily in early pregnancy. I let myself in with my key, and then I heard voices in the living room. One was Anne's. The other was a male voice. I realized Richard Neal was there, and Anne had lied when she said their affair was over.

"I stood in the hall for a minute, trying to decide whether or not I wanted to confront them or just leave. I decided I'd let enough go on behind my back. So I walked into the living room to find Anne alone. When I told her that I knew Neal was in the house, she denied it. But she was very agitated, and it was clear to me that she was lying. The door between the kitchen and the dining room that was always left open was closed. So I figured he was hiding in there, waiting for me to leave.

"I was upset because I'd driven all the way back to be with her and Wynne, and now she obviously didn't want me there. I told her I'd heard Neal when I came in. I told her I wanted the affairs to stop. No more lies. I told her I wanted her to promise that she'd never see Neal again. I told her that if she did go on seeing him, I'd divorce her and take Wynne.

"But she laughed in my face. 'You'll never get Wynne. He's not yours. A divorce is fine with me. Leave now and don't come back.'

"But I said, 'Of course I'm coming back. Wynne is my son. And we have a baby on the way.'

"She was extremely agitated by this time. She hit me on the cheek and screamed, 'Get out and don't come back!'

"I ran out of the house, got into my car, and squealed my tires as I made a U-turn to head back to Charlottesville. That was when I saw Allison standing in her usual place by the streetlight. I realized that she'd seen and heard everything. I felt so violated that this stranger knew the most intimate details of my life.

"I started driving, and then it dawned on me that I had no place to go except back to the hotel. I stopped and bought a six-pack and drank as I drove because I was so upset. Quinn was still asleep when I got back, so I tore up the note and got back into bed with her. The next day, I drove her to her car and headed home. I was desperately hoping that Anne was over whatever had upset her the previous night and hoping that Neal hadn't persuaded her to leave me. But when I found her dead, I had no doubt who'd done it because Allison was standing only a few feet from the house when I left. I didn't think Anne was in danger because I thought Neal would stay the night with her."

"Why didn't you tell your previous lawyers about this?"

"I didn't tell Brad because it just made me look guilty. He was sure I killed Anne because I was a philanderer. I didn't tell Brendan because I was ashamed of sleeping with Quinn that night and because telling him that Anne was going to leave me meant she'd have taken Wynne and that gave me a motive to kill her."

"Neal could be the killer."

"No, he loved Anne. I'm sure he was there that night to talk her into leaving me. He'd left his wife, and he wanted to marry her. Besides, his DNA wasn't on the bat. It was Allison. Somehow she managed to get in after Neal left."

"The trouble is we still don't have any evidence to prove that. Dr. Vom Saal says her DNA isn't on the bat."

"Even if it was, it's too late anyway," Ed said. "Thanks for everything that you've done. You took on a big load at the last minute. Give Brendan my thanks, too. And take care of Wynne. And Claire."

"They found her. She's going to be okay."

"Thank God."

* * *

"Thou anointest my head with oil; my cup runneth over. Surely goodness and mercy shall follow me all the days of my life."

"It's five to nine," Ed heard them say.

"Open the curtain, then."

Ed heard the swish of the heavy fabric and the clicking of the little metal hangers sliding along the metal track as they opened the curtain to reveal him to the witnesses behind the glass window who had come to watch him die. The needles in his veins hurt. He willed himself to block out everything except his memory of Anne's voice reading aloud from the *Four Quartets, "In the end is my beginning."*

JOURNEY BY NIGHT AND BY DAY

"It is obvious that we can no more explain passion to a person who has never experienced it than we can explain light to the blind."

T.S. Eliot

CHAPTER FORTY-NINE

March 2, 2017, 89 Rue des Filles-du-Calvaire, 3rd Arrondissement, Paris

Morgan Thomas found it hard to sleep past three a.m. No matter when she went to bed, she always awoke in the dark hours before dawn crept over the streets of Paris. She attributed it to habit. When her husband, Pierre Moreau, had been battling cancer two years earlier, she had sat up with him in the wee hours of the night when he was in too much pain to sleep. Her body had become accustomed to light sleep and early awakening.

Now she lived alone in the lovely two-bedroom apartment on the Rue des Filles-du-Calvaire that had been her home with Pierre for over thirty years. The spacious rooms were filled with sunlight by day and moonlight by night.

Paris had been her home since 1980. After she had fled Sullivan and Cromwell and her passion for Ed Carter in 1977, she had landed a slightly less boring job at King and White's New York office. She had spent the next two years trying to stay awake in conference rooms while the partner she worked for took depositions in securities fraud cases. Two years into the King and White job, her marriage to Jay Thomas had ended and so had her patience with the intricacies of securities fraud. Relying on her fluency in French, she had negotiated a transfer to King and White's Paris office where she had finally found her niche in international law. Three years later, she had met Pierre, a banking executive with Société Générale.

They had had a happy marriage. Neither of them had wanted children, so they'd grown especially close because it was just the two of them. Their careers had given them the money to enjoy the things they both loved: travel, fine food, the ballet, and the opera. But during the past two years of her widowhood, Morgan had regretted having no son or daughter to share the grief of Pierre's passing. She had retired from King and White four years ago, and now time hung heavy on her hands except when the firm called her to pinch hit for someone in the international department. It happened infrequently, but Morgan kept her passport at the ready, just in case.

She went to the kitchen and made a cup of tea with lemon. She considered reading but decided to turn on the television instead. Although neither she nor Pierre had much interest in television, they had a digital subscription that allowed them to watch CNN when they chose. As international business people, they needed to keep up with the American point of view.

It was nine p.m. in New York, and Anderson Cooper was rehashing Mckenzie Fitzgerald's downfall as a Supreme Court nominee. A panel of three long-faced experts consisting of a Harvard law professor, a retired Ninth Circuit judge, and a partner from the Washington D.C. boutique appellate firm of

Harper, Spalding, were damning Ms. Fitzgerald for her rookie failure to record Quinn Fairchild's alibi evidence in the Ed Carter case. Behind the panel were blowups of Mckenzie's professional portrait from the Goldstein, Miller website and Ed Carter's most recent mugshot.

Morgan stared at the picture of Ed. Surely that wasn't— but it was. The Ed Carter whom she'd been so deeply in love with, the Ed Carter who had been so deeply in love with his unfaithful wife. He was scheduled to die in just twenty-four hours. She put her teacup on the coffee table and stared at the screen for a long time without paying any attention to the commentary.

Ed didn't kill Anne. Of that she was sure. She smiled as she remembered his dark-haired, brown-eyed good looks that had melted her heart every time she had been near him. The old butterflies filled her tummy as she remembered walking down the long hallway to his office, full of anticipation, and pausing just outside his door so that she could hear his soft Virginia accent as he talked on the phone. And then there had been those gloriously stolen minutes in those tawdry by-the-hour rental rooms and the unforgettable look on his face when she'd invited him to dance on the library tables. That night she had gambled on her hunch that a passionate man was longing to have someone help him break through the conventions that imprisoned him. And she'd been even more deeply in love with him because she'd been right.

Ed Carter was that one-in-a-million male who had everything a woman could possibly want. He was wealthy, good-looking, and intelligent. But above all, he exuded qualities rarely obvious in a man, nurturing and caring. He was born to be a husband and father, and Anne Carter had been an unforgivable fool for throwing all of that away.

Sitting in front of the three arrogant talking heads who were unconscionably feeding on the helpless carcass of the ingenue Mckenzie Fitzgerald, Morgan let herself remember what she had kept locked in her heart for more than thirty years. While she had loved Pierre, he had been the antithesis of Ed. He had been a sophisticated international businessman, who would have been decidedly out of place in a nursery. He'd made their childlessness feel acceptable and appropriate.

But Ed had been an entirely different story. Morgan had longed for a child with Ed. She'd fantasized about standing over a crib with him, gazing down at the baby their passion had created. Back in the days of the gritty hotel rooms, she'd even considered skipping a pill or two to make her dream come true. But she had stopped short of deception because she loved him, and she had known how miserable he would have been if she had trapped him with a pregnancy that he had trusted her to avoid. After all, she knew better than anyone else that he was already dealing with betrayal because Anne Carter was sleeping with her husband.

* * *

The assassination of Mckenzie Fitzgerald finally ended, and Morgan turned off the television. She made herself another cup of tea.

Anne and Jay had met in the fall of 1975 at the firm party to welcome new associates and their spouses. Ed had never known that his wife was head-over-heals for her husband. Nor had he known that was the reason Morgan had approached him in the library that day. She'd been looking for revenge because Jay was having sex with Anne Carter in their marital bed while she was dying of boredom in the Sullivan and Cromwell library. Anne's husband was handsome beyond belief, so why not turn the tables on Jay? Except she wound up turning the tables on herself because she fell in love with him. It would have been so convenient, she reflected, if Ed had accepted her invitation to run away together. Then Anne would have had Jay, and Ed wouldn't be facing death tomorrow.

But he didn't kill her. He loved her too much to kill her. I loved him more than any man on earth, but he wouldn't leave her for me. What can I do to stop it? You know what you can do. Go read the letters. The ones you've always been too hurt and afraid to read.

* * *

Jay Thomas had died in a car crash on a winding road in Provence in July 1990. He had rounded a curve at a high rate of speed, slipping into the oncoming traffic lane. He and his wife, Pamela Vannier Thomas, the daughter of the chairman of the department of comparative literature at NYU, had been killed instantly.

The gendarmes had come knocking on the door of 89 Rue des Filles-du-Calvaire a few weeks later to tell Morgan that Jay was dead; and she, his ex-wife, was his only next of kin. They had informed her that his belongings would be delivered to her within the week. Pierre had frowned and then given a classic Gallic shrug. How inconvenient to be the recipient of one's former spouse's property, more than a decade after their marriage was over.

She'd had a few nostalgic moments over Jay's record collection and the expensive sound equipment that the police truck had brought. He'd bought some of those albums in their Duke days before he'd shattered her dreams of being married to a reliable husband and equal partner. But in the end, she'd had no qualms about donating all of his belongings to the Soeurs Servantes du Sacré-Coeur, except for his papers. Those she had gone through carefully and tabbed each one. There were his scholarly papers, his attempts at poetry, his letter to Pamela, and his correspondence with Anne Carter.

She had peeked at the letters between Jay and Anne, but she could not bring herself to read them. The story of Anne's unrequited love for her former husband was too much for Morgan to bear, given that Anne's spurned husband had been the great love of her life.

But now, at four a.m., on the night before Ed was scheduled to die, Morgan made herself read the decades old words that might prove her hunch: Jay had killed Anne Carter.

2425 Grove Avenue, Richmond, Virginia, November 7, 1983
Dear Jay,

Ed took Wynne and me to Charlottesville this weekend. Some horrible woman followed us to the bookstore where I had asked Ed to take us.. She was this great, hulking creature from one of Ed's classes. Apparently, she's been looking after Wynne during Ed's office hours. Wynne made a fuss about seeing her. I suppose Ed is sleeping with her. He sleeps with his students to punish me for not loving him. This one is really horrible. Dark and threatening. He shouldn't have left Wynne alone with her.

I hate the life I'm living with a man I don't love. I've been in love with you since the moment I saw you that night at the Plaza in the midst of all those boring lawyers. I want to be with you and to have Wynne grow up knowing you're his father. Please end this game that you've been forcing me to play. I want to be your wife and the mother of a brother or sister or both for Wynne.

Love always,

Anne

Chelsea, New York City, November 10, 1983

Dear Anne,

I am engaged to Pamela. Her father is the Chairman of the Comparative Literature Department. He has converted my contract position to tenure track. I am now an assistant professor of Comparative Literature at NYU. I would be an utter fool to choose life with you and Wynne over the life that I am going to have with Pamela as the son-in-law of Professor Marcel Vannier. Why do you keep bothering me? I have told you repeatedly that I haven't the slightest interest in being a father to anyone.

Sincerely,

Jay Thomas

2425 Grove Avenue, Richmond, Virginia, November 14, 1983

Dear Jay,

I am shocked and hurt. I have called and called, and you refuse to answer the telephone. Ed will be in Charlottesville this weekend. Wynne deserves to know his father. If you don't come to see him while Ed is away, I will bring him to New York and introduce him to your fiancée. I'm sure you haven't told her about us.

Love,

Anne

Chelsea, New York City, November 16, 1983

Dear Anne,

Resorting to blackmail is unbecoming, but I will come down to Richmond on Saturday so that we can talk sensibly.

Jay Thomas

Morgan shivered at the thought of the besotted and defenseless Anne inviting Jay into her house that night. The next envelope she picked up held newspaper clippings of Anne's obituary and of Ed's arrest. Jay had written at the top of one of the pictures of Ed being led away in handcuffs a quote for Shakespeare's *Twelfth Night,* "Why am I a fool?"

It was all damning evidence, but the final envelope was the worst of all. Jay had kept his tickets showing his travel to and from Richmond on November 19 and 20, 1983. He'd arrived late on Saturday afternoon and departed early the next morning.

He'd stayed at a small hotel in the Fan District, close to 2425 Grove Avenue.

The hands of the clock were nearing five a.m. The first faint streaks of dawn were visible in the east although it was still very dark. Morgan counted backwards on her fingers to determine what time it was in New York, eleven p.m. So in California it was eight o'clock.

She found Mckenzie Fitzgerald's office number and dialed it. A bored night secretary informed her that Ms. Fitzgerald was in Virginia on family business and was not to be disturbed. Morgan explained that she had evidence that could save Ed Carter's life, and she needed to reach Mckenzie at once. The bored voice said that she would take the message and relay Morgan's phone number to Ms. Fitzgerald, but she could do no more than that.

Morgan hung up and sighed. She had no confidence that Bored Secretary would transmit her message. She googled Ed Carter's attorneys and discovered that Brendan Murphy was his current defense attorney. She tried his number at Craig, Lewis, and Weller's Richmond office where it was also eleven p.m. A night secretary with a soft Virginia accent explained that Mr. Murphy was in the hospital and that Jeffery Ryder had taken his place. With great regret, she informed Morgan that she could not give out Mr. Ryder's personal cell phone number, but she would most certainly let him know that Morgan had called. She hung up and tried the Governor of Virginia's Office. But there was no night voice there, only a recording that said his office would open at eight thirty in the morning.

She considered her options; but in truth, there was only one.

Flying out of Orly at seven fifty a.m. Paris time, she could reach Richmond in eighteen hours. Or by eight p.m., just one hour before Ed was scheduled to die. It might be enough time to save him, or it might not. But her heart said she had no choice. She must go.

She booked her flight and ordered a limousine from the service King and White used. The drivers all knew her, and she could rely on them. By the time she had finished dressing and throwing a few items into her carry-on bag, the limo was waiting downstairs. She made sure she had the set of old letters and hurried out to the car. She told herself that she'd succeed; Ed wouldn't die tonight.

* * *

Morgan landed in Lisbon at nine twenty in the morning. It was four twenty a.m. in Richmond, so she knew the chances of reaching anyone there were slim. No one had called her and left a callback number while she was in flight. Maybe that was to be expected since everyone was probably asleep, but couldn't any of those secretaries have awakened Mckenzie Fitzgerald or Jeff Ryder with her life-and-death message? She was worried that everyone she had spoken to had thought she was just some sort of weirdo seeking attention. She was convinced that her messages hadn't been delivered.

Since Mckenzie Fitzgerald had been under the gun for her failure to help Ed early on, Morgan felt that connecting with her was her best opportunity to save Ed's life. Surely Mckenzie would jump at the chance to redeem herself. It was one twenty in the morning on the West Coast, but Morgan dialed the main switchboard at Goldstein, Miller, which was the only way she had to try to reach Mckenzie. The night operator assured her that her earlier message had been relayed to Ms. Fitzgerald. She promised she'd give her Morgan's second message as soon as Mckenzie woke up and called in for her messages. But of course, it was four thirty in Richmond, and Mckenzie was asleep.

She had three hours and thirty minutes before she could board her flight to Newark. She paced the airport restlessly, trying to reassure herself that someone connected to Ed's case would call her as soon as they all woke up.

Just before her flight was finally called for boarding at twelve thirty, she managed to get through to Craig, Lewis, and Weller in Richmond where another sweet, southern voice told her that it was seven thirty in the morning there, and Mr. Ryder was at the prison in Jarrat with his client. The voice promised to pass along her message as soon as Mr. Ryder became available for messages. *Of course that isn't going to help,* Morgan thought, *because I'm about to get on an airplane and turn off my phone.*

She asked the Craig, Lewis operator if she could put her in touch with Mckenzie Fitzgerald only to be told that Ms. Fitzgerald was attending a breakfast meeting with the governor and could not be disturbed. Morgan begged her to send a message to Governor Reynold's office telling him that she was en route with evidence that would prove Ed's innocence. But the voice would only promise to communicate that message to Mckenzie as soon as her meeting with the governor ended.

Morgan boarded her flight, reassuring herself that she'd have plenty of time to get in touch with Ed's attorneys when she landed in Newark a few minutes before four o'clock. Surely in the two hours and thirty minutes before she took off for Richmond, just before six thirty, she'd be able to find someone to tell Governor Reynolds that she was on her way. It was too late to go to the courts, so reaching the governor's office before nine p.m. was her only hope.

She ate only a little of the lunch Air Portugal served and drank some tea. Afterward, she tried to doze, knowing that by the time she reached Richmond, she would have been awake for close to twenty-four hours.

She hadn't expected to fall fully asleep, but she did. She awoke with a start because the plane was in an uncontrolled drop. She heard the pilot's voice on the intercom telling everyone to put on seatbelts and to remain seated. He regained control of the plane's altitude, but after a few seconds, the plane dropped sharply again. Some overhead bins popped open, and smaller pieces of luggage fell out. A few passengers screamed. The flight attendants took their seats and begged for patience. The pilot came back on and said there was turbulence on the descent to Newark. He'd been instructed to circle the airport and wait for the wind to die down.

Morgan looked at her watch. Three thirty. Surely they'd still be on the ground close to their scheduled arrival time of four p.m. She had nothing to worry about. Even if there was a line at immigration, she had two and a half hours before her commuter flight to Richmond took off.

But in the end, they were an hour late landing, and the immigration wait, even for citizens, was forty-five minutes long. Morgan made calls while she stood in the line but failed to reach anyone on Ed's defense team. She arrived at the United Express commuter gate at six, just twenty minutes before her flight to Richmond was scheduled to depart.

After she boarded the little plane, but before it took off, she finally reached a night operator at Craig, Lewis in Richmond who told her that Mckenzie was now at the hospital with Claire Chastain, Jeff Ryder was with Ed, and Justice Moreno had lifted the temporary stay that she had issued earlier. She closed her eyes and asked the Universe to let her arrive in time.

The flight attendant closed the little jet's doors, but the plane didn't budge. Through her window, Morgan saw freezing rain. She prayed they'd get off the ground before the plane had to be deiced. They were already ten minutes past their departure time.

Morgan stared at her watch. Ten minutes grew into fifteen and then finally, twenty. At last, the commuter jet began to taxi toward the runway. Morgan began to breathe again. But then the pilot informed them that they were fifth in line for takeoff. Finally at seven, they were cleared to go. Arrival time was now eight thirty.

As soon as the flight attendant was up and moving around the cabin, Morgan summoned her. She was a kindly, heavy-set woman in her forties, who looked as tired as Morgan felt.

"What can I get you?" she asked.

"Nothing to drink. I'm going to need your help getting off the aircraft."

"Of course. I can call ahead and order a wheelchair for you."

"No, not that kind of help. I need to be the first one off the plane, and I'm going to need a police car at the gate to drive me to Governor Reynold's office. I'm an attorney with King and White on urgent business for a client."

The flight attendant looked her over carefully and apparently decided she looked like the sort of person who would need to go straight to the governor's mansion after a transatlantic flight. Morgan was glad that she'd worn her black cashmere power overcoat.

"I can promise to get you off ahead of everyone else. The police transport is a different matter."

"Please try. A life depends on it. And Governor Reynolds is expecting me," she lied.

* * *

The flight attendant was as good as her word. Morgan was the first person down the steps, and a Richmond police car was sitting on the tarmac. She was relieved to see that the freezing rain had stopped. The night was now clear, crisp, and very cold.

"I'm Sergeant Petree," the uniformed officer informed her, "United Airlines said you need to get to the Governor's Mansion ASAP." He was about thirty, very fit, and lean, wearing a police-issue raincoat over his uniform.

"Faster than that," Morgan said as she climbed into passenger seat of his car. "It's eight thirty-five, and Ed Carter is scheduled to die at nine."

"Civilians ride in back, ma'am."

But she ignored him. "Please, hurry!"

As soon as they hit I-64, Morgan said, "Can't you go faster?"

"Not unless I turn on the siren."

"Turn it on, then."

Sergeant Petree gave her a sideways look, hesitated for a moment, and then switched on his overhead lights. The siren began to wail. Morgan saw the speedometer jump from seventy miles an hour to just under a hundred. She closed her eyes and prayed.

When she felt the car begin to slow, she opened them again. They were in downtown Richmond, taking the Fifth Street exit. "Nearly there," Sergeant Petree said. Morgan's watch said seven minutes to nine.

Sergeant Petree turned into the circular drive in front of the mansion and stopped at the front door. The house was dark except for a light at the center of the white-columned portico. Two state troopers stood guard by the massive green door.

Morgan jumped out of the car and ran up the steps. One of the troopers moved to block her, and the other reached for his gun. Behind her she heard Sergeant Petree call out, "She's okay. Let her in and take her straight to Governor Reynolds. She says she's got evidence that Ed Carter is innocent."

The trooper with the gun holstered his weapon. The other opened the front door and hurried her through the hall and upstairs toward what she assumed were the living quarters.

"This better be good," the trooper muttered, "or you'll be in jail in about ten minutes." He stopped in front of a pair of massive white doors and knocked hard.

A gray-uniformed maid opened one of them and stared at Morgan. She said, "What's going on? Governor Reynolds is with Pastor Kaplan, praying until the execution is over. He can't be disturbed."

"I've got evidence that Ed Carter is innocent. My ex-husband killed Anne Carter to silence her about their love child. I've got to see Governor Reynolds at once." She shook her briefcase full of Jay and Anne's letters at her.

Suddenly a tall gray-haired man in pajamas and a bathrobe appeared. Morgan could see a man in a clergyman's collar standing behind him. She thought how odd it was that a man could go about his usual bedtime routine while another man was being put to death.

"What's all this about?" he demanded.

"She says she's got evidence that Ed Carter is innocent, Governor Reynolds." Sergeant Petree had caught up to them. He was breathing hard from running. "United Airlines requested police transport for her as soon as she landed. She's flown all the way from Paris to see you."

"You'd better come in then," the governor said. "But first, get the warden on the line down at Greensville. We've got less than a minute before they knock him out."

THE WEDDING

"Sometimes things become possible
if we want them bad enough."

T.S. Eliot

CHAPTER FIFTY

Saturday, June 26, 2017, Belle Grove Plantation Bed and Breakfast, Port Conway, Virginia

At five o'clock, Jeff looked out the window of the Madison Suite and studied the lawn and the river below. The three hundred guests, glittering in evening dress, were assembled in rows and rows of white chairs, waiting for the bride and groom. White orchids and roses and white ribbons had been tied to the chairs that lined the aisle that led to the arch of flowers placed with the river in the background.

He could smell the hors d'oeuvres that were going to be the light first course after the wedding. And the Beef Wellington with red wine and shallot reduction that, with fresh green peas with mint and herb roasted potatoes, would be the main course for the sit-down dinner under the tents. Dessert would be three kinds of wedding cake because Claire could not make up her mind between vanilla, chocolate, and carrot. Tyndall had hired a fifteen-piece orchestra for dancing under the stars, and Wynne had insisted on fireworks over the river for the grand finale at midnight with the orchestra playing Handel's *Water Music*. The lanterns were hung, the lights were strung. The tents were up. Michelle said it was the biggest, grandest wedding so far at Belle Grove. And she was all the more delighted because Claire was a Turner bride.

At that moment, Claire was in the Turner Suite with Mckenzie and Ellen, who were helping her with the final assembly of her Vera Wang gown and veil. Jeff, Wynne, and Tyndall were dressed and ready to go downstairs as soon as Father Jim summoned them. Wynne had forgiven him completely for counseling Ed to tell the truth about his father because identifying Jay Thomas' DNA profile on the bat had helped to save Ed's life.

Jeff looked out the window again and saw Ed and Morgan sitting next to Brendan and Emma. Wynne had bought a farm near Charlottesville where Ed could have rest and quiet and long walks through the fields every day with his Golden Retriever puppy named Eliot. Morgan had taken up permanent residence in New York but visited the farm often. She and Ed had planted a garden full of vegetables and flowers, and she taught him cooking techniques that she'd learned from the various French cooks who had worked for her and Pierre. Sometimes Ed flew to New York to spend time with her, but he was still adjusting to life outside of prison, and the ceaseless bustle of New York rattled him. He preferred the quiet of Windsong Farm.

Jeff studied Joel Whitby sitting next to Jenny Miyamoto in the row with two empty chairs: one for Mckenzie, stand-in for mother of the bride, and the other for Tyndall, who no longer had any reservations about his daughter's marriage. No one blamed her now for betraying Joel's confidence about

Mckenzie's mistake because without the national and international attention that it had drawn, Morgan would not have crossed the Atlantic to save Ed. *The Universe works in strange ways,* Jeff thought. *Wynne was heartbroken when he learned Ed was not his father. Mckenzie was hurt when she lost the Supreme Court nomination. But out of those two things came what we all wanted most: justice for Ed.*

Michelle appeared in the doorway and said that Father Jim was ready for them to take up their places for the wedding on the lawn by the flower arch. The orchestra, which Jeff knew had been playing Vivaldi only because Wynne had informed him this would be the music for greeting guests, now shifted to Pachelbel's *Canon,* again because Wynne had told him the name of the processional for everyone except the bride.

Jeff and Wynne walked with Tyndall to the Turner Suite and left him there to escort Claire. Then the two of them linked arms and followed Michelle downstairs. Just before Michelle opened the back door, Wynne paused to give Jeff a hug. "Thanks for being the brother I always wanted."

Before Jeff could say anything in return, all eyes were on the two of them, and they were walking down the path through the chairs toward the arch. Jeff saw his father with his girlfriend, Elaine, and his brother, Ethan, with his pregnant wife, Mary Sue. And he smiled at Beth Rafferty and Abby sitting with Bryce Daggett. Abby waved, and he waved back.

All the people he loved were here in this place, and there was nothing to fear from Allison Byrd, who had been extradited to San Diego to stand trial for the murder of Quinn Fairchild. Wynne moved into position, and Jeff took his place. Ellen came next as maid of honor, and then the music changed to Wagner's familiar *Bridal Chorus.*

Jeff smiled as Claire walked toward him on Tyndall's arm, her face glowing. She was wearing a long-sleeved, lace column with a short train that was exactly the mixture of sophistication and elegance and that was the essence of the woman he loved. For so many years, when he hadn't wanted a wife, she'd been beside him as his closest friend, refusing to desert him even when the world shunned him. But now that he so dearly wanted a wife, she was the one he wanted.

He smiled as Tyndall placed her hand in his, and she smiled back as Father Jim began with words from Anne Carter's favorite poet. *"Love is most nearly itself when here and now cease to matter."*

TO THE READER

Keeping Secrets is a work of fiction. Inmates on Virginia's Death Row survive an average of seven years after conviction, and as Brendan tells Wynne, Virginia courts are some of the most skeptical in the nation when it comes to doubts about the validity of capital convictions.

In California, where I live and practice law, the average time on death row is twenty-five years from conviction to execution. So were the story set in California, Ed's thirty years spent waiting to be executed would not be as much of a fictional stretch. However, I wanted to set this story in Virginia for many reasons.

First, when Professor Edward Wynne Carter III introduced himself to me, and asked me to tell his story, I knew at once that he was an old-school Virginian, born and bred. I had the privilege of working in Richmond, Virginia, as an associate attorney for Hunton & Williams upon graduation from law school, and I met gentlemen like Ed Carter during my time there.

Second, although I was raised in Tennessee, my family and my closest friends all live in Virginia, and I wanted to weave a story from my memories of being with them and of living in

Richmond. I lived at 2425 Grove Avenue between 1982 and 1984. It was a very happy experience. I loved the quaintness of the Fan District, and I missed it after I moved north to Washington, D.C. and eventually to San Diego in 1985.

Third, in 2013, I met Michelle Darnell, the innkeeper at Belle Grove Plantation at Port Conway, during a visit to my family in Richmond. At that time, she was getting ready to realize her dream of opening her bed and breakfast at the plantation, and I was on the verge of realizing my dream, publishing my first novel, *Dance for A Dead Princess.* Over the years, as our dreams have found success with travelers who have enjoyed Michelle's hospitality at the plantation and with readers who have been entertained by my stories, we have talked about a novel set at Belle Grove that weaves the history of the house into the fictional narrative. I liked the challenge that it presented, and when Ed Carter asked me to tell his story, I knew that Belle Grove was going to be an important part of it.

If you visit Michelle and Belle Grove, you will see the matchless beauty of the house she has created. And as she says, the one thing she knows inside and out, is hospitality. And there is plenty of that at Belle Grove. If you do visit the plantation, you will be able to see the historic outbuildings where Allison Byrd camped while she stalked Wynne and Claire. You will be able to stroll on the lawn where Claire and Jeff walked by the river on that cold February day and where Claire's wedding eventually takes place. You will be able to visit the library where she was kidnapped and see the Hipkins-Bernard Suite where Allison hid before the wedding. And perhaps most interesting of all, upstairs you will be able to view Carrie Turner's etching on the window in the Turner Suite.

A word about the death penalty. *Keeping Secrets* is meant to be neither pro nor con. I know many people on both sides of the issue. At the present time, the United States Supreme Court still takes the position that the death penalty does not violate the Eighth Amendment's ban on cruel and unusual punishment. However, as Mckenzie and Joel discuss in the story, that conclusion has come more and more into question in recent times. It is true that the states have had great difficulty finding a completely humane way to take a life in the name of justice. And lawyers for the condemned have raised many valid arguments against the practices currently in use. But whether the Supreme Court changes its view on the compatibility of the Eighth Amendment's guarantee against cruel and unusual punishment with taking a life in the name of justice remains to be seen. This story is not meant to advocate one outcome or the other. It is meant to be the story of an innocent man's brush with death and his experience during the last sixty days of his life.

A heartfelt word about errors. I write fiction at night after a full day of complex law practice. I have never been a perfect person, and the editors and proofreaders who work with me are not perfect, either. There is nothing that hurts my feelings more or those feelings of those who proofread for me than a snarky comment such as, "She needs an editor!" I have several and I, too, am an editor. We try hard to find the errors, but none of us are perfect.

If you like my stories, please overlook the occasional error that you may find. Even better, please write and tell me what you've discovered. But for anyone who is looking for absolute perfection, please don't look here. Find a truly perfect author to read. I'm out of the running for that distinction.

And for those of you looking for absolute realism, this is not your story. Until 2015, when a federal judge issued an order barring these practices under the Eighth Amendment, prisoners on death row in Virginia were subject to automatic solitary confinement, physical isolation from visitors and other prisoners, and other harsh conditions. While my description of Ed's execution is accurate and realistic, I have taken some liberties with the terms of his living conditions in prison to lighten the bleakest part of the story. If you want realism, I can send you one of my appellate records to read; but I promise you that it won't be nearly as much fun to read as my fiction.

My heartfelt thanks to everyone who has enjoyed my stories. I am so thrilled to hear from you when you take the time to write to me. My goal is to entertain you and to keep you up until the very last page. When you tell me I have succeeded, I am over the moon with joy.

Thanks to everyone who has taken time to leave a review on Amazon.com. or Goodreads. Reviews help attract new readers. And with more readers, I can practice law less and write more novels.

I love to hear from you directly at dhawkins8350@gmail.com. You can connect with me on Facebook at https://www.facebook.com/DeborahHawkinsAuthor and on Twitter at @DeborahHawk3. My websites are my Word Press blog at https://dhawkinsdotnet.wordpress.com. and my author website at deborahhawkinsfiction.com. There is a link on both sites to sign up for my mailing list for advance notice of new releases.

Deborah

NOVELS BY DEBORAH HAWKINS

MIRROR, MIRROR, A Legal Thriller
THE DEATH OF DISTANT STARS, A Legal Thriller
DARK MOON, A Legal Thriller
RIDE YOUR HEART 'TIL IT BREAKS
Winner Beverly Hills Book Award 2015

DANCE FOR A DEAD PRINCESS
Finalist Foreword Reviews, 2013
Honorable Mention, Beverly Hills Book Award 2014

Made in the USA
San Bernardino, CA
15 January 2019